I

The woman across the square says that she's my mother. I don't believe her, of course. But these days all it takes is a seed - a suggestion - and then self-doubt starts seeping in.

She nods and waves at me whenever we see each other. She probably thinks that she keeps herself together pretty well, what with the rouged cheeks and dark red lipstick. But her grey hair is wild, spraying out from the sides of her head. And her fringe looks like she's hacked at it with a pair of garden shears. She's stooped, which shows that age is getting to her, but she still tends the half-dead geraniums in her window boxes, which shows that she's still somewhat with it. Still, I don't hold out much hope.

We've only spoken a few times over the past eight years. When I first moved here, she gave me the whole "Ciao bella," thing, and rabbited on for a bit about who she was, how nice it was to see new faces, and who a few of the neighbours were. A year after that, and everyone was gathered in the square after the disaster, as if we were awaiting the second coming of Christ, and she pawed at my arm, anxious and seeking reassurance. The penultimate time, she was just as solicitous, peering up into my face, but there was a sentimental quality to her attention. She patted my hand and had this beatific smile. I didn't think I was going to get away the right side of sundown. When she eventually let me go, she left almost regretfully, as if she had something she wanted to tell me. She kept on looking over her shoulder as she shuffled towards the door to her building. I just thought she was lonely.

The last time we met, she made a beeline for me, skirting a small pile of rubble and a dead dog, and took both my hands in hers. Don't you remember me, bambini, she said. Of course I do, I replied, you're Rosa from across the square. She looked around her, to make sure that no one was listening, and then told me that she was my mother. I laughed. I probably shouldn't have, but it was such a bizarre thing to say. I didn't know if she was simply losing her mind, or if she meant it figuratively, as in, during these hard times, we all need to look after each other. I made light of it. What else could I do? I told her she was the sweetest lady I'd ever known, and that I'd see her again soon.

That was over a month ago. Then, yesterday morning, I found a postcard tucked under my door. How she got through the outer doors,

I've no idea - I'll have to have a word with Filippa. Anyway, the postcard was a view of the town from the river in the 1920s, before the Germans came to stay. I imagine that she's got a huge stack of old postcards over there, and that she goes round stuffing them under people's doors for no good reason. Anyway, she's invited me round for coffee today, and I'm already running a few minutes late.

I'm going of course. We all have to stick together in these unsteady times. Still, I intend to swap our cups if I get a chance. I could do without a dose of strychnine or arsenic, thank you very much. It's not that I don't trust her, but it pays to be careful. I've made it this far, and I don't intend to be poisoned by some deluded old crow.

I'm taking my knife, of course, and I've even got dressed up for the occasion. I'm wearing a little black dress - the one with dropped, gauzy shoulders - and a pair of heels, which I can kick off quickly if I need to. I'm taking my beige corduroy bag, slung across my body - hard to pull off, but easily accessible - and an exciting but worthless necklace made of miniature gold baubles.

In fact, I saw Rosa not two minutes before, beckoning to me from her window. To be honest, I'm feeling a little nervous, but intrigued.

I wonder what she wants.

On the way out I see Filippa. She's sitting in her

little cubbyhole, staring at the wall again. The red, shapeless cap she wears is looking greasier than ever, as is her dark blue uniform. She used to be a ticket inspector, and still dresses like one. She glances at me with distracted eyes and nods, not bothering to move from her chair. She has that heavy-set, listless quality that some would call bovine, but that would be cruel. I give her a gracious smile and sweep past.

The front doors to our block are about nine feet high - two vast slabs of ancient wood painted dark brown. They've been reinforced over the last couple of years with extra planks and metal struts, and the one on the left - the one that doesn't move - has half-a-ton of breeze blocks stacked behind it. I scan the square quickly through the peephole and then begin the rigmarole of undoing all the various bolts and latches. I can only hope that Filippa secures them again as soon as I've left, otherwise what's the point in having them?

The square's empty, of course. Little rivulets have cut through the dust and gravel as a result of the recent rains, creating rivers, tributaries and deltas - the sort of things scientists would have kittens about if they saw them on another planet. Here, they mean nothing, and my foot puts paid to a watershed or two as I pass. The sky overhead is grey and lowering, but also luminous, so much so that it almost hurts my eyes.

There's a sun up there, trying to get through.

I knock at the door to Rosa's building and wait, casting glances to either side. I suppose I'm getting more anxious about being outside, but there's not a lot I can do about that. The idea of ending up as a crazy cat lady is terrifying, but perhaps inevitable. Next year, I'm going to take a hiking tour in the Alps, but I've been saying that for the last five years, so by now it's just a pipe dream, or rather a mantra that I keep repeating to myself to prove that I've got my sights set on far horizons. As if.

The door opens slowly to reveal the burly, square-set figure of Hilda, the concierge. She's like Filippa on steroids with a dose of gumption for good measure. She's not as formally dressed as Filippa, sporting her ubiquitous blue jumper and dirty jeans, but she's far more effective. I see her some mornings, running errands around the town, crossing the square, back and forth, back and forth, like some busy bluebottle. She's not scared to be outside - she doesn't seem to give a damn - and I suppose her imposing physique has something to do with it. She's a little shorter than me, but about five stone heavier - the sort of woman you'd want on your side in a fight.

Ciao, I say, I'm here to see Rosa. She nods sullenly, still eyeballing me the whole while, and opens the door just wide enough to let me through. I get a glimpse of a still-shiny parquet floor before the door closes behind me, and I imagine this is how it feels when you go to prison. I feel intensely vulnerable: Hilda's behind me in the darkness, and if she wanted to jump me, I wouldn't stand a chance. She could kill me within seconds - it'd be that simple.

I find the stairs thanks to some meagre light let in by a distant window, and begin to climb. This block isn't so far removed from my own, except that the wooden stairs are slightly wider, slightly grander, and there's a more obvious atmosphere of damp. I imagine Hilda scrabbling around on the roof with a hammer and a mouthful of nails, trying to fix down stray tiles before winter hits. She certainly looks capable of it. Sadly, I can't imagine Filippa leaving her cubbyhole, and imagining her doing some practical, useful task is impossible. It's like trying to press together two pieces of a puzzle that won't fit. But the real issue here is maintenance, not Filippa's ineptitude. I've been putting it off for months, all through the summer. But now we're in the last days of August, I need to start getting things done. I make a mental note to draw up an action plan as soon as I get home. Preparedness makes us powerful.

From the stairs, the parquet floor reasserts itself all the way to Rosa's door. As I stand there, I realise that I've brought nothing except myself. I feel naked and churlish, and vow to make a cake and drop it round in the next couple of days. I'll have to be especially effervescent to make up for this sad oversight. With this in mind, I plaster a gracious smile across my face and knock three times as loudly as I can. I imagine that Rosa's hearing isn't all that it could be, but my knuckles don't thank me, stinging from their impact with the steel-plated door.

Several minutes later, the door opens soundlessly, and I see Rosa standing there, hunched in the half-light. Bambini, she coos, stepping aside and ushering me inwards. I look over her head, peering around for signs of anyone else, but don't see anything. Her flat's quite grand - its ceilings are higher than mine, and its walls encrusted with landscapes and portraits in gilt frames. It's open plan too, which perhaps makes it seem larger than it actually is. The parquet floor continues, bordered by walls of deep dolphin blue and a spotless white ceiling with a large glass chandelier. I could live like this, I think, and clutch my hand to my heart, take a deep breath and give it the whole bella casa thing, tutting and saying how much I love the chandelier and the long Prussian blue drapes.

She nods, smiling, and ushers me over to the window. She's got a small table and two chairs set up there - the wooden slatted ones with metal frames that you see in cheap cafes. On the table is a small glass vase - probably a shot glass, in fact -

which contains an oversized daisy. It's one of the most beautiful things I've seen in a long time, and I feel myself beginning to well up. I turn, one hand clasped to my chest again, hoping not to see Rosa rearing up at me, carving knife in hand, and ask her where she got the flower from. Luckily, there are no carving knives to be seen. She smiles, bows her head slightly and points upwards. At first I think she means that it's come from Heaven, but then I realise she must mean a rooftop garden. My mind boggles with visions of Elysian Fields up there as she ushers me into a chair. Maybe the gardens or balconies are on the far side of the roof, where they can't be seen from the square. I decide to make it my life's work to find out what's up there.

On the table is an aluminium coffee maker sitting on a cork matt. The coffee maker is immaculate, but has a dull patina across the metal which can only be the result of years of use. Steam is still spilling from its tiny mouth, and the aroma is incredible - dark and rich, enough to make me start salivating. Rosa pours the coffee into two bone china cups with a shaking hand, then bustles off towards the kitchen.

I look out across the square, staring straight into my flat, and half expect to see a pale woman with a bob of dark hair staring back at me. Thankfully, I don't. Instead I realise that Rosa is my future. If I survive that long - a good thirty years or so - I'll look exactly like Rosa, and probably behave like her as well. The realisation hits me like one of those proverbial thunderbolts, a flash not so much of inspiration but of dread and desperation. If I don't do something soon, this is exactly where I'm headed.

Thankfully she returns to break my train of thought with a plate of madeleines. They're all tumbled together, still steaming, and I realise that she's just taken them out of the oven and knocked them out. The smell of citrus is overwhelming: if I wasn't salivating before, I am now. She motions for me to take one. Grazie, I say, picking one off the plate in as ladylike a manner as I can muster. The sponge is warm, soft and airy all at the same time: sugar, lemon and the scents of summer spill over my tongue. It's the best thing I've tasted for years.

Rosa takes a seat and eats daintily, like a wild bird pecking at the ground whilst looking around for predators. I finish the madeleine and make appreciative noises. She gestures for me to take another. I do so, and it disappears. This is how people are lulled into a false sense of security before they're murdered - I know that, but still I can't help myself. I throw caution to the wind, even sipping at the coffee before Rosa. The deep roast with the hint of crema on top is a revelation. Why doesn't my coffee taste like this? I take another sip - longer this time. It feels risky -

9

like having unprotected sex with a stranger - but I don't care. Que sera, sera. If I end up dead, my body jammed down a builder's rubble shoot at the back of the building, then so be it. At least I'll have enjoyed the coffee and cake.

I make more appreciative noises and try to make small talk, but it seems that Rosa is quite happy just to sit there contentedly, eating and drinking and nodding her head like a small bird, so I decide to pitch right in. Rosa, I say, taking one of her hands in mine, the last time we met you said that I was your daughter. What did you mean by that?

She puts down the remaining quarter of her madeleine, looks at me and smiles. It's a sad, wistful smile, and as she takes my hand, I realise that she's trying hard not to cry. I said it, she says, because it's true. I widen my eyes a little. Just wait here, she says. Have another cake.

She gets up and shuffles off through a half-open door to what I can only assume must be her bedroom. I try to quash images of her reappearing with a blunderbuss as I stuff down another madeleine. I take another as well. Maybe I'm just a pig deep down inside, but I can't help myself. They're just too good.

When she reappears she's clutching a black leather-bound book in her papery hands. Returning to the table, she sits right next to me. She places the old photo album on the table and opens it to a page near the front, and for a second I feel as if I'm looking at a picture of my younger self. It's a photo of a dark-haired woman, slim and smiling, clutching a child. The child that I never had. It takes me a few seconds to get a grip of myself, but then I realise that the woman is Rosa and that the child - the child smiling up at me from a park bench - is me. Or at least that's what Rosa is trying to insinuate. I scratch at the side of my head and find myself wincing before I manage to smooth my features over. The kid - about two years old with dark, slightly wavy hair - does bear an uncanny resemblance to photos I've seen of me in the past. But then again, lots of kids look roughly the same, right?

I give it the whole, que bambina thing, suck in a deep breath and ask Rosa if the pretty woman is her. She nods solemnly, with the corners of her mouth turning up slightly at the implicit praise. And that's me? No! Surely not. A lovely, lovely child though. She must have been so very proud.

She shakes her head, raises her hands and lets them fall back to her lap. I was proud, she says, so very, very proud. But it only got worse. Worse and worse as the years passed. I raise my eyebrows, hoping for some clarification. The feeling, she says. The heavy feeling, the feeling of death. It only got worse. My husband, she says, making a walking motion with her fingers, was long gone. In the end, she couldn't leave the house, couldn't look after the child. She had, she says, and this time tears actually pool in her eyes and leak down her cheeks, to give her away. To give me away. To the sisters, so that someone could look after me properly.

I sit back, wide-eyed, one hand clasped to my chest. Rosa's story isn't as implausible as it sounds. I was born in this town, and my parents moved back to Britain when I was four. And grudgingly I have to admit that I do look quite like Rosa - especially her younger self. I look more like her than my own mother, but that could just be coincidence. Still, my parents never mentioned anything about my having been adopted. And I think it would have come up at some point, surely. I haven't spoken to them in almost ten years. I wonder what they're doing. Toiling under leaden skies on a pig farm somewhere in Wiltshire, no doubt. I shudder at the thought.

It seems that now we've broken the ice, Rosa's on a roll. You were everything to me, she said, everything. You'd play out here - here, in this very room, so quietly, while I slept. You were no trouble at all, and you used to look up at me with those big dark eyes before you could talk. Ah, but I couldn't let you become some feral child. My love for you meant I couldn't let you suffer because of my inability to look after you. You needed more - someone to do things with you, someone to be an example for you. The sisters are severe, perhaps, but good. I knew that they'd find a family for you. And I was right.

She stares at me with her imploring, water-logged eyes, and I begin to feel things shifting around within me. It's an odd sensation - not so much like the grinding of a joint, but perhaps like the grinding of tectonic plates deep below the Earth's surface. I feel the whole basis of my reality shifting sideways. It's obvious that she believes the things she says, but that doesn't make them any less fictitious. The question is, why do I find myself so willing to believe her?

I didn't want to say anything, she says, her voice becoming more strident. When you first came back, I knew it was you, returning to the place of your birth. But you had a life, and I didn't want to intrude upon it. You had gone away, but you'd come back - what a blessing! And you lived on the opposite side of the square from me: at first, it was enough to know that you were near, and that you were well. But now, with things being what they are... she raises her hands again and lets them fall in that gesture of helplessness... how could I not speak out? How could I not tell you? Perhaps it was selfishness. Perhaps, perhaps. I don't know. She starts shaking her head slightly.

I take her hand in mine once again and pat it. When she looks up, tears speckled with black mascara run down her cheeks. I realise that she's waiting for me to reply. I shift in my chair. I'm feeling guilty, and all I've done is trough a few madeleines.

But that's not the point. We can be guilty through inaction. Rosa seems to know this well enough. The point is that I've got a decision to make. Do I become complicit in her lie, or do I reject her? She's opened up her heart to me, and she seems to be speaking from experience. Maybe she did have a child when she was young, and she did give her away. Her pain seems real enough. Or maybe through the onset of dementia, privation and hunger she's simply transferred emotions from another event to this fabrication. Maybe she's just seeking closure from some unresolved trauma and sees me as the vehicle for doing so. The mind works in mysterious ways, especially when you spend most of your waking hours thinking about food.

To lie, or not to lie? Once upon a time, this would have been much more straightforward. I'd have let her down gently, maybe been vague, but certainly not entered into an old woman's redemptive fantasies. But now? Things are not the same as they once were. We all know that. And allegiances are hard to come by. Everyone mistrusts everyone else, even people from other buildings. And to insist upon the hard facts now might scuttle any chance I have of forming an alliance - however tenuous - with Rosa. And although I'm ashamed to admit it, part of me is wondering what I might have to gain.

I smile sadly and look down. You're very brave, I say, very brave, to tell me this. After all these years. I can only imagine how hard it must have been. But what you must understand, I say, looking up at her, and sitting up straighter, is that I have lived a life, and that I do have parents, and that they're - for all I know - still alive.

All of this is true, of course. But it makes Rosa move back slightly, and her eyes widen with alarm. But they're a long way away, I continue, and we haven't spoken for years. But they're not the people who brought me into this world, who loved me first. That, I add, was you.

I bring my hand up to my face in a fanning motion, glance out over the square and swallow as hard as I can. This is all so sudden I add, that I don't know what to say.

Rosa takes both of my hands in hers. There's been a lot of hand-clutching today, and I must admit that it's made me slightly uncomfortable. I've never been a particularly tactile person. Physical human contact has become a rarity for most of us, and it feels welcome but also intrusive. As does expressing oneself, which I've never been much good at. It's one thing to have these thoughts and feelings running around in one's head, and quite another to express them to another person. Even if they are all lies.

I know, she says, nodding, I know. You have

a life - a past - and I have no right to intrude upon it. But maybe we could get to know each other again. Maybe we could spend some time together. And maybe one day you could think of me, not just as Rosa across the square, but as who I really am: your mother.

I'm taken unawares by her eloquence. And with it she's so reticent, but so sincere. To my horror, I find that I'm actually welling up. Once this happens, it's as if some chain reaction's been set in motion, and years of withheld emotion pour out of me. My face crumples and tears start to run. I lean forward, arms outstretched, looking for comfort like a young child who has just hurt herself. Rosa does likewise, and suddenly we're both embracing, both crying. I'm wracked by heaving, uncontrollable sobs. Part of me - the part that still contains a modicum of moral fibre - is horrified. Another part - let's call it the wannabe actress part - is jubilant. Well played! Wherever this is coming from, don't stop! Who says that method acting is dead? Plus, you'll feel better for it. Cleansed.

I don't know how long the crying goes on for. The moral part of me has retreated in horror, along with my sense of time. Eventually, the sobs begin to subside. When I can breathe properly, I sit up straight, hold Rosa at arm's length and look searchingly into her tear-stained face. It's good to be back, mamma, I say. It's good to be back.

I stagger through the streets, a hollow woman, head filled with straw. The encounter with Rosa has left me empty, vitiated. I feel as if I've run a marathon, been to a funeral, or both. I'm surprised to find that I also feel angry, as if I've been put upon, put in an impossible situation. At first I don't actually realise where I'm going - I just seem to be walking without apparent purpose, as fast as my ridiculous shoes will allow - and when I realise, I'm immediately resigned to it. There's still enough daylight left, and I still have my knife in my bag.

The buildings pass me like the washed-out facades of a movie set. They're uniformly high and grey, with occasional signs of life amid the boarded up windows: red geraniums - why's it always geraniums? - and drying underwear. All of the ground-floor shops have been boarded up or their metal shutters lowered, like curtains pulled in grieving houses. I weave my way through the detritus of the streets: a mangled bicycle, a leaning stop sign, until I find myself in another square. It's grander than the one I live in - long and rectangular - and the buildings are more impressive. Parts of it are cobbled, and to my right, several dead trees rise above a row of benches. A multitude of cafes once spilled on to this square. Years ago, this was one of the town's main hubs - a place where couples would come and sit, children would play, teenagers would flirt, and old people would stroll. It was blessed by both the evening sun and an absence of traffic. But now those halcyon days are little more than idealised memories, like those of a happy childhood.

But I don't let the past deter me. I cut diagonally across the square, heading for a flat-faced building with a round window that leers from its front like a single eye. Behind the severe apex of its roofline, a squat tower stands like a miniature hat. A scrawny buddleia nods from one of the tower's arches, the merest of ornaments.

When I get to the front doors - large and oaken, studded with iron - I start hammering and don't stop. Aprire la porta, I shout, not giving a damn if other people can hear me. I keep knocking and shouting like a woman possessed. I haven't felt this feisty - or determined - in years.

Of course, the survival instinct hasn't entirely left me. I'm aware that I'm glancing around, making sure that no one's creeping out of their buildings, like rats at twilight, or that nobody's got the drop on me and is about to brain me with a saucepan.

There's movement on the other side of the door, and I stop my frantic hammering. There's a small slit at head height that resembles a letterbox, and a metal slot behind it slides to one side. In the gloom beyond, I can just make out a pair of eyes.

Hello, I say, smoothing the front of my dress down and smiling, trying to appear less manic. Is it true that there used to be an orphanage here, as part of the convent? The figure inside nods. And do you still have records, I ask. I've just found out that I might have been adopted from here and, well, I want to make sure.

The woman on the other side explains that all the records were kept electronically, of course, but that more basic entries were made on paper as they always had been. If I was alone, I was more than welcome to come and look. Until nightfall, of course. I smooth my hair back, clutch my bag more tightly and nod my grinning head like a young journalist on her first case. A human-sized door opens in the giant door, and I'm swallowed by the convent.

I follow the nun through the dark entrance-way, and we skirt a small quadrangle. Beyond the arched colonnades a square of dead grass lies beneath its choking blanket of ash. I don't ask the nun her name, just follow the dark swish of her habit. I suppose I should be more appreciative, but I'm preoccupied, and she's not the chattiest of gals. Glancing down, I notice that my knuckles are actually bloody from hammering on the door. I glance up to the heavens, still in actor mode.

And that's when I see them. Small, silent figures clutching the stone balustrades above us and staring down with big, dark eyes. From what I can see, they look well dressed, in simple if old-fashioned clothes. But the most notable thing about them is that they don't move. Is this a result of the sisters' well-known discipline, or because they're on the edge of starvation like everyone else?

This vignette of silent children hits me hard. I almost stop and stare. Instead, I simply catch a toe on a protruding flagstone and stumble forwards, barely stopping myself from face-planting. As I straighten up and try to regain a semblance of dignity, I realise that there's no laughter. Not even a stifled giggle. Nothing. Apparently not one of these children has thought that this fancy lady in her ridiculous shoes almost losing some teeth was worthy of a chuckle. Not one. Have they been drugged? I glance up at them and smile to appear friendly, cover my embarrassment, and to show my appreciation for their not having laughed. I immediately wish that I hadn't. It's then that I realise there are literally dozens of them. They've got the swarthy look of people in Victorian photographs - they don't seem to be dirty, but the dirt's so ingrained that it's just become part of their natural complexion. There are boys, girls, some in their early teens, some still toddlers. I've always wondered where all the children went, and naturally I just feared the worst. But the answer is that most of them have ended up here in this family of flaxen-haired and immobile ghosts.

Of course, their futures are palsied and bleak, no more substantial than those of the ghosts they resemble. They've survived this far, obviously outliving their older and apparently stronger relatives, but what do they have to look forward to? No racing around on scooters, flirting or foreign holidays for them. And what happens when they reach a certain age? Do the nuns put them to work, or simply kick them out? No doubt most of them will succumb to hunger or illness long before their age becomes problematic. I feel myself welling up, but I can't afford another emotional episode now, certainly not after my interview with Rosa. So I suck in a deep breath, attach my eyes to the nun's back and try to clear my mind.

When we get to the corner of the quadrangle the nun turns to me and says, mind your step. There's a light in her eyes, and the corners of her mouth turn up slightly, the bitch. Oh well, fair play. I'd have done the same. We descend several steep stone blocks to a small, arched door. Here she retrieves a set of gaoler's keys from beneath her habit, opens the door and steps down into darkness. For a second, I'm loath to follow her. It's the survival instinct kicking in again - fear of the dark, the unknown. Apparently we developed it at one point in our evolution when we were hunted by big cats: seeing as cats have good night vision and we don't, we were right to be afraid. Unfortunately that often leads to cause-less alarm, such as now. I centre myself, suck in another deep breath and step down.

The darkness below comes replete with its own rich atmosphere of damp: it's humid and earthy, and envelops you instantly. Luckily, be-fore I can get very far or embarrass myself again, a small flame winks into existence. As she lights the oil lamp in her hand, the nun's face is caught in the yellow light, rendering it as waxen and sal-low as beef dripping. She stares at the flame for a second, then looks up at me and says, the spirit of God was hovering over the waters. With that she turns and descends.

I follow, trying not let the steel ferules on my heels create too much of a clatter, or to lose my footing again. And I realise that this is how these women must live their lives - in hope. That one day they'll be united with God, and that all the ills of this world will be washed away. I'm hit by a sudden stab of jealousy: if only I could have such faith the days would be easier to get through. This, of course, just makes me feel churlish. How must this calm, undemonstrative woman see me? As a stroppy, self-important cow no doubt, demanding her time when she has bet-ter things to do, such as keeping children alive.

At the bottom of the steps the nun pauses and raises the oil lamp. There's something about the image - a solitary, robed woman holding a light above her head - that is worthy of an oil painting, or at least a photo. It reminds me for some reason of the old painting called The Light of the World, the one of Jesus looking furtive, which is weird as the two images have nothing in common apart from the lamp.

Sturdy arched pillars recede into the darkness around us, holding up a ceiling of sagging stone. The nun smiles again, and I'm not sure if it's because she's marvelling at the aged grandeur of this place, or because she's about to whip out a knife and try to kill me. What do they feed the children anyway? Skinny, neurotic women who stumble into their clutches? And then it strikes me that I would make pretty poor eating; any curves I ever had have long since disappeared. I'd be stringy at best.

To be fair, as impressive as this place is, there's a lot of junk down here. Paint pots and rolls of old wallpaper cluster around the pillars, and pieces of abandoned furniture lurk around the edges like insane relatives who've been locked away. The nun plunges onwards, and we soon find ourselves in the far corner of the cellars - the dank place where people get bricked up in gothic novels. Here the lines of the arches have been destroyed by the interposition of a dozen shelving units, the sort that men buy for their garages back home and are inordinately proud of. Lining these shelves is an impressive array of leather-bound tomes and stacks of mildewed papers. They must go back several hundred years. It's a genealogist's wet dream.

So, asks the nun, what year were you looking for? I smile coyly and look away, that would be telling, wouldn't it? What's the most recent you've got? The nun shrugs, obviously unimpressed by my attempt at humour. She hums a tuneless tune to herself as she moves along the racks. At the last of them she squats down and wipes a hand across several of the leather-bound spines. Here they are, she says, the last of the historical entries. I give her an arch look and kneel down next to her, trying to do so as elegantly as possible. The floor is cold, and the position makes me feel as if I should be praying.

I pull the last tome out and begin flicking through. There are literally hundreds of entries giving names, dates, and the sparsest of biographical details. All of the first names you'd expect, the Marcos and Marias. Of course names are given in full, and some are so long as to be almost laughable. It's amazing that anyone could bestow such lavish names upon a child, but not their love or care. But I'm not here as a sociologist, so I skip forwards quickly. The entries end halfway through the book. At first, I'm perplexed. I look up at the nun.

There must be some mistake here, I say. Where are the most recent entries? You're holding them, she says. Provision for orphans was handed over to the state in the nineteen-sixties. Having said that, she adds, smiling again, you do look very good for your age.

At first, I don't get it. This is what hunger does to you: it dulls your wits, often putting the obvious just beyond your grasp. But what, I ask, are all the children doing up there? Did I imagine them? Are they really ghosts? No, she says, speaking calmly as if to a small child, they're real enough, poor souls. Times are hard, she adds, shrugging, and certain elements of the social fabric have fallen through. We couldn't just stand by. What would you have us do, leave them out on the streets?

No, I mutter, of course not. It's just that... it's just that, I've been told I was adopted from here, And now I see that's impossible, because of the dates. She smiles at me. It's probably all the sympathy she can muster, poor woman.

Could this whole adoption sequence be something that happened to Rosa when she was young? Perhaps it's something she's reimagined, casting me as her younger self, and then fashioning an idealised reunion with her own biological mother? It's possible. But how old's Rosa? She looks old - in her seventies at the very least

- but that's probably just the effects of privation: everyone looks older than they are. I determine to look for her in this last volume to see if she's actually the one who's been adopted. Okay, so what's her surname?

Kneeling there, I try to think of the few times we've met, but draw a blank. She must have told me her full name, right? If she has, the details escape me. On the front of her building, was there ever one of those little buzzer panels with the names pencilled next to the buttons? I wrack my brains, but get nothing. Although she says she's my mother, Rosa is apparently an absolute enigma to me.

I'm sorry, I say, it's just that... my train of thought trails off, a not uncommon occurrence. I feel something touch my shoulder. I flinch reflexively, and find the nun's hand there. It's quite alright, she says, lots of people come here, trying to find loved ones or looking for details of their past. I wish I could say that most of them find what they're looking for, but they don't.

On my way up out of the cellar, I keep my eyes fixed firmly on the floor. In the quadrangle, I daren't look up. I'm terrified of meeting the eyes of those children. They'll see me for what I am: a vain, self-interested fraud of a woman. My contributions to this dying society are minimal. I'm not fit to be in the presence of this nun who gives so much, who offers so much hope in these dark times.

The convent spits me out like the whale rejecting Jonah. And I find myself spinning through that wide, dust-paved square, heading automatically for home, despite the hollowness in my head. As my stagger settles into a broken march, my self-recrimination turns to anger.

I've been played, put-upon in the most callous manner. How dare Rosa offer me hope, based as it is on a fabrication? Perhaps we're all living on stories at the moment, on made-up truths that stop us having to face the awfulness of our lives. And that's all well and good, but when we involve others in our wish-fulfilment sagas, then we've crossed a line. The feelings of warmth and closeness I experienced have suddenly been converted into emptiness and gall. How dare she lie to me? How dare she?

The intensity of my rage makes my head swim, and I abandon all of my usual cat-like precautions, clattering though the grey streets like some pissed-up member of a hen party. No one does this sort of thing to me. No one.

As I re-enter our square, I can't even bring myself to look up at Rosa's windows. She's let me down more than she can ever know, and I realise, as I rap my still-bloody knuckles against our door, that there's only one solution.

Rosa will have to die.

I'm not a rash person. I never have been. So I get home and sleep on it. It's one of those fourteen-hour sleepathons that are so common amongst those of us who are clinging on. Dreamless, it's just a black tunnel of oblivion leading to tomorrow. One day, I figure, that tunnel will be never-ending, or will lead nowhere. And that'll be that.

When I wake, I find that my resolve has been sharpened, twisted into something gnarled and uncomfortable. Have you ever seen a fulgurite? It's where lightning strikes sand and fuses it. You're left with these weird, convoluted shapes that people sometimes find, like a root crop from the depths of hell. That's how my resolve feels: spiky, asymmetric and alien. It's not a thought I've really ever entertained before - that of killing someone - but now it doesn't seem unnatural. Let's be honest: the vestiges of civilisation have all slipped away, leaving nothing but the will to survive. Around here, the best one can hope for is that each block of flats will come up with some form of self-governing system. Thousands of years ago, when times were hard, the old and infirm were no doubt culled or simply left to die. If you can't contribute, why should you get a share? And no, this isn't some kind of right wing eugenicist style of thinking I've lapsed into. You've got to look at context. In times of plenty, things are different. Very different. Even morality. In fact, especially morality. The things I've seen and heard about in the last seven years would never have happened - could never have happened - a decade ago. They'd have gone against the common good and therefore quite rightly been seen as crimes. But now? Now all bets are off.

But there is one stumbling block, as I've mentioned: the block itself. Around here, for whatever reason, it's been agreed by some kind of unconscious consent that stuff stays within each block of flats. If I die, then someone like Filippa can quite happily trawl through my stuff and take what she wants. It's like a cross between a house viewing and a car boot sale. When you die, they fling the doors open and people come in and take what they want. At first, it was like the January sales: people queuing up outside, shoving each other, fighting over the choicest pieces. Now, it's a much more civilised affair. Imagine people visiting a National Trust house, or some other stately home. There's ordered queuing, if any, and people are polite, respectful and keep their distance from one another. Despite what most people think, hunger can have some surprisingly civilising effects.

So if Rosa dies, who gets her stuff? The people still living in her block. Not me. And if I'm going to go to all this trouble, I want some material gain into the bargain. I noodle with this problem for a while over a large cup of rather watery black coffee while staring at Rosa's flat. She never pulls the curtains, I notice, just leaves them open like most people do to try to soak up as much daylight as possible. Once upon a time, you could have got old duffers to hand stuff over to you in their will, but now that's not feasible. Wills are laughable, as are any agreements scratched out on bits of paper. Common consent and brute force carry the day. There are no lawyers left.

Anyway, the first rule of killing someone is staying alive yourself, so when I see Cornelius sidling his way around the square I lean out of the window and whistle to get his attention. I shout his name, wave and give him my most ravishing of smiles. He pauses, looks back as if he's about to cross a road, and then cuts across the square. Minutes later he's sitting in my kitchen, and I'm brewing up some more weak coffee.

Cornelius is one of the few men left alive around here. It used to be said that a good man is hard to find. Now it's hard to find a man at all. Most have been claimed by the demands of their own metabolisms, or by periodic outbreaks of violence. Is Cornelius a good man, though? That's a hard question to answer. As he reclines in the narrow confines of my kitchen, one leg folded over the other, peering out of the window, it's hard to tell. Although he's dressed nattily in a dark grey suit with matching waistcoat, brown shoes and a crimson handkerchief in his top pocket, he's not what you'd call an attractive man. He's always been lean, but that's not really the problem. The problem is his head. It's slightly too big for his body, a leathery potato-egg with grey stubble for hair and restless, shifting eyes that peer out from his deep-set sockets as if he's looking at you from miles away. I know this sounds unkind, and who am I to talk, seeing as we're probably all sporting lollipop heads by now? But the fact is that for such a slender man, Cornelius's head is formidable: it looks like it's something he could kill you with. In fact, his daintily folded hands are oversized as well. And for a white man, they're inexplicably tanned: it's as if he's commandeered a sunbed and is making good use of it. If I had to sum Cornelius up with one word, it would be swarthy. And natty. And shifty.

I clear my throat as I sit, trying to tear Cornelius's attention away from Rosa's flat, and place two cups of my poor excuse for coffee on the kitchen table. When he finally manages to wrestle his attention back to me, I wonder whether he's thinking of killing Rosa too. Maybe a lot of people are. My mind boggles. Maybe I'm late to the party, and there's actually a whole line of people forming a virtual queue to get hold of Rosa's stuff. I shove the thought to one side, smile as winningly as I'm able, and fold one leg over the other, mirroring my guest's sitting position. I've never quite worked Cornelius out, but if he's straight, I'd bet that he's a leg man, seeing as he's so long-limbed himself. And my legs have always been my best feature: long and slender, with just the right amount of muscle tone. Of course, most of that muscle's gone now. But although I'm a little scrawny, around here I'm probably something of a catch.

Why thank you, says Cornelius, in a voice that's too deep for his body but just right for his head. He picks up his cup, blows at the steaming liquid and eyes me over the rim with glittering grey eyes. Sadly, he doesn't look down at my legs, but hey, a girl's got to try. Still, his eyes hold mine, and it seems that he's intrigued by me in some kind of asexual way. To be fair, I probably am looking rather enigmatic. I'm wearing a maroon blouse and pencil skirt, a faux diamond cross and have quickly slathered on enough mascara for a slutty, rock-star look.

So, he says, a nascent smile splitting his old-time rugby ball face, what can I do for you? I increase the width of my own smile to Cheshire-cat proportions and pick up my own cup. I'm a master of mimicry, my talents wasted beyond the stage.

Oh, nothing untoward, I say, just the usual bits and bobs. Some guttering, and some roofing tiles. Cornelius purses his lips and shrugs slightly, as if this is no big deal. In fact, I add, I've got a list. I stand slowly and give him the slightest of twerks as I turn my back on him. Whatever it takes. I retrieve my list from a kitchen drawer and slide it across the table to him before resuming my seat.

He scans it casually and shrugs again. Most of this I can do, if you give me a couple of weeks, he says. The diesel, though, that'll be expensive. I flatten my mouth in mock consternation. Without the generator, some of the people in here won't make it through the winter. I'm aware of that, he says, still looking at the list and thrumming his fingers on the table, but what can I do? My hands are tied by the supply lines. And as for flour, you've got to be joking.

Why, I ask, throwing my hands up, is flour the first thing to go? It makes no sense. He shrugs again. Who knows? I suppose that people around here are still trying to make bread and pasta. I've got sacks of rice - hundreds of them - but as for flour, it's like gold dust.

He gives me an oily smile, and I know that I've got his full attention, although I'm not sure in exactly what manner. Okay, I say, substitute the flour for rice if you have to - just get us something with carbs and calories. He nods his head slightly, as if he's some kind of humble servant, and goes back to scanning the list.

And what's this last entry, he asks, looking up at me with his quick grey eyes. I take in a deep breath. Has he seen that I've added it more recently? This morning, in fact. Or have I written it more aggressively, or perhaps in bigger letters? I smooth my hands down my skirt and try to compose myself. Is it such an odd request?

Rat poison, he asks, lifting one faint eyebrow. You're not planning on making a bomb, are you? I look to the heavens and scratch my forehead to hide my relief.

Some of the people have complained about rats in the roof space, I say. They say the scratching's keeping them awake. Crazy I know. And sometimes you can hear them in the walls.

So? Put some earplugs in, he says. Ignore them. I'm not sure if he's genuinely suspicious, or just pulling my leg. He gives me that oily, ambiguous smile again. Is it an expression of amusement or complicity?

With everything being so scarce, the merest gesture or change of expression can be significant. It's exhausting. We all long for the old days, where you could go to a supermarket and get whatever you wanted, not simply because of the vast selection of goods, but also to avoid the necessity of haggling. People like Cornelius are essential in the new world order. They're connected, and they can get stuff by hook or by crook. Often they were criminals, business owners or builders in their past lives - people who were close to existing supply chains. Now each goes under the unassuming title of il servitore. Of course this term plays down their importance and the latent menace that they can hold over people. The efforts of your servitore can mean the difference between life and death, and woe betide anyone who gets on the wrong side of theirs.

The problem with Cornelius is that, unlike some servitore, he's highly educated, and shrewd besides. He was a quantity surveyor in his past life, and his grasp on human need goes well beyond the simple logistics of supply and demand. It's as if he can see into your soul, work out what you're most desperate for and then use this knowledge to his advantage. He also holds a dual passport - he's originally from Bolton, of all places. And while you might think that his being British creates some kind of kinship between us, it doesn't. Perhaps he understands me a little better, but this makes me easier to read and thus easier to take advantage of. Linguistically, I suppose it's helpful - we swap between English and Italian almost on a whim - but that's about it. But since there's no one left in the block who's sharp enough to order supplies, it's up to me. But to be frank, I do enjoy the challenge.

I laugh. Ignore the rats? That's easy for you to say. Sometimes it sounds like they're doing gymnastics. Some of the residents have said that it reminds them of the spirits of the dead, come back to haunt them. Anyway, does that list sound okay?

Well, he says, looking back at the piece of paper and taking a deep breath, some of these items are a little tricky. But what we really need to discuss is payment.

Fair enough, I say. But I'm quite busy. Let's walk and talk. If Cornelius is surprised at all, he doesn't let on. I grab a pair of rubber gloves and a set of keys from the sideboard and head out of the kitchen, then the flat. Cornelius follows calmly in my wake.

When I get to the entranceway I shout, Ciao Filippa, just to make sure that the ponderous slab of flesh is awake, and add that I'm heading down to the basement, just so she doesn't think that we're being attacked by tomb raiders. Unlocking a door beneath the stairs, I plunge into a stairwell that descends almost vertically into the ground. Mind your step, I call backwards, then clatter onwards, leaving Cornelius to fend for himself.

Unlocking a second door that is both narrow and warped, I push aside a sheet of thick plastic and step into the basement. The humidity and blazing white light hit you simultaneously. It's a surprising, unsettling combination, because with air this damp you're expecting a sultry, leftover light, the sort you'd get under a jungle canopy. Plus, with the weather being what it is, you just don't get days this bright any more.

Cornelius follows me in and stops dead beside me. Oh my, he says, despite himself. And in that moment, I know he's mine.

Spread out before us under the blazing light of twenty halogen tubes is an oasis of greenery, a market gardener's paradise. Set out in narrow, ordered rows we've got green beans, peppers of all colours, cherry tomatoes, medium-sized tomatoes, beefsteak tomatoes, aubergines, herbs, and towards the right hand wall, an explosion of courgettes whose deep yellow flowers gape at the ceiling like the mouths of some exotic alien brood. The peppers, tomatoes and aubergines glisten in the fierce light, dragging the branches of their poor parent plants towards the flagstone floor.

As I start uncoiling a hosepipe from its bracket next to the door, I turn to Cornelius as if I've just remembered something. Oh, and could you add a hundred metres of hosepipe to the list? We've got the connectors and timers, but have run out of hosepipe itself. We want to set up a self-watering system. This lot's a real pain in the arse to water.

I turn the tap on, close my thumb over the end of the hosepipe and start watering the peppers. I'm pleased to see a rainbow pulsing through the fan of water, adding to this scene of opulence. Lowering my eyelids slightly, I pretend to be lost in my own little world, lost in the therapeutic nature of the task. Cornelius steps in closer to my shoulder. Is he invading my personal space? Perhaps a little, but that's no bad thing.

Well, this is very impressive, he says, his oversized head nodding sagely. Very impressive indeed. You think so, I ask, looking at him with feigned surprise. This is just something Mr Moretti and I knocked up in our spare time - a project if you will.

In fact, Mr Moretti hasn't been well of late. Sadly, he's developed a nasty, persistent cough that he hasn't been able to shake. Normally, he's a small, hale and hearty man with slicked-back hair, a twinkle in his eyes and a ready smile. He's what you'd call industrious, not one for moping around. When the plants on his allotment on the edge of town finally gave up the ghost, he transferred his attentions to the basement. In fact, I'm taking a bit of a gamble here. We've never shown this place to anyone outside our block, and this is the kind of resource that people would kill for - literally - but I'm assuming that Cornelius is too shrewd to come back with a posse and a battering ram.

Oh, I add, we've got some chillies along the back wall, and a few cannabis plants. For medicinal purposes only, you understand; we haven't gone all gangster. I smile at him, and play at the demure little woman doing the watering. I'm sorry, you were talking about payment?

Over the past few years, the use of money -

of actual Euros - has been in decline. And things that used to hold value - trinkets and family heirlooms - have become virtually worthless. Bartering is back in fashion, and fresh fruit and vegetables are rare, making this place something of a goldmine.

I move, my hand twitching water over the peppers, leaving Cornelius suddenly stranded at the end of the row. His gaze is lost in the green leaves, as if he's remembering more abundant days, when plants like this actually grew in the ground. I'm sure we can come to some arrangement, he mutters.

She glowers at me over the pale blue tablecloth, her eyes shaded by a dark fringe, her shoulders hunched. Even the oversized daisy has wilted under her gaze. Bovine was perhaps too harsh an adjective to apply to Filippa, but ursine fits the bill here. This bear of a woman looks as if she may well launch herself across the table at me in a flurry of nails, teeth and slobber. In turn I fantasise about beating her to death with one of my stiletto heals.

Meet Ursula. Ursine Ursula. Until five minutes ago I was only dimly aware of her existence. I'd seen her around, of course, but she's rather unremarkable looking, and generally keeps herself to herself. What with Hilda the concierge to add into the mix, it's obvious that this block is tenanted by some formidable women. No wonder no one's taken advantage of a little old lady like Rosa yet. For her part, Rosa sits between us, eyes cast downwards, a beatific smile on her face. She radiates that calm happiness that we tend to associate with people who have undergone some kind of spiritual awakening, and are slightly bemused to find themselves still in this world. There's a smugness about her, and smugness is not a good quality.

Ursula, she says, gripping the other woman's bear-like hand. I'm so happy. Yesterday I met my daughter after more than forty years. She's come back to me after all this time, come back a grown woman.

I suppress a smile. Come back an old woman, I think.

When she was taken from me, her new parents took her back to England, but she returned here like a homing pigeon. The lord moves in mysterious ways.

I scowl slightly. Taken from me? So the narrative's changed already, has it? Yesterday she gave me up. Today I was taken from her. It looks as if keeping up with the shifting tides of Rosa's mind might be a challenge in itself. No one ever said dealing with senility was easy.

She reaches out and takes one of my hands in hers. I'm careful to lengthen my fingers, showing off my red, glistening nails to their full advantage so that Ursula's suffer in comparison. Ursula's originally from Germany, says Rosa, from Bavaria, so you two should have something in common.

She hasn't formally introduced us, and this statement doesn't really help. It feels like I'm being set up on a lesbian date, or being told as a kid that I really should get along with so-and-so. Another ex-pat, eh? The place is swarming with them. I suppose it's because we're so close to the border.

So, I say, airily, how long have you known Rosa? Fifteen years, Ursula says in a deep, guttural voice. Her lips barely move. She doesn't look away, smile or show me any sign of welcome whatsoever. I'm assuming that Ursula is a younger friend, confidant and carer to Rosa. Which means that as far as I'm concerned, she's a stumbling block. A rather large one.

I'd assumed that I'd been innocently invited over for lunch, but now that doesn't seem to be entirely the case. Unless I'm much mistaken, I'd say that this whole thing has been arranged - or at least suggested - by Ursula so she can get a good look at me. Of course, I don't discount jealousy as a motive. I notice that Ursula hasn't been retrospectively adopted by Rosa. If you had to choose a daughter, there would be no contest.

You two children please excuse me, says Rosa, rising slowly to her feet. I've got to finish the lunch.

So, I say, crossing one slim leg over the other and waving one hand in an admittedly theatrical gesture, where are you from originally?

Herrsching, says the bear. It's a small town, on a lake.

It sounds lovely, I add. So, why did you come here?

It's complicated, she says.

And I realise that Ursula is going through some profound inner struggle as we sit here listening to Rosa bustle about her kitchenette. The only thing being said here is what's not being said.

But while I'm sympathetic, Ursula's glowering demeanour and clipped answers are sucking the life out of me. I try to maintain my smile, but it's withering on the vine.

It's true, I say, as if trying to justify Rosa's lie. I was born here. I don't remember it well - just an impression really, of white walls and sun. Of high buildings and blue sky. Narrow streets. And smells - but we always remember those, don't we? I remember the smell of a bakery. Of course, it's not in the same place as I remember. But it's still here. Or, rather, it was. I've always loved Italy. Well, the Mediterranean in general. It's the people - they're so much more open, so much warmer, don't you think? I've always thought that's because of the weather. The sun makes everyone feel so much more content. Well, I add with a shrug, it did.

The sadness of this last statement stops me mid-flow. No one likes to be reminded of how much they've lost. My attempt to bolster Rosa's lie has ended in blather, and I decide to stop talking. Even Ursula seems embarrassed. Yes, she says, deciding to help me out. It was beautiful here. Once.

Luckily, Rosa intervenes, swinging two white plates on to the table. My eyes widen. What, I ask, salivating already, are these? Sitting on the wide plate are half-a-dozen miniature red lobsters, drizzled with a red sauce. A small green salad and lemon wedges finish the plate.

Gamberessas, says Ursula, staring at me from beneath the protection of her fringe. I squint at her, not willing to admit that there's a hole in my vocabulary. Okay, I say, but where from, we're nowhere near the sea.

Rosa re-joins us with a plate of her own. No, bambina, she says, throwing her hands up in mock exasperation. They're not from the sea. They're from the river. Ursula traps them with nets, sticks and trickery. The river is full of them! Little aliens. When she gets some, she brings them to me, and we have a feast.

Rosa pats Ursula's hand, and as she says a small prayer of thanks, I twig that they're cray-fish. Admittedly, I'm not as sharp as I used to be.

We launch into them with gusto. I haven't eaten anything since Rosa's madeleines the day before, and I'm starving. We break the little bodies apart with our fingers, suck the juices and pry the flesh out with metal crab forks. I can't remember having ever eaten anything so unctuous, so exquisite. The sweetness of the flesh, the simple, piquant sauce, the acid zest of the lemon: all combine to put me in a heady, decadent daze. It's all I can do to stop myself groaning with pleasure.

Rosa's right, says Ursula. They're aliens. These are American crayfish. They're an invasive species. They've taken over large parts of Europe.

I have an image of giant lobstermen marching down the streets of the town, taking over. It's both ridiculous and unsettling. It's our duty, then, I add, to eat them. Rosa nods sagely. Her beatific smile has returned, this time no doubt a result of an imminent food coma.

To my chagrin, I realise I'm the first to finish. Despite her redoubtable appearance, Ursula eats daintily, as does Rosa. I've torn through my crayfish like a savage, and their dismembered bodies lie scattered across my plate. I use the napkin to wipe red sauce from my mouth and fingers as elegantly as I'm able. Can I just say, I add, trying to cover the mess I've made with my exuberance, that they were fantastic. My compliments to both the chef and the supplier. Ursula nods at me. Rosa just makes eye contact. Her bemused, slack smile is becoming creepy.

After an awkward wait in which I realise - to my horror - that I'm quite full, Rosa springs back into action. As she's bustling about, I try to help clear away, but Ursula's got the drop on me. A big, fishy paw lands on my shoulder. Don't worry, she says, this is my job. I grit my teeth and smile up at her. Just before she removes her hand, she squeezes. There's nothing untoward in it - nothing you could object to, and certainly nothing to make you cry out. Still, the message is clear. As her strong fingers clamp around my shoulder blade and clavicle, she's saying, you may be more elegant than me, but I'm stronger. Much stronger.

Rosa returns with meringues topped with fresh berries and a red coulis, of all things. This time, I do actually gasp. Berries, I say, forgetting my manners, where the hell did you get them from?

Rosa taps her nose and looks up to the ceiling. Whether she's indicating the bounty of God or their roof, I don't know. Assuming it's the latter, I ask, what have you got up there, the Garden of Eden?

They don't reply. They're too busy cracking the meringues and chasing berries across their plates. No wonder the women in this block are so formidable, with food like this.

Coffee follows, but the conversation is both sparse and stilted. Rosa still seems lost in the funk of her newfound happiness. At least I've done some good: I'm her prodigal daughter, bringing hope to her last days. Her aura of blissful contentment is a personal thing, however. She's like a saint who's achieved perfect peace, but whose gaze is turned inward and whose enlightenment isn't shared with the rest of the world. Perversely, her happiness creates a rather sombre mood, and Ursula isn't the chattiest of gals.

After a polite amount of time, I make my excuses and stand up. To my no great surprise, Ursula does the same. I thank Rosa for the lunch in the most effusive fashion, lean over and kiss her. Ursula follows suit, closes one big paw over the old lady's shoulder, and follows me to the door. We leave Rosa sitting there like the subject of some old still life, the weak light of late August casting a pale glow across her face. Her smile remains, and I wonder how far gone she is. It's hard to tell. From my limited experience, people with dementia often have lucid spells interspersed with periods of complete bewilderment. They can chat away one minute, and forget the simplest of things the next. But whatever the state of her mental health, I'd say she's not long for this world.

With our final Ciaos dying in the spacious flat, we step into the dark corridor. I don't attempt to engage Ursula in conversation - there's really no point. I just turn and start moving.

Hearing the door close behind me, I continue at an even pace, a condemned woman walking down death row.

For some reason, I start counting in my head. I don't even get to three before I hear a low, guttural, hey! I turn, smiling sweetly, but before I can even see what's happening, a hand closes around my throat and I'm shoved into the wall. I'm so skinny now that any impact hurts, and my shoulder blades blaze with sudden pain. Despite expecting something like this, I find myself physically caught off guard. My head is flung backwards an inch or two, and I bite my tongue. Not too badly, but still, it's annoying. The metallic taste of fresh blood invades my mouth.

I can sense rather than see Ursula's face next to mine, can feel her hot breath on my cheek. This is probably how people feel a split second before getting mauled by a bear: their understandable fear is mixed with acceptance. She's much stronger than me, so fighting her off won't work unless I'm extremely lucky. And it's too late to get my knife.

I don't know what game you're playing, she says, speaking in heavily accented English, and pausing between words just so I don't miss anything, but I don't trust you. So if you are lying to Rosa just to get some of her things, or trying to get free food, you should stop. Stay in your own block. If I see you again...

To emphasise the implicit threat in this last statement, she punches me in the stomach with her free hand. The blow isn't that hard, but as I'm pressed up against the wall, it hurts more than it should, knocking the wind out of me and doubling me over. I'm dimly reminded of the phrase 'folding like a hooker punched in the stomach by a fat man,' and it seems appropriate here. I'm half-expecting some more whispered threats in hard-edged gangster-style Italian or plosive-laden Bavarian, but Ursula isn't one for small talk. What I do get is another swinging fist. This time I see it, and turn my head just in time. Her hook makes contact with my left eye socket, but it really doesn't hurt that much. I offer up a stifled cry, however, just to make her think it does.

I let my legs go and crumple slowly to the floor, starting to snivel. Ursula bends over me and says, show yourself out. I nod frantically in the gloom like a contrite child. Between the crocodile tears that leak down my face, I watch her walk down the corridor and count her steps. I sit there, legs akimbo, like the proverbial beaten hooker, until she gets to a door on the left. Ursula's strong, nondescript figure is caught for a second in grey half-light, and then disappears.

Pushing myself upright, I kick my shoes off, pick them up and hunch my shoulders slightly. Ursula's a bit shorter than me, so I adjust my stride accordingly and walk soundlessly down the corridor, following her footsteps. After thirty-six strides I find myself directly outside a door. It's number twenty-seven. I back up the way I've come, put my heals on and descend the stairs with a slow, rickety gait, clutching the handrail and making as much noise as possible. Twenty-seven, eh? By the time I'm back on the ground floor, I'm smiling again, my mind racing through different scenarios. I do love a project, and the planning stage is often the most enjoyable part, when possibilities seem endless. The unconscious seems to revel in having so much freedom, but at the same time a concrete purpose. Don't bring me problems, I whisper to myself, bring me solutions.

I stumble towards the light emanating from Hilda's concierge station - a beacon of dim yellow in the darkness - and prepare myself to give her the briefest and saddest of farewells. One must be prepared to share one's misery around. Why be selfish with it? Other people share good cheer, so why not misery? Plus I want her to see how weak and pathetic I am. Basically, I slump against the doorway, with a forlorn little smile on my face. I blink in the dim glow from some fly-spotted and ancient forty-watt bulb before I realise that the tiny room is empty.

I suppose I should explain about concierges. People like Rosa and I are not living in the lap of luxury. At the present time, nothing could be further from the truth. Back when these flats were built, they certainly weren't too shabby - witness the parquet floors, wide staircases and wrought iron balustrades. That was well over a hundred years ago, and back then, such places generally had a concierge, along with their small architectural nods to the Art Deco movement. Since then, of course, the concierge has become a relic, a vestigial organ in the history of private housing. But since things went south, they've come back with a vengeance - at least around here. They're essential for security in such barbarous times.

Peering into the darkness that leads to the front door and back over my shoulder towards the stairs, I hold my breath and listen, but can hear nothing other than the beating of my heart. Where's Hilda? I'd always assumed she ran a pretty tight ship, so I'm surprised to see her room empty and unlocked. Still, that's what perpetual hunger can do to you: it can make even the most meticulous of people careless.

It also slows down one's thought processes. For example, it takes me a few seconds to see the opportunity in front of me. I slip my heals off and look around again for good measure. I step quickly into the musty, hallowed space of the concierge station and scan its contents. Luckily, it's very similar to Filippa's. There's an old wooden desk sporting the aforementioned flyblown lamp and a cafetiere squeezed in against one wall. A wooden swivel chair is pushed back from the desk, but since I'm not here to collect antiques, it doesn't really concern me. The obligatory safe lurks beneath the desk, but its contents are probably no more valuable than a handful of dust. It takes me a second or two to spot what I'm looking for, as it's surrounded by a plethora of post-it notes, postcards and a calendar of Italian landmarks. It's a wooden key cabinet, about a foot wide and fronted with iron mesh. Behind the door, brass keys glisten in the weak light like gold coins. Bingo.

I lean backwards and peer out towards the stairs. I can't see or hear a thing. Could it be this easy? A sense of glee starts to rise up inside me, only to be quashed by the thought that this could be a trap. But then again, who's got the energy to set a trap these days? I snap back upright, step forward and turn the cabinet's tiny steel key. It's a little creaky, but it turns easily enough. The click as it unlocks, however, is appalling. It's probably quite quiet, but in my heightened state, it sounds like a gunshot. Still, there's no going back. The keys hang on little iron pegs, and while half of them are missing, number twenty-seven is present and correct. Within seconds, I've extracted Ursula's keys, dropped them in my handbag and shut the small door.

That's when I hear the front door slam. My heart lurches as I throw myself sideways out of the room. I'm no doubt silhouetted against the light, so I stagger towards the door.

Hey, what are you doing? The voice is closer than I'd have hoped, but I keep moving towards it. Thank God you're here, I say. I couldn't open the front door. It feels as if I've been fumbling around for hours.

Hilda's redoubtable bulk emerges into the light. With her short hair, shapeless blue jumper and dirty jeans she looks like an off-duty car mechanic. She stares at me with her small, icy eyes, and for a second I'm worried that she's going to pull out a ratchet and brain me.

You've been crying. It's a statement, not a question. I look down and nod, as if ashamed. I wring my hands, contorting one over the other like a couple of snakes mating. Yes, well, I say, I got a little flustered. I'm claustrophobic, and... you know how it is.

It's obvious from the way she continues to stare at me that she doesn't know how it is. I wonder if she's ever been scared in her life. I wonder how she sees me. As a simpering girl? No, I'm much too old for that. Probably just as a scrawny, neurotic woman, which is about right.

At first I think that she's not going to believe me. I'm not sure if it's my tear-stained face, downcast eyes or hands that convince her. Actually, I'd bet it's my hands. They're my worst feature, the hands of a tall but effeminate man, oversized but expressive. Still, it seems as if they've carried the day as Hilda steps to one side and ushers me over to the front door.

How was Rosa, she asks. Very well, I say, with an excess of enthusiasm. She seems happy. Imagine that in these times!

That's good to hear, says Hilda, finding and opening the large door with ease. A pall of weak light wafts over us.

Yes, I say, smiling bravely despite my tears. We've found out we're related and it seems to have... well, I don't know. It seems to have brought her some comfort. Hilda stares at me and nods, and I decide to leave before I say anything stupid. Thank you, I say, touching her shoulder and lurching out into the square. It's about two o'clock now, as bright as it's going to get, and overhead I get a glimpse of the white circle of the sun trying to peer through the shifting skeins of cloud. Eventually I hear the door clatter back into place. It's an impressive, booming sound - the sound of a castle door slamming shut.

It's a good thing I've got the key.

II

Standing in front of my mirror, I assess the damage. There's a reddish mark on my neck, presumably where the ends of Ursula's fingers dug into my skin. It's no surprise. I bruise as easily as the proverbial peach. What does surprise me is my left eye. Within hours it's become surrounded by a purple smear, as if some overenthusiastic Goth has been allowed to do my makeup. The streaks of grey in my dark hair are down to age, though, and I can hardly blame Ursula for getting older. Still, I'll blame her for everything else. People like her are the reason the world's in the shape that it's in. They create animosity, sow doubt and suspicion, and are generally opposed to people getting on. The fact that she's got good reason to be suspicious is beside the point.

I smear some foundation on my neck and put on my sunglasses. Their large black lenses conceal my black eye, giving me the look of a starlet desperate to avoid the advances of the paparazzi. Almost unbidden, the rictus grin that I've been trying to suppress rises up to the surface of my face. As I think I've already mentioned, I do love a plan. And now it seems I've got to come up with two.

It doesn't take long for the last vestiges of summer light to flee the sky. By five o'clock dusk has made a murky pool of the square. Rosa's light comes on, as do several others in her block, including Ursula's. Leaving my own light off, I sit in the open windows just behind my small balcony and watch. I've propped a small pair of binoculars on my table, but I find I don't need them. My eyes are as good as a hawk's. I watch Rosa fuss around in her kitchen for a while, coming and going, shifting things about and generally just fannying around. Ursula remains stubbornly hidden behind cream coloured curtains, however, which is vexing. Even hawks can't see through curtains.

With Rosa, I can afford to take my time, come up with something elegant, perhaps even lyrical. Ursula, though, is another matter. As I mentioned before, she's simply a stumbling block - something in my way that needs to be removed as quickly and as efficiently as possible. The trouble is, I know nothing about her. I could simply go in and stab her - I've got her keys after all - but that would arouse suspicion. I've got to make the whole thing look like an accident, and that's hard to do when you don't know somebody. I could make it look like she's drunk too much and taken a fall, but that'd be seen as suspect if she doesn't drink. I could go down the overdose or suicide route, but that'd be harder to make stick if she turns out to be as even-keeled as a Dutch barge. She certainly doesn't look like she's got too much imagination.

Eventually Rosa's light goes out, and I find myself prowling round the house like a big cat looking for prey. Ursula's light goes out shortly afterwards, leaving me literally and metaphorically in the dark. I used to be fairly quick-witted, but this slow starvation of body and soul has dulled my mind. Inspiration has dried up over the years, leaving me reliant on plodding, pedestrian thinking, trying to link cause and effect like some struggling school kid.

I don't get much sleep. I snatch a couple of hours on the couch, but that's it. Even then, my dreams form a disturbing tableau of food, flowers and dead people. So many have died over the last few years that you can't escape dwelling on death. Before the impact, people would die quietly, in nursing homes or hospitals. Now, we're all subject to this slow, relentless decline. People often simply die in the streets where they're standing or walking, their grey corpses as common as benches, the life literally hollowed out of them. You can't imagine that there was ever any spark or vitality there at all. They remind you of the preserved corpses of a different age, wizened by the passing millennia, or the cadavers of mountaineers, their flesh scoured away by the relentless wind. These forlorn, fallen people just lie there until the dogs get to them, or the industrious tenants of some well-organised block cart them away. There's no mourning, no wailing, no outpourings of grief. In fact, it's as if all of the highs and lows of life have been evened out: the mountainous highs have been ground down to dust, and the valleys of grief have silted up. We're just left slogging through this grey dust, knowing that one day we too will collapse.

I think that's what I hate most about this new world order - the mundanity, the sameness of it. If I have anything approaching a mission left in life, it's to add some colour and vibrancy back into our days, accent them with joy and mark them with sorrow.

As the grey vestiges of dawn leak into the square, I realise that I'm exhausted. I've got nothing. Nothing to show for my hours of wakefulness other than brain fog and the first signs of a headache. Still, I'm nothing if not persistent. When inspiration fails to strike, you just have to work through it. I throw my balcony windows open and sit back on my chair, a blanket over my legs to keep the chill off. My coffee machine gurgles away in the background, producing another insipid brew. To be honest, I can think of far worse ways of spending the day. I'm almost content.

But by mid-morning, nothing's changed and

I'm getting restless. Rosa's up and pottering, but Ursula's curtain hasn't so much as twitched. I imagine her sprawled out on her bed, a big bovine lump, chewing the air.

The trouble is, I still know nothing about her. She's originally from Bavaria, and she's stronger than I am. And she doesn't like me. It's hardly a psychological profile. As I sip my fourth cup of watery coffee, I realise that I'm not getting anywhere. Maybe be I should just go over there and knife her.

My mind, filled with self-disgust, starts wandering. Inevitably it turns to food. I remember the warm, vanilla-scented madeleines Rosa produced the day before, and then there was yesterday's feast. Crayfish in red sauce. That's it - crayfish! I jump out of the chair and do a little victory lap of my living room, waving my arms in the air like an athlete thanking the spectators for their support. That's the other thing that I know about Ursula - she traps crayfish. Thank God for them and their tough little invasive hides.

Now it's time to get to work.

My bedroom used to be neat. It's not as if there's a dearth of storage: around the double bed in the back wall are built-in wardrobes in pale blue. To the side is a freestanding dressing table with three drawers. But even this ample storage has been unable to swallow the vast amounts of clothes I've gathered over the last few years. They sit in black plastic bags around the edge of the room like donations to a charity store that have yet to be sorted.

My memory's still good, though, and it doesn't take me long to find what I want. In the wan light that leaks through the white, diaphanous curtains, I dress myself with the solemnity of a priest preparing for mass. When I'm done, I shuffle over to my floor-length mirror with my eyes closed. I adopt a hunched, knock-kneed posture and let my mouth fall. Taking a deep breath, I open my eyes.

Standing before me is a glamorous geriatric, a starlet gone to seed, an elegant woman bowed by privation and the passing years. A grey baize coat is cinched tightly around her meagre waist; a large-brimmed, shapeless hat adorns her head; her feet are enclosed in cheap navy blue trainers, and the only real dash of colour is provided by a paisley scarf she wears about her neck. I smear some red lipstick around my mouth. Gangster granny eat your heart out.

This will be me in twenty years' time, if I manage to live that long, but the thought annoys me, so I shove it aside. I've already seen my future self in Rosa, and I really don't need any more visual reminders of my inevitable decline. I straighten up, take the hat off and shake my hair out, but it's too late. What do I have to look forward to? Sitting on my balcony drinking neat gin, watching the sun disappear over the roofs in its weak, sulphurous glow? Great, really great.

Hurrying back into my living room, I flounce down on to my seat, kicking one long leg over the other in an outward show of vitality. It doesn't work. My mood has been soured, and I'm resentful. Sometimes, it just makes you wonder why you bother. Why not just lie down with an assortment of prescription drugs and a bottle of vodka, and let it all go? And then I realise that far too many people have done that already. I'm still here because I haven't done that; I haven't totally given in to despair. It's meant to be a cheering, rousing kind of thought, but it isn't. It's just irritating. I sit there staring at Ursula's windows with my arms folded.

Come on you bitch.

Her curtains twitch open. She's framed by the window for a second, and disappears. Only then do I realise that I'm massively underprepared. I've squandered so much time! I run back into my bedroom, find an ex-army backpack and chuck in a bottle of water and my knife. I throw it down by the door and put my lumpheaded walking stick next to it. The stick is fashioned from a single piece of wood, and the handle is formed by a polished, fist-sized knot. It's certainly got some heft to it. I return to my seat, sit there twitching for two minutes and then go and put some more coffee on. The game's afoot!

It takes her over an hour to leave her flat, the lazy cow, and I'm not far behind. The good thing about Ursula is that she doesn't look around. If she did, she might see a little old lady hobbling along. This little old lady follows her doggedly from a distance, and sometimes - when Ursula is out of sight - even breaks into a run! From above, it must look strange - one following the other, like a ghost following Pac-man through his maze. And the streets are a maze - they're bound by winding, high grey walls and populated by nothing other than bags of rubbish and stray dogs.

Heading past a looted supermarket and a boarded-up pharmacy, we find ourselves on the outskirts. We follow a road that winds past a row of villas whose white walls have been besmirched by the relentless dust, and then proceed out of town. This is where I'm most vulnerable. There's nowhere to hide, and although the views of the rolling hills and distant mountains open up, I can't enjoy them. I hunch forward, keep my gaze fixed on the ground and tap along lightly, trying to appear as harmless as possible.

The road descends, with a rocky bluff rising up on our right, and soon - at the first bend - Ursula drops off the road, taking a rocky path down to the river valley below. She's instantly out of sight. I stop, straighten up and suck in a deep breath. It's really hard walking bent over - I don't know how some of the old folk do it. I give her a minute or two, and when I'm sure she's a long way ahead, I take the plunge.

As Ursula's still out of sight, I skip down between the rocks and boulders, weaving my way between cypresses that point like dark spears at the sky. The path switches back and forth, and I ski-turn some of the corners, sliding into the loose scree and flinging my walking stick out for balance. You've never seen such a sprightly octogenarian! As I near the bottom, though, I slow down, take a stumbling step on purpose, just to get myself back in character, and proceed at a stately pace, stick probing the ground, eyes straining through dark glasses. I'm Lucretia Fiori, an eighty-two-year-old who once had a husband and a career in the civil service, but who now has little more than memories of her carefree girlhood and a desire to roam the local countryside, hunting for sustenance. Just to prove my point, I stop at a sloe bush, rip off a branch and stick it out of the top of my backpack at a jaunty angle.

At the bottom I sit on a large rock and get my bearings. The valley's still steep, but it's opened out a little. We're on a bend in the river: across from me, the inner curve is wooded and serene. Some of the leaves of the trees are still green, though most are already yellow and some have fallen. Even so, it looks like an idyllic place, with stepping stones set across the river to reach it. I decide that I must come back here one day for a picnic, before the weather really turns.

On this side, a long spit of sand arches out into the water. It must be about twenty metres long, and the fine white sand reminds me of holidays I've had years ago. That's the problem these days - everything you see or experience makes you nostalgic. Anyway, at the end of this singular spit stands my quarry, Ursula. She's leaning out over the water, hauling on a line.

I stay on the rock, as if catching my breath - which isn't far from the truth, as I've slalomed my way down here like an Olympic skier - and slowly stand. I pitch myself forward and make my way along the sand spit, stick sinking awkwardly into the yielding surface.

Up ahead, Ursula hauls a netted trap from the water, squats down and pulls it in to her feet. She's wearing a grey plaid shirt and slacks, and you can see her muscles work beneath the fabric. If I get this wrong, I'm in trouble. Still, with her attention upon the trap, she's facing away from me. I close the distance between us quickly.

When I'm about five metres away, she notices me. Peering over her shoulder, she squints at me suspiciously. I offer up a little wave with one shaking hand, lower my gaze and keep moving forwards. Luckily, when I next glance up, her attention is once again firmly riveted on the trap.

What have you got there? I ask, throwing my voice into a high-pitched, wheedling croak.

Crayfish, she says, glancing quickly back at me. Would you like some?

The offer leaves me stumped. I'd imagined Ursula as some heartless, selfish bitch, and here she is offering to share sustenance with an old lady. Then again, I remind myself of what she represents to me: a stumbling block. A stumbling block and no more. She's probably one of those people who have no sympathy for people their own age, but think that pensioners are cute.

I stare down at the trap, more to distract myself than anything else. I can't believe what I'm seeing. The trap - a netted tube about a metre long by half-a-metre in diameter - is packed with crayfish. Their fat, armoured bodies boil over each other in a restless motion that makes me feel suddenly nauseous.

That's quite a catch, I say, voice breaking with admiration. If you could spare a few... She doesn't look back at me, but I see the edge of a smile etched on her face. She pushes one hefty hand into the side of the trap where it's swallowed by the roiling red mob.

In a split second, my senses fire up. Everything leaps into greater clarity, and time slows. The crayfish turn lazily, and Ursula's hand doesn't move at all. I grasp the walking stick by the stem with both hands, letting it slide forward as I retract it, until I'm gripping its wet end and the heavy knot of the handle is back behind my shoulders.

Ursula must have sensed the sudden motion, as she turns her head towards me, eyes widening. I swing. The walking stick descends in a vicious arc. She raises one arm slightly and hunches her shoulder, but her other arm is still caught in the trap, so she can't move much. Even so, it's enough. The walking stick catches her shoulder and glances off the back of her head. It's not a clean hit, but it's enough to pitch her forward into the water.

The great splash breaks the spell, and time's back on. Before I can react, she's managed to twist herself around, and although she's still submerged, she's facing me. I scream like a banshee and wade in, stick pile-driving down on to the surface of the water. I've got to press home my advantage, but I'm suddenly too close, and realise that I'm going to have to get my hands dirty. With the stick held between my hands, I lunge at her, trying to pin her neck to the riverbed.

This isn't as easy as it sounds. Her hand pulls free of the trap, and she manages to grab me by an elbow, twist me off balance and push me to one side. I lose my footing and plunge face-first into the water. This isn't going as well as I'd hoped.

It gets worse. Before I can right myself, I feel strong hands closing around my shoulders and neck. They're the hands of a murderer, and I wonder how many poor souls she's dispatched over the last few years. I thrash and scream again, but succeed only in emptying my lungs of air. The pressure around my neck increases. I have flash-backs to the hallway the day before. If it ends like this, I wonder whether I'll get the chance to come back and haunt Ursula. It's a pleasant thought, but would be something of a consolation prize.

I feel my strength start to go. I'm on the edge of blacking out. This really galvanises me. Through the choppy waters, I realise that her body's off to one side. I manage to grab one of her arms, pulling her down towards me. Luckily, I'm pretty flexible, and with the last of my strength manage to fling one leg up and catch Ursula in the midriff. That, combined with the fact that I'm pulling her downwards, pitches her headlong into the river.   Her grip fails, and I'm on my feet in an instant. This time, I'm not going to mess it up. Shrieking like a banshee, I throw myself on to her back, wrap one arm around her throat and clamp it there with the other. It's an obvious hold, but effective. She's stronger than me, but from this position she can't reach me: it's all that she can do to keep her head above water. Still, she manages to push herself round, and I soon realise she's trying to drag both of us back to the shore.

This won't do. I'm not ceding the advantage to this lump of a woman. And then it comes to me. What do crocodiles do? They roll. I ratchet my arm further into Ursula's throat, take three quick, deep breaths and throw myself to one side. She's heavy, but my momentum is enough to bring her down on top of me. The waters foam and splash around us, but I keep my grip. As she lashes out above me, like a beetle on its back, I let my mind wander. I wonder what Rosa's got in that little roof garden of hers. I imagine it as some English garden, huge curving sections awash with flowers, bisected by narrow gravel paths and curved wedges of lush green grass. There are apple trees too, a little seat that resembles a piece of Stonehenge, and a small pond, awash with lilies, their white flowers burning like stars against the dark green. And then this evolves into open, alpine meadows, Sound-of-Music style, and I'm running free, careering across the undulating landscape beneath a bright sun, its warmth gilding my limbs, like a carefree child.

To give her credit, Ursula does struggle. She realises that this is it, that her life is leaving her, and she puts in a sterling effort. Eventually, though, her limbs start to slacken. I count to six, and then she's still. With the last of my breath, I make a shushing sound into the water, as if I'm trying to calm a truculent toddler, and release my grip. Scrambling from under her dead weight, I break the surface of the water, gasping and twisting like a fish, surrounded by falling water that catches the light like jewels. I wade back to the shore, and turn to inspect my work. Ursula lies there, staring up at the scarfed sun, her body a floating hulk.

I look down and inspect myself. The grey baize coat has lost its shape, and come undone. The black top I'm wearing is now plastered to my skinny body; I may not be much to look at, but it's obvious now that I'm not some little old lady. I'm going to have to try to dry off a little before heading back into town.

Then I hear it - a sudden, spasming intake of breath. I look over at Ursula's body - her head jerks back, and in a slow, horrible rolling motion, she turns on to her front. Slowly, ever so slowly, she raises her head until she's fixed me with those baleful eyes. She's not dead! Jesus - what does it take to kill this woman? Before I panic and give way to fears that she's some kind of zombie, the rational part of my mind takes control. There's no way that she's fully with it after what she's just been through. Slowly, keeping my eyes fixed on hers, I wade out and retrieve my walking stick. I circle round towards her, making sure I'm just beyond her reach. She breathes with slow, laboured gasps as she squints up at me, black hair plastered to her forehead.

And it strikes me that this is a turning point. I could spare her. But then what? I'd have to move out of town, find another place to hole up, and that would never do. I'd probably be raped, knifed and robbed within days. And there's no way I could stay in town with Ursula alive after this. I don't think this is something we'll be able to laugh off over a cup of coffee and a slice of cake.

So I grip the stick tightly, like a batter approaching the plate. Ursula doesn't have enough breath to talk, so I do it for her. Yes, I say, I'll see you in hell too. With that, I swing the walking stick as hard as I can. She doesn't have the strength to move quickly enough, and the knot of wood catches her squarely on the temple. There's a faint clicking sound, and then she slumps forward, face down in the water. I stand up straight and toss the walking stick back behind me.

I resist the urge to slump down into the water myself. Instead I take a couple of paces backwards and collapse on the sand. What now? There's no way I can hide the body - I don't have the strength. And it would be pointless anyway. Pretty soon people will notice she's missing. I splash some water over my face, and realise how cold it is. The frigid sun has barely warmed it, despite the passing of the so-called summer months.

To be fair, I thought it would be worse than this. I thought that killing someone would involve passing through some phase of gut-wrenching horror. But in reality, it felt like killing an animal - a regrettable but necessary act. And by the end, it was a mercy killing. Poor, dumb Ursula.

Bovine until the very end.

A few hours later, I'm picking my way back through the grey streets. It's barely past five, but dusk seems to have already set in. The high-level haze seems to be thicker than ever, which can't be the case, but whatever, not much sunlight seems to be getting through. Still, I'm thankful. Earlier I headed downstream a little and tried to dry my coat out on a rock. I sat wedged in a patch of spiky undergrowth, hoping that I was hidden from view. As far as I could tell, the only company I had was a buzzard, which circled ceaselessly overhead, waiting for me to die. I wasn't particularly sorry to disappoint him, and now here I am, Lucretia Fiori, tapping her way feebly back through the streets, skirting the edges of the cliff-like buildings. If you accosted her, you'd realise that she was soaking wet, and that her bag was not only fit to bursting, but writhed with a life of its own.

I shouldn't have taken any crayfish, I know, but the thought of their warm sweet flesh was just too much. So I hauled out about two-thirds of the catch and wedged poor Ursula's arm back into the trap for good measure. By now the little bastards will probably have eaten her hand off.

At the edge of our square, I pause. There's no one about. A couple of lights are on, of course, but there's nothing I can do about that. I mustn't break character now, must hold my nerve until the end. Even so, I quit my circuitous tapping and cut diagonally across the square. Despite my best intentions, I find that I'm holding my breath and casting glances from side to side. I'm just waiting to be accosted at any moment by Hilda, with Rosa standing just beyond her shoulder, nodding like a golem.

Only then to I realise just how much my bag is moving. Glancing down I see - to my horror - that the zip has started to work its way open. I fumble with it, but as I'm doing so something dark rises up like a turd in reverse, and falls from the edge of the bag. As soon as the big a crayfish hits the ground, he's scurrying away, pincers raised. What the hell? I don't have the self-control to stop and retrieve him, so I just press on, my face a mask of dismay.

I force myself to open our block's front door with the methodical slowness of a little old lady, and resist the urge to slam it behind me. Then I take off my coat and stalk confidently past Filippa's concierge station. I needn't have bothered: she's asleep in her chair, snoring quietly, head supported by her lack of neck and the thick collar of her uniform.

After a quick, adrenaline-fuelled jog up the stairs, I'm back. Inside my flat I lean against my door and sink slowly to the floor with relief. I've done it. Phase one of the plan is complete, and no one other than a bunch of crustaceans and a lonely bird of prey saw a thing.

Dinner is a riotous affair. I dress in some new stockings, my highest heels and my little black dress. I add one of my ex-fiancé's black suit jackets, by way of contrast, and an old top hat that I found years ago in a charity shop.

The crayfish get dumped into my biggest pan of boiling water. If they weren't squirming before, they are now. Look lively boys! I slam the lid on just to prove a point: there's no escape.

While I'm waiting, I stick on some Sinatra and dance my way around the flat. With my walking stick in one hand, I'm all Liza Minnelli in Cabaret, sultry and innocent by degrees. I leave the windows open - it's no crime to have a party - and even enjoy the cold air sweeping in sheets into my flat. I slam a half-empty bottle of vodka on to the table along with a shot glass.

The crayfish only take minutes to turn a lovely, deep red. They're the same colour as wet terracotta, and remind me of the sunsets we've had over the last few years. I pour them out on to the largest of my chopping boards, and they fill it completely. Sitting at the table, I arm myself with some nutcrackers and a skewer and set to work.

Slathered with a simple dressing of lemon juice and olive oil, and plastered liberally with pepper and sea salt, they form a veritable feast.

It's the most memorable meal I've cooked in years. As old blue eyes croons, I begin to pile up crayfish shells like some grisly memorial. Native or not, they make great eating.

When I'm done, I pour myself a shot of vodka and sit back, replete. In the last two days I've probably consumed more protein than I have in the last two years, and right now it feels good. To Ursula! I say, and knock the fiery liquid back. I'd like to carry on partying, but it's as much as I can do to clear away. Once I've cleaned myself up I crawl into bed, suit jacket and all, and fall asleep as if someone's hit me over the head with a stick.

The next day I'm not so good. I should be exultant, over the moon with my success, but I'm not. I feel cold, as if winter's already invaded my bones. It's not food poisoning, as I don't feel sick, so reckon I must have picked up a chill from the river.

I pull the duvet over my shoulders and mope about my flat feeling lonely, which is ridiculous. Most of us have felt lonely for the last seven years. Of course, you're thinking that this is psychosomatic, that my sudden illness is my body expressing my sorrow and regret for killing Ursula. Sorry, but I'm calling bullshit on that. Let's straighten this out: I had no ill feelings towards Ursula, but she made her intentions towards me quite clear. If she'd shown a bit more warmth or humour, I might have found the task more unpleasant, but she didn't. Plus she attacked me in the corridor, which made my decision and its execution so much easier.

Sitting in the chair by the window, I stare over at Rosa's block. How long before they realise Ursula's missing? How many people are even left in that block? I have no idea.

Just as I'm considering going back to bed, there's a knock at my door. I cringe down into my duvet, imagining a queue of identical policeman in the hallway, ready to take me away. It's a startling vision: their white, implacable and plate-like faces loom down at me like something out of a Kafka novel. I must really be ill.

I consider sloping off to bed, but tell myself to get a grip. Still trailing the duvet, I move soundlessly to the door. The peephole reveals Cornelius, his head swollen to planet-sized proportions by the fish-eye lens. Grudgingly I let him in, giving him a sad little smile as he enters. Maybe now he'll want to ravish me, seeing how vulnerable and forlorn I look. The sad thing is that I might not even say no.

In his easy-going, dandyish way he crosses the room and seats himself in my chair. Hard night, he asks, or are you just succumbing to the inevitable malaise, the ennui of our times? I stand there, feet losing their warmth on the cold floor, and stare at him. No, I say. I've just got a bit of a chill. What brings you here?

Well, he says, looking sprightly, and inspecting a gold pocket watch that he pulls from his waistcoat, I thought I'd give you a little update on your order. Companies used to do that, didn't they, when the internet still worked?

How very thoughtful of you, I say, dragging a chair away from the table and placing it midway between the door and the window. I slump down into my duvet, and am thankful for its soft, quilted padding.

Yes, I say, they did. But am I having to pay for this service? I raise one eyebrow. Am I flirting? To be honest, I have no idea.

No, of course not, he adds, smiling. I was just passing. One has to keep hustling, or so they say. His smile widens and he looks at me with dancing eyes. It's then that I realise he's amused by the state I'm in; he's obviously one of those people who feeds on the misfortune of others, who gains energy in direct proportion to how much others are suffering. Sicko. He's certainly not eyeing me with any sense of admiration or attraction, which is understandable.

Your order's progressing well, he says. There's only one item that we can't source: the rat poison. We've got a warehouse full of plastic traps. What's hard to get is the actual poison itself. What with an increase in recent demand, and the fact that the factories stopped operating years ago...

He doesn't finish the sentence, just leaves me to join up the dots. Is there anything I can do, I ask, raising my eyebrows a little, to procure any, or to speed the order along? I snake one leg out towards him and give him an enigmatic smile. To his credit, Cornelius doesn't take the bait. I decide he has an aversion to sweat-soaked, feverish women. The loser.

I can get you a terrier, he says. That should certainly discourage them. In fact, I saw one as I crossed the square. He was facing off against a crayfish, of all things.

My stomach contracts, and I feel suddenly queasy. Can he smell the remains of the crayfish in here? I inhale slowly through my nose. I don't notice anything, but it's possible that the air is saturated with that sweet, fishy smell and that I've become unaware of it. Does he know what I've done? Is he mocking me? I tell myself to get a grip. It's just fever-induced paranoia.

Really, I say, how strange!

Cornelius shrugs. I didn't expect it to be much of a contest, he adds. But the crayfish reversed expertly up one of the downpipes to your block, leaving one hungry and disappointed dog. If you've got a spare leash lying around, I'll go and fetch him.

That's just what we need around here, I say, rolling my eyes, another mouth to feed. Plus, the last time I checked, dogs weren't that keen on vegetables.

True, says Cornelius, very true.

Once I've shot the breeze with Cornelius, I head out again. I feel the need for some kind of solace. I still feel ghastly, as if I've got a dose of flu, Covid-19 or both. Which of course is ridiculous, as my social contact has been severely limited. I don't see the dog that Cornelius was yammering on about, and I don't see the bloody crayfish either. In fact, I don't see another soul, which isn't uncommon.

After a ten minute controlled stagger, I'm sitting in Santa Maria's, the smaller of our two churches. Again, I'm on my own, but the place has a down-at-heal feel. I decide that this must be because of dust that has blown in and created a gritty, sandpapery feel underfoot. With most places running a skeleton staff - if you'll excuse the pun - cleaning is one of the first things to slide. Plus the churches are left open during daylight hours, so I figure they've taken a lot of traffic in the past few years, and have developed a kind of psychic fatigue as a result.

Still, it's pretty enough. I sit towards the back, my gaze channelled towards the altar by the stone pillars that rise from the floor like dead trees. The altar itself is bathed in an otherworldly light provided by stained-glass windows that ooze electric blues, purples and oranges. I contemplate some of the mysteries - the Word made flesh, the Immaculate Conception and the Resurrection - in a vague and unconnected way. I'm not terribly religious, and never have been. In fact, I've always been quite dismissive of religion, although some part of me has always yearned for that quiet, contented faith that some people seem to have. Now more than ever, of course.

In fact, I'm sure I heard it once said that religious faith and an appreciation of the aesthetic are one and the same thing. Why else would churches have stained glass windows and frescoes? Why else would mosques be inlaid with ornate tiles and call people to prayer in such a dramatic manner? Contemplating the mysteries of God certainly does lead to awe and wonder, and the mythologies themselves are obviously more poetic than factual. I decide that it's all really just about finding beauty in what can be a rather messy existence. As Keats said, truth is beauty, beauty truth. Fundamental concepts and tropes endure, and thus have a timeless elegance. And that's how mathematicians find beauty in equations, surely. They transcend time and space.

Sitting here has made me appreciate one thing, if nothing else. Rosa's death must be an aesthetic phenomenon. It must have a timeless appeal, must bring to the fore the tragedy implicit in the human condition. It must also give us hope for the future, even if it is a piece of theatre. Any fool can kill an old woman. It's making Rosa's death signify something beyond itself that is the hard part. In short, I realise, I want to turn Rosa into a saint. I want to turn this deluded old woman who's on the edge of dementia into a beacon of hope for humanity in these trying times. On her own, and in life, there is no way that Rosa can realise this lofty ideal. But in a well-performed death, she can be transformed, the base metal of her being transmuted into existential gold.

I'm overcome by a deep upwelling of joy. I realise that I've got to elevate Rosa to the status of a piece of art, have her cut down and then watch the pathos come pouring out. She will fall, but her memory will rise up. She will become much, much greater than she was before, a guiding light for those who linger on.

Sadly, practical concerns tend to cut through the highest of aspirations and emotions. The pews are as hard and unforgiving as ever - even more so now I've lost any padding I ever had - and my backside has gone numb. I stand up, jig around a little, but sitting back down just leads to the numbness returning in seconds. I could wander around, could inspect the stained glass windows, but reckon that since they're modern they're bound to be less impressive close up. Some things are best contemplated from a distance, lest they lose their mystery.

Still, my visit's been as overwhelming success. To put it plainly, I now need to big Rosa up. I need to create some momentum, an ad campaign of sorts. Procuring poison will probably be the easy part.

The rest of the day passes in a daze. I schlep around the flat in my duvet and keep tabs on Rosa's block. There's a sudden flurry of activity just after nightfall, when a whole bunch of lights come on. Have they finally realised that Ursula's missing? It didn't take them long, to be fair. The stories of people who've been found dead in their flats are beyond counting, so to find out that she's not there after thirty-six hours is pretty good going. But still, it's night now: they've missed the boat and will have to wait until morning.

I don't sleep much. I catch a couple of hours on my sofa, hours that are polluted by dreams born of my fever. They're grotesque, but strangely vivid. In one I'm underground, hunting through tunnels that could have been sewers or caves, with a fiery brand held aloft. When I come to a side tunnel, something scuttles back into the darkness. But scuttles is probably the wrong word, as this thing is big. It fills the tunnel, hard carapace scraping along the walls. Before anything else can happen, I wake up, and for once I'm thankful.

Just after first light, my fever breaks. Sweat pours from me in liberal streams, and it's as much as I can do to keep swigging water between periods of unconsciousness. My duvet becomes a sponge, and each time I wake up it's wetter than before. By midday the filling starts to pile up in protest, forming dense ridges beneath the sodden cotton. This fever could be the death knell for my duvet. Where the hell am I going to find another one?

I try to keep apprised of events across the square, but in my wretched state it's difficult. There's a flurry of activity at about ten - Hilda and a couple of other women are milling around the front door, but that's all I manage to see. I'm woken by occasional bangs, which I take to be knocks at my door. Several times I creep over and peer out, but there's no one there. I decide it's the fictional rats coming back to haunt me, and let it slide.

Another whole day passes in a daze. On the fourth day, I rise again. With my sickness sloughed away, everything seems fresh and vibrant. My vision seems sharper, colours are brighter, the texture of the rag rug in my bathroom is exotic. I bake some bread, and the smell is as lavish as anything ever served up for a Turkish sultan. In fact, as soon as the bread has cooled, I decide to take a trip to see my long-lost mother. I pop the bread in a wicker basket, pull a tea towel over it and don a scarlet headscarf. As I step out into my corridor and descend the stairs, though, I realise that I'm still weak from my sudden illness. Venturing out into the daunting expanse of the square I feel like Little Red Riding Hood heading off into the forest.

Hilda greets me at the door with a wordless nod, and retires to her cubbyhole before I can say anything charming or stupid. As I work my across the parquet floor and up the wide stairs, my steps ring with the finality of someone approaching the gallows. The place has a sombre, haunted air, and only then do I realise that Ursula's keys are lying in the bottom of the bag that I've slung so carelessly over my shoulder. If Hilda searches me on a whim, I'm screwed.

It takes Rosa an eternity to get to the door. She seems smaller and frailer than I remember. In the sharpness of my post-fever vision the creases on her face look like valleys, her hair the finest of wire wool. She's wearing a dark, floral print dress, which is fair enough, but the black cardigan she's thrown carelessly over the top has seen better days. She seems to have lost all the pep she ever had and, to be frank, this simply won't do. It's pretty hard to make a martyr out of someone who's half-dead already.

In a split second I realise that it's up to me to inject some energy into this scene. I sweep into the room with the perky verve of a fifties starlet.

Mama! I say, parking my basket on her little table, come va? I've been so ill! I widen my eyes at her as if I've had a brush with the Grim Reaper himself. She shuts the door behind me and works her way over to me, her gaze on the floor. I made you some bread, I say, not to be put off by her lethargic, shambling gait. A great sculptor can only work with the block of stone before them, and I'm beginning to wonder if mine has more cracks than I bargained for.

When she gets to me, she casts an eye at the bread and pats my hand. Bene, bene, she says, then moves around me and plonks herself into a chair. Mama! I cry, still wide-eyed and theatrical, what's wrong? Are you sick? Do you have the fever too?

She shakes her head. It's these times, she says. People - pfff! - they disappear. Slowly at first, but now - how many of us are left? She looks up at me with a heartbroken gaze. There's humanity there. I can work with this, I tell myself. I can work with this.

Mama, I say, as if about to scold a child, what do you mean? First it was signor Rosato, she says. Then Emilia. Now, Ursula. I sit next to her, take her hand in mine and fix her with a concerned, searching gaze. What are you saying, Mama? You're making no sense! Even I'm impressed by my air of innocence and credulity. My talents were wasted in the classroom. I should have been

on the West End stage, the silver screen or some
dingy hole in Edinburgh tearing my own hair out.

It's Ursula, she says, taking my hand in hers
and patting it gently. She's disappeared. She's not
in her flat. And her spare keys have gone! We had
to use the key that she gave me years ago to get in.
We've searched the block - even the attic! We've
sent search parties around the streets. She's not
here. She's gone. Perhaps to somewhere else, perhaps a better place. She shakes her head sadly, and
I see tears starting on the underside of her lids. It's
then that I realise that she really cared for Ursula.

Okay, I say. When was she last seen? Where
was she? Rosa shakes her head, as if my questions
are those of a child. There's only one place she
might be, says Rosa. Down by the river. I frown.
The river? Yes, she continues slowly, still patting
my hand, down by the river. With her crayfish.
My frown deepens. What do you think she's doing
down there, I ask. Camping?

Rosa doesn't smile, but doesn't chide me either. It's the only place we haven't looked, she
says. Hilda would go, but her hip is bad. There are
a couple of other women who could, but they're
too scared. Like ghosts already. She looks up at
me, and I can see the defiance in her eyes. This is
good! We need that fire, that will to survive.

There must be someone, I say. There must
be. She shakes her head. Only you, bambina. Only
you. You're fit - agile, like a runner! Could you do

this thing for us? Poor dear, sweet Ursula.

I think that applying the adjectives "dear" and "sweet" to Ursula might be pushing it, but I hold my tongue. Inside I'm smiling. This is going much better than I expected. Without even trying to, I've suddenly become indispensable to Rosa's block.

However, I hide my sudden glee by frowning. My face must be as deeply lined as Rosa's. Okay, Mama, I say, taking a deep breath. I don't mind going, but -what time is it? Eleven already! If I go, I'll have to start soon to get back before dark. Where is it, this place she collects crayfish - do you know?

Il burrone, she calls it. The gorge, the ravine, the gulley. The Italian word sounds as if it's got something to do with donkeys - burros in Spanish. The two languages are remarkably similar.

Hilda, she says, Hilda can tell you how to get there. Okay, I say, but I've got to go now. We both rise in unison, and kiss each other. Enjoy the bread, I add. I'll be back before nightfall. If I'm not, well... for once I'm at a loss for what to say. Well, enjoy the bread, I add. And then I'm off, whirling out of the room like a glamorous super-hero ready to face the forces of darkness.

An hour later I'm dancing my way down the steep switchbacked trail towards the river. Hilda's instructions weren't half bad, actually, and I listened to them with a look of studied concentration on my face. I popped back to my flat, put some trainers on, put a knife and a small torch into my bag, and here I am, tripping the light fantastic. I'm surprised how little time it's taken me to get here. The sun's at its zenith now, a paper disk floating above the layers of haze. Even so, I'm still conscious of time, of not wanting to get caught out here. I'm like a mountaineer on a summit push, ever fearful of night closing in.

By the time I get to the riverbed, I've actually had some time to mull over what Rosa and the rest of her block expect of me. If Ursula's body is still there, then what? Report back, I guess. There's no way I could lug her body back single-handed. And as they don't have anyone else able-bodied enough to get down here in the first place, how am I meant to retrieve the body? I guess that's a hurdle I'll have to cross when I get to it. Still, it's good to know that they're so short-handed. With Ursula out of the way, I could become indispensable as a fetcher of sorts.

I make my way leisurely along the sand spit. It's warm enough, and a light breeze blows grains across the exposed skin of my ankles. I don't really know what to expect but - to be fair - I don't actually feel that daunted. Ursula's bloated, waterlogged corpse, its arm eaten off by crayfish? There are worse things in this world, I tell myself.

At the end of the spit I stop. Placing one

hand above my eyes to block out the meagre glare, I peer at the river. The water rushes along the shallow bed happily enough, hurrying here, eddying there. Starting from where I stand, I scan the area before me with long, lazy glances, assuming that her body has been washed downstream some way. Nothing. Not even the floating remnants of a crayfish trap.

Sighing, I make my way back along the spit and start picking my way over the rocks and boulders of the river's edge. A short while later, I reach some spiky bushes, and I negotiate these as well as I'm able, scratching my legs and splashing through the water where I have to. After a hundred metres or so I stop, body sweat-glazed with the effort. I scan the waters. Nothing. I repeat the process once more, twice more. By now the river has narrowed, pitching into a gorge. The bank has disappeared, and to go any further, I'd have to wade on into the fast-flowing waters.

Dissatisfied, I beat a retreat. It takes me some time to make my way back, and I plonk myself on the large rock at the base of the path and cast my eyes up and down the river. My legs are aching and scratched and my heart's beating hard within my chest. Annoyed, I keep scanning the river. Eventually I have to admit that there's nothing there: Ursula and her traps have disappeared into the ether. The current doesn't seem strong enough to have taken them far downstream, and it's so shallow - surely she would have been snagged by a rock or branch before getting far?

Sadly, I'm forced to head back. As I make my way up the rocky path, past the abandoned villas and then through the grey streets of the town, I start to wonder if Ursula is actually dead. She recovered pretty well from being strangled, and maybe the blow to the head wasn't the coup-de-grace that I'd thought it was. I imagine her water-logged figure lurching around the streets at night: her torn crayfish trap is attached to one arm, and she wields it like a hammer. Within the mesh confines of the trap, however, her skin has been stripped away, leaving a whittled pink mess where her forearm used to be.

I don't know what I'm expecting, but back at Rosa's block there's no huddled group greeting me at the front door and asking questions in hushed, reverential tones. In fact, no one greets me at all. It takes five minutes for Hilda to open the front door, and when she does, she doesn't say a word. It's up to me to shake my head and say that I found no sign of Ursula. She sighs and retreats to her concierge station. I can't believe it - I'm absolutely flabbergasted. After all I've done for them!

I stalk upstairs in a foul mood. Rosa greets me without enthusiasm. It's as if she's forgotten about my mission, or as if she's just assumed Ursula was dead anyway. Once again it's up to me to add the energy. I waltz in, drop my bag on the table and throw one leg over the other as I sit, revealing my scraped legs. Not a sign of her, I say, throwing up my hands up in the air for emphasis. Rosa just retreats to the kitchen, shaking her head. Would you like some coffee, she asks.

Coffee! I have to stop myself from shrieking the word out in exasperation. Are these people for real? That would be lovely, Mama, I manage between gritted teeth. There are only two reasons for such subdued reactions: they'd either given up hope of Ursula's body being found in the first place, or they know I did it and are rubbing my nose in it like an owner rubbing a puppy's nose in its own mess. Telling myself it's the former, I take a couple of slow, deep breaths to calm myself.

The listlessness of these people is astounding. Killing Rosa could be a lot easier than I'd thought. Maybe I should be aiming higher, looking further. Suddenly dreams of declaring myself queen of the whole square start to run through my mind. I see myself sitting on some makeshift throne atop one of the blocks, a wooden effigy of saint Rosa by my side as fireworks go off overhead, marking the night sky with trails of purple, orange and blue.

As Rosa brings coffee and slumps down next to me, the visions continue. I could flood the square, bring in gondolas and rowing boats, and spend warm, leisurely afternoons punting across the calm, dark waters, rowed by wretched minions. Of course, the only thing missing would be someone to share this with, a partner in greatness. Sadly, no one springs to mind. There's got to be someone out there - sad eyed and gaunt, but with a malicious smile - who I can share all of this with. But right now, I have no idea where he is. Maybe I should start looking.

Daydreams aside, I realise that it might be me who's setting the wrong note here. These people need my help. Mama, I say, leaning forward and taking Rosa's hand in mine, Ursula's not at the river. Do you have any idea of where she could be? The old lady shakes her head, reminding me of a child trying not to cry. Patience, I tell myself, patience. You've checked all the rooms, you said, and the attics. Have you checked the basement? She nods. What about the roof garden? Rosa shrugs. She wouldn't be up there, she says, her voice a whisper.

Perhaps not, I say, pressing my advantage. But don't we owe it to her to check? She might be up there, camping. Having a lovely time! Come on, I'll come with you. It might not be likely, but we've got to be sure. Let's go together, for Ursula. I squeeze her hand and smile sadly. To give her her due, she nods and says, va bene. We finish our coffee in silence, leave the flat and walk up the wide staircase hand-in-hand. It feels like a woman taking her elderly mother for a walk, perhaps to visit places they used to go when they were much younger, or to pay their respects to a loved-one in a churchyard. As we make our way up the dingy stairwell, I start to feel choked up. I haven't felt this close to anyone for years. Rosa's my mother now, and I'm going to enjoy her company for as long as I'm able. With the elderly, every day is precious.

Eventually we come to the top of the building. We make our way slowly along one of the corridors. Does anyone still live up here, I ask. Only Signor Rosario, says Rosa. He used to be such an active man, but since his wife died six months ago, we barely see him. He is a small and proud man and keeps to himself. She shakes her head at the damage that's been wrought on society in the last seven years. We forget how fragile life on Earth really is: crop failures, food shortages and bang - before you know it, a large proportion of the population have starved to death. You can't feed many people with mushrooms and vegetable gardens in your basement. It's all very well, but at some point you just need calories.

Halfway along the corridor we come to a door on the right that's ajar. We sneak through the gap like burglars, and are soon inside a dark flat. Mama, I whisper, trying to sound naive and vulnerable, doesn't someone live here? Hush now, my child, she says, and a warm sense of affection floods through me. My child! No one's ever called me that! No, she continues, the people who lived here moved away years ago, soon after the skies darkened. The flat is smaller than Rosa's, and rear-facing, if that makes sense. We pass some kind of kitchenette and proceed across an open-plan living room like two explorers braving a desert. It's odd to think that people once lived here: all of them gone now, all of that life force lost, or simply shunted elsewhere. We pause at patio doors, and Rosa moves the old net curtains to one side with care. The door itself opens with a sound like the shrieking of the dead, its metal underside scraping in its runnel.

As we step outside, we're met by a cool afternoon breeze. We're in the last days of August, but it feels as if winter is just around the corner. Normally this kind of thought would lower my mood, but not now, not with the prospect of clapping eyes upon this block's garden.

We're on a small roof terrace, and to either side a plethora of plants rises from old containers that have been press-ganged into a new existence. Buckets, oil cans and even an old boot have become the home of vegetables and herbs. Courgettes pour from redundant corners, another plant vomits aubergines into the cooling air, and in the corner sprouts a banana plant of all things! Beans ascend makeshift canes, and assorted herbs mound up around our feet.

Mama! I say, this is wonderful - an oasis! An Eden! Rosa nods and moves forward again, picking her feet up with pride. When the catastrophe stuck, she says, we all got together and turned these terraces over to general use. We all came to work up here together - those were the days! We were like a swarm of bees, a load of little communists! Look at what we achieved!

At the end of the garden we step up on to a packing crate, and then on to a walkway made of scaffolding boards. A handrail has been put in between vertical wooden posts, but even so it's a harum-scarum drop into an odd-shaped courtyard below. As we make our way along this precarious path, I notice that vines are trailing above our heads, snaking their way through a wonky trellis, with bunches of luminous grapes hanging over our heads like an inheritance.

We pass several more rooftop gardens, each equally as packed and verdant as the first. Then we come to a set of packing crate steps. Clutching an even flimsier handrail, we make our way upward. Now I really do feel like a mountaineer, staggering up the final slope of some incredible eight-thousand-metre peak. We arrive at a wide plinth of wood, surrounded by more makeshift rails and a few pots. Wooden chairs cluster around a small tiled table. We're at the top of the block now: the peak of the roof is just a couple of feet beyond this plinth. This place is like an eyrie - high but secluded. I've certainly never caught a glimpse of anyone up here from my flat.

Taking a slow turn, I realise that you can see right out over the town from here - a perfect panorama. The roofs slope away in a charming assortment of colours, textures and angles, and I realise how lucky I am to live somewhere so beautiful. To the north the mountains begin to rise: the horizon is dominated by their hard grey ridges and slopes, their summits slathered in snow.

We used to come up here, says Rosa, pulling out a chair, Ursula and me. We'd come up here just to sit in the meagre sun. She was a good friend. I take a chair and sit across from Rosa. It pains me to see how much I've hurt her. I reach for her hand, and she puts it quietly into mine. I'm sorry, Mama, I say, so sorry. I pause, trying to be tactful. But at least we've found each other. We won't be lonely now, either of us.

It's not late, but the sun is already beginning its slow descent through the thick layers of haze and dust, and it burns a filthy, spreading orange in the western sky. The year's on the turn, and despite the profusion of plants up here, it's been hard not to ignore signs of premature decay: the yellow mottling on some of the leaves, the undersized aubergines, the clusters of unripe grapes like green marbles. Some of it will come good, for sure, but some of it won't. As I've said, at the end of the day it's about calories. With a sack of rice or flour you can survive for months. A couple of courgettes won't get you very far.

Still, at least I've found this place. This is where I'll erect my throne. This is where I'll light my fireworks. This is where I'll place my statue of Saint Rosa, carved from a water-weathered log dragged up from the river below. This is from where I'll rule. And this is where I'll anoint my successor.

People thought that Rome or the Third Reich would last forever. I'm not that naive. But still, I aim to put my stamp on this little passage of passing time in which we find ourselves. We need some positivity, some continuity, some glamour in these hard times.

Maybe another day we can come up here for coffee and cake, I say to Rosa, squeezing her hand. Come on, I say, let's look for Ursula. So we descend and wander about the other balconies. But she's not there. She's not there at all.

I stay with Rosa for a while and then creep along to Ursula's flat. I cast furtive glances down the stairwell as I pass, but Hilda must be in her concierge station. The door to Ursula's flat opens easily, as if it's been periodically checked and oiled. They're running a tight ship over here, and no mistake. I close the door quietly behind me.

It's funny that I didn't end up actually using Ursula's key when I killed her; now I'm going to see if there's anything in here worth nicking. It's not the most uplifting of sentiments, I'll give you that, but times are hard. I'm loath to turn a light on, so I take out my torch and start making my way furtively around the flat in the thin beam of light. I feel like a professional, moving soundlessly in my sneakered feet. I come across the obligatory furniture: a cupboard full of glasses which can, quite frankly, stay where they are. In a drawer I find another torch and some spare batteries. I take those. Again, this is open-plan living, so it's pretty easy to navigate my way around.

I'd left Rosa back in her flat not five minutes before, and she seemed tired but positive, like someone who's actually done something useful. I've suggested that we go on a little scavenging expedition tomorrow. She didn't say no, simply smiled and said, we'll see, we'll see. I'll get her out, no problem. She needs some exercise and fresh air. We don't want her getting frail before her time.

I pick my way carefully into the kitchen. The floor tiles gleam with a pearly-white sheen in the torchlight. So, Ursula, what do we have here? In the cupboards I find a yellow packet of caffe d'orzo, half-a-bag of sugar and a kilo of flour, Farina"0", all of which I take. There's also a can of sardines and a packet of red paper serviettes. They'll be good for Christmas, I think, rolling my eyes. That's it. There are a few vegetables in the fridge that are starting to turn, so I leave them where they are. No secret stashes of food here, unless she's got stuff stacked under the floorboards.

I fare little better in Ursula's bedroom. I don't know what I'm expecting to find - handcuffs and sex toys? But there's nothing like that. It seemed she lived a pretty frugal existence. There's a dead iPhone, and a few novels, but I leave them where they are. There isn't much in her wardrobes either, but I do find a pair of black winter gloves, and those go in my bag. Straightening up, I head back into her lounge and stop in the middle of the darkening room. I can't help but wonder what sort of existence we're living here. It seems to be one of slow attenuation, of things settling, clocks and batteries running down to zero. Ursula didn't have much stuff. Neither does Rosa. Neither do I. There's no excess, no wealth; no one's thriving any more. Energy is dissipating, feeling failing.

Where could it be better than this, I wonder? Did you ever see those documentaries about the potential ravages of global warming? The maps of the shrinking coastlines around the world were always fascinating, until you realised how many people would be affected: how many people would be displaced, how many die of cholera or other hideous diseases. And at the end

97

of those programmes they'd always try to put a positive spin on things. Humans are adaptable, they'd say. Humans are the most adaptable species to have ever walked the planet. Apart from cockroaches, ants and flies, I'd think, but hey. And then they'd give you a little something to buoy your flagging spirits: in a world of runaway global warming, new lands would emerge. And there would be this graphic of the Antarctic ice sheets melting, revealing vast lands last seen when the dinosaurs ruled the Earth - a new Eden where the sun doesn't set for half the year.

And I wonder if anywhere on the planet is like that now? What would happen if we all jumped on a freighter, hit the North African coast and started heading South? Would we find that the Sahara has been converted into a network of oases, gleaming like strewn jewels in the sun? The desert as the new Mediterranean, its waterholes and plantations joined by Venetian canals, towering palms and the neon wildfire of bougainvillea?

It's an arresting image, and it leaves me stranded, speechless in Ursula's flat. Have other people already worked this out? Has there already been a mass migration into the depths of northern Africa? With one-way traffic into Europe for decades, does that count as reverse colonisation? I have no idea, but I realise - sadly - that I'm stranded here, on this bank and shoal of time.

If I'd had the energy to run, that time is long past. We have to make the best of where we find ourselves at any given time. And, for sure, there are worse places to be.

Making my way over to a window, I peer out across the square. Inky shadows have settled into the corners: it's a scene caught perfectly between night and day. The sky still retains a certain luminosity, but everything down here on earth has lost its colour, the lines of the buildings sketched in with pen and ink. People don't often use lights after dark - it's not worth firing the generators up for - but, strangely enough, there are a couple on in my block. One in the top left, one on the ground floor. There's also one on in the middle. I locate the edge of the block, count over and up. When I realise that the light's in my flat, my vision lurches sideways. I feel sick, as if I'm about to faint, or as if I've just been hit on the head. I clutch at the top of a chair to steady myself, just about managing to keep my gaze steady. Did I leave a light on? Not bloody likely, but there it is. There's a light on, over at the Frankenstein Place... great. Is that how I'm going to think of my flat from now on? I shake my head. I've got to get a grip.

It's simple enough. There's someone over there, wandering about my flat, doing exactly what I'm doing over here, but with much less caution. I run a hand through my hair and suck down a deep breath. And that's when I see a figure, standing back behind one of the floor-length windows. It moves out of sight, and seconds later the lights go off.

Sweat pricks at my temples. I try to clear my throat, but my mouth is so dry that I can't. I don't want to move, but I know I've got to go back and face this thing. Over here, even in the half-dark, I feel exposed. I leave Ursula's flat in a pall of silence and head noisily down the stairs, slapping my feet against the steps, squeaking my hand along the railing and coughing. I give Hilda a cheerful "Ciao" and head out into the inky darkness of the square.

III

The image of the figure, lit from behind, burns hard in my mind's eye as I cross the square. I couldn't tell if it was a man or a woman, but it was adult. Sadly, its features were obscured by the bright background, the yellow light of hell. It could have been anybody.

I make my way inside, notice that Filippa isn't at her station, and make my way quickly up the stairs. The wooden steps creak, but once I'm in the corridor, the parquet floor and trainers combo renders me silent. As I take the knife from my bag, I can't help thinking, how now brown cow? Whoever's in there is in for a nasty surprise.

No light filters out from under my door, and I turn the key in the lock with a slow, steady hand. I push the door open hard, and slap the light switch with my other hand. My flat bursts into being: it's familiar yet pallid, its colours lost in the sudden exposure. Something moves in the darkness of the hallway behind me, and I step quickly into the doorway. I scan the hallway, but I've been blinded by the light. I don't hear anything, so assuming it's one of our mythical rats, I slam the door shut.

The lounge looks just as I left it: it's easy to see that there's no one in here. For some reason I find myself rushing to the window. I peer out into the square, but my vision is again hampered by the light . I stare across at Ursula's flat but - thankfully - it's still dark.

I spin quickly, and turn my attention back to the flat. I remember seeing a documentary years ago about how the SAS cleared compounds in Afghanistan. The basic concept was, go in hard as surprise gives you the edge. Even if you get hit by a round or two, the guy on your shoulder will get the job done. I decide that this tactic might not actually work here. When I'm queen of the square, I'm going to form my own militia.

I work my way steadily over to the kitchen, step forward and stick my head round. It's a small room, and there's no one in there, unless they've jammed themselves into one of the cupboards, which seems unlikely. I edge my way out, press a hand to my bedroom door and fling it open. I slap the light on and step back, knife drawn. Again, no one. Crouching down, I peer under the bed. Then there are the built-in wardrobes. I pull each open in turn, knife raised. Nothing. Getting all gung ho, I kick open the door to the bathroom and wade in like a marine. Nothing. I do a five-minute recce of the whole flat, but there's no one here. Since the generator's obviously still on, I put on the kettle and make myself a cup of coffee, using Ursula's packet of caffe d'orzo. If you can imagine coffee made out of acorns, that's what this tastes like. It's not unpleasant, just something that cowboys or peasants from the middle ages might have concocted.

So what's going on? Either I got it wrong when I saw the light on from Ursula's, and was actually looking at someone else's flat, or there was someone in my flat, but they got away before I turned up, or I'm just going crazy and imagined the whole thing. If we can't rely on our own mind in times like these, then we're lost. There's no meals on wheels, social services or nurses coming round to check that you're all right. There's the solidarity of the block, but that's the only sort of safety net there is.

Despite the fact that caffe d'orzo's meant to be caffeine free, I have a terrible night. My mind just won't shut up, lurching from one thing to the next. When I do actually sleep, my dreams have a gaudy, hallucinatory feel. Maybe I haven't fully got over my illness.

Whatever the case, the next day when I turn up at Rosa's flat to take her out, I look like I've pulled an all-nighter. Still, with a paisley scarf wrapped around my head and a pair of sunglasses hiding the dark smudges under my eyes, I'm back in my fifties movie star persona, purposefully failing to avoid attention.

When Rosa comes to the door, I'm glad to see that she's ready, bundled up in a cream cashmere coat, with a leather bag slung over one shoulder. Her grey hair's loose and a bit unruly, but there's a gleam in her eye which I'm glad to see. Ciao bella, she says. Where are we going?

As we clatter down the stairs, I try to address the question. Mama, did you ever read that book, going on a bear hunt? She looks at me quizzically. Okay, well, never mind. It's a kid's book. No, we're going scavenging, to see what treats we can find. I've got a couple of ideas. Did you bring the madeleines? Yes, she says, smiling proudly and patting her bag. Good, I say. I've got the coffee.

I squeeze her hand as we head out into the square. A raffish wind is blowing, scouring dust from the stones, and blowing it up into our faces. Despite this, the day has that clean, airless quality that you often get up near the mountains. It's raw but vibrant. Energising.

We make our way through the streets, corkscrewing into the oldest part of town. It's also the highest part, lying just below the bell tower of the largest church. The streets of the old town are narrow and confusing, and I soon realise that I'm lost. Plus I haven't been here for years. It's the perfect place to get mugged, stabbed or raped, so I've given it a miss for the last seven years.

Rosa doesn't seem to mind, though. She looks about with the eyes of a child, perhaps remembering better days. Soon we stumble across what I'm looking for: the Strada d'Oro. When I first moved here, even though I was an adult, this was always my favourite place to visit. It was a street packed with shops: a toyshop, a sweet shop, an ancient haberdasher's, a cobbler's. It was a street stuck in a time warp, its shops still able to exist because of their small size and obviously low rents. If anyone visited, they would end up here at some point. And there was Marco's, the best cafe and gelateria combo in town.

Of course, everything's locked down now. The antique shop even has boards nailed over its wide windows. It's a tragedy really, but what can you do? The rusted iron cowbell above the ironmonger's rings mournfully in a sudden surge of wind, and a couple of leaves skitter away across the cobblestones, as if we needed reminding that winter was coming.

Halfway along the street, we find what I'm looking for: the Venetian mask shop. Its once resplendent window is boarded up, its door locked for the last time. When people are starving, papier-mâché masks aren't on the top of anyone's shopping list. I pull my foot-long crowbar out of my bag like a magician and wedge its end between the door and the doorframe. Rosa lays a hand on my arm. My child, she says, what are you doing?

I smile at her. It's quaint to see how she's still hampered by social conventions. The people who owned this flat have probably died or fled south years ago, and Rosa's worried about their door. I smile back at her. Borrowing a few things, I say, and shove the handle of the crowbar inwards. There's a dry but satisfying splintering as the door gives way, juddering inwards. As we move tentatively inside, our eyes adjust, revealing the hidden splendour of the mask shop.

This is how Howard Carter must have felt when first peering into Tutankhamun's tomb. The slow, wonderful revelation, the falling away of the veil. From low tables, masks rise in mounds, covering the walls and depending from the ceiling. Edges of gold and whole faces of pearly white glow throughout the twilit space. It's an unsettling sight, as if you're being studied by the denizens of some nether world. Beautiful female faces, animal masks and grotesque masks with long, tapering noses all stare down at us. Mama! I say. Che bello!

Okay, I say, moving into the centre of the room and looking about in a daze. We need a mask for each of us, and then six smaller masks. So pick one for yourself, and then three of your choice. I'll do the same.

Of course, I choose something glamorous - a Tre Ricci style mask - it's very feminine, but the three crimson curls sprouting from the top of the head give it a sense of gaiety. Rosa chooses a simple half mask in gold. When we've picked the six smaller masks, we stuff them all in a sack and head back into the street, closing the door reverently behind us. I don't know about Rosa, but I feel like a proper criminal.

There's an old toyshop a couple of doors down, and we get in there as well without too much ado. The interior of this shop is more practical, but crammed. We manage to pick up a couple of multi-coloured footballs, a frisbee and a giant shuttlecock. We also find a lightsaber, a puzzle, a few dolls and a dozen small soft toys. They all go into the sack. As we make our way back along the Strada d'Oro, I realise that Rosa hasn't once asked me what we're up to. She's just gone along with everything, which makes life easy for now, but what does it say about the future? Casting vague worries aside, we head downwards.

The nuns take some convincing. I'm not surprised. If I were in their position, I'd be exactly the same. Rosa's a good Catholic, though, and this is something I've counted on. When my energetic but ultimately vain entreaties fail, Rosa steps into the breach. To be fair, I haven't told her what we're up to, but she picks it up pretty quickly. Think of how good it will be for the children, she says, to get some fresh air, to be out-side, to explore! The nun behind the door doesn't really have a response to this. And it's not as if we've come to prey on the kids. Or to sell them overseas. We're a forty-something woman, her mother and a bag of toys.

Yes, says the nun, eventually, but it is our duty to keep them safe, you must understand that. Safe, I reply, but not cloistered, not shut away for the rest of their lives! Besides, we won't be going far, and we'll bring them back before nightfall, of course. She stares out of the peephole with dubious, unflinching eyes.

I tell you what, I add. You choose the kids. About six will be fine, and throw in a sensible older kid as well. That should do it. Hell, I add, forgetting where I am, you or one of your sisters can come along as well. It'll be fun!

I don't know if fun is foremost on the mind of this woman. I suppose nuns aren't exactly known for their high spirits or frivolity. And I suppose I must look like some female version of the Child Catcher with a giant sack thrown over one shoulder. But still, my words must have had some effect, because after a while she says, wait here.

So we wait for what seems like half-an-hour. We chat a little as the wind puffs little billows of grey dust across the square, but really, we're too keyed up to talk. Eventually, though, the door to the convent cracks open and a sad little procession of children is ushered out. There are six of them, and they seem to have been arranged in height order, the smallest first. They're led by a little girl with dark wavy hair. She's wearing a long-sleeved white top, a brown corduroy dress, thick tights and leather shoes. She looks like something from the nineteenth century. The kid behind her - a little boy not much bigger than she is - sports a grey flat cap like an old man from Yorkshire! They all keep their faces turned down, and none of them makes eye contact with us. The nuns may have broken their spirits and dressed them like Victorian orphans, but you can't deny that they're clean and well turned out. The girl at the back has a thick wedge of black hair and empty green eyes. I'd guess she's in her mid-teens. She certainly looks sensible, if not exactly dynamic.

Hello children! My name is August, I say, and this is my mother, Rosa. Today we're going on a little outing. We're all going to have a lot of fun. Come on – follow me!

Everyone experiences this to some degree, but I often find there's a great disparity between my expectations and reality. In my mind's eye, I'd imagined us skipping through the streets, hand-in-hand, and then frolicking over the hills like the von Trapp family. It's not that I don't try. As we go, I try to engage the little girl in conversation. Instead of replying, she just stares up at me with dark, baleful eyes. I try a couple of different avenues, but she remains mute. Don't the nuns teach these kids manners? The whole speak-if you're-spoken-to thing? I remind myself that these are potentially damaged kids. They've witnessed society as we know it falling apart, have seen things that no child should ever have to see. And they haven't had the maturity or emotional tools to deal with any of it. Few of us have.

Feeling suitably chastened, I reach out my hand to the little girl. But instead of taking mine, she holds my gaze and puts both of her hands behind her back. What's your name, I ask, smiling. Again, I get nothing. Regan, Samara? Never mind. It doesn't matter.

As we wend our way through the desolate streets, I try to strike up a song or two, but after a couple of verses my voice trails off in the dead air. So we troop on in silence. Me, then Rosa, then the kids, then our nun-of-the-day bringing up the rear. We must resemble a work detail returning to a gulag rather than a bunch of kids heading off on a picnic.

I'd intended for us to get out into the fields, or what's left of them. And again, this image ends up being complete pie in the sky. I'd always thought that Rosa was slow, but she's sprightly compared to this lot. Their pace can only be described as glacial. Do they have to walk at this speed around the convent? Or is the influence of the nun at the back retarding their progress, slowing them down like the gravity of some giant planet? I don't know, but at this rate it would take us a week to tear ourselves free from the town's shackles.

For a few minutes we wander on aimlessly, my mind threatened by a rising sense of panic. If we can't make it out, what are we going to do with them? And then I've got it. We hang a couple of rights, going back on ourselves a little - which no one seems to notice - and then burst into a small, oddly shaped square bounded by high, cliff-like flats. In the middle of this square is a small play park, surrounded by dead plane trees. I hear a couple of murmurings behind us, and I instantly know I've made the right decision. What kid doesn't like a play park?

The place is enclosed by a low fence, which will no doubt serve to reassure our nun. All of the apparatus - including the climbing frame - is made of weathered grey wood, which is at odds with the plastic trim which is rendered in bright primary colours. The effect is cheerful but incongruous. To be fair, the place looks in good nick, as if it hasn't been used for the past seven years, which it probably hasn't.

We enter through a low gate and I plonk my bag down next to a bench. Rosa and the nun deposit themselves there, apparently wearied by the short walk. Figuring that handholding isn't going to work here, I decide to lead by example. Come on kids, I say. I give them an amused smile, nod towards the swings, and break into a jog. A minute later I'm lounging on an undersized swing. I figure that these kids are a little on the scared side, so I decide to take it easy instead of tearing around like a madwoman. To be fair, it doesn't take long for them to get into it. They disperse, and are soon exploring this new, exciting space. When they realise that it's okay, some even start moving faster than a death march, and whispered voices become louder. The little girl with the wavy hair sits on the swing next to me, rocking slightly. This time I don't bombard her with questions, just let her be for a bit. I'm pleased to see that Rosa and the nun are chatting away. Bingo.

I kick my legs forward, then pull them back. Forwards, backwards. Forwards, backwards. I do this in a slightly exaggerated, pantomime manner. Slowly I start to move. Casting a glance sideways, I see that the little girl is trying to copy me. Soon, I'm swinging easily. The little girl, on the other hand, after initially making some progress, ends up jerking back and forwards. Her timing's off, and it's soon obvious that she's going nowhere fast. I look at her with a tight-lipped, complicit smile and nod slightly, as if to say, I know, it's hard, isn't it? Would you like a push, I ask.

She stops her jerking motions, stares up at me with wide dark eyes, and nods. I come to a stop, go around behind her and start pushing her swing, gently at first. As I can't see her face, it's hard to say how she's reacting. I reckon that she's about four - five at the outside - and I realise that communication isn't the strong suit of kids this young. After a bit I ask, higher? She nods slightly, and I propel her to a slightly-less-than-lame height. I give it a couple of minutes, then ask, higher? She nods again. You're the boss, I say, and before long she's flying through the air, her little hands clutching the chains. It's hardly a white-knuckle ride, but I'd bet it's the most fun she's had in a while.

After what seems like a long time, I start to slow her down. When she comes to a standstill, she turns, gives me the briefest of smiles and runs off towards something that looks like an old wooden roundabout. For a second, I feel all fuzzy inside. By now the other kids have got into it too, and are climbing or running about, shouting to each other. For a second it sounds as if life is proceeding as usual. As if the last seven years have been a bad dream from which we've all collectively awakened, and can now go back to work and play the way we did a decade ago.

But as I wander the perimeter of the park, smiling benevolently and keeping an eye on my charges, my feet end up kicking up the long-dead leaves of the long-dead trees, and the veneer of ash that coats everything like a second skin is a reminder that everything has changed, and that very little has remained the same. Still, humans are adaptable, and it's that adaptability that will see us through. And it strikes me that one of the problems we've had is a lack of people or ideals to live up to. Politicians have let us down, celebrities simply slunk away. In the past there was God and the saints, but their ranks need refreshing. What we desperately need are new points of reference in this troubled world, examples that we can look up to, venerate, and draw strength from. And that - of course - is where Rosa comes in.

By the time I get back to them, the two women are getting on superbly. Rosa seems animated, and the nun has even cracked the barest of smiles. It's all coming together. Taking my bag, I spread a red-and-white checked picnic blanket on the sandy, gravelly ground in front of the bench. It's only then that I realise that the nun is the same one who showed me the records the other day. For a horrible, sinking moment I wonder what I've said to her. To be fair, I draw a total blank. My memory has suffered over the last few years, I won't deny it. Lack of food and despair has certainly done for some of my brain cells and synapses. Either that or I've got early-onset Alzheimer's. My nan died of the disease, so I've always had my worries. Still, I decide that it doesn't matter what I've said. Like a populist politician, I decide that anything can be laughed off or shrugged away if it comes back to haunt me.

Mama, I say, have you got the cakes? Without drawing breath, Rosa passes me her bag. When I realise that she probably gets on with the nun much better than me, a stab of jealousy passes through me. But then I realise that it's no big deal. These two women have probably both lived in this town all their lives, and have a wealth of stories and gossip to share.

I place Rosa's exquisite madeleines on a paper plate and place them in the centre of the blanket. Then I take two flasks from my bag, and pour caffe d'orzo into little paper cups. I hand a cup to Rosa and one to the nun. They take them with a grateful nod and keep on talking. If I achieve nothing else today, at least I've introduced these two and got them chatting. For a second or two I feel like some glamorous socialite, bringing people together.

Still, the little cups of coffee bring me back down to earth. Kids in Italy drink caffe d'orzo, but usually with milk. And that's where we're lacking. Cows are in short supply and as I don't know any farmers, the kids are going to have to go without.

Children, I say, turning and waving one hand in the air, snack time! They stop what they're doing and converge on us warily, as if they're animals lured in by food but expecting a trap. Here, I say, offering the cakes. Sit down on the blanket. Here's coffee. The kids obediently sit crosslegged on the rug and accept the small cups of coffee without complaint. I then proffer Rosa's madeleines. These are very special cakes made by my mother, I say, indicating Rosa with a flip of the hand and a smile. I had some just the other day. They're made with lemon, and are so soft! She made these this morning. They're still warm. Go on, take one.

They all take one. The older girl, who's wearing a long dress, boots and denim jacket, takes one too. What's your name, I ask, smiling. Cara, she says, smiling back at me from beneath her black fringe. Of all of them, I want to make this older girl feel special. Little kids are often more resilient, rendered emotionally pliable by their lack of understanding. They adapt easily. Cara may be the most affected of all of them.

Perhaps unsurprisingly, this pauper's banquet takes less than two minutes to complete. To my surprise, most of the kids actually drink the coffee and don't seem to mind it. But still, pretty quickly the blanket is strewn with crumbs and discarded cups. It'll never be the same again.

Okay, I say, I'm now going to read you a story. If you want to go off and play, that's fine, but I think you'll enjoy it. It's called, *We're going on a Bear Hunt.* I find that I'm nervous, which is strange as I used to be a teacher, but I start reading with gusto, and soon find that I'm on autopilot. I bought a copy of this book years ago. Like a lot of kids' books, the simple language and the refrain make it ideal for teaching English. I was so impressed that when I saw an Italian copy I bought it on a whim, just to see - I suppose - how the two stacked up. It's not bad at all, and now it's coming into its own. When look up, I realise that all of the kids are looking at me, spellbound. Encouraged, I press on.

A few minutes later one of the girls who must be about eight wanders off. Cara goes after her like a good older sister would. That's fine by me. The kids are a bit rubbish at repeating the refrain, but again, that's okay. They stare at me, and mutter away, but at least we've got some interaction going. When I've finished, they continue staring at me. I give them a storyteller's sly, unctuous smile, and say, now children, off you go and play for a few minutes, and then we're going to do our very own bear hunt! Off you go now!

It takes a moment for the spell to break, and then they're scrambling away, calling out to each other and heading in different directions. Perfect. Rosa gives me a clap, her eyes shining, and says, bravo, bravo! They loved that. It was as if you had them hypnotised! Grazie, I say, bowing my head slightly. I hope they enjoyed it. Enjoyed it, says the nun, they loved it! As she doesn't strike me as the most effusive of gals, this is high praise indeed.

Still, I say, no peace for the wicked. I dig the plush toys out of the sack and ball them up in my hands. For the next five minutes I lurch through the dead undergrowth, behind the tree trunks and around the climbing frame, trying to remain inconspicuous as I hide the plush toys about the perimeter of the park. I let the kids play for a bit, then call them back to the bench. They come as obediently as well trained dogs.

Okay, I say, around here lots of little animals are hiding. They're small and devious, and could be in nooks or crannies, or sitting up high, but they're all inside the fence. See if you can find them!

And with that they scatter as if someone's thrown a bomb amongst them. Within what seems like a seconds, a cry goes up. Our little boy with the flat cap is frantically waving something that can only be described as a crimson seahorse with legs. Bravo! I shout - keep going! Again, an activity that I'd thought would take ten minutes takes two. Soon enough all of the kids are back in the centre of the park. It didn't take long, but they're all smiling, so I guess it worked out well enough. The only problem is that our grey-capped lad - Massimo - has two toys. Cara has none, which isn't surprising, as she was helping some of the other kids. Massimo, I say, which one do you want to keep? He looks at me as if I'm playing a trick on him, then stares down at the two plush toys. To my surprise he keeps the mutant seahorse. I ask him to give the white, long-limbed bunny to Cara. She looks at me and nods, and for a second I think she's gong to curtsey. When I'm queen of the square, I think, that's what I'll do: I'll insist that everyone bows and curtsies when they greet me.

I smile, and beneath my benevolent gaze the kids rush off for a last blast, each clutching a small plush toy. When we round them up half-an-hour later, they're flush-faced but ready to roll. We wind our way back through the streets with the calm, satisfied air of people who have just spent the whole day outside. Even the nun picks up her pace. She may not have chatted to another adult in a long time, so our little outing may have been just as beneficial for her as for the kids.

Outside the grand door of the convent, our nun accosts me. Thank you, she says, eyes shining, the children enjoyed that so much! That's very kind, I say. Only then do I realise that we didn't even get to use the masks! Look, I say, I know that you look after a lot of children. Maybe some others would like to come out with us? We could do this regularly - I've got more games that we could play, I say, patting the sack. Really, she asks, looking as if she'd just received an unexpected gift. That would be wonderful. When would you next like to come?

I don't know, I say, throwing an arm out in a carefree gesture, how about tomorrow? Same time? Two o'clock? The nun nods. That would be wonderful. I'll have six more ready to go. And with that she ushers her young charges back into the convent, and the door closes behind them, leaving Rosa and me alone in the square. We walk home arm-in-arm. Thank you Mama, I say. You made all that possible. Did you see how happy those children were? She never would have agreed to let them out if it hadn't been for you. Rosa nods and clutches my arm more tightly, as if only now realising how much the outing has tired her. Then she looks up at me, a small, curious smile upon her lips. Would you like me to bake some more madeleines for tomorrow? That, I say, echoing the nun's words, would be wonderful. Wonderful.

It never ceases to amaze me how quickly we can reconstruct our world. We can't change much, to be sure, but we can effect change quickly. It doesn't take a lot. A smile. A gesture. A moment's thought before lapsing back into previous patterns of behaviour. Showing warmth instead of irritation. Saying something generous instead of cynical.

Before we know it, Rosa and I are running daily outings to the play park. We're forced to raid the toyshop and mask shop several more times to keep our supplies replenished. By the tenth day, every kid in the place has been out at least once. Our nun - Anna - establishes a rota and comes with us most days. If not, she sends a substitute. It doesn't take me long to realise that Anna is pretty organised, and is probably the most active member of nunnery, which is something of a worry.

The kids genuinely have a blast. We take different groups each day and go through something of a similar routine - with a few variations, to be sure. When we've taken every kid to the play park twice, it strikes me that we've got to come up with something else. By now we're well into September, and we've only got a few weeks of half-decent weather to play with.

Searching for inspiration, Rosa and I spend hours some mornings tramping the streets, looking for interesting places to go or shops that haven't been completely looted. We don't achieve much, but we do start to get a little fitter - which is no bad thing - and bolder. Of course we don't go out in the dark - we're not stupid - but it does make me realise how much time I've spent inside over the last few years, and how bad that is for one's mental health. Of course, during the first year the air was so bad that going outside was problematic. But now there's really nothing holding us back other than our own fears.

One morning on the edge of town we come across a shop we've never noticed before. It's been plastered with hardboard, and by shining my torch through the gaps and peering in I eventually work out what's inside. It's a hell of a job getting the door open, but when I do we're confronted by racks of rods, reels, salopettes, jackets, boots and bait boxes. Most items still have a waxy or metallic sheen, suggesting that this shop was shut up pronto and has been undisturbed ever since.

Mama, I say, turning to Rosa, are you thinking what I'm thinking? No, she says flatly, which does her credit. Very funny, I say. Have you heard the expression, give someone a fish and they eat for a day, but teach them how to fish and they eat forever? She looks at me as if I've taken a turn for the worse and shakes her head. No, she says, I haven't. I wave an arm in the air as if to dismiss the topic. Well, it's something like that, I add.

That evening, exhausted after an afternoon at the play park, we drag ourselves up to the roof of my building. I haven't been idle in the last few weeks, oh no. I've persuaded a couple of people that we need a lookout station, and have fashioned - with Filippa's help - a deck not dissimilar to the one on Rosa's block. If you appeal to people's sense of fear and anxiety you can achieve anything. We needed a clearer view of the buildings around us, I argued. And we needed a clearer view of the mountains, in case raiders came down. Of course, I was just making stuff up. What I really wanted was a triumphal plinth so that I could survey the whole of my future domain - the square itself.

With the help of Mister Moretti - replete with cough and DIY skills - and Filippa, we managed to drag a wooden pallet up and install it on the very apex of the roof. We propped it up with cut-down wooden crates and lashed it to a flue, but it's essentially just a floating platform. I just hope it's heavy enough to stay in place when the next storm hits. We even installed a handrail and laid part of an old wooden ladder down on to the tiles for access. I have ideas of erecting a small bothy on it, replete with wood burner, allowing us to create a twenty-four-hour watch rota, but this will take a bit more persuasion on my part.

Still, as it stands, my new platform is ideal for fishing practice. It seems absurd, but I've never been fishing. Whether this leaves me at a substantial disadvantage in life remains to be seen. But still, how hard can it be? We've brought two rods up, and have tied the hooks on already. We've also managed to get up here without taking an eye out, which is something of an achievement. Having said that, Rosa sways somewhat on the platform, giving me the vapours. It's as if she's already had a couple of shots for Dutch courage; either that or she really needs to work on her core stability. I really want to attach her to the hand-rail with a carabiner. Sadly, this isn't an option.

We practise baiting the hooks with dead leaves, which is easy enough. Then I perform a demonstration cast, pulling my arms back like a javelin thrower, and let it rip. The result is less than spectacular. The hook flops on to the roof about six feet in front of me. It's then that I real-ise we've forgotten all about floats and weights. Surely they'd make a difference? But the box with all of that stuff is downstairs, and the thought of going back down fills me with dismay. Instead, I decide to watch Rosa, and it's a good thing that I do. Instead of throwing the rod up and over her shoulder, she swings it in a low, wide arc. I drop to one knee and duck. The rod barely passes over my head. Mama! I shriek, what are you trying to do? Kill me?

Instead of replying, she simply chuckles. Looking up, I see that her line has disappeared straight over the front of the building and is now dangling somewhere in the square below. It's as if she used to be a champion fly fisher and just for-got to tell me. Va bene, I say. You can teach the kids. We'll just have to line them up on your left so they get to keep their heads.

As the sun sets in a bloody contusion of cloud, I watch Rosa as the warm, dying light ani-mates her face. She's smiling and humming an old tune to herself. She looks content, and I wonder if she actually thinks she's fishing. And at that moment I realise that try as I might, I'll never know all that much about her. What song is she humming? Even if she told me, it would mean nothing. And it strikes me how inscrutable people are, and that even when surrounded by loved ones, we still live very much alone.

It takes a bit of persuasion, but ultimately Rosa's aura and voice of reason carry the day. Anna even agrees to shunt our departure time forward by an hour. I don't think that actually affects or alters the timing of the convent's day in any way, but even shifting things by an hour seems like asking a lot: the idea's met with a sense of mute consternation that's expressed in little frowns, scowls and shakes of the head. The nuns are running a pretty tight ship - but perhaps a little too tight. I realise that once they lock in on a time or an event, that's it. Spontaneous they are not. I begin to wonder if their lives are animated less by God and more by routine.

Still, we're heading in the right direction. By spring, I might well be leading day trips to the next town, and by summer - who knows? Maybe we really will be frolicking through the alpine meadows like the Von Trapp family. Stranger things have happened.

But right now we're heading down the rocky switchback path into the gorge. It's narrow and treacherous, but the kids are the least of my worries. They make light work of the obstacles and uneven footing, and if they stumble they just carry on. They're fine. It's Rosa and Maria I've got to worry about. Rosa actually fairs better than I'd thought, but our resident nun is flat-footed, lacks coordination and seems to have the ankle strength of a toddler. She lurches about alarmingly, trying to use her upper body to stabilise herself, and clings to Rosa as if she's the last piece of wood on a sunless sea.

As I descend behind the line of children, I can't help but stifle a smile. I cast occasional glances back over my shoulder, and leave the oldies to struggle on. Anyone would have thought I'd asked them to walk over hot coals. As soon as we get to the bottom, the kids start playing on the rocks and fanning out on to the sandspit. When Rosa and the nun reach us, they plonk themselves down on the rock at the base of the path, breathing heavily, looking a little worn and still clutching each other's hand. It's quite touching actually. Still, neither of them actually complains about the descent.

I haven't told Rosa that this is where Ursula had her crayfish traps, for fear that she'd baulk and refuse to come down, either due to the slope or from some morbid fear. If Rosa knows where she is, she certainly doesn't let on. Still, the fact that she's actually got down here - something that she wouldn't even have contemplated several months ago - shows that I'm breathing life into the old girl yet. There's not much point in killing a corpse.

I decide that we'll fish from the spit. There's nothing for the lines to get caught on, and the sand is dry enough for the kids to sit on if they want to. We get them set up fairly easily, each with a rod and an old jam jar of dried mealworms for bait. I leave the demonstration bit to Rosa. She's a natural teacher, has more patience than me and has a pretty good cast on her. If she's been fishing before, she certainly hasn't mentioned it, but I have my suspicions. Maria bustles about, helping the children, getting them to watch Rosa and generally sorting them out with a minimum of fuss and effort. She's in her element. Suddenly, it strikes me that I'm redundant. I've got them here, and now my work is done.

It's a horrible feeling. Stepping back, I realise that the whole scene before me is tinged with grey, as if an artist has put a wash of lead solution over the canvas. The vibrancy this place had at the end of summer seems to have gone, and I can't help but wonder why this is. The cliffs seem greyer and craggier, and even the water - despite the fact that it's running faster - has been imbued with a leaden hue. As it's been raining more over the past couple of weeks, a lot of ash has probably been swept down from the mountains. This has no doubt tinted the water, mingling with the sand particles and generally putting a downer on everything. Plus there's the slow dying of the light, which is natural enough at this time of year. I just hope it's these tangible things that have created this pall of grey and nothing more sinister.

Whatever the cause, the realisation that the colour has been leeched from this place pains me. Here I am, trying to add some vivacity back into life, and it's being stripped away by the day, faster than I can comprehend. Mood soured, I decide to do a little exploring. I head across the stepping stones towards the patch of trees nestled in the far side of the bend. Soon enough, my feet are wet. The icy thrill of the water is unexpected, but it's easy going, even if some of the stones are submerged. When I get to the far side I look back: all the kids are absorbed in what they're doing; Rosa and Maria are moving freely between them, offering advice. No one's even noticed I've gone.

Looking up, I realise that the trees here are larger than I'd thought. They bend out over the rocks and water with riven, twisted trunks. I recognise a few ashes and a couple of sweet chestnuts. By now, only a few lemon-yellow leaves cling to their branches, the first flames of a forest fire.

I make my way tentatively forward, as if I'm doing something unseemly or furtive. Slipping between a couple of large rocks, I pick my way around dead branches and through drifts of crisp leaves. There's not much undergrowth and I move easily. There's a special quality to this place: the grey trunks are thick and rise in gnarled, twisted forms that seem to have been extruded from the very earth itself. The few leaves that cling to the limb-like branches above hiss and witter in the light wind. It's as if I'm entering some ancient grove, a small conglomeration of trees that has existed before the dawn of civilisation.

This sense of sanctity only intensifies the shock I feel when I emerge into a clearing. But this isn't any old clearing: the remains of a fire sit in its centre, and a blackened kettle hangs from a tripod of sticks over the ashes. The floor of the place is packed hard, and a ring of rocks has been pulled into place around its perimeter. On the far side of the clearing, the cliff wall rises vertically. There's a small opening at its base. I quickly scan the trees, but can't see anyone. I still feel exposed. I look back over my shoulder. Nothing.

Creeping up to the fireplace, I take a look at the kettle. It's cast iron with probably a two-litre capacity. You could cook in it every day and it would probably last for years. It's not the sort of thing you just leave lying around. Which means that someone is still here. And then it strikes me - what if it's Ursula? What if she didn't die? What if she managed to crawl out of the water, survive the first few nights huddled up in this wood, and then set about regaining her strength and plotting her revenge?

The thought really freaks me out. My pulse skyrockets, and I can feel beads of sweat bursting along my temples and spine. I cross the clearing quickly, looking about in an exaggerated, manic fashion like a kid learning to cross a road, and pause by the edge of the small cave. Even though it's not very deep - I can actually see to its far end - it still exudes that chill dampness that all caves do. Looking around one last time, I duck my head and plunge in.

I don't know what I'm expecting to find - maybe a bracelet that says URSULA, a handwritten diary detailing her resurrection? Of course there's nothing like this. There are a few blackened pots and pans inside the cave entrance and, at the rear, a low platform of sticks that has been lashed together to form a rudimentary bed. On top of it lies a brown, crumpled sleeping bag that has an ex-army look to it. Ursula could have made that bed frame - she's the sort of person who could thrive in such Spartan conditions. There's an oil lamp and a black rucksack by the bed. I delve in. There's a high-tech hunting knife in a sheath, a pack of playing cards, a large box of matches. There are side pockets too, and I'm about to start checking them out when realise that there's only one way out of the cave. If

Ursula or whoever-else comes back, I'm trapped like a beetle in a bottle. My heart lurches again, and I scramble out of the low cave, banging one arm against a wall, heart trip-hammering in my chest until I'm outside again and gulping down the sweet, delicious air. I keep glancing around, totally on the edge by now, and stagger back across the clearing and through the trees.

By the river I perch on one of the large, jagged rocks and try to calm myself. I breathe in through my nose and out through my mouth, trying to lower the amount of carbon dioxide in my blood, desperately trying to re-establish a normal breathing pattern. I don't know how long this takes. Five minutes? Probably ten. Eventually I make my way back over the river, resoaking my feet, and approach the little group on the sandspit. Ciao bambini, I say to the little girl with the ruffled hair. She's sitting cross-legged, holding her fishing rod as if she's some kind of real-life gnome. Caught anything yet? She looks up at me with her big dark eyes as if I'm a ghost and doesn't say a word. Never mind, I say, adopting my most patronising tone. If at first you don't succeed, try, try again.

I work my way further into the group. They're all totally preoccupied, living in the calm sense of expectation that must be peculiar to fishing. There's no sense that I've been missed or am needed in the slightest way. People always think that they're unique, that their specific skill set or personality can't be replaced. And if you've survived this long, you start to think it's for a reason, that you must possess some rare quality enabling you to keep going where others have faltered. But in the end it's not true. You've survived because of luck or a quirk of your metabolism, nothing more. And you can die, or be replaced, and it makes no odds. For example, I've started these excursions, but they could continue without me. It's an edifying, galling thought, but it does offer some consolation: we're all free more than ever to do our own thing. Just like our man-or-woman-in-the-woods has done.

Plastering a grin on my face, I make my way over to Rosa. Mama! I say. Come va? She nods, slowly. Bene, bene. And then she turns to me, her grey eyes shining like wet, cracked stone. They love it, she says, casting a hand around her like a net. Look at them! This is probably the best day they've had for years - thank you. Thank you. I find myself choking up. Rosa has certainly begun entering the territory of sainthood. I take her hand and squeeze it gently but firmly. Thank you, Mama, I say, my voice barely more than a whisper, I couldn't have done it without you.

A cry goes up behind us, breaking our love-in. As Rosa turns and heads off with her bucket to land the latest minnow, I take a seat in the middle of the spit. The sand is dry, and still contains the barest hint of warmth, the waning imprint of the last days of summer. Our nun stands at the end of the spit, arms folded behind her back, staring at the water like a figurehead riding the grey seas of the Atlantic. It's a stirring image, and it makes you wonder whether everything will actually be okay, whether civilisation will slowly crawl back from the brink of collapse, shake off the dust, and start to rebuild itself. Are these women the right people to lead the way? I can't think of any better. What we need now is compassion married to strength. And that, in a nutshell, is what the nuns bring to the table. As I'm sitting there, a certain reflective calmness washes over me. It's a strange sensation, and not one I'm used to. It could be what they call contentment.

When the hue and cry have died down, Rosa wanders back, bucket sloshing. Look what Massimo caught, she says, waving the bucket beneath my nose. I look down at the hunched, lumpen form of a crayfish. It churns slowly around in the water, a mealworm still gripped between its pincers. I feel my stomach sink, and am forced to compose myself. Well done Massimo, I say, nodding. Well done.

Mood soured, I try to change my train of thought. Despite the crayfish, it's obvious the kids aren't catching much. Perhaps it's because of the choice of bait? Dried mealworms aren't the most dynamic of strugglers: I'm pretty sure desiccated rats' turds would work as well. Pushing myself up, I retreat along the sand and begin to skirt the shoreline on the near side of the river. I clamber across the rocks until I reach the first of the thorny shrubs, and then work my way along a little further, ignoring the scratches and scrapes. Eventually I come to what could be loosely termed earth. Finding a flat rock, I start chopping at the ground and within a couple of minutes I'm almost a half-a-foot down. I can't believe what I find. Were there this many worms before the impact? If nothing else has benefitted, it seems that the humble earthworms are having a great time. I scoop up the biggest handful of earth and worms I can carry and stagger back to the spit.

Bambini! I cry, come and see what I've got! The kids drop their rods and scuttle over, as if they've just woken from a trance. In my hands the worms writhe, their tapered heads searching the air. Cries of disgust go off around me like grenades. The kids' response is predictable, but just goes to show how little time they've spent outdoors during the last few years.

I drop the worms at my feet, and we watch in horrid fascination as they try to escape, their bodies elongating and stretching in a display of mindless - and ultimately futile - activity. Now, I say, worms will make better bait because they'll move around more, attracting the fish. Fish generally don't look for things that are already dead.

They want something that's alive, that's fresh - something that's got plenty of life to it. Massimo - fetch me your rod. Now, bear in mind that this doesn't hurt them. They don't feel pain like you and me. They'll be just as happy on your hook as they would be in the ground.

Even as I say it, I know that the last sentence is a lie. Picking up one of the most energetic worms, I press Massimo's hook into its side and then, with one deft movement, push it through. The worm writhes horribly, and some kind of dark goo seeps from its side. A collective cry of Euwwwww! goes up from the group, and I can't say I'm surprised.

Standing quickly, I go to Massimo's spot and, taking advantage of my height, cast the damn worm as far as possible. It sinks in the rolling current, and is thankfully lost to view. Massimo reclaims his rod, and I go back to the worms and encourage the other kids to bait their hooks with them. There are a few gasps, and even a couple of tears, but I give the more reticent ones a hand and we get the job done. In the new world order we're going to need people who can show a bit of grit: baiting a hook may seem like an odd way to kick-start personal growth, but for these cloistered kids it isn't. Soon enough, all of them have resumed their former positions, and the struggles of their pierced and now drowning worms are quickly forgotten.

Time passes. It could be an hour, maybe more. We're all caught in the present, when past events and future plans become as irrelevant as they actually are. Never before have those words, upon this bank and shoal of time, seemed more apt. Maybe it's because we're sitting on a sand-spit, or because we're all part of some group flow state. But it shows what simple things we are, caught up in the implacable march of time, bounded and defined by it, like worms struggling in a river.

Anna, guarda! The shout brings me back from my half-arsed philosophical reverie. It's Silvia, a quiet girl of about twelve with long dark hair and mournful eyes. I've never really heard her talk, so her voice is something of a surprise. As is the fact that she's on first name terms with the nuns. Who knew? Our nun disengages herself from the front of her virtual ship and wanders over to see Silvia, as do I.

Have you caught something, our nun asks. Silvia steps into the river and plunges her arm into the shallow water. When her hand comes back out, she's clutching what looks like a human bone. Appalled, my mind begins whirring. It's a humerus, by the look of things, and probably that of an adult.

What is it, asks Silvia. It's a bone, I say, stepping over to the girl, as a chill sense of impending doom spreads up my legs and back. If you throw it in, you get a wish. Really, asks Silvia, looking at me with the wide eyes of a small child. I look into her cherubic face bordered by a severe fringe, but can't see any traces of irony. How unsophisticated are these kids? They've spent way too much time with the nuns, learning about God.

Sure, I say, nodding. Silvia stands, turns and hurls the bone out as far as she can into the river, which isn't far. Do you want to know what my wish is, she asks, staring up at me with a beaming smile. No child, I say, stroking a hand across her head. Keep it to yourself. That way it may come true.

What am I saying? I wipe a hand across my mouth and scour the riverbed with my eyes, hoping but dreading to see a pronounced hint of white poking up from the stones and gravel. I feel suddenly sick, and glance up at the sky to hide my discomfort. The sun's still high, buried behind its perpetual blanket of cloud, dust and haze.

Okay children, I say, clapping my hands together and trying to adapt a cheerful, Mary-Poppins-esque tone, it's time to go! A collective groan sounds around me. August! August! Can't we stay a bit longer? Please. Please! Rosa comes over to me and regards me with her calm grey gaze. Let them stay a little longer, she says, half-an-hour. Look how much fun they're having.

I'm surrounded by a small circle of upturned eyes. Bene, bene, I say. Half an hour. I just don't want to get caught out here, that's all. Rosa runs a hand down my arm in a calming, maternal gesture, and it's all I can do not to hug her. At times like this, I'm so happy that she found me. I'm so happy that I'm her daughter.

By the time we actually pack up to leave, I'm hopping between the various kids, helping and cajoling like some mad aunt who's got to get back for her evening dose of gin. I wax lyrical about the paltry fish that we've caught, and even agree to carry them back as long as we get going pronto. I gather all the rods under one arm, snatch up the bucket in the other hand and lead the way off the spit and up the rocky path. But in less than a minute, I've gapped the rest of the group. The children, it appears, have been greatly fatigued by sitting on their backsides for the last few hours, and haul their skinny frames upwards with just enough energy to keep the fires of life burning. What's wrong with them? Even Rosa and Maria make their way upwards, chatting happily, without the slightest difficulty - that's how slow we're going. At any moment, I'm expecting one of my young protégés to rush back to the river and pull out a crisp clean skull from the water. Alas poor Ursula! Rosa, I knew her... it's amazing how you can find some pithy Shakespearean epithet to fit any eventuality. Damn his eyes.

When we finally get back to the road, I

breathe a mental sigh of relief. As we head back into town, the rational part of my mind tries to reassert itself. That could have been anyone's arm bone. So many people have died in the past few years - they're beyond counting. And who's to say it was a human bone anyway? Last time I checked, I couldn't find my diploma in comparative anatomy anywhere.

And of course, there's no way Ursula's body could have decayed that quickly. Still, no amount of reasoned argument can stall my mounting sense of unease. When we get back to the gates of the convent, I hand the bucket of tiddlers over to Silvia. The kids all gather round and stare down at the handful of fish. So, we can really keep them, asks Massimo, staring up at me. Of course, I say, waving a hand through the air, as long as Anna agrees.

At this point, of course, I'm expecting Anna to baulk, and to have to tip the fish down the drain in front of the children. Instead, she comes over and hugs me, resting her head momentarily on my shoulder. I hope my shock doesn't show, as I couldn't have been more surprised if she'd pulled out a shotgun and let me have both barrels. The children have had a lovely time, she says, pushing herself back from me and clutching my shoulders. Haven't we children? In unison, they all shout Si! A couple of the younger ones start jumping up and down. At least one of them starts clapping. I just stand there, stunned, like a yokel who's won the lottery. So have I says Anna, turning a beatific smile upon me. She drops her hands slightly, squeezes my upper arms and then prises the bucket from my grasp. We'll take good care of these. These can go in our pond, where the children can see them every day. I know it's a lot of effort for you, she says, but could we perhaps go again tomorrow?

I find myself nodding. For sure, I say, why not? At this point, Massimo pipes up, can you take us again tomorrow, he asks. Anna turns to him, calm but firm. No, child, but if August agrees, we could go again next week. Massimo starts bouncing on his toes with the energy of a toy that's had its batteries replaced. Who am I to stand in the way of enthusiasm? Of course, I add, we may as well get in a few trips before the weather turns.

I listen to myself as if I'm hearing someone else talking. What am I saying? I'm glad the children enjoyed it, I add, and then with a cheerful wave Rosa and I take our leave. On our way back, she links her arm through mine. You're doing something wonderful, she says, giving hope to those poor children who have lost everything. I'm very proud of you, she says, stroking my forearm as if it's a dozing cat. It's a team effort, Mama, I say, pulling her in towards me. It's all I can do not to start crying.

That night, I'm not good. If I sleep at all, it's only for a few twenty-minute stretches. O what can ail thee, lady-at-arms, alone and palely loitering? It's the riverbed that I can't escape. Waking or asleep, I scoop handfuls of sand and grit from the chill waters, and in each are white, porous shards. The fractured, shattered bones constitute the very stuff of the riverbed itself. At some point there's an actual skull in there too, silted-up eye sockets staring at me.

I know it's pathetic. I know it's the height of folly. But I can't shut my mind up. It just keeps chuntering away, returning to the riverbed again and again, and that bone. It's as if my own mind's turned against me, and wishes me harm.

I realise that - sooner or later - I'm going to have to locate Ursula's body, to actually find out what happened to it, or I'll never really be able to relax.

The next morning, wreck that I am, I gather up a few things and head over to Rosa's an hour early, hoping that she won't mind the intrusion. The thought of going fishing again today makes me want to run screaming for the hills, but I dutifully gather up the rods and find another bucket.

When she opens the door, Rosa seems genuinely pleased to see me. The smell of vanilla wafts through the gloomy, high-ceilinged space of her flat. More madeleines, eh? I ask, giving her a weak smile. I sometimes imagine that your entire basement is full of flour.

Rosa stares at me intently. Bella, she says, what's wrong? I wave a hand through the air, as if to dismiss the topic, but I know I won't be able to. In fact, I don't want to. Pre-empting this little collapse, I've brought over a leather-bound photo album which I now place on her table. If I'm going to be upset, at least she's going to think it's about something that doesn't make me a murderer. I sit and lay a shaking hand on the album. Rosa pulls up a chair and takes one of my hands.

Mama, I say, I've got something to tell you. She nods, reaches up and pushes a strand of hair back from my face. It was that bone, I add. I can't get it out of my mind. It's just made me recognise all the things that I've lost. That we've all lost. And it made me think of Marco.

She smoothes my hand in hers. Who's Marco, she asks, talking to me patiently, as if I'm a child who's being bullied. Marco was my fiancé, I say. We were going to get married, and I drove him away.

As soon as I've said that, I hunch forward and start weeping uncontrollably, my body shaking in gasping sobs, tears falling to the floor. I feel a hand on my back, soothing. But I can't stop. Everything just comes pouring out. I cry for what must be a solid ten minutes, overcome by a sense of loss as old and as deep as the universe itself, a sense of loss that seems as intrinsic as space and time.

Rosa, to her credit, doesn't say a word. She just lets me get it all out of my system, stroking my back patiently and waiting. Eventually, the sobs and tears start to abate. I wipe at my face with the back of a hand, and wonder how ghoulish I must look. This isn't going to be something that a splash of cold water can solve.

What happened, she asks, stroking my hair. Then I realise that I'm not off the hook, that I'll have to follow through with my story. Again, part of me wants to run, to brush it off, but I know I can't. This, I say, patting the old photo album, this happened. But first, I say, pulling a large photo from inside the album, this is him.

I hand the oversized photo over to Rosa like a kid doing show-and-tell. I've stared at it so many times over the last few years that I know every mark and blemish on its glossy surface. Rosa stares at the photo, nodding. He looks like a film star from the nineteen-fifties, she says. At this point, I know she's being generous. Marco was good looking, but in a cheeky, devil-may-care way, rather than in a leading man way.

In the picture, he's standing somewhere high up above the sea, one foot on a low brick wall. He's at a friend's wedding, and is wearing a white shirt, waistcoat, beige trousers and brown brogues. He's looking directly at the camera, his mouth rising in an amused smile. His dark eyes twinkle, and you get a sense that he knows how charming he is. He also looks as if he's having a great time, as if he's got a group of mates there with him, and that while they're having their photos taken they're telling jokes and taking the mick out of each other. Behind him, the sky is clear except for a couple of cirrus clouds, as if someone's added them in as an afterthought. The land falls away, and you see water to one side and fields to the other. For some reason the place reminds me of the rocky outcrop where the church in the film Mama Mia is located.

We were together for six years, I say. And eventually he got the balls to ask me to marry him. I was so excited: I had this image of a big Italian wedding at the Catholic church, you know, and growing old together. And maybe kids. At this point I have to stop myself from crying again. It's almost too much, the thought of what we've lost, of what will now never happen. So much potential has been wasted, so many futures have simply disappeared.

What happened, she asks. She stares at me, eyes slightly widened, face creased with compassion, voice soft and soothing. It's as if I'm seeing her for the first time. The saint I've been so consciously trying to create is already here in front of me, fully fledged. What would I do without her? The thought is sickening.

Again, I realise that I'm going to have to follow through. I take a deep breath. What happened is that I found this, I say, laying a hand gently on the leather-bound cover of the album. Rosa hitches one eyebrow, doing a fair impression of Doctor Spok. If I weren't so upset, I'd laugh. Again, I realise that I've got to give something. Slowly, I push the photo album towards her. I found it not long after we moved in together, I explain. Under his socks, of all places.

Rosa takes the album as if it's a Bible from the fifteenth century, lays it on her lap and slowly begins leafing through it. She nods as she goes, turning the pages reverently. They're very good, she says. Tastefully done. She stops about halfway through. Her left hand rests on a photo of a tousled-haired girl who's probably in her twenties. It's hard to tell because she's facing away from the camera, looking out of a high window. Shuttered flats are visible on the other side of the street. Sunlight lances down into this manmade canyon, catching the edges of her silken nightdress which is probably pink, but it's hard to tell because the image is in black and white. One hand pushes down into the mattress, keeping her torso upright. Her legs are pulled up behind her, giving the whole scene a relaxed but voluptuous air. A slim crescent of sunlight catches the curve of her hip beneath the nightdress.

A pretty girl, no doubt, murmurs Rosa. Who

is she?

I shrug and wave a hand through the air again, as if to make light of the question. I've no idea, I say. I don't know who any of them are. When I first discovered it, it was like someone had smacked me in the face. My heart was beating frantically. I put it back, but I couldn't get it out of my head. I'd think about it day and night, wondering who they were. As you can see, there's no writing, no names. There are twenty-seven different girls in all.

They're good photos, says Rosa, very poetic. Not slutty. I'm actually shocked that Rosa would use this term, even in a negative construction. It makes me wonder how much we actually ever know about other people. Absolutely, I say, agreeing with a little too much enthusiasm. I'm no artist, but even I can see that. They're tasteful, mysterious. Not revealing. And the girls, of course, are all pretty. It's sad to say it, but I'd much rather have found a stack of pornography.

Rosa closes the album slowly and replaces it on the table. She crosses one leg over the other, places her hands in her lap, and waits. So, I say, struggling to verbalise this experience for the first time, I put the album back under the socks and tried to forget about it. Except that I couldn't. My mind kept going back to it, just churning away. Every spare moment I had when he wasn't around, I'd dig it up and leaf through it, looking for clues. But there weren't any, and that was the most distressing thing. There was nothing for my mind to fix on, so it just kept going over and over the same thoughts, the same suspicions. As you've seen, the photos are revealing, but opaque. I didn't know any of the girls, had never seen them around town. I even scanned a couple at work and did internet searches, but I found nothing. It was literally driving me crazy.

And so... says Rosa. I look up and away, tears brimming along the lower edges of my eyes. One day I confronted him. I had to. If I hadn't, I'd have gone insane. As you can imagine, he was defensive, which just wound me up. It all became more and more fractured, less rational. I ended up shrieking, are these pictures of all the girls you've been out with, like notches on your bedpost? The last phrase throws Rosa, and I've probably got it wrong. The English probably doesn't translate. That really got to him, I add. We had this awful shouting match. No, he said. I used to have a photography business, a couple of years ago. These are all that's left of it. It went bust, because I'm bad with money, didn't get people to pay me and got drunk too often. These are just my favourite pictures, okay?

Nodding my head slowly, I continue. The strange thing is that I believed him. And what's the problem, really? He likes girls, and has a few pictures of them that he took in a previous life, before me. But I couldn't let it go. I became obsessed. Was he seeing any of them? Why had he never offered to photograph me? He said I'd never asked, which was true. It just went on and on, and I couldn't let it go. I kept picking away at it, trying to find out details, torturing myself, but he wasn't forthcoming. He got resentful. Things started to deteriorate. After one argument, I told him to get out.

I stood there in the bedroom while he packed a bag. I watched him, fuming. As he walked past me, he glared at me. I felt wronged, triumphant, vindicated. But as soon as the door closed, I realised what I'd done. I'd destroyed something that had once been so precious. I wave both hands in front of me like a helpless, frightened bird. I've been here before. I'm right on the edge of losing it, of having a full-blown panic attack. I breathe in slowly through my nose, exhale through my mouth.

But Rosa's not letting me get away with anything just because I'm suffering from a sense of imminent doom. She just sits there, waiting. Implacable. Like a chief justice, or a member of the inquisition. Waiting for me to tell the whole truth.

I take another steadying breath, and the panic begins to recede. Okay, I might be over the worst now. But Rosa's not having it. And? She asks. Is there anything else my child?

I glare at her like an angry teenager. Well, I don't know where he went after that, I say. I know he didn't have any family nearby. Maybe he went and shacked up with one of his whores, I say, giving the album a petulant shove. Rosa shakes her head slightly, and I'm back to being a kid again, a kid who thinks she's already an adult. Okay, I say, finally giving in, finally crushed by Rosa's obdurate silence. The impact happened several days after he left. How many people have died? Sixty, seventy percent of the population? More? Nobody really knows.

And again I'm trying to excuse myself, to give good reasons for what happened. An image comes to me, an image of the worm in my hand, struggling to escape as the hook is pressed into its flesh.

The truth is, I say, that I never saw him again. I don't know if he had anywhere to go. As far as my conscience is concerned, I killed him.

IV

I have to know who's living down by the river. My mind chatters away constantly, giving me no peace. Could it be Ursula, somehow miraculously brought back from the dead? And where the hell is her body if not? It takes all the willpower I've got not to head back to the river one evening. But I daren't. The stories about things that have happened to people out at night - especially single females - are too gruesome. It's fascinating how thin the veneer of humanity and civilisation can be: in times of stress it's shown to be not much thicker than a layer of paint. I don't risk it. I wait until the weekend.

Before I'd gotten involved with the kids, all of my days had just merged into one another. I didn't even know what day of the week it was most of the time. Falling in with the nuns, though, has reestablished my sense of time. The life of the convent - its daily prayers, meal times and other religious observances - have gone on as always, giving a sense of solidity and - dare I say it - purpose to everyone who lives there. The nuns have always recognised the power of routine, and I must say that I'm starting to feel some of the benefits.

So, at first light on Saturday, I head out. I wrap up, as the days are getting colder now, and make sure that I've got a knife and a torch in my bag, just in case. I also take my wooden, lump-headed walking stick. I throw it jauntily over my shoulder as I walk through town, whistling. All I need now is a bindle and I'd look like a right-regular hobo.

When I get to the top of the rocky path, I stop and peer at the mountains away to the north. The grey ridges and snowfields lurk in the distance like the promise of winter to come. Having said that, it's a surprisingly clear day - I don't think I've ever been able to see so far. Maybe the air's clearing? Maybe, and of course it will do by degrees over the years. But there's still that sad smudge in the upper atmosphere that hangs over us like a death sentence.

As I make my way slowly down the path, I realise that being obsessive is probably my defining characteristic. It's exactly what happened with Marco. I couldn't get past the album, and wasn't satisfied with his explanations. Being a little obsessive is one thing, but I'm on a whole different level. I need answers, even if my search for them leads to my looking like a serial killer returning to the scene of the crime to gloat.

Well, if monomania was good enough for Captain Ahab, it's good enough for me. Of course, I don't know who I'm going to find down here, if anyone. But I've got to know.

When I'm halfway down the slope, I stop at the end of a switchback and peer down at the small clump of trees on the other side of the river. And then it strikes me that Marco could be the person living there, surviving in the woods on the edge of civilisation. He might be biding his time in the wilderness before coming back to reclaim me like some modern-day Lancelot. I can actually see him, standing on the edge of that clearing, his cheeky half-smile pulling at one side of his mouth. For a second, inspired by this image of chivalry and tenacity, I feel heady and giddy. I step off the path and perch on the edge of a rock. I take a few deep breaths and find - to my horror - that I'm beginning to well up. I know it's little better than a schoolgirl fantasy, but I clutch at the image of Marco tightly, trying to preserve it - to enjoy it for a few seconds before it falls prey to the ravages of my scepticism.

Ever since my confession to Rosa, I've felt lighter, freer, happier. But at the same time any little thing sets me off, has me crying like a small child. It's cathartic, for sure, but it's also wearing. The question is, is this the new norm? Is a weepy, wavering August going to take the place of the tough, skinny bitch that has survived for so long? Have I lost my edge? These days, edge isn't something that's monopolised by high-fliers or extreme sports junkies: we all need some just to get through the days.

So I take a deep breath and tell myself to man-up. Can you think of a more male-oriented phrase? Me Tarzan, you Jane. Grrrr. Anyway, for some reason it does the trick, and soon I'm bounding downwards like a loon, eager to find out who may be palely loitering in the woods.

I trip back over the stepping stones, chagrined at my now wet feet, and try to pick my way silently through the trees. I soon realise it's impossible. All the leaves have fallen and lie in drifts calf-deep. I may as well be walking on castanets. I try to hop up on to a rock here, pull on a tree branch there, but at the end of the day it makes little difference. If anyone's within earshot, they'll hear me. And it strikes me how desolate this place actually is - in our brief summers, sure, it has the look of an oasis. But now, with winter right around the corner, I realise how little shelter these denuded trees will offer someone living here. Most of them are very old, their grey trunks riven, twisted and split; their narrow, leafless branches won't provide much protection from the winds and snowstorms howling down from the mountains.

The clearing is as I remember it, but more open. With its swept interior and ring of rocks, it could be the scene for some kind of gladiatorial death match. But the fireplace is still there, as is the tripod of sticks. The kettle, though, is nowhere to be seen. I move slowly around the circle towards the cave, keeping an eye on the trees. Part of me wants to call out a cheerful greeting, just so I don't disturb whoever-it-is who lives here. Another part of me thinks I'm a moron for even entertaining such an idea. At the end of the day, surprise may be the only chance I have of getting out alive.

I pause at the edge of the cave, running my hand down the porous rock, and give myself a moment, like a heroine in some classic Hollywood movie who's about to make a big decision. Standing there, one leg slightly cocked, an inquisitive frown upon my face, I imagine myself in black and white. I must really look the part.

That's when I hear it - a rustling of dried leaves. I turn, heart lurching, and see movement in the trees behind me, the way I've just come. This totally throws me - I'd expected to find someone here, but now they've found me. And I'm trapped, totally trapped, my exit cut off by rocks and a thick layer of undergrowth. I shrink back against the cliff face, one hand clutched to my chest, still in film heroine mode.

A tall figure emerges from the trees. It's instantly clear that this is not Ursula. It's a man, and although he's obviously skinny, he's well over six feet tall. He looks wiry, but strong, as if he could snap my neck like a chicken bone. At first I don't think he sees me. He's carrying the blackened kettle and wearing a wax jacket, lumberjack shirt, dirty jeans and boots. A wide-brimmed hat hangs low over his dark brows. He's got a beard, and locks of peaty hair hang from beneath his hat. He's probably about my age, which might be helpful in my quest for survival: kindred spirits, shared cultural references and all that.

When he looks up at me and smiles, I realise that he's known I've been here all along. He raises the kettle slightly, and asks me if I'd like some tea. He widens his eyes as he says this, as if we're sharing a joke. I nod by way of response. I don't know what it is about him, but I instantly feel at ease. He takes his time securing the kettle over the fire, obviously not considering me a threat. When he's done this, he moves to the side of the clearing, finds a fair-sized rock, and picks it up as if it were a bag of sugar. To my dismay, I realise that he's even stronger than I thought. He deposits the rock by the edge of the fireplace, waves a hand at it and says, please, take a seat. I've just got to grab some sticks.

As soon as he's left the clearing, I move slowly over to the rock and do as he says. Despite its size, the rock's rather low, so I end up squatting on it - hardly a flattering position. I pull my knees up, clamp my arms around my legs and probably end up looking more like a child awaiting a beating than a movie starlet.

It doesn't take him long to return. He kneels down by the fireplace, deposits a load of dried leaves beneath the kettle and lights them with a plastic lighter. Then he begins stacking a succession of increasingly large sticks up around the nascent flames. Soon enough, he's got a blaze going beneath the kettle. The fire's comforting, mesmerising. It looks like a teepee that's gone up in flames. All the while he's doing this, he doesn't look at me once, which I find both reassuring and aggravating. Am I that hideous? Still, all of his movements are calm, unhurried and assured. I find myself feeling more relaxed than I have done in a long while, which is perhaps a worry. Is he simply lulling me into a false sense of security?

So, he says, finally looking me in the eye, nice to see you again. What brings you down here? I immediately tense up. What do you mean again, I ask. He shrugs, smiles and pokes the fire with a stick. Well, you're down here most days with a load of kids, so it's been hard not to notice you.

Well, in that case, I snap, you could have come and said hello. His smile widens. True, he says, but you always seem to be having such a good time - I've never wanted to intrude. A bearded redneck emerging from the woods might spoil the mood.

Huh, I say, you're not that intimidating. That's good, he adds. When you've been living on your own for a while, you lose track of things - especially of how other people might see you. I always think I look like the Yeti. I roll my eyes. Don't flatter yourself, I say. He chuckles, and a smile breaks out across his face. Under the beard, it's obvious that he's probably quite an attractive man. He doesn't come up with a response, which is gratifying: just so long as he recognises that he's not going to win a war of words with me. But to stop the sudden silence becoming awkward, I reach out a hand.

He regards it with amusement for a second, as if unsure of how to proceed, leaving me wondering whether I've committed a social faux pas. These days shaking hands has become a lot more common. Everyone's become so wary of one another that the traditional Italian clutching and air kissing has died a death, except between well-known acquaintances. And that's fine by me. Never having been that tactile, I've always been uncomfortable pawing at people I don't know.

When he finally takes my hand, I'm horrified to see how it disappears into his workman's palm. His fingers are the size of chipolatas, darkened and shiny with use. He gives my hand a perfunctory squeeze, and it's done. It always seems strange, he says, shaking hands with a woman. Of course, this makes me bristle. Well, you could have kissed me, I say, but the moment's passed.

What the hell's wrong with me? Am I actually flirting with this guy? I tell myself to rein it in. He could be a criminal, an escaped murderer hiding on the edge of society. Kindred spirits and all that.

Well, I'll remember for next time, he replies, smiling. I realise that I'm actually enjoying talking to a man for once. Since most of them have died, it's been a while. I've always been a bit of a man's woman, and I enjoy the banter, the back-and-forth. Somehow, Cornelius doesn't count. We're so dependent upon him that I'm always on my guard when interacting with him: he's so inscrutable that it makes me tense; I'd hate to think that he could get one over on me. With this guy, it's different. I feel far more relaxed.

I'm August, I say. August, he says, as if amused. That's an unusual name - for a girl. I nod enthusiastically. It is, I say. My parents were teachers, so they always used to go away for the whole month, exploring other countries and having a great time. Until I came along, of course. And you?

He nods, staring at the fire. I'm Joe. Joe Moralis. It's funny, he adds, when you hear your name again after so long. It sounds odd, like somebody you used to know. Still, he says, raising his eyebrows, strange times, eh? So, he says, fixing me with his hunter's eyes, what brings you here? Is this a social call?

Again, I find myself nodding enthusiastically, like the class swot. Absolutely, I say. I'll be honest - I found your little campsite the other day, and I just wanted to see who lives out here. I just had to know, I add. Curiosity and all that.

I see, he says, nodding sagely. Excuse me a second. He unbends himself slowly, rising up to his full height like a golem pouring itself upward out of the earth. As he skirts the fire and heads back to the cave, I feel absolutely dwarfed. I'm tall for a woman - five foot ten at last count, but this guy is built on another level, like a bridge, a crane, or some other vast metal structure.

He returns with two white tin cups and hands me one. They remind me of the cups my parents had when we used to go camping, decades ago. They're just as old and chipped, and when he gives me one, I turn it over in my hands. There's something reassuring about it: it's a link to the past, which implies that there might be a future.

Opening the top of the blackened kettle, Joe tosses three teabags in. It won't be long, he says. And I'm afraid that I can't offer you milk, of course. I frown. Well, I am disappointed, I add. I'd have thought you had a cow tethered up around here somewhere. I know, he says, shrugging, it's disappointing. But I do have sugar.

I'm sure it'll be fine, I say. I haven't had sugar in hot drinks since I was a kid. But when he pours the tea several minutes later, I wish that I'd accepted his offer. The tea is dark, bitter and scalding hot. I clamp my palms around the tin cup, but it's so hot that I have to set it down for a minute. Joe does not. He sips at it and grins at me. Not exactly a fine espresso from your local cafe, is it, he asks. I'm just impressed you can make tea over a fire, I say. Which brings me to the question, why are you out here? There are quite a few flats going for free.

Joe shrugs and looks away, as if remembering happier times. In my last job, I was a glaciologist, he says. I spent a lot of time in the Alps. I stuck it out up there for a bit, after everyone else had panicked and run off, but the weather got worse, and the higher up you are, the worse the dust is. So, seeing as my dad was Italian, I thought I'd work my way down into Italy. Plus, it's a long country. If things got too cold, I could keep going for a good five hundred miles, and then I could always hop across to North Africa if I had to. But when I found this place, I liked it, and just stayed. Hardly anyone knows I'm here: I don't disturb them; they don't disturb me. It works perfectly.

So, I say, frowning, where are you from originally? Somerset, in England, he replies, grinning. The land of apples, ditches and Avalon. I roll my eyes. I thought there was something in your accent, I reply, in English. You should have said. But you do speak Italian very well.

Very kind, he says, lapsing back into the broad vowels of the West Country. Like I said, my father was Italian. I studied it on the side at Uni, and I've spent lots of summers out here.

I quickly fill him in on my background. He nods and maintains his smile. Another ex-pat, I add, who'd have thought it? I think, he says, still holding my gaze, that a lot of Italians have relatives in the South, or simply know the land better, and have chosen to decamp permanently. And fair play to them. Still, I've always preferred the North. It feels a bit more... like home. I nod sagely. But what about all this, I ask, waving my hand at the clearing, the cave. Why stay out in the elements?

Don't tell me, he says, that you've never wanted to go camping? I suck on my teeth. Sure, but not forever. He shrugs. I'm a bit of a solitary beast. I don't like being beholden to anyone, and out here I'm not. You can live on your own terms - a quiet, peaceful existence, you know? Out here, there are no temptations. When he says this, he fixes me with his dark eyes and tilts his head just a little. He doesn't look away and I'm forced to. A cold hand of static walks its way up my spine, and I just hope I'm not blushing. For a moment I'm lost, then I remember the tea. I pick it up and sip at it appreciatively, casting my eye around the clearing. I take a deep breath. In through the nose, out through the mouth.

Eventually, I clear my throat. It must get cold here, though, in the winter. He shrugs. It does, for sure. But I think the pros outweigh the cons. I replace my empty mug on the ground. Something tells me that it's time to be going, that I don't want to outstay my welcome. Well, it's been lovely meeting you, I say, sounding suddenly as prim as some Victorian governess, but I really must be going.

Stay longer, if you like, he says. It'll be light for a while yet, he adds, as if pre-empting my next point. I smile at him. True, I say, but I've got some errands to run. Well, some shops to rob and some houses to loot, if you must know. He raises his eyebrows. Quite the little criminal, eh? For a second I have an image of this man's long, swarthy body beneath me. I'm pale and naked, twirling my bra around my head and riding him like a cowgirl on acid. I need help. I really do.

Let me show you out, he says, levering himself from his shallow rock. I stand too, feeling suddenly self-conscious and bashful. Like really, what is my problem? He ushers me across the clearing, and I have to admit that I feel chaperoned and safe. Well, it was nice to meet you he says. Feel free to pay me a visit any time. As you can see, I'm not that busy. At the edge of the clearing I stop and turn to him. I'll think about it, I say, trying - and failing - to sound coquettish. And maybe - who knows? Maybe one day I'll invite you up for coffee.

I cringe internally. What am I saying? I'm trotting out tired euphemisms already? Suddenly I see why this man might want to shun social interactions. At least he wouldn't have to talk to idiots like me.

That would be lovely he replies, smiling knowingly. Although, I say, trying to throw in a barrier like a workman lobbing down cones, you may have to spruce up a bit first.

He looks down at himself and laughs - thankfully. At least he's not easily offended. I can do that, he says, meeting my eyes once again. You'd be surprised at just how well I scrub up. I look pretty good in a tux.

I laugh too, and actually pat his chest! I need to get out of here before anything else goes wrong, before I humiliate myself even further. It's then that I spot the cross in the woods. It's about three feet high, made of two wonky grey branches - driftwood I suspect - that have been lashed together with twine. It protrudes from what seems to be a low mound covered with yellow, drifted leaves and fallen twigs. I feel my whole body tense up.

What's that, I ask, clearing my throat and pointing at the cross. That, says Joe, is a grave. A grave? I say, sounding like a parrot. For whom? He shakes his head. I don't know. A woman. I found her over by the sandspit. She must have been there about a day, as the birds had already started picking at her. She was well and truly dead. I couldn't leave her there, so in the end I dragged her body over here. It's the only place hereabouts where the earth is deep enough to dig a decent grave - hence the trees. You have no idea how hard it was to dig. I broke one spade, and couldn't use my hands for days, they were so blistered.

Who was she, I ask. I pitch my voice at cheerfully disinterested, but it comes out more like a terrified croak, the sound of a toad about to get run over. He glances back at me and shrugs. I've no idea, he says, she used to set her traps here, out on that spit. I set all of my traps upriver, so there was no competition. I saw her a few times, but I never spoke to her. Still, I felt like I did the right thing, you know? And it's strange, whoever she was, it's some kind of company. Does that sound strange?

No, I say, shaking my head a little too fervently. We all need companionship these days, and I suppose we find it in different places. I must be going, I say, looking up at him weakly. I've got all of those shops to rob, you know? Well, he says, smiling down at me, you enjoy yourself. And I look forward to that coffee.

For the rest of the day and night, the question

of whether Joe saw me kill Ursula obsesses me. I replay our conversation a thousand times in my mind, analysing it meticulously. For one run-through, I'll conclude that he has no idea, that his features just portrayed a solemn honesty, his perhaps once-optimistic nature tarnished by the times. Two minutes later - literally two minutes later - I'll have convinced myself that the opposite is true. The corner of his mouth turned up a little, his eyes widened - both the marks of a knowing, insincere smirk. He knows, I think. He knows, and he's just hiding it well, using it for future leverage. What that might be, of course, I have no idea. The whole process, needless to say, is exhausting. The hours pass in a state of heightened awareness, adrenaline seeping into me as if I'm mainlining a hospital-grade bag of the stuff.

Of course, Joe said nothing about who killed Ursula. He just said that he found her. Any sane human being would conclude that I'm in the clear. Occam's Razor and all that - the smaller the number of assumptions, the more likely the explanation is to be true. It's much more likely that Joe simply told me what he knew, rather than purposefully omitting his knowledge of my involvement in Ursula's death. You see? It's exhausting. I want to let myself off the hook, but some part of my mind keeps me on it, struggling like one of those poor worms we sent to watery graves. That's the trouble with obsessive thinking - one obsession often leads to another. Where will my erratic thought process lead me next? I've no idea. That's what makes me so much fun. That's what makes me so special.

I barely sleep. By Sunday morning, I'm a timid, creeping wreck, and I can't see how I can carry on. The question of why I'm so keen for Joe not to know I killed Ursula is one that's best avoided. I think it's because if I want him to like me, I have to appear to be a certain type of person. It's perhaps to do with how we, as women, are always trying to please men. We're always trying to project this idealised and often wholesome image of ourselves. At school, I was always the perfect student: studious, well behaved, a constant high-achiever. And I think that has far more to do with a received sense of personal identity than it does with being naturally academic or intellectually inquisitive.

By the time the grey fingers of dawn have touched the sky, I'm on the edge of a full-blown panic attack. The thoughts won't stop swirling in my mind, like dead leaves falling unbidden from autumn trees. Rosa and I often spend the weekends apart, but I soon realise that I've got to have some company, that I've got to break this chain of pointless rumination. So I dress simply in a long coat, dark glasses and a Paisley headscarf - a splash of colour in this washed-out world - and head over.

At Rosa's block, Hilda eyes me suspiciously. She's used to my popping round, but never on a Sunday morning. I'm here to take Rosa to church, I say. This seems to do the trick, and she lets me in, but she seems to know that something's wrong. I can't help but feel that my card's been marked, that I'm going to have to be extra careful from here on out.

Rosa accepts the news of our imminent journey with a solemn nod. Her hair seems greyer, wispier than ever; her eyes seem more unfocused, as if she's looking inward, peering out over a promised land that only she can see. Is there time for coffee, she asks. I throw my hands up in the air. Of course, I say. There's always time for coffee! She puts it on and hurries to her room. When she reappears five minutes later, I get a shock. She's dressed exactly as I am - long coat, dark glasses, Paisley headscarf.

What's with the get-up, Mama, I ask, as we sit down to our tiny cups of espresso. Do you like it, she asks, smoothing down one sleeve and running her hand over the scarf. She then tilts her head upwards, as if to catch the light or avoid the paparazzi's gaze. I've always wanted to be a film star. I grit my teeth and sip my coffee. You look lovely, I say. At least this will give me something else to chew over for a bit.

The inside of the Santa Maria's is sombre, but enlivened by occasional shafts of direct sun-

light that angle down through the stained glass,
throwing faint spears of blue and purple through
the gloom. Direct sunlight at this time of year?
Could things be improving? I swallow my sense
of hope and stare at the front of the church,
at the altar and the surrounding windows. I've
never been religious, and I'm still not, but I've always liked churches. The calmness, the sense of
safety and solace they provide. At these times I
envy those who truly have faith: it must a lot of
comfort, must make sense of much that we see
around us. Although I reckon that sometimes the
explanatory power of religion must be stretched
a little thin, what with everything that's gone on.

We're the only people in the church, and although it's soothing, something's missing. Before
the altar stands a lectern, and on it lies a large
Bible, already open. While part of me's surprised
that it hasn't yet been used as toilet paper, another part of me's delighted. Come on Mama, I
say, let's go and have a look at the Bible - let's
see what the last person in here was reading. She
follows me without protest, and we're soon gaz-
ing down into the gothic script of the giant book.
Older texts, with their archaic turns of phrase,
are generally where my Italian starts to struggle,
but staring at the open Bible, I realise that I get
the gist easily enough. So many of the words are
simple or repeated that it does make sense.

The last person in here was reading Genesis,

perhaps predictably enough. And the Earth was without form, and void; and there was darkness on the face of the deep. And God's spirit moved over the face of the waters. Or as near as dammit. I've always liked that section - the sense of unchained potential and expectation. It's dark, sultry, almost sexual. And then God shows up and pumps his seed into the world, and here we are.

I know what, I say, clutching Rosa's arm. Let's each read a section, as if we're the priest. We can choose whatever we want. Rosa casts a glance at the door of the church, then looks back at me, eyes wide. She's got the air of a child about her. A child about to do something naughty. Do you think that would be allowed, she asks.

I wave a cursory hand through the air. Of course, I cry. Who else is here? It's just you, me and God. Go on, take a seat. I'll start. Rosa does as she's told, and after a pregnant pause, I launch into Genesis, giving it a good go, giving it my best Italian preacher impression. It feels empowering to be belting these ancient words out to the back row, and I can see why people go all Evangelical. It's freeing, inspiring. It must be something along the lines of what it feels like to sing for others, if you're actually good at it. I don't think drunken karaoke counts.

When I get to the whales and wild fowl I wind it up. Rosa looks up at me and claps quietly, her face full of glee. Once again she reminds me of a small child. I wonder whether this is just simply sweet, or whether she's actually regressing, being channelled back into her early years by the ravaging effects of dementia. Without any medical tests, it's hard to say, but I do wonder. You see? I told you it was exhausting being me. My mind just won't shut up.

Your turn, I say. Rosa approaches the lectern with a sense of trepidation. As she stands behind the oversized wooden pillar and platform, she looks small and frail, like someone who has been cast adrift in this world. But when she starts reading, everything changes. Her voice is thin and haunting, but behind her querulous tone lies the conviction of deep-seated belief: it resonates through her words, much as the spirit of God must have resonated through the dark Earth in Genesis. I'm utterly speechless, bound in by the power and purity of her words. I did well to choose her. She's got the stamp of sainthood on her already. She's a martyr in the making.

We alternate several times, and go from staring at the other in hushed awe, to giggling like schoolgirls. It's cathartic and confusing. We have the sense that we're doing something we shouldn't be, but at the same time, we're reading the words of God. Or the words of God watered down a little. Or the words of God as bastardised by man. Whatever. You get the idea.

So Rosa's up there again, and quite frankly

I'm amazed that this little old lady can project so much power. Brother will betray brother to death, she chants, and a father his child; and children will rise up against parents and cause them to be put to death. Matthew 10:21, she adds.

Of course, this is pretty much what happened after the impact: with no sun for months on end, some people lost the plot and turned on each other. Those with egos, those who needed to dominate soon found themselves on the outs. Those who could cooperate did just that, and got on with things. They did so quietly, calmly and with a sense of resignation. The meek shall inherit the Earth. And so it was.

Cornelius is back. He worms his way into my flat like a neighbour's cat. A cat trying to curry favour and expecting to be fed. Any titbits, he asks. It's an odd word, but I assume he's referring to food. Sadly, I have to keep him sweet. I eye his oversized head with open distaste. Has it got bigger since the last time I saw him, or has he just got thinner?

Years ago I saw an astronaut getting interviewed. Can you imagine it? An astronaut. A man who'd been on the International Space Station. Anyway, this guy said he'd once had this epiphany: that everyone has their own struggles. No one's breezing through life, contrary to what they might want you to think. To me, that statement was life-changing. It made me a little less neurotic and self-obsessed. A little. Everyone's struggling - not just you. As far as empathy goes, that's a great mantra.

Anyway, I wonder what struggles Cornelius has been going through. All I see is this lounging, well-dressed dandy, but I'll bet most of his days are spent hunting around insalubrious places and doing deals with people who'd just as easily stab him as look at him. He's made a niche for himself all right, but I bet he doesn't maintain his position easily.

I make a great show of going through my cupboards, rhythmically drumming on a few empty shelves. I can't help but think there's some bluffing and counter bluffing going on here, but I'm too weary to work out the details. To be fair, my supplies are getting a little depleted again. I'm going to have to start trapping crayfish like Ursula did, or fashion myself a bow and go rollicking through the countryside looking for deer like some modern-day Diana.

I find a packet of Matzos. I pull them out and wave them cheerfully at Cornelius. I've got these, I say, giving him a winning smile. I'll put some coffee on to wash them down with, I add, hefting the pack he's just given me. Cornelius nods and I get to work. Coffee is the lifeblood. It's one of the only things I insist he bring every time. I can go for days without food, but coffee? That's not even funny.

When the coffee's ready we sit for a bit, trying to choke down the world's driest crackers with tiny sips of espresso. It's not an ideal combination. The rest of my order is downstairs in the hallway, with Filippa keeping a beady eye on it from he concierge's station. Great, I think, at least half of it will have disappeared by the time I get down there. Cornelius is in a whimsical mood, but we chat away easily enough. When we can enunciate through the floury paste that clogs our mouths, that is.

Oh, by the way, he mumbles, I got your poison. He pulls a plastic pouch from a deep pocket. The plastic's clear, and you can see the bright red grains inside. They look like blood clots. I take the packet and squeeze it between my fingers. It feels like some type of uber-healthy granola, packed with nuts and seeds. It's called Ratter. A cute cartoon rat with crosses for eyes sits beneath the name. It's industrial strength, says Cornelius. It only takes a few grains to kill a rat. The trouble is, you don't want the damn things to die under the floorboards or anywhere you can't get to. Apparently the smell is awful. He bestows an unctuous smile on me, as if this is something he's just heard.

Then he reaches out and lays one of his leathery hands on mine. I couldn't have been more surprised if he'd slapped me in the face. Here we go, I think. He's finally succumbed to my womanly charms. Would I actually sleep with him? The answer is probably not, but I'd certainly lead him on a bit, just for the leverage.

I hope, he says, looking at me solemnly, with only the merest hint of a smile on his mouth, that you're not thinking of doing anything foolish. There are very few capable people left, and it would be a great shame to lose you. This block, he says, looking up and around at the ceiling, would crumble without you. I doubt anyone in here would make it through the winter without you driving the bargains that you do.

At first I don't get it. Then I realise that he's trying to dissuade me from doing away with myself. Then I'm slightly offended - so he wasn't really making a pass at me? Overtly sexual advances are much easier to process that displays of genuine concern. Does Cornelius really care? I find the thought unsettling.

Waving my free hand through the air, I laugh. Of course not, I say, still incredulous. We really do have rats. They're a right pain in the arse.

Okay, says Cornelius, his eyes still staring at me, as if he's trying to look into the very depths of my soul. It's just that the rats in our block died a long time ago. I always thought that rats and cockroaches would inherit the earth. It seems I was wrong about the former.

Well, we breed them pretty tough over here, I say, slowly pulling my hand away. Thanks for your concern, I add, but I'm absolutely fine. Oh, and your payment's over there by the door. He glances over at the two carrier bags stuffed with home-grown vegetables, the thin plastic stretched tight by the curved weight of the produce. The bags have an almost voluptuous quality to them, seeming to hark back to a time when women actually had curves.

Thank you, he says, sidling over to the bags and pulling them effortlessly from the floor. These will save a few people, I can tell you that. And no, I'm not being dramatic. Until next time. He nods, pulls the door open and leaves without fuss. Am I going crazy, or does Cornelius actually have a conscience? Maybe. Just maybe. But whatever else is going on with him, I'm pretty sure he smells a rat.

Monday is much colder. We wrap up warm, but as we tramp out beyond the natural windbreak formed by the buildings, an icy wind hits us, stripping away any spare heat we might have had. The kids don't seem to notice it at first, but after a couple of hours sitting on the sand, they're shivering and ready to go. Not even the catching of fish seems to lift their spirits.

Our nun Anna also seems less than enthusiastic: my quipping about us being fishers of men

doesn't even get a response. It's then that I realise I'm trying to push what's an ostensibly summer sport into the winter. Without all the gear
- the tents, portable stoves and balaclavas - we
can't really expect to carry on much longer. Reluctantly, I call it early, and we tramp back into
town. Sadly, the kids look relieved.

We do stick it out for the rest of the week,
but by Friday I realise we've wrung out all the
joy from fishing that we're going to get for this
year. I've got to come up with something else,
and sharpish. I'm preoccupied with this question
as I make my excuses, leave the kids with Rosa
and our nun and head over to the woods. I make
as much noise as I can crossing the drifts of desiccated leaves, just to make sure Joe doesn't think
I'm some armed intruder and go all Rambo on me.

It doesn't take more than a minute for me
to work out that nobody's there. I take my time,
wander around the clearing, and even check the
cave. But all of Joe's stuff is still wedged in against
the back wall, so I figure that he can't have gone
far. It's a shame not to be able to speak to him in
person, as I was looking forward to a bit of banter, but that can't be helped. I've written him a
note - replete with a crude map - and I leave this
on the edge of the fireplace, weighted down with
a small rock. It's a formal invitation to my place
for coffee. It might be a bit risky, but I've got to
return the favour - that's simply politeness. Be-

sides, I've got enough knives to keep him at bay. If he actually turns up, that is.

It's then that I hear the whistling. It's faint at first, and I can't quite place the tune, even though it sounds familiar. I stop and watch Joe as he skirts the base of the cliff, negotiating large rocks and tree limbs as if they weren't there. If it weren't for the whistling, I wouldn't be able to hear him. Hello, I say, before he enters the clearing proper. I see him stop and stiffen slightly. Then he scans the clearing, sees me and relaxes. By the time he's actually walking towards me, a large grin splits his bearded face, and his eyes have a bright, come-hither quality beneath the wide brim of his hat.

Well, fancy seeing you here, he says in English. We've got to stop meeting up like this - people will start talking. He's just as tall as I remember, and I'm glad to see he's wearing a different shirt this time - an old denim number. I twirl a finger through a lock of my hair, and hope the grey doesn't catch in the weak light.

I came to invite you round, I say. The note's by the fireplace. I wave hand in its general direction. All the details are there.

That'd be lovely, he says, frowning slightly. That'd be lovely, it's just that... As his voice trails off, I raise my eyebrows, refusing to let him off the hook. Look, I say, if you've had a better offer, I understand. No, he says, looking at me in an

almost bashful manner. I'll be there. It's just...
maybe don't expect too much. I haven't social-
ised for a long time. I'm probably a bit rusty.

For some reason, I find this slight display of
vulnerability touching. Well, I say, drawing out
the word, it is pretty tricky. And things have
moved on a lot in the last couple of years. Eti-
quette changes, you know? First of all, you have
to bring me flowers. And supply a cake. And then,
of course, you have to address me as Your High-
ness, or else I set the dogs on you.

He smiles at this. You shouldn't joke about
dogs. I've had a couple of dodgy moments with
wild packs in the last couple of years.

Really, I say. I'm surprised you don't have
your own pack. I could see you as some modern-
day dog whisperer. His face clouds suddenly. I had
a dog a couple of years ago, he says, but when he
died, I didn't want to replace him. It would have
seemed wrong somehow. But I still miss him, you
know.

Again, I find myself strangely touched at
this odd confession of fidelity. I'm sorry to hear
that, I say, smiling slightly. But I'm guessing that
he had a pretty good life, with you. Joe nods and
smiles. Yeah, we had some good times together.
Well, I add, glancing back towards the river, I've
got to go, but maybe you can tell me about him
tomorrow.

Joe nods and holds my gaze. Yeah, he says.

I'd like that. I'll see you then. I give him a cursory nod, turn and walk away. A nervous, expectant energy ripples through me, and the fact that his eyes are no doubt lingering on me as I leave only adds to the tension. Mission accomplished.

When I get back to our little group, I find that my sense of elation is out of place. The kids are huddled down in their coats, and some of their lips have even started to turn blue. Rosa and our nun are standing at the end of the spit, staring downstream, their conversation broken by the cold. Okay kids, I say, time to get packed away. There are no cheers, but no words of protest either. And I realise that we've come to the end of an era. Will we start fishing again next year? Who knows. It's a long way off. We've still got to get through the winter first. And these days, most of us struggle to think more than a day or two in advance.

It only takes us five minutes to get ready, but it isn't soon enough. The kids are cold and monosyllabic. What a difference a couple of weeks can make! As we grind up out of the river valley, I'm once again preoccupied by what we're going to do next week. Should Rosa and I take a week off? You couldn't say that we haven't earned it, but at this stage we've built up a lot of trust with these kids, and it would be a shame to lose it.

When we reach the road, I pause and look

back out towards the mountains. It's then that I notice a thin stream of brown smoke pulling itself up into the air.

I point the smoke out to our nun. She just crosses herself and starts hurrying the children along. The source of the smoke can't be seen because of the rolling land, but its source is perhaps five miles away, between us and the glowering grey of the mountains.

Mama, I say, catching Rosa by the sleeve, what's that? We both shield our eyes against the white of the sky and peer at the rising smoke. It's too much to be coming from a domestic fire, or even a bonfire.

She shrugs and sighs. Probably those devils from Monte Fiore again, she whispers, as if saying the name out loud is somehow taboo. Looting and pillaging. Did I tell you about the time my father sold his car to a man from there?

As we wander back into town after the children, I'm barely listening as Rosa launches into an extended anecdote about how her dad was ripped off by some shady character from Monte Fiore half a century ago. The town's a little smaller than ours, but a fair bit rougher: football matches between the two were usually tense, and the fans often got stuck into each other. Derby day was always interesting.

Back home, I start desperately cleaning in preparation for Joe's visit on the morrow. The place isn't actually that bad, but I've always been a bit of a clean freak. Two hours later the whole flat smells of bleach and furniture polish. I light a joss stick, just to take the edge off, and place it on the kitchen table. As the blue smoke pillows upwards and merges into the air, I'm reminded of the rising smoke we saw earlier. Whether or not it has anything to do with the residents of Monte Fiore is almost impossible to say, but it can hardly be a good sign. Why would anyone bother to burn down a building? But then again I tell myself that winter's coming, and that this is when people do crazy, desperate things. At least ten per cent of the population won't make it through the next five months, so it's no wonder.

Joe's late, but acceptably - almost fashionably - so. When I first open the door, I do a double take. The straggly beard is gone, leaving an angular face, with chiselled cheekbones and dancing eyes. If I were in a period drama, I'd swoon quietly into a corner. Giving the theatrics a miss, I clear my throat to hide my surprise and usher him in. He smiles at me as he enters, and I feel a glow of warmth in the pit of my stomach. Maybe it's the first signs that the permafrost of my emotional life is finally melting.

You scrub up well, I say, closing the door. Please, take a seat. He wanders in and sits at the kitchen table. I'm once again impressed by how tall he is, the size of his hands. He's combed his longish hair back, and strands of it frame his face. Leonine, I think, and cringe inside. So, I say, you found it okay?

Yeah, no problem, he says. Your directions were pretty good. I only had to knock at about five blocks first. I give him a sidelong look, and notice that he's smirking. Apart from that, he says, they were great. I roll my eyes. I would have thought glaciologists were good at navigating through unfamiliar terrain. I guess I was wrong.

I turn my attention to my old espresso maker. Its aluminium surface is covered with a dull patina and dark coffee stains. As I fill its bottom, spoon coffee into the midsection and then screw the two halves together, I see that my hands are shaking. What happened to the ice maiden of my youth? Maybe she never existed other than in my head.

Pushing this thought to one side, I scoop up the cake and bring it over to the table. It's sitting on the biggest plate I could find, and I'm not ashamed to say that it's a miracle of rare device. I've even managed something approaching a mirror glaze. I've never made anything quite so extraordinary.

Joe's eyes widen. He couldn't be more surprised if I'd placed John the Baptist's head down in front of him. My God, he whispers, where did you get this? He looks up at me from where he sits, almost alarmed. It's as if he can't believe that such a thing could be.

I wave a hand casually through the air. Oh, it's just a little something I rustled up. I had to borrow a few things from a friend, but there you have it. Voila. I curtsey and smile at his continued amazement. Round one to me, I think.

I didn't know you could get chocolate any more, he says. Generally you can't, I say, but I've got contacts. I can get most things within a few days. He gives me an arch look and furrows his brows. Don't tell me that Amazon Prime has risen from the flames, he says. Very funny, I reply. No, some things have gone for good. But the Mafia are here to stay.

He shrugs. Well, that makes sense. So, have you got vast stores set in for winter? I shake my head and mentally urge the coffee maker to boil. No, not really, I say. We've got some staples, some vegetables, but it's probably not enough to get us through. I actually think that each year things have got slightly worse. I don't know where we'll be at in February. We'll probably have to resort to eating each other. He doesn't reply, just turns his head and stares out of the window.

You know, he says, I never believed in all of the end-of-the-world stuff. Even global warming. It wasn't great, but I assumed the planet would adjust, reset itself to a new normal. When the dinosaurs were around - and long before that - the Earth was considerably hotter, with far more carbon dioxide in the air. Things change over countless millennia. I always thought that the Apocalypse was just fiction - a symbolic device used by us to, well, explore ideas about our own death. I didn't expect the apocalypse to be real.

As his words trail off, the coffee starts to boil. I pour it into two espresso cups and refill the coffee maker, almost scalding my hands in the process. Well, I say, bearing the cups over to the table and taking a seat, that's not quite how it is. This isn't an apocalypse in the true sense of the word, is it? This is more of a slow strangulation. A fade away... not a burn out.

He shrugs. Yeah, no one ever said that the end of the world would be easy. As a scientist, I do feel obliged to point out that things will gradually improve as more and more particles fall from the atmosphere. It just might take a while.

Too long for some, I say. I mean, I always thought something big would happen. I'm not sure why. Maybe I was just caught up in the drama of it, you know? But I thought it would be something else: Covid, Trump, Brexit or the Chinese financial crash.

I never thought it would be a giant rock. I thought they had all of those covered.

Joe shrugs. They did. But of course they didn't have a handle on things that came from beyond the solar system. How could they? Those rocks are like the stealth fighters of the asteroid world. We were just unlucky enough to get in its way. Where's Jupiter when you need it, eh? Plus it was a lot denser than they thought. Hence the amount of ejecta, and the spectacular blocking of the sun's light.

He smiles at me, and in his eyes I see the deep sadness that afflicts us all. There's only so much loss that the human animal can recover from.

In an instant, though, his face brightens. So, he says, are you going to cut that cake? I'm starting to salivate. I giggle. Oh, I'm sorry, I completely forgot.

And there's actually some truth to that statement. Talking with Joe is engrossing. It's a quick back-and-forth, free from the lacunae that plague my conversations with Rosa. It makes me realise how much I've missed talking with someone who's actually compos mentis.

We eat in silence. The cake tastes just as good as it looks, which is something of a miracle. I serve us both a second helping, and fetch the second round of coffee. When we've finished, more than half the cake is gone.

God damn, says Joe, sitting back, that was amazing. I didn't think I'd ever eat anything like that again in my life. Thank you. My pleasure, I say. It was nothing. He fixes me with his dark eyes, and I feel a slow shiver run up my back. You weren't a baker in a previous life, were you?

Oh please, I say, slapping him lightly on the shoulder, spare me the flattery. Why, he says, leaning forward, and still holding me with his eyes. Because I'm not used to it, I say, turning away and hoping I don't look as flustered as I am.

I decide not to mention the false starts, the wasted ingredients and the tears that went into making this one cake. It probably cost me the equivalent of a month's food. Just to impress this man who I don't know, I've basically risked starving myself over the winter. I've played Russian roulette with my food supplies.

If you think that was good, you should try my red velvet cake, I add. I don't know where this has come from, as I've only ever eaten red velvet cake once in my life, let alone actually made it. But I can see it in my mind's eye as if it's actually sitting in front of us: a quarter of it's missing, revealing its three red layers of sponge separated by white icing so thick it looks as if they've been applied with a hand trowel. There must be some reason for this vision but I can't quite fathom it, and I don't have time to work it out right now.

So, he says, still leaning forward, how come a pretty lady like you lives on her own? Sweet lord, I think, don't blush. I sit back a little, feigning indignation. I had a fiancé once, a long time ago, I say, but I got rid of him. Joe raises an eyebrow. Anyway, I add, sounding defensive, what about you? Why do you live like the local hermit?

Joe sits back and looks past me out of the window. Well, he says, I once had an Italian girlfriend. I'd met her the year before the impact. We were kind of long-distance, you know? She was about ten years younger than me. After the impact, she decided to head south with her brother and their parents. I guess she didn't think I was such a good bet in the long run. I'm sure she was right.

I'm sorry to hear that, I say. But I think she was wrong, if it helps. Joe shrugs. Well, I'm still alive. That's about as much as can be said. I shake my head. Hardly. But you know, it strikes me that someone like you - who's obviously intelligent and able-bodied - would be a great asset to this town. There aren't many people around here who fit that description.

No thank you, he says, that's not my cup of tea. As you may have already guessed, I'm something of a lone wolf.

That's a shame, I say, compressing my lips a little. Good men are hard to find, as the saying goes. How are you lined up for the winter? He shrugs. I've got a few staples, he says, but not enough to get me through. But I'm a hunter, so I'm used to food coming in fits and starts. I'll supplement my diet with a bit of fishing and foraging, and I should make it. I'll tell you what, I'm pretty lucky with where I live. Crayfish are the gift that keeps on giving. Invasive species my arse. I love the little critters. Miniature lobsters for dinner a few times a week. I can't complain.

I had some once, I add. They were amazing. That woman you buried, I had some of hers. She lived in the block across the square, the block in which my mother lives, in fact. One day, she just disappeared. We always wondered what happened to her. I guess we know now.

Joe sits takes one of my hands in his. I'm surprised, but also feel a sense of reassurance. I found her like that, he says, peering at me with his dark, searching eyes. You know that, don't you?

I feel like making some quip about his sounding guilty, but I don't. I nod in agreement like the girlfriend of a criminal who's doing time for something he swears he didn't do. Do you want any more cake, I ask, smiling brightly.

Well, he says, mirroring my smile and releasing my hand, we don't want it to go to waste, do we? I save two modest slices for me and Rosa to eat tomorrow, and we demolish the rest. In my previous life I'd never have thought about eating three slices of cake in one go. But now, when you're almost constantly in a calorific deficit, it barely touches the sides. I make more coffee, and soon we're both riding a sugar and caffeine high.

We become so giddy, in fact, that I decide to take Joe on a quick tour. I'd always thought of our block as functional rather than elegant, but now

I realise that it's more like something out of 1984 than anything else. The corridors are dark, have a hint of damp, and in many places the plaster has peeled itself from the walls. It's obvious that the place has been missing regular maintenance. While I'm good at driving a hard bargain, I'm no handyman.

And as much as I hate to admit it, it's also obvious that I'm trying to impress Joe. He makes a few polite noises as we move about, but there's no wow factor, no roof garden as in Rosa's block.

I take him into one of the empty flats. While it's neat and tidy, it's also unspectacular. We gravitate towards the windows and look out over the square. The view isn't much different from the one in my flat. This is old Elyra's place, I say. She was as nutty as a fruitcake, but great to have around. She did a lot of the cleaning and other bits and bobs. It looks like we miss her, I guess. She didn't last two years.

That's the only trouble with places like this, says Joe, still staring out across the square. You rub shoulders with ghosts.

I can't disagree. Around here the dead out-number the living by at least three to one. Across the square, I notice that Rosa's light is on. I see her pass in front of it, a living ghost. Still, there's certainly a lot more to be had from Rosa before she flees this mortal coil. The thought's quite depressing; a change of scene might prevent me becoming maudlin. Hey, I say, would you like to see the basement?

Sure, says Joe. As long as it's fully stocked with wine.

Don't get your hopes up, I say, ushering him out and then pushing past him. As our arms briefly touch, electricity fizzes up my arm. I twitch my backside a little as I stride ahead of him, but it's so dark he probably doesn't notice. Hey ho.

Actually, I say, there's no wine in the cellar. Most of that got drunk within the first couple of months. We've got something far more valuable.

I'm intrigued, he says, his voice right behind me. We descend into the belly of the building. I haul open the heavy door, push my way through the plastic, and we're in. The familiar humidity, earthy scent and blinding white light hit us all at once. My God, says Joe, it's like I've stumbled into a sci-fi novel.

Not bad, eh? I reply, grinning at him. This is the reaction I'm after. I'm now solely responsible for everything you see here. Feel free to call me green fingers. To be fair, the vegetables are even more impressive than when I showed them off to Cornelius. I think harvesting some of them has given fresh impetus to the plants. They've been coming on strong ever since.

I saunter along one of the rows, with Joe following mutely in my wake. You think it would be a burden, I say, all of this. But I've got it down to a fine art. It probably takes me no more than ten minutes a day now. The worst bit is getting the compost together, but the less said about that the better. I bend forward and fondle a couple of firm beefsteak tomatoes. I don't know how long it's been since I began to find fruit and vegetables erotic. I straighten up slowly, and turn as I'm doing so. I hope I'm making this as obvious as possible. I don't think we've got time for misunderstandings.

To his credit, Joe takes a half step towards me, and places his hands gently on my hips. I feel suddenly self-conscious, unnerved by how prominent my hip bones must be. Let's just hope he likes skinny bitches. As if in response, he pulls me against him, and lowers his head towards me. He's so tall and the light's so bright that his features are thrown into overwhelming detail. His face could be that of an ancient carving, or a totem, replete with a wry smile and the devil in its eye. And then we're kissing, and I close my eyes and try to enjoy the moment.

He tastes, predictably enough, of chocolate and coffee, which is just as well as I'm sure I do too. But there's a stronger scent to his body, lurking in the background. To my surprise, I find that it's not unpleasant: it's the scent of wild woods, of earth and sweat. It doesn't take me too long to realise that it's actually quite a turn-on. Our tongues soon come into play, probing into each other's mouths with the slow pull of ice cream scoops. To my surprise, I find that I'm getting aroused pretty quickly. Judging by the hardening in the front of his trousers, he is too.

We carry on necking like hormonal teen-agers for a couple of minutes before I pull away. Wow, I say, wiping a strand of hair back across my head, that got serious quick. He smiles that wry smile and tries to move in again, but I've got my forearms locked between us, which pulls him up. Maybe we could continue this another day, I say, tilting my head to one side coquettishly. After all, I hardly know you.

His smile widens, and I feel relief wash through me. If he wanted to rape me here and now, I wouldn't be able to stop him, and he'd get away with it Scott free. Of course there are no police left, and I think about the countless stor-ies I've heard, of how women have suffered. Of course, my lady, he says, still fixing me with his devil's eye. I shall continue to woo you at the soonest opportunity.

All right Shakespeare, I say, pushing play-fully at his chest, it's a deal. But I'd like more of that fancy talk. Everything you say, from now on, in iambic pentameter, if you please. He arches an eyebrow at me. I think you forget that I'm a sci-entist, he says. English, perhaps understandably, was never my strong point.

I shrug. There are other languages we can speak, I add. Now he raises both eyebrows. Other languages, he asks. I take it you're not referring to Italian.

V

The canonisation of Rosa continues apace. The next day, we take a group of kids to the church. As Santa Maria's is so close to the convent, the nuns let us take a dozen kids at a time, with no chaperone. We've shown that we're trustworthy, and the nuns simply adore Rosa.

We read at random. That's how the game works. We flick through the pages of the old book, trying to find pithy passages. Try saying that when you're drunk. Of course, Genesis is a favourite. As are the Epistles. But really, everything's on the table. Since it's all from the Bible, we know that we can't go far wrong. But choosing short extracts and reading them out of context gives the whole process an abstract, revelatory air. The words of God at random - a pastiche of holy declamations.

I'm nothing to shout about. I'm simply volume and theatrics, a poor television presenter trying to mask a lack of understanding and empathy with enthusiasm. Still, I give it enough oomph that the kids listen without complaint.

I sometimes wonder if the nuns sedate the kids - there's no way I could have sat that quietly at their age, but then I suppose constant hunger does sap one's energy. To me they listen politely, but when Rosa speaks, you can tell that they really hear. As she steps up to the lectern for the first time there are rustlings and murmurings, as if the kids aren't sure about what to expect. But as soon as she starts reading, they fall silent, bound beneath her spell. Whereas I enjoy the words, it's obvious that Rosa adores them, believes in them, and lives them. We've never talked about religion, but it's obvious that she has a faith that's as inspiring as it is mysterious. After her first reading, I get the kids to clap, and we alternate from then on. Seeing the kids listening agog to Rosa is strangely gratifying.

After about twenty minutes or so, we pause. Would anyone like to come up and read, I ask. Silence. Little faces look at us as if we've asked them to commit blasphemy. It's okay, I add. We're just reading from the Bible. You can read as much or as little as you like. But silence prevails. Stony ground indeed.

Luckily the older girl from our first excursion is in this group, sitting behind the others and just taking everything in. Cara, I say - and I can see she's surprised that I've remembered her name - come up and show the little ones how it's done. Her green eyes widen with surprise, but I smile massively and beckon with one hand. She has no choice. Slowly she levers herself upright, exactly as Rosa might, extricates herself from the pews and steps tentatively forward. How sad, I muse, that this may be the only time that she walks up an aisle. Then I catch myself, and am annoyed. What kind of received patriarchal rubbish is that? And anyway, where was my white wedding? Stuff like that didn't matter then, and matters even less now. Still, it strikes me that Cara has probably grown a couple of inches since the summer: she's less bulky now, her hair is less wedge-like, and she seems more like a young woman. If anything, though, it's her attire that surprises me. She's wearing a pink scarf in her hair and a pair of stonewashed denim dungarees. I can't believe the nuns would let her come out in anything so informal on a Sunday: she looks more like Madonna from the Eighties than Madonna from the Bible.

Cara looks at me with trepidation as she approaches the lectern, so I nod enthusiastically. When she's alongside me, I lean forward and whisper, it's okay, just turn the page and read a paragraph, or whatever you like. Just show the little ones how it's done. Cara flips through the pages of the giant book, and comes to a halt at random. As she starts to read, her voice is a little querulous at first, but it soon picks up impetus. Soon her words are resonating through the church.

And the angel came in unto her, and said, Hail, thou that art highly favoured, the Lord is with thee: blessed art thou among women. And when she saw him, she was troubled at his saying, and cast in her mind what manner of salutation this should be. And the angel said unto her, Fear not, Mary: for thou hast found favour with God. And, behold, thou shalt conceive in thy womb, and bring forth a son, and shalt call his name JESUS.

The last word brings her up short, and she looks at me, stunned, as if in the grip of some kind of revelation. It's a bravura performance by any standard. I nod my head and start clapping, and the other kids follow suit. But then Rosa bustles past me, arms outstretched, and hugs Cara warmly. The girl stiffens, but then I see her relax in Rosa's embrace: her eyes close and she's enjoying that physical contact, that moment of oxytocin release that we all crave. The nuns do a great job - don't get me wrong - but I'd guarantee that they're not tactile, mothering types.

Who else would like to read, I say. To my surprise, every child raises a hand. Bingo, I think. Once again, somehow, Rosa has worked her magic.

We work our way through the whole group, for better or for worse. It's obvious soon enough that the nuns - while not fans of backslaps and

Greco Roman wrestling - have done a great job in teaching these kids to read. There are a few stumbles here and there, but with such an old text in such an old font, it's not surprising. Some kids are more fluent than others, but every kid can read, and that's got to be an achievement in these trying times.

Last up is the little girl with wavy hair. Again I remember her from the day of our first excursion. If I'm not mistaken, she's wearing roughly the same clothes as she was then - a brown corduroy dress, this time augmented by an oversized black rainproof. At the lectern she stops and peers up at me with her large dark eyes. Like I thought, she's probably no more than four or five years old. Cara accompanies her like an older sister.

Sorry, I say, talking quietly, I don't remember your name. It's Abril, says Cara. It's a Spanish name – her mum was from there. Abril doesn't say much, but sometimes she tells me things.

What a lovely name, I say, looking down at the little girl, a very unusual but lovely name. As I straighten up, I try not to clutch my hand to my chest or make any other histrionic gestures. We forget, these days, I think, that grief - although commonplace - is still something that most of us have to deal with on a daily basis. Where's this little girl's mother now?

I smooth the dark outcrop of Abril's hair:

it's unruly and wiry like mine. She steps up to the lectern and starts leafing through the Bible. When she stops, she peers at the page, points her finger at a passage and then looks up at me expectantly. It takes me a few seconds to understand that she wants me to read for her. And I guess that's fair enough – she is very young.

And beside all this, I begin, between us and you there is a great gulf fixed: so that they which would pass from hence to you cannot; neither can they pass to us, that would come from thence.

I stop abruptly, pulled up short by the impact of the words. Abril looks up at me, gives me the briefest of smiles, and returns with Cara to her seat. Well done, I say, well done everyone. Rosa's so emotional that she can't even speak. She simply stares at the floor, clutching her hands together, and mutters bambini, bambini, bambini. It seems like an odd mantra, caught between pity for these kids and seeing them as hope for the future.

Still, as we start ushering the kids down the aisle and back to their cloistered lives, I can't help thinking about the "great gulf" in Abril's reading. These days, there's a great gulf between all of us. Eight years of days that barely break will do that to people.

T.S. Eliot was wrong. April isn't the cruellest month - November is. There's the dwindling of the light. And then the jollity promised by Christmas is still so far off. We keep up the readings with the kids, rotating groups, but like everything else, the magic soon wears off. In my memory, nothing compares to that first group we took - that sense of both trepidation and elation. We seem to be just going through the motions now, but I'm determined not to stop, not to lose momentum. It's so easy to lapse into apathy. And that's something I'm not prepared to do. How many people have died in the last few years because they just couldn't see the point in going on? It strikes me that the gulf between us all is only too real, brought on by years of isolation and grief.

One afternoon, standing on the high plinth above Rosa's block of flats, we see not one fire, but two. They burn in the rolling countryside between us and the mountains, and are too big to be fires that serve any purpose, unless someone is roasting whole teams of oxen. No, these fires are lit out of frustration or anger, their brown smoke seeping straight upwards into the sky. It could be the people of Monte Fiori, or the barbarian hordes coming down from the mountains. Hopefully these aren't the first signs of some aggressive, expansionist policy on the part of our neighbours. But times are hard and I wouldn't be surprised: if you don't have what you need for the coming months, one way to get it is to simply go and take it from someone else. Stories of towns attacking each other are rife, and it strikes me that there's a curious circularity to this narrative. In medieval times and right up through the Renaissance, Italian towns were often at war with each other, and even families within towns were sometimes at loggerheads. We're right back there in some senses: one rock the size of a mountain was all it took.

In the spirit of bridging gaps, I've invited Joe over again. Not having mobile phones that work is proving to be a pain in the backside, at least as far as dating is concerned: I was forced to hike down to his camp and leave another note. He arrives fashionably late, as is his wont. But as we engage in small talk and drink coffee, there's an undertow, a sense of expectation that I'm finding just so much unwanted pressure. It's threatening to sour my mood, as are the fires that Rosa and I witnessed earlier. I suggest to Joe that we take a walk around the town, get some fresh air. At first he looks mildly surprised, but agrees readily enough. Perhaps he was hoping to get his leg over in short order. Oh well.

As we leave the building, Filippa bustles out of her cubbyhole, doffs her greasy cap and opens the door for us. I couldn't have been more surprised if she'd slapped me in the face. I obviously do a bad job at hiding my surprise, because as we step out into the square, she gives me a knowing wink. What the hell, I think, now I've got Filippa on my case? Thanks sweetie, I say, giving her what I hope is a ravishing and sarcastic smile. I put my hand on the small of Joe's back to propel him out as quickly as possible.

We wander aimlessly for some time, mainly in silence, which - strangely - isn't actually uncomfortable. Joe takes everything in as we go, his dark, hawk-like eyes range from the tops of buildings to boarded-up windows. It's as if he's looking for vantage points and potential threats, and he probably is. Despite this, he does seem more at ease in the open air, slightly less like a caged animal. Or maybe just an animal that's pacing up and down in a bigger enclosure.

After a while, I start talking. It's more of a monologue than anything two-way, and I soon find that I can't stop. Joe turns out to be a surprisingly good listener: he remains impassive, but attentive. I lament the fact that everything's been compartmentalised. The whole world now seems to be little more than a succession of boxes: the individual in their flat, the blocks facing off against each other across the square, the square itself, and then towns, cities and villages pristine in their isolation. How did it come to this?

As if on cue we step into the main square. The convent stands over to our left, its single Cyclops eye sullen, the buddleia growing on its bell tower apparently dead. As we pause there, the dam really bursts. I tell him about the fires. About Monte Fiori. It's clear how worried I am. He gives me an arch, amused look. If you're worried, you need to get organised, he says.

Huh, I say, rolling my eyes, it's not like I've got a lot to work with. I don't think forming a local militia is really on the cards. What have we got? A couple of octogenarians and Filippa. And you saw the state of her. That's where all the kids live, I say, nodding towards the convent, determined to change the topic. Their parents, their families are all long gone. You should see how many there are - it's a tragedy. And there's nothing we can do apart from take them on day trips. Do you ever feel completely ineffectual?

As we move off, Joe shrugs. No, but only because I've recast my life in different terms, he says. As far as I'm concerned, my existence is completely superfluous - I'm not part of anything any more. I'm just me. People might say that's selfish, which is fine - that's their opinion. Does a lone individual lack meaning? Only if we define ourselves solely as social animals.

Grey, empty buildings rise around us like man-made cliffs. The empty windows look like the burrows of creatures that have long-since fled.

He gives me one of his wry, racy smiles, and I think that's what does it. I move towards him and put my arm through his. If he's surprised, he doesn't show it. He simply pulls me in and we fall into step. We lapse into an easy silence once again and wend our way back to my flat, looking no doubt like two lovers past their prime out for a Sunday promenade. I feel the sudden need for a corset and bonnet. Joe would look pretty good in a top hat, but I don't reckon we're ready for role-playing just yet.

Back in the flat, the warm glow inside me starts to fade. We're back to that sense of expect-ation, and I don't really know what to do with it. Look, I say, it's getting late - well, it isn't, but it is getting dark. Would you like to stay for din-ner? Really, asks Joe, raising an eyebrow. Yeah, really, I say, feeling suddenly flustered. I won't poison you either, at least not intentionally. Joe nods and that wry smile returns to his face. Well, he says, I think the risk-to-reward ratio is accept-able. That would be lovely. Is there anything I can do?

I turn away quickly, trying to hide my smile. Well, yes, I say. There is one thing. You can open this bottle of wine. I go hunting in one of the low cupboards and pull out a dusty bottle. I wipe one hand down the label and locate a corkscrew. It's a Barolo, I say, so about as local as it gets. I hand the bottle to Joe, and he scans the label as if it's the frontispiece of some religious text. As-tounding he whispers. I'd pretty much resigned myself to never seeing a bottle of wine again in my life, and certainly not anything this good. Let's hope it's not corked, he adds, giving me a wink.

I find two wine glasses and Joe starts working on the bottle. If I wanted to reduce tension, I've gone the wrong way about it. I can't believe, he says, levering the cork out of the bottle's neck, how much willpower it must have taken not to drink this. Well, I say, I thought I'd save it for a special occasion - and if this isn't one, I don't know what is. Joe pours the wine and as we stand facing each other, I wonder how this tall, shabby, attractive man came to be standing in my kitchen.

I'm not very good at making speeches, he says, holding my gaze, so I'll keep it short. I'm just so happy I met you. I twist coyly under the weight of this compliment, and hope I'm not blushing. Huh, I say, trying to hide my discomfort, you're only here for the booze. That, he says portentously, as if quoting from somewhere, depends entirely upon the quality of the vintage.

We clink glasses and sip. There's a touch of harshness, and I worry that the wine's corked. But I quickly realise that this is because I haven't drunk anything like this for so long. Seconds later a rich, textured warmth floods my mouth and gullet. Sweet Lord, breathes Joe, staring down at his glass. That's wonderful. I take another sip and have to agree with him. This wine is red nectar sent from the gods across the intervening years of greyness, reminding us of when summers were golden, and quaint notions like hope and love could actually flourish.

We both sit and drink slowly, savouring every drop. The wine is exceptional, breathtaking. I can't think of enough adjectives to describe it. But drinking it brings back so many memories of what we had, of what we've lost. We sit in silence for some time, both mired in bittersweet thought.

Eventually I break the reverie. Well, I say, shaking my head slightly, as if to dislodge loose memories, I did invite you round for dinner. And is certainly isn't going to cook itself. I stand, go to the cupboards and start hauling ancient staples out on to the sideboard. There's the ubiquitous plastic bottle of table salt, packets of dried instant yeast that are five years out of date, and a paper bag of malted, mealy flour that I practically had to sell a kidney for. I've got an old CD player next to the hob, and bang on some Glen Miller to keep the mood upbeat.

The vegetables - of course - are going to be the stars of the show, and just as I've pulled a bag of them from my defunct fridge, Joe sidles up behind me and runs a hand down my hip. Need a hand, he asks, trying to keep his voice sweet and innocent. I turn and arch my back to look up at him. Yes, I say, pursing my lips at him. You can go back over there like a good boy, enjoy your wine and amuse me with witty remarks.

He rolls his eyes and retreats. Jesus, he says, I just wanted to chop some vegetables. Being witty sounds much more taxing.

I pull a mixing bowl from a cupboard and start dumping flour into it. You've got a lot more legwork to put in, I say.

That's okay, he replies, I always was a leg man. I turn on him. Is that your idea of wit? If so, I might have to ask you to leave.

Okay, okay, he says, holding up two placatory hands. I just wanted to gauge what level we were working at. I snort and dump two sachets of yeast into the flour. A much higher one than that, I add.

Cooking pizzas from scratch is always a bit of a labour of love, especially without a bread maker or anything quite so useful or decadent as tinned tomatoes. What's perhaps most disturbing about this little scene is how we've slipped back into stereotyped gender roles - his opening the wine, my cooking and fending him off. Of course, it's me who has enforced them, and to be fair, he has offered to help. I do sometimes wonder what my mind's up to. Perhaps it's harking back to the past in search of the security of the nuclear family. But that model's been dead for a long time, so playing the role of housewife is curious to say the least. Still, I can hardly invite Joe for dinner and then make him cook it, can I?

Time ebbs and slows as the dough rises; silences blossom and are replaced by idle comments. We savour the wine and each other's proximity. It's strange, but we don't feel like the strangers that we are: there's a connection here, as if we share some deeper bond. I preheat the oven for about half-an-hour, obviously wasting gas, but I want pizzas that are crisp, not ones that resemble dead lettuce. The chuntering of the oven meshes perfectly with the music, setting off the high-pitched fusillades of the brass section with a loose undertow of white noise. When the finished pizzas finally appear, the smell of tomatoes, roasted vegetables and sizzling olive oil fills the kitchen. I stick them on boards, slice them and then deposit them on the table. Looking down at these two brightly coloured, aromatic circles of life, it's hard not to think that I've created something wonderful.

They taste just as good as they look: the searing crunch of the bases, the rich acidity of the tomatoes, and the sweetness of the peppers and caramelised onions all add their separate notes. Joe shakes his head and eats in studied silence. When he's demolished two slices, he looks up at me and holds me with dark, baleful eyes. For a second I think I've done something wrong, and am about to shove my chair backwards and retreat. That, he says, pointing down at the pizza, but not looking away from me, is the best thing I've eaten - ever. I'm... well, I don't know what to say. I'm amazed.

Again, I feel self-conscious. He may be amazed, but I'm just as surprised that anyone would say anything so complimentary to me. Once upon a time I'd have described myself as self-confident, but years of relative isolation have rendered me ill-equipped to deal with praise.

I pour the last of the wine to cover my confusion. There isn't much left, but we finish it in silence, both feeling replete, both enjoying a rare moment of relaxed satisfaction. As I'm on the verge of standing up to clear away, his hand closes over mine. The strength of it is unnerving, and as he squeezes, I feel fragile bones in my hand clicking against each other. Thank you, he says. That was wonderful. Now allow me. As he washes the dishes, he regales me stories of daylong hunts. Ten years ago I'd have found anything to do with hunting distasteful, but now I can actually appreciate the cunning of it, the practice of such a complex craft. Darker tales of avoiding bands of armed, roaming men follow. He laughs several times, apologising for boring me when he's doing nothing of the sort. It's sweet: despite his apologies he carries on, his words buoyed up on a tide of enthusiasm. To my surprise, I soon find myself admiring him for the dangers and hardships that he's passed.

Joe's competence could be the difference between life and death around here, especially if things start to get a bit tasty this winter. I don't think my interest in him is Machiavellian, but the thought gives me pause. I rise slowly, feeling - if not confusion exactly - a certain muddying of my motives. Am I really an automaton, always trying to gain advantage, even subconsciously? Or should I just cut myself some slack: years of playing the game of survival are bound to make anyone calculating. Why don't we retire to the lounge, I ask, trying to play the gracious hostess. I smile weakly.

I'm in the process of standing when he catches my wrist and turns me towards him. I stare up at him defiantly, mouth closed. Thank you, he says, and leans in. I let him kiss me, not responding at first, but there's only so much provocation I can take. I soon relent, opening my mouth to his probing tongue. He pushes me gently up against the doorframe and his hands explore my midriff. After years of virtual starvation, at least I'm not conscious of my weight. I would say my belly's flat, but really it's hollow. His hands drop slowly, exploring the fronts of my thighs. This time, I don't push him away. Instead I push my pelvis against his, wind my hand round the back of his head and pull him even closer.

I should go through some coquettish pre-amble, but we're not living in some period drama and - to be frank - I can't be bothered. Besides, these days you're never sure that you're going to get the chance to do certain things ever again, such as having sex.

I do consider getting him to take me where we stand, but the height difference and clothing might prove something of a hindrance. Instead, I grab him firmly by the front of his shirt and drag him into my bedroom. He needs no second bidding. As soon as we're over the threshold we start tearing off each other's clothes, kissing when we can. And as soon as we're naked, he lifts me, throws me back on to the bed and stalks over me. We kiss frantically, both hungry for each other. He enters me straight away. Not that I have any complaints - I'm wet already. Soon we fall into synch, quickly getting used to the mechanics of each other's bodies. As his rhythm builds, I end up staring at the ceiling in a state of distraction, my mind contemplating the cracks in the dull ivory paint. To my surprise, I find a wave of pleasure rising rapidly within me: it builds, and builds, and builds and comes crashing down. I arch up beneath him and then find myself thrashing like a surfer caught in a wave's swash. Drops of his sweat hit me in the face, but I don't care. Open-mouthed I gasp as he kisses and bites the soft skin of my neck. It's clear that my orgasm has brought him to the edge, and he ploughs on, his body bucking against mine until he's coming inside me.

We both collapse into separate, sweating heaps, breathing hard. We don't say anything. We can't. For some reason, all I can think of are the words 'Sweet Jesus.' I say them again and again in my mind, each time adding more and more emphasis to each of the words. Eventually I reach out. To his credit he squeezes my hand gently. I cast a sidelong glance towards him and he turns, giving me a wry smile and a wink. It should be cheesy, but somehow it seems endearing. I smile and settle back into the pillows. Sweet Jesus.

When we've recovered, I tease him a little. So, I say, is that why you came round? A quick shag? Wham, bam, thank you Mam? He props himself up on one elbow and shrugs. Well, he says, it had crossed my mind. But I've got no complaints. I shove his shoulder. I should hope not, you cheeky bugger, I add, rolling my eyes. I reckon you had this planned all along.

A voice inside me is saying, take it easy. I often end up pushing people away, and I don't want to do the same thing here. As far as I recall, drawls Joe, you invited me round.

Yes, I say, but I didn't expect this. I'd say you took advantage of me. Easy, August, I say to myself. Easy. Don't go making any accusations, even in jest. Joe shrugs again. I'd say I took advantage of the situation, wouldn't you? Yes, I say, moving in and kissing him. That sounds about right.

Within half-an-hour, we're back at it, but this time we're less rushed. We've got time. I actually even ride him cowgirl-style for a few minutes. I look around for my bra so that I can twirl it around my head, but it's nowhere to be seen. We finish off with a bit of missionary. We start slowly, but can't help ourselves, and are soon rutting like deer. To my surprise, I come again. When our slick bodies finally separate, I'm awash with the afterglow of pleasure. But that little voice just has to chip in, taking the gloss off the moment. Don't mess things up, August, it says. Don't mess things up.

Night falls, and we stay together. The temperature's dropping each day, so before we finally turn in I throw several blankets over the duvet. I sleep well, but wake periodically, my dreams alive with outlandish, carnivalesque figures that prance and lurch through the shadows of a benighted netherworld. It's dramatic, entertaining and somewhat disturbing, but by the time I wake up in the morning, I feel like a whole new person. Joe's still there on the left side of the bed, sleeping soundlessly. Strange, but in the space of twelve hours my life seems to have changed beyond recognition.

We while away the morning together, lazing and

lounging through the long grey hours. We spend most of the time chatting, and thankfully the words come to us just as easily. We don't have sex again, and somehow that's a good thing. It'd be a shame to do anything that would detract from the night before. And, to be fair, I am a little sore. Hey, he says at some point, looking uneasy, I should have asked you this last night, but I must say I got carried away. It's just that, well, he says, clearing his throat, I assume you're doing something for contraception, right?

I widen my eyes and clutch the duvet up to my chest. Oh my God, I say, didn't you use something? Very funny he says. Condoms don't grow on trees, you know. I know that he's not buying it, so I give him a gentle shove in the chest. Relax, I say. I haven't had a period in years. Too skinny. So unless you've got syphilis, we're in the clear.

After a lunch of a couple of odds and ends, Joe heads back out to the river. We kiss on the threshold, but it starts to get a little heated, so I push him away. Go on, I say, get back to your cave. When we next meet, I shall bring you a sack full of crayfish, my lady, he says, bowing gallantly, enough for a veritable feast! My stomach twists at the thought of food. Especially crayfish. Do you really think that will sweeten the deal, I ask. And what makes you think there will be a return visit? To be honest, he continues, I just assumed. His tone is light, but I can see that there are the tiniest pangs of hurt in his eyes. Excellent. Well, I say, draping myself against the doorway, maybe if you play your cards right. Maybe. But we need much more of the 'my lady' chat.

As soon as he's gone, I prevent myself from swooning against the back of the door. Instead, I start cleaning, which is a little backward, as most people clean before guests arrive, not after they've bolted. Still, with my hands occupied, my mind's free to roam over everything that's transpired. Part of me wishes that I'd been a little nicer to Joe when he left, but I know this is me doubting myself for no good reason. A touch of meanness adds to the frisson, and he certainly didn't seem put out. Of course, my mind grinds over every little detail of the past twelve hours, obsessing, chastising, speculating and generally being quite annoying. I do perhaps regret not setting up another meeting, but I don't want to appear to be some simpering fool who's been made complete by having a man in her life.

That afternoon, though, I find myself at a loss. We haven't arranged to take any of the kids to the church, as it's a Sunday. What should we do now? Before I know it, I'm in the throes of a panic attack, clutching the back of a chair and gasping like a fish drowning in air. I shake my head, grip the chair until my knuckles turn white, but nothing seems to work. Eventually, after what feels like years - but what is probably only twenty minutes or so - I start to calm down. I sit on the chair, pushing my knees together and laying my hands demurely on my lap. I imagine that this is the posture a young girl would adopt when being interviewed for a place at a boarding school. For the best part of half-an-hour I stare across the square at Rosa's window. I know she's in there, but I can't see her. It's still just about light outside, so she hasn't yet turned on her lights, which might have helped me locate her. I think about going over for a chat, but decide against it. I don't know if she'd understand what's just happened between me and Joe, but maybe I'm not giving her enough credit.

Instead, I reach for the landline for the first time in ages. Taking a deep breath, I dial my parents' number from memory. I used to call them every weekend, even as an adult. I put the handset up to my head and listen to the empty expanse of the dead line. I hold on to the phone as if it's the last thing in the world that might give my life meaning. Despite what I tell myself, I'd do anything to talk to them. Anything. Even hearing one of their voices on the answerphone would really be something. But of course, there's no chance of that. After ten minutes of listening to nothing, I put the phone down. Then I start weeping. Catastrophically. Uncontrollably. And part of me is amazed at how I can lurch from a state of joy to absolute devastation in the space of a day. I don't know if I can take much more of this. I honestly don't.

Eventually, there's nothing for it but to crawl back into bed. I get to sleep quickly, and am soon walking through dark, glistening streets. I seem to be alone, but after a while I realise that there's something else there too. Something lurking in the shadows. And I don't think it's human. Eventually I've had enough of running and I stop to confront it. It shifts in the darkness of an alleyway. As it moves forward slowly, I realise that it's big - about the size of a small car. Its body makes a squeaking, chitinous sound as it moves, and it's preceded by the smell of rotting fish. I gag and step backwards. A thick red claw emerges, its bulbous, curved edges catching the white light from a streetlamp. Then a lobster-like head breaks through the darkness, all mouthparts, antennae and black, staring eyes. I scream. I sit bolt upright, heart hammering, forehead slick with sweat. I don't get back to sleep.

Monday morning, at first light, I wander through the streets in an effort to clear my head. It's well below zero, with a scorching, flapping wind coming down from the mountains. As such, I'm huddled down into as many layers as I've been able to strap round my emaciated frame. I've also found a new accent piece - a grey bobble hat which matches my long woollen coat. Needless to say,

I've abandoned the movie starlet look of the summer and have gone for something that I like to call 'Winter Frump.' All I need now are some grey, shapeless leggings that sag at the arse and knees, and my look will be complete. As I move towards the outskirts of town, I seriously consider visiting the defunct retail park to see if I can find some.

Sadly, this doesn't come to pass. As I emerge from the abandoned villas above the ravine, I see a huge cloud of brown smoke rising up into the air. At first, it's so near that I think it must be coming from Joe's camp, but then I realise that it's coming from somewhere just beyond - from a property no doubt slumped in a crook of the land. Not being able to see the source of the fires is vexing, but they must be houses or farms nestled in the landscape.

In the past, the fires have seemed distant, but this one can't be ignored - it's right on our doorstep. I think about carrying on, about dropping down the rocky path to tell Joe, but decide against it. I've never been one to simply get a man to solve my problems, and I'm not about to start now. Instead, I turn and hurry back into town. Once there, I call a block meeting in my room, which involves me going round and knocking on the doors of the surviving residents and getting them to come to mine, using free coffee as a sweetener.

It's not a rapid process. But in just over an hour we have the great and the good of the block assembled in my lounge. They may be good, but they're certainly not great, and there aren't many of them. The most promising of them is Nicholas, or Saint Nick, as we refer to him. He's about my age, a tall pale man whose most distinguishing features are his wave of black, greasy hair and pronounced Adam's apple. The only problem with Nick is that he's painfully shy. It's hard to get a word out of him at the best of times, and these are not the best of times. You get the impression that the Covid-19 lockdowns of long ago and the creeping isolation post-impact have suited him down to the ground. He sits slumped in one of my chairs in dirty jeans and a thin windproof, his eyes at once sullen and restless, which is quite an achievement. At least he's able bodied.

Then there's Maria Gonzalo, and older but spry woman with a penchant for floral skirts and berets. Can I do anything, my dear, she asks. And sadly, this is her default setting. She's like a parrot, constantly asking this question, but then not actually doing anything. We've all just learned to say, no, grazie, and continue on with what we were doing. But, if she had a super power, it would have to be benevolence.

Then there's Mr Moretti. With his gardening and handyman skills, he's been a great asset to the block. But that cough he developed towards the end of the summer has refused to go away. He sits, wrapped in a lumberjack shirt, coughing into one hand, rarely making eye contact. He's shrunk somewhat over the last few months, and his slicked back black hair is thinning noticeably.

Then there's Lucretia, a small and still-plump housewife of middle age, whose orangey bob seems about fifty years out of place. She sits with arms and legs folded, feet barely reaching the floor. She's gnome-like and hostile. Her husband died years before, and this seems to have taken her raison d'etre away. She used to be distant and superior, but now she's just distant and terse, rarely deigning to speak to anyone. If you wanted a definition of resting bitch face, she'd be it.

Then, of course, there's Filippa. She took some persuading to leave her cubbyhole down by the front door to come up here, even for a short meeting. She's still wearing her uniform, its dark blue trousers and jacket displaying a satin-like sheen from so much use. Bless her, a sense of duty seems to be all she's got to cling to. She stares at the floor, sullen and preoccupied. With what, I have no idea.

That's it. The only survivors from what used to be dozens and dozens of residents. The other thing that strikes me is the lack of children, or even young adults. The young and the strong have fled or succumbed to starvation, leaving us: the weak, the inept and the lost. I wonder which category I fit into. All of the above, knowing my luck. So here we are: the last half-dozen, like an old pack of eggs that has been shoved to the back of the shelf and forgotten. How the hell am I going to do anything with this lot? I can make fishers of kids, but I doubt I can make militiamen out of my fellow residents. We may just as well lie down in the streets and die. Our bodies will probably provide better obstacles than anything we could fashion.

Silence slowly settles, and they all end up looking at me. Even Mr Moretti stops coughing and looks me in the eye. We used to have a laugh, him and me, working in our little slice of paradise in the basement. Sadly the fight seems to have gone out of him, and I doubt that he'll be much of an ally. This all seems so pointless that I almost start talking about the guttering, just to save these good but defeated people from worry. Still, I've always thought that you've got to face things head-on. And having a purpose, even a pointless one, is often better than having none at all.

Okay, I say, resting my hands on the back of a chair. Recently, fires have been spotted in the countryside between us and Monte Fiori. Mr Moretti purses his lips, and for a moment I think that he's going to spit on the floor, either to clear

some phlegm or at the thought of our neigh-
bouring town. There have been several fires, I
continue, trying to hide my disgust, and each
has come closer. The last one was on the other
side of the ravine. Of course, I say, pressing onwards, I have no proof, but I assume that a group
from Monte Fiori are heading south, adopting a
scorched earth policy as they go. Maybe they've
run out of supplies, maybe they're looting and
pillaging, or maybe they're engaged in some final
death march. I don't know. It could be none of
the above. But somebody's out there, and they're
burning stuff.

I pause like any good orator to let this sink
in. So, says Mr Moretti, coughing hard into his
hand and looking back up with watering, rheumy
eyes, what do you suggest we do about it? I
suggest, I say, pausing again, that we get organised. We need to arm ourselves, to set a watch,
to build barricades. If we don't take action now,
we might find ourselves waking to the smell of
smoke before too long. Besides, I say, trying to
end on a more positive note, preparedness makes
us powerful.

Mr Moretti glances up at me, takes out a
handkerchief, and spits. Facisti, he says. I don't
know if he's referring to my words or the citizens
of Monte Fiori, and I suppose we'll never know.
Augusta, he says, adding an 'a' to the end of my
name and making me sound like a Caesar. You've

always had good judgement, and have provided well for us. You may be right, he says, shrugging, or you may be wrong, but a little caution goes a long way. However, you cannot do much, he adds, wafting a limp hand at the assembled group, with the likes of us alone. You need more people to have any security: the smallest area you need to secure is the square. If you can do that, there may be some hope of peace. If not, and we're attacked... here he makes a pfff noise, no doubt signalling a block of flats going up in flames.

I nod. Mr Moretti has never given me bad advice before, and I'm sure he's not going to start now, even if he is at death's door. Okay, I say. You're right. If everyone is in agreement, I'll go and talk to Rosa across the square. She knows everyone hereabouts. A few people nod. Mr Moretti clears his throat again, then looks at me and asks, how about that coffee?

We meet under a louring sky in the centre of the square. Rosa has done a great job. Tens of hunched, shivering ghosts have gathered around me. It's way more than I had hoped. Still, I need to be quick - a heaviness in the air threatens snow.

A week ago, I say, I saw a fire out in the countryside between here and the mountains. Two days ago, there were two. This very morning, there was a fire not five kilometres from here, beyond the ravine. My fellow residents, my friends.

Someone is coming. It may be raiders from the mountains, or devils from Monte Fiori. I don't know. But I do know that we need to be ready to defend ourselves. If we are not ready, all may be lost. This winter could be our last. Bene, bene, someone mutters, and I don't know if they're commenting on my plan or the idea of an imminent death.

The only way in and out of our square is by the three corners, I say, pointing to each darkening gulf with outstretched arms, twisting like the mechanism of some doomsday clock. The fourth corner is simply a join between two buildings, so we're lucky. Tonight we will block each corner with a sturdy barricade, post an armed guard at each, and high above us, I add, indicating the platform on the top of Rosa's block, we shall post a sentinel with a bell. Forewarned is forearmed, my friends, I add with a smile. After tonight's efforts, we shall all sleep better in the knowledge that we are safe. Are there any questions?

There are none. Some people shift from foot to foot, restless. Others simply stand there as if they're already dead. Okay, I say, let's do one barricade at a time - rapid progress will keep us motivated! We'll do the northwest entrance first, I say, indicating the corner that leads most directly to the ravine. Build a base of sandbags, I add, a metre high if we can. And then bring up any old furniture from basements and pile it on top. Let's go!

To my surprise, people surge into motion. Luckily, there are a lot of sandbags positioned around the doors of the blocks. They were put there to prevent flooding. Slowly, working in pairs or threes, people start taking the uppermost of these bags and carrying them over to the entrance. They're not easy to shift, having become concrete-like over the years, but they are to hand, which makes all the difference. After a couple of hours and a lot of sweating and swearing, we've got the base of a wall almost a metre high.

In the closed corner of the square is a low mound of sand that was dumped there years ago, for the express purpose of filling sandbags. Hilda - an enterprising soul if there ever was one - disappears into her block and comes back clutching a handful of hessian sacks. Several of the older folk help her fill them, scrabbling around the sand pile like geriatric children in some absurdist play.

Supply lines form as if by magic, and soon the building of the second barricade has begun. Meanwhile, the first is finished off with a layer of old wardrobes, cabinets and tables - the detritus from the flats of the dead. The barricade soon reaches the height of a tall man. Excellent, I say, throwing my hands in the air. A couple of ghosts hang about me, smiling. And this, I say, pulling at one leaf of a large folding mirror that forms a door on the top, is genius! Bravo! Let's get some lights on it, and we're done.

I go off in search of Filippa. It doesn't take me long to find her. She's carrying a sandbag towards the second barricade with the mute indifference of an ox. Let me help you, I say, grabbing one side of the bag so that we're carrying it between us. In reality, this doesn't help much. She's still carrying most of the weight, and we're now lopsided. Still, the gesture is there. After we've deposited the bag on the growing wall, I put an arm around her shoulders and walk her back to the first barricade. For the first watch, I say, we need someone steady and reliable - someone who's professional - someone who can show the others how it's done - someone who can set an example. Filippa, I can't think of anyone better for that job than you. Will you do it? She doesn't protest, just nods mutely. Exactly as I'd hoped.

It looks like someone has taken me a little too literally. In my short absence, the first barricade has been adorned with a string of ice blue Christmas lights. They're obviously meant to be used outdoors, as each bulb glows brightly, forming small halos of white in the chill air. An old storm lantern and a plastic camping lamp finish things off. Okay, I say, exhaling and patting Filippa's shoulder, you'll be stationed here. This is the most important barricade. I have faith in you. We all do.

One of the ghosts transforms into the hunched form of Mr Moretti. He peers up at me with his rheumy eyes, and I wonder if I've been laying it on a bit thick with Filippa. Bene, he says, bene. I'll get her a gun. And with that he shuffles back to the block, leaving my mind to boggle at the arsenal that he may well possess. Filippa simply stares at the barricade, as if familiarising herself with her new surroundings through the act of rumination. I pat her shoulder again. I'll get you your chair. If there's anything else you want, just let me know. She turns her head and gives me a weak smile. No, grazie, she says.

As the work continues, Rosa and I draw up a provisional rota. It's pretty sketchy, as finding individuals who are both able-bodied and compos mentis is tricky. Still, we write it up and tack it to the door of her block. Then we start making our way upwards to the roof. To my surprise, Rosa seems particularly spry and energised: I suppose having a common goal will do that to a person. I hold her hand and guide her along the wooden walkway on the roof, although she doesn't seem to need any help and eventually pushes my hand away. Good. This is good.

Before we know it, we're standing on the high platform. The wind scours us, sucking away both the oxygen and the heat from our bodies. Mama, I cry, we're going to need to put some kind of shelter up here. A sentry wouldn't last five minutes. Rosa nods enthusiastically. Maybe we should give them a fire and some hot chocolate too, I add. And a hot water bottle, she chimes in, smiling at me. It's good to see her so lively, so animated. Below us, work in the square continues apace. The second barricade is almost finished and the third has been started. Never in my wildest dreams did I think that we'd get all of them done so quickly. It just shows what people can do when they come together. Random oil lamps, gas-powered camping lights and propped-up torches glow across the square, making it look like an enchanted, benighted land. It's the most beautiful thing I've seen for a long time.

I look up to see if I can see the whites of the mountains in the encroaching darkness. I can't, but what I do see drops my body temperature by a couple more degrees. Beyond the ravine, the large fire burns brighter than ever. Its yellow flames are clearly visible, licking upwards into billows of brown smoke. It looks as if the eternal bonfire has moved one step closer.

I clutch Rosa's arm in a grip that's probably too tight. Mama, I say, with a sigh of resignation, look! Bene, she says, nodding slowly. It looks like we were just in time. Well done, August. Well done. But my grip only tightens on her arm. I feel her jerk away from me in protest, but I hold on. I feel suddenly sick, nauseated by a sense of dread that starts rising through me like a dark, filthy tide. Mama, I say, turning her to face me, and staring into her eyes. I don't expect you to understand this, but I've got to tell you, otherwise I'll go crazy. Mama, I've taken a lover. He's a wild man - he lives in the woods, over there in the ravine. Just beneath where that fire is. I've got to go to him. He's not safe.

August, she says, shaking her head a little, as if she's upset with me - a mother disappointed in her teenage daughter. This is all very sudden. Very sudden. What are you talking about? A wild man? When did you meet him? And why haven't I met him? I'd like to see what kind of a man he is. And I hope you wait until you are married to...

Yes, yes, I say. All in good time. But now I must go to him. From where he lives, he probably has no idea that there's a fire nearby. Rosa shakes her head again. Go, if you must. Love must come first. But make sure you return to us, bambina. As you can see, we need you here. I need you here. She grips my arms, and peers at me. She may be welling up, but really it's too dark to tell. Come on, Mama. Let's go down. I won't be long.

Rosa follows me reluctantly. I leave her stranded in the square, an immobile ghost amongst the restless dead. Within minutes I've returned with my bag, knife and a torch. I give her a quick wave and head over to the first barricade. Filippa's there, an old rifle slung over her shoulder, the satin sheen of her suit glistening under the Christmas lights. She peers out into the dark streets though the doorway created by the great folding mirror. She might not be the brightest, but no one could ever accuse her of not doing her duty.

As I begin to climb the barricade, I feel a hand on my leg. I turn and glare down at Mr Moretti, who doesn't release his grip on my calf. Where are you going, he asks, scowling. I shift my leg a little and he lets go. There's someone who lives outside the town who I've got to warn, I say, or he might not last the night.

Mr Moretti glares at me, and I glare back. Within a second or two he's worked out that I'm serious, and that no amount of persuasion is going to hold me back. Bene, he says, and reaches into a pocket. Here, he says, take this. He passes me a gun - an old service revolver, by the looks of it, that could have come from the First World War. It's loaded, he adds, so be careful - there's no safety catch. The gun's heavy, but reassuring. I nod at Mr Moretti and clamber over the barricade. Then I'm gone, flitting through the streets like something that doesn't quite belong there, like something on the edge of things.

Strangely, I'm not scared. The murky shadows are comforting, as if I'm moving through a familiar element, my element. The wind sighs and bustles about me like the people who used to walk here. Before long I've reached the outskirts of town and am gliding along the road between the villas, dancing between patches of deeper darkness. There's a full moon, but it isn't the white luminous disk that we remember. It's a pale smear that barely penetrates the underside of the ash clouds that encircle the globe. Still, it's better than nothing, providing me with just enough light to stop me from breaking my neck. When I stop at the top of the path, the huge fire seems no more than a stone's throw away. The great yellow flames and roiling clouds spill upwards as if drawn up the flue of some invisible chimney. What in God's name can they be burning - a fuel depot? I pull out my torch, turn it on and dance down the switchbacks like a mountain runner, impressed by my own agility. This is all very well, of course, but if I give away Joe's location with the torch, then it doesn't matter how quickly I get down. Still, somehow it seems that speed is of the essence.

The river is more of a torrent now. The stepping-stones have long-since been submerged by the raging waters. As I step in, I have to resist the temptation to gasp or cry out. It's ridiculously cold, as if I'm entering a river of dry ice. Steeling myself, I press forwards. The water's quickly up to my thighs, and I can feel my body heat being washed downstream. My teeth start to chatter, and before I'm halfway across, I can no longer feel my legs. Then - as luck would have it - my foot slides off a slick, rounded rock and I cry out. I plunge an arm forwards, and just manage to re-gain my balance before I go in. Needles of water reach up my sleeve, cutting at my thin skin. How loudly did I cry out? It sounded to me like a shriek, but did I really have enough air in my lungs for that? Part of me wonders what it would be like to kick my heels up and let the current take me. The mountain waters would numb me, and I'd slip off into an eternal, dreamless sleep. So many people have taken their own lives since the impact. When you're caught in the middle of an extinction event, it's easy to lose hope. Still, I bet not many floated themselves down river, dying Ophelia-like amongst the water and weeds. I wonder whether I'd look as elegant as that Vic-torian painting of her. Probably not. I'd probably end up half-naked and nibbled by fish. Still, fish or no, the thought's so alluring that I almost do it. It would be much easier this way.

Then I remember Joe. His life may well be in my hands. Which makes me wonder why I'm out here, risking life and limb for someone I barely know. It's because you're a good person, August, a little voice inside me says. Which makes me laugh. Once you've killed someone, can you ever classify yourself as a good person? I doubt it. Then I stub my toe on a rock. Despite the cold, pain resonates through me, a bronze gong. I re-mind myself that to live is to suffer, despite the manifold pleasures we may enjoy along the way. So I keep moving, pushing one leg after the other through he dark, pounding water, until I emerge on the other side, bedraggled and rat-like.

I bushwhack my way between the gnarled trunks of the trees, the shattered rocks, and the drifts of dry leaves. As I emerge into the clearing, I call out Joe's name in a stage whisper. My voice sounds fragile. It's the voice of a woman on the edge of hysteria, or hypothermia, or both. I call out again. Nothing.

The image of Joe striding out of his cave with his rifle and shooting me as an intruder turns up unbidden. I love my mind. I really do. I wonder if this method of dying would garner me more points for the Darwin Awards than simply letting myself float off downstream. I decide that it would. Getting shot by someone you're trying to save at least has some irony to it.

The fireplace contains ashes. I squat down and rub some between my fingers. There's no heat here. None whatsoever. And now a new fear takes me. What if he's left? What does that make me? A pathetic, scrawny bitch trying desperately to save someone I once slept with. Loneliness I can deal with, but I do object to looking like a mug.

There's nothing else for it. At the risk of getting shot, I turn on my torch. Joe, I whisper, my voice an aggressive hiss. Approaching the mouth of the cave, I hear some movement inside. Joe!

Then I hear the unfamiliar but very recognisable sound of a rifle's bolt being drawn back. Who is it? The voice is Joe's - thank the Lord - but there's an unsteady quality to it. It's me, I hiss. I've come to get you. Is it okay if I come in?

I don't wait for a reply but move forward, the beam of my torch playing along the ground. Joe's sitting up on the edge of his bed with a rifle trained on me. This isn't the happy-go-lucky survivalist I remember, but then again I have turned up unannounced in the middle of the night. Still, it's interesting to note that your paranoid fantasies can be close to the mark: I wonder how close I was to getting shot?

Even in the half-dark, Joe's eyes seem sullen and track me as if I'm a wild animal. I sit down next to him, cramped and uncomfortably close. That's when the smell of alcohol hits me. As if realising I've noticed, Joe shunts himself away from me, makes the gun safe and lays it on the bed. It doesn't take me long to spot the empty bottle of whisky on the ground. Having a little party out here, I ask, trying to sound upbeat.

He doesn't respond, just stares at me. I try to hold his gaze, but can't, and am forced to look away. I suddenly feel uncomfortable, unwanted. August, he says, look at me. Before I can react he reaches a hand out and grabs me by the chin. He turns my face to look at him. He's not exactly hurting me, but I decide to see where this is going before I swat his arm away. Look at me, he says. Before the other day... before I met you, I was fine. All on my own. Self-sufficient. Not exactly happy, but... and now? Now you're here, in my head. I think about you all the time. All the time.

I push Joe's hand away and adopt a business-like tone. That's very flattering, I say. And I'm glad I made such a strong impression, but right now we have bigger fish to fry. There's one of those fires - you know, where people have been burning buildings? It's just above us, more or less. You're not safe here. We've got to go. You can come back to mine.

No, he says, shaking his head. I'm no good in a town. I've got to be out here. On my own. It's for the best. I stare at him, and realise that I'm starting to shiver. I let my senses play out into the night, and hear distant shouts and their dull echoes in the ravine. I grab Joe's arm and squeeze it as hard as I can.

I'm not leaving you here, I say. This isn't the time to be making lifestyle decisions. This is about survival. Can you hear them, the devils from Monte Fiori? As if on cue, a loud shout cuts through the night. You're not safe. Later on, you can do as you please, but I'm not leaving you out here.

Maybe it's the pressure of my fingernails on his arm. Maybe it's the fact that I don't look away. But Joe sits up straighter, his eyes suddenly a little more animated, a little less inward-looking. Perhaps he realises that his feelings aren't going to go unrequited, that the simple fact of my being here says something.

Okay, he says, as if a switch has been flicked in his head. Just let me grab some stuff. Then he's on his feet packing a rucksack. He moves about methodically: all traces of the self-involved drunkard have disappeared. In less than two minutes he's towering above me, the rucksack on his back, the rifle over his shoulder. Ready, he says. And I don't know if it's a question or a statement, but it doesn't really matter. We creep out of the cave and away through the trees. As we stand in front of the river, he takes my hand. Thanks for coming to get me, he says. And then we're wading out into the icy water, hand in hand. And this time it doesn't feel nearly as cold. This could be because I'm already soaking, but it's probably because - as they say - hope springs eternal. Suddenly it seems as if there are possibilities: before I met Joe there was only a slow drifting towards death.

And I don't feel as if I'm the weakest link here either. If I've survived this far, I've got to have something about me. So we cross the river as equals, each helping the other, and as we do so a sense of joy - ridiculous in its intensity - wells up within me. When we get to the other side we stop and turn. The fire rages up into the night sky, its billowing yellow flames brighter than ever. We look at each other, smile, and wend our way up the rocky path. We soon gain the road, and as we walk into town, the everlasting bonfire recedes. For once I feel like I'm going the right way.

VI

The devils of Monte Fiori. It sounds like a something you'd see on a fresco in a medieval church, the deep reds and ochres chipped away by time. I know we vilify the other, quickly casting them as folk devils to ensure our own solidarity. I get it. Politicians did it all the time to galvanise a population and ensure they stayed in power. It's one of the oldest tricks in the book. The question is, have I done it for my own ends, unconsciously or otherwise?

The question bugs me until I wake up to a pillar of brown smoke rising from the edge of town. The edge of our town. People stand in the square and gawp up at it; some of us head to the top of Rosa's block and peer at it from the rotting roof gardens there. We chat as ghosts will, and all come to the conclusion that one of the villas on the road above the ravine has been torched. The problem is, no one has the willingness or the balls to go and check. Apart from me.

I leave Joe in my bed. He's sleeping off the whisky from the night before and it's just as well.

I don't think he'd be too keen on me sticking my neck out like this. Still, I can't help it. An almost morbid sense of curiosity drives me on, sending me plunging through the town in a route that's as circuitous as it is confusing. I flit from one side of the streets to the other, ducking behind abandoned cars, piles of sand, whatever's to hand. My inner Tomboy's really coming out these days. I think it's from finding that you're way more physically capable than you ever thought you were. Part of me wishes that I'd traded in at least some of the wine drinking in my previous life for marathon running. Being a skinny bitch would have held some real-world advantages, other than just feeling lithe. But the truth is, I'd much rather be moving than simply stuck in the square or my flat. As long as I keep moving, anxiety seems to be transformed into excitement. Plus I don't actually feel that scared. I've got my knife in the bag slung around my shoulder, and Mr Moretti's revolver clasped in one sweaty hand. What more could a girl want?

Figuring that our visitors will expect any resistance to come from a central location, I hike up the Strada d'Oro, which brings back memories of happier times. In fact, even a few months ago, at the end of August, things seemed simpler. As I flit past Marco's gelateria and the toy shop, a heavy sense of nostalgia descends on me. Then there's the mask shop and - sure enough - the splintered marks where I forced the door open with my crowbar. Ah, happy days.

Then I'm into it, snaking down from the heights of the old town through alleyways and narrow streets until I'm on the road above the ravine. I crouch down in one of the front gardens behind a cluster of pots, barely shielded by dead stems, and peer out. The brown smoke rises up only a stone's throw away. I'm almost there. I move towards it, keeping in close to the villas, clambering through wasted front gardens, over dead hedges and between the rising knives of cypress trees. It doesn't take me long to close the distance, and while I acknowledge that curiosity can be a good thing, part of me just wishes I'd stayed at home, sleeping next to Joe. Sometimes ignorance really can be bliss.

The closer I get, the more I notice the heat. At first it's a slight warming of the air, but then it hits me: a wall of warmth, radiating from the burning villa. And then there's the acrid smell of things being burnt that shouldn't be: rubbers, plastics, odd fabrics. I hunker down behind a bush - a Hebe, I think it is, with succulent leaves and blue flowers that are at odds with everything else around here - and peer out. There's only one villa between me and the one that's on fire. Brown smoke rises in predictable torrents from empty windows and is sucked up into the empty air. Since it's daylight the flames aren't visible, but the destruction they've wrought is clear enough. The white walls are blackened, the windows put out by the heat, the red-tiled roof starting to collapse.

Then I see them, standing in the road. Five men milling around, swigging from bottles and laughing. They wear grey and brown shapeless clothes: hoodies, puffer jackets, low-slung jeans. In the middle of them stands a radio, booming out some kind of tuneless house music. And they are all guys - and relatively young too. Which is strange. You rarely see gangs of blokes together these days. The ones who haven't been finished off by their own metabolisms are usually in more mixed, family groups. But here we have at least five male pyromaniacs. What a treat.

As I watch them, I try to differentiate between them. Pretty quickly I realise that I don't recognise any of them. They're certainly not from around here. There's a squat, wordless one furthest away from me, and then there's an older, scrawnier one to the right who's wearing a brown parka with his hands thrust down into the pockets. He stares into the fire, looks about as if he's on something, and periodically squawks with laughter, not necessarily in response to something that's been said. With his back to me is a tall, slim younger guy who has a certain swagger to him. He takes several swigs from a green bottle, points at the others, shouts loud comments and laughs a lot. He could be their leader, or he could just be the drunkest or most opinionated of the lot. It's hard to tell. He wears a satin grey baseball jacket inflated by numerous layers, including at least one faded plaid shirt. He too, like the older guy, looks about him a lot, but with a more studied air. When he looks this way, I feel an icy hand reach up my back. His head's shaved, and his dark eyes are intense, but that isn't what scares me. It's the fact that his face - his whole head - has been smeared with ash. Thankfully he turns away. Then I realise that the other two also have similarly grey, shaved heads, adorned no doubt with the remnants of their former fires.

Beyond the squat man stand several large white plastic containers, their contents surely used to start the fires. I wonder how much they've got left. I also wonder where they got it from. Petrol is like gold dust these days. These guys could live the life of Riley if they decided to sell it. But I suppose starting fires is the more exciting option. I suppose you've got to give them marks for style. And psychopathy.

So these ash-smeared men mill around, basking in the warmth and spectacle of their fire, which is fair enough. It's important to enjoy your achievements, and these blokes seem pretty satisfied with what they've done. But what are they going to do next? That's the question. Part of me wants to simply step out into the road and challenge them, see what they have to say for themselves. Of course, this isn't a good idea. I haven't lost all sense of reason - at least not yet. Above the crackle and hoosh of the fire it's also difficult to catch what they're saying, and I don't hear anything other than a few random words and expletives. And if I get any nearer I run the risk of being spotted, which isn't gong to be worth it. All I can do is gather as much information as possible, and then get back to the square.

So I hunker down, determined to see if I can find out if there are any more of them. Luckily, it's still early, and any noise I make settling down is covered by the sound of the fire. I pull my coat tight about me, and wonder what we should do. Maybe we should send a delegation out to meet them? But still, rocking up in someone's town and setting buildings alight is hardly a peace offering. Maybe we should confront them and ask them politely but firmly to leave? The thing is, I don't reckon we'd appear intimidating enough. Unless we sent Hilda on her own with a baseball bat. That'd do the trick.

Peering out from behind my Hebe, I try to work out if these guys are armed. I can't see any weapons, but it doesn't mean that they're not. If they've laid them on the ground or propped them up somewhere I'd be none the wiser. I check my watch. Minutes pass but seem like months. After ten, I begin to shiver. It's not excessively cold, but I'm not moving and my body fat's probably in the single digits. What should I do? I can't stay here for much longer, but I haven't learned much either. When I hear a loud crash behind me, I'm horrified, but also glad that the decision has been made for me.

Peering round slowly, I see two men saunter out from the villa behind me. One is carrying a large wide screen TV, the other an old hi-fi system. In the absence of a reliable electricity supply, I can only assume that these items are simply more fuel for their fire. The first man is big, bulky even by yesterday's standards, clad in a grey jacket and grey jeans. The second man is much younger; he's scrawny and swathed in a shapeless army surplus coat. They seem to fit the description of tradesman and apprentice, but I could be wrong. Both have the hairless, ash-smeared heads that look like pencil erasers.

I don't move, and hope that they will just walk on by, their attention focussed on the defunct electrical goodies they've just snatched. Sadly, my hope is misplaced. Halfway down the short flight of steps, the big man notices me crouching there like some squatting gnome. He pauses a second, as if in shock, then bellows, Marcello! Vieni qui! Pronto!

I need no second bidding. Like a hunted rabbit I break my paltry cover and - to the two men's surprise - run straight past them, heading back the way I came. Some vestigial impulse about not dropping electrical equipment hampers them, and by the time they've even started to give chase, I'm well on my way. When I reach the corner of the street leading back up to the old town, I pause and glance backwards. To be fair, I wish I hadn't. Sure enough, the two pencil-headed looters are heading towards me through the gardens, but they're making hard work of it. The bigger one looks as if he's wading through heavy surf - he's all high knees and waving arms. The kid is sprawling around within his coat, trying to keep it out of his way. They're not really a threat - I know I can get away from them, especially with my knowledge of the streets. The real problem is the slim young guy who must be Marcello. In contrast to the other two, he's jogging down the road itself, obviously intent on saving energy. He's got the easy, loping stride of a hunter or long-distance runner. As he locks eyes on me a smile splits his grey face in two. Then I notice the hooked machete that hangs loosely from his hand. I turn and run.

The buildings pass me like the backdrop of some nightmarish cartoon, punctuated by the push and pull of my breath. My legs flutter beneath me, working on automatic, but it still feels as if I'm stationary and everything else is moving. However, I soon realise that I'm gaining height, being propelled upwards by a sense of panic. I've heard the stories of lone women who get caught by gangs of guys, and they're really not worth relating. Raped, tortured, enslaved, killed. The list of outcomes is no more than a list of bland words, but each victim's plight a specific, awful tale.

As soon as I've gained some height, I turn. Marcello's still there, grinning, eyeballing me and climbing easily. I jink right, run along the old wall of some derelict garden and then head upwards once again. When I reach the top, I'm gasping, my legs awash with pain. But at least it's all downhill from now on. I pause in a tiny, empty square on the apex of the hill. No sign of Marcello. This is no time for lollygagging, so I drop straight down the Calle D'Oro, feet dancing daintily over the cobbles. I'm at one with my surroundings, descending as soundlessly as someone who's already dead. As I'm about to plunge into the streets of the town below, I risk a glance backwards. That cold hand reaches up my back again, icing my skin. Marcello's right there, the hooked machete now held horizontally, that fixed grin adding a glint of white to his grey face. How can he run so quickly? I notice how his long stride eats up the ground, how poised and efficient he is. His running style might well be a thing of beauty if it weren't for the fact that he's chasing me.

As the streets level out, I try to push on, but there's no fifth gear, just a sense of impending exhaustion. I'm pushing firmly into the red, and I wonder how long my body will be able to keep this up. I glance back over my shoulder, and see that he's closer still. And it's at this point that I realise that I'm not going to make it, that he'll catch me well before I can reach the safety of the barricades.

The gun. How I can have forgotten about it? Especially as it's been slapping against my back for the last five minutes. I slow my pace, move my bag round to the front, and pull out the revolver. I just hope that Mr Moretti's kept this thing in good nick, and that it actually works. And that it's loaded with real bullets. If it isn't, I'm in trouble.

I choose an open section of road and come to a halt on a corner. I spin and hold the gun level in both hands, hoping that I look like one of Charlie's Angels. I would shout something, but I can't. It's as much as I can do to keep from keeling over. Marcello slows to a saunter, holding both hands up, letting the machete dangle from its wrist strap. Ciao bella! He shouts. It's okay. I just wanted a chat, but you took off too quickly. What could I do, he asks with a shrug. I had to follow you. I didn't mean to frighten you.

I take a few seconds to compose myself. Glancing about me I realise - to my horror - that I'm not sure where I am. We're so used to staying in our flats that my familiarity with the town has dwindled. And now's not a good time to have lost my bearings. Some part of me thinks to hell with it, just shoot him. Anything that comes out of his mouth is going to be lies, so what's the point in talking? To my credit and consternation, another part of me rails against this. You've got to give people a chance. Plus, if I kill him now, I'll be none the wiser as to what these eraserheads are actually up to.

Very funny, I say, still breathing hard. Maybe you could have left the machete at home, in that case? In fact, I think you can drop it now. He peers at it, still smiling. What, this? He looks at the machete dangling from his wrist as if it's a harmless object, something he didn't realise he was carrying, like a pen.

Go on, I say, drop it. With one hand he pulls the wrist strap up his hand, bends at the knees and lays the machete on the ground before straightening up. He doesn't take his eyes off me the whole time. You've got to admire his poise, I guess. In normal times he'd be quite a catch: good-looking and intense. Now, these qualities just make him more dangerous.

Well done, I say, good boy. I give him a wry smile, let's keep this up, shall we? Now, who are you? He squints at me, as if trying to remember something. Or maybe some of the ash has run into his eyes, dislodged by sweat. I think you may know that already, he says, from Fabio's outburst. My name's Marcello. And yours? I raise an eyebrow. August, I say. August, he repeats, his frown deepening a little. That's an unusual name. Unusual, but pretty. But it's not Italian. Where are you from August?

Never mind, I say. I'm still breathing hard, and have to concentrate to appear calm. What are you doing here, and why did you set that building alight?

What, he says, his frown turning into a smile, that villa? He drops his gaze, purses his lips and shrugs. It's the gesture of a career criminal accused of something, replete with indignation and disbelief. We were just cold, he continues, bringing his eyes back to me. We needed to warm ourselves. What better way than using an old building as a bonfire?

This isn't your town, I say. You can't just come here and start burning things. Where are you from? Marcello cocks his head to one side. No, he says, you're right. It's not our town. But it doesn't sound like it's your town either. Where are *you* from, August?

That icy hand reaches up my back once again. I was born here, I say. My mother lives here, but I've spent a lot of time in England. Part of me sees the necessity of sharing information with this man if I'm to get any out of him, but another part of me is appalled. Why am I telling him these things? I think I'd make a terrible interrogator. Now, where are you from, I ask, trying to regain control of the conversation.

I'm glad you like it here, he says. And I'm glad you've decided to stay, although some of my friends might not think the same. In my opinion, these days we need all the pretty girls we can get, wherever they're from.

Very good, I say. But flattery's not going to get you very far, especially when mixed with xenophobia. Now tell me where you're from - and what you're doing here. I'm a patient person, but don't push it. As if to emphasise my words, the gun twitches in my hands. To his credit, Marcello doesn't so much as flinch.

Okay, he says, exhaling. We're from Monte Fiori. I nod: so far so good. Have you ever been there, he asks, looking at me from under his eyebrows, as if he's ashamed of something. A couple of times, I say. Bene, he says, bene. A lovely place - or it was. Now - what can I say? For years we did quite well, but slowly things have begun to fall apart. The electricity started to go, our greenhouses didn't get enough light. Plus, it's a difficult place to get to, as you know. It's hard to get supplies in. Even the criminals began to leave. And then there was nothing. Just us. Things just got worse and worse. People began dying left and right. There was nothing we could do. Some even descended to the level of animals, eating each other - imagine that! The hand of death has settled on Monte Fiori, casting us out into the ashes of this world.

It's no different in most places, I say, sneering. Well, apart from the cannibalism. What makes you so special, and what makes you think you can come here and start lighting fires?

Marcello shrugs and fixes me with his eyes, a grin slowly emerging upon his face. We're similar to everybody else, he says. We're no better, no worse. But we have been awakened. We are, he says, his grin deepening, what you might say in English, woke. My sneer returns and I hope he understands the depth of my contempt. It sounds to me as if you've commandeered that word, I say, in much the same way as you're trying to commandeer this town.

I can't agree with you, he says. Some people say the rock that struck us was a warning from God. Whatever it was, it was a wake-up call. But what happened? Soon people fell back into the old ways, continuing on with their pathetic lives. Complacency has almost claimed us again, and the world is fading away August, fading away day by day into the grey. We're fighting against that. That's what we're here for: we believe it's better to burn out than to fade away.

And that malevolent, age-old grin splits his face in its full glory. I swallow hard. His mission statement sounds pretty much like my own, and it takes everything I've got not to tell him.

Really, I say, and how are you doing that, by setting buildings alight? His grin deepens even further, becoming a rictus worthy of someone who's dead. There are other ways as well, he adds: ways I'd love to show you. It's as if his veneer of charm has suddenly shifted, revealing the real man beneath. Dread washes through me, and I feel my whole body begin to tense up.

What's with the ash, I ask, trying to lighten the tone. Our humanity has been taken from us, continues Marcello. We're here to reclaim what we've lost - our humanity, our masculinity. There are some lines from the Bible - I've got them memorised... I brought fire from amongst you; it has consumed you, and now you are ashes on this earth, in the eyes of all who behold you. Profound, isn't it? When we have reclaimed what is ours, we will wash, but not before.

Very impressive, I say. But what do you want to reclaim - this town? Marcello shakes his head. You misunderstand me, bella. We want to reclaim ourselves. What we see around us, he adds, nodding at the buildings on either side of us, is simply our means of doing so.

Don't get ahead of yourself, I say. If you think you can come here and take over, you've got another thing coming. You and your men need to go. I'm sure there are other places where you'd be more welcome. And I'm sure you'll find yourselves along the way.

The sound of shouting tears my attention from Marcello. Behind him, the two looters lurch into the street. The young kid is still slapping around in his coat, the bigger man stumbling forward as if he's crossing a battlefield. Beyond them, in the depths of the old town, I can hear voices calling: it's no doubt Marcello's other men, trying to work out where they're going.

The two looters come to a halt a few metres behind Marcello. You see, he says, shrugging. We're not going anywhere. Why don't you put the gun down, bella? I'm sure we can all get along. You can introduce us to your friends. If they're as pretty as you, I'm sure we'll all have a great time. Marcello bends slowly at the knees, picks up the machete and straightens again. He can't lose face in front of his men, but this isn't helping his cause. I'm warning you, I say. You and your men need to go. Now.

He doesn't respond, simply stares at me from beneath his louring brows. With his bald grey head and hooked machete he looks like something out of some obscure mythology: Eraserhead, bringer of death and ashes. Bella, he says, his voice syrupy and rich, put the gun down. Let's all see if we can get on. This world's too full of hate already. Let's join forces. Together we can reclaim what we've lost.

His voice is hypnotic, I won't deny it. But when he starts to move forward, the gun goes off. It's as if my body's on automatic, or being controlled by an operating system that I'm not aware of. Even so, Marcello seems to know me better than I know myself. He pivots at the waist, and the bullet meant for him goes past. I watch as the young boy behind him crumples, thrown backwards and collapsing as the shot hits him in the upper chest. I turn and run, the concussion echoing in my ears.

If the shot has given him pause, it doesn't take Marcello long to get his act together. I can soon hear his footsteps and breathing behind me. This is what being hunted feels like, and after shooting the kid, I doubt I'll get much mercy from him. I consider turning to shoot again, but dismiss the idea. If I miss, I could lose an arm. This thought keeps me going. I hang a right and there - like Elysian fields - I see one of our barricades.

Help! I shout in English, help! I can't see anyone there. The barricade seems to be abandoned, an unmanned barrier of broken furniture. I glance backwards over my shoulder, and Marcello's right there - a grey-headed, grinning fiend. I jink to the left, and am dimly aware of the machete slicing through the air, just where I was. Help me, I yell. The barricade's looming up now, but I'm going too fast to stop. Instead, I take a deep breath and jump. I land on it like a cat that's climbing a tree, my shin smashing into something hard. I hop to one side just as the machete crashes down where my foot had been, sending splinters of wood into the air. Reflexively, I kick backwards and feel my heal hit home. Then I'm scrambling upwards. I hear a voice, see heads emerge on the other side of the barricade. A cry of August goes up, and then there's Mr Moretti, an improvised pike in his hands, stabbing downwards into the space below me. And then I'm over the apex, turning and aiming. I see a whirling figure that must be Marcello, but he sees the danger, jinks as the gun goes off and then he's running back up the street. He ducks around a corner and is gone, like something hideous and seductive returning to the depths of my unconscious.

The debrief takes place in the square, with me sitting in the dust, the gun between my feet, desperately trying to catch my breath. Mr Moretti's there, pike in one hand and the other on my shoulder, a look of concern on his face. Rosa's there too, clutching rosary beads between her hands and staring at me with the eyes of a dying saint. I've got a small crowd, and I tell them everything I know, which admittedly isn't much. As I leave out the metaphysics, it seems I know almost nothing, and it certainly doesn't seem worth the risk I just took.

When I'm almost finished Joe turns up, tall and glowering, with his wide-brimmed hat and his hands thrust deep into the pockets of his waxed jacket. When I finish the story of my exploits, Mr Moretti pats me on the shoulder and

Rosa kisses me on the head. You're very brave, my girl, she whispers, very brave. But it's Joe who hauls me up, offering me a long, strong arm. I wipe myself down, but my backside is filthy from sitting on the floor.

What were you thinking, he mutters as we head back across the square. What do you mean, I say, looking up at him. He doesn't reply, but when we're back in the flat he throws his hat down on a chair and turns on me. August, he says, shaking his head, you could have got yourself killed - and for what? His dark eyes bore into me, and his arms hang at his sides.

I've no doubt that he's just expressing concern, but I'm in no mood to be placatory. Hold on a minute, I say. I invited you here to my flat, but that doesn't mean you get to tell me what to do, okay? This is my place. My rules. Someone needed to get this lot organised, and it's a good thing that I did. That bloke and his little bunch are deluded and dangerous. They're not messing around. And now we know more about them, thanks to me.

Is that what this is to you, he asks, stuffing his hands into his pockets, a chance to take control? I stare at him, incredulous. A what? I'm trying to save these people's lives! But apparently, he adds, you're not too concerned about losing your own. Maybe not, I say with a shrug. If something happens, so be it. Que sera, sera. Well, says Joe, exhaling through his nose, maybe it would interest you to know that I care. I raise my eyebrows. How very kind, I say. Maybe next time you can come along and hold my hand, just to make sure I'm okay. I push past him and head to the bathroom, feeling a perhaps unreasonable anger. Still, I'm in no mood to deliberate the ins and outs of my actions.

I bang the immersion heater on and treat myself to a bath. Compared to what baths used to be, it's probably just a shallow, tepid pool, but it feels like luxury. I get dressed in some old cargo pants, a navy jumper and some Doc Martins I haven't worn in years. They're as comfy as I remember. If things are going to get a bit tasty around here, I need to be dressed for it, not swanning around in Gucci and heels. I find Joe in the kitchen, stewing, his long body stretched out in a chair.

Fancy a coffee, I ask. It's my default question, but why he couldn't already have got me one is beyond me. Perhaps I've been on my own too long for cohabiting to work. We'll soon see. He nods like a child who's just been told off. Beyond his sprawled form the grey of the day is deepening. It's already starting to get dark. We could be in for a long night.

I join Joe at the table, and as I sip the espresso, I feel myself begin to calm. I hadn't realised how keyed up I was. They'll come back at night, I say, trying to make conversation, against my better judgement. Joe nods. Now that they know where we are. Go on, I add, why don't you just say it? Now that you lead them here, August. Joe shrugs and peers out of the window. It's a bit late for all that, don't you think? But I don't let it go. A bit late for what, I ask. He turns to look at me, his dark eyes unreadable. For petty recriminations. What's done is done. We just have to adapt.

I want to snap at him, just for being so reasonable, but I've nothing to say so I don't. We just sit and watch the buildings of the square and the patch of sky darken through successive gradations of grey. Slowly, as the minutes pass, I feel the need to talk building up inside me. It's not that I feel awkward - that really isn't the case with Joe. It's just that I haven't had anyone to confide in for so long that I can't help myself.

I clear my throat and shake my head. I shot a young boy, I hear myself saying. He can't have been more than seventeen. Joe looks up at me. He doesn't say a word, but his silence is an invitation to confidence. I shrug. I was aiming at Marcello, the ringleader, but he twisted. The boy was standing behind him.

Joe raises his eyebrows. Do you think he's okay? I shake my head. The bullet hit him in the chest and knocked him down. I don't think he's got much of a chance. Joe reaches out and takes my hand. His hand is double the size of mine, and strong. I'm sure if he wanted to break my fingers he could. It's an unsettling thought. In these times, he goes on, strange things happen. It's not our fault. You didn't bring them here. They came of their own accord.

I look away, back out the window. I want to tell him that I feel like I did bring them here, that I created them, that they're here because of me, but it sounds too unhinged to put into words, so I don't. For a second I think I'm going to cry, but there's nothing there, nothing at all.

Joe's got an old head torch - it's just the sort of thing he would have. Plus he's squirrelled away enough batteries to last him a couple of years. My torch - a small, steel-bodied Maglite - still works too, which is something of a miracle.

Strings of Christmas lights adorn the barricades, run from generators in the basements. Oil lamps and candles are in abundance too, giving the whole square a festive feel. It really feels like some winter wonderland, but the aesthetics are at odds with the tension we all feel, creating a discordant vibe. Still, Mr Moretti's come up trumps again, lighting a bonfire in the centre of the square using palettes and old furniture. We don't have a lot of combustible material, and I know a lot of people around here would baulk at such apparent waste. In reality, though, the bonfire's a godsend. It creates a focal point, one you can keep coming back to as you mill around. Its warmth and light are both cheering, pushing away the cold, the darkness and the pessimism. It reminds us of future days of blue skies and security, when we can sit with others eating, drinking and telling stories, simply revelling in the company of other human beings and our place upon this Earth.

Looking into the fire, I can't help but remember Guy Fawkes bonfires from the past. That was an odd celebration, quintessentially English in its sense of macabre. The old Guy perched atop the bonfire, limbs being shed as the flames reached him, papier-mâché head lolling forward on a crooked neck, eyes glinting beneath his wide-brimmed hat. And then the flames would eat him alive, and our own chilling fears of the other would be exorcised with this annihilation of our national scapegoat. How very pagan.

It's while I'm thinking about Guy Fawkes that we hear the first shout. It comes from beyond the barricade nearest the ravine, the one Filippa's made her own. At first, I don't recognise what's being said, but I get it soon enough. August, the cry goes. August. August! The vowels are dragged out like the droning of summer bees.

I look at Joe. He looks back at me. Wordlessly we move towards Filippa's barricade. We see her there, perched behind the makeshift mirror door, peering out into the darkness, the old rifle clutched in her hands. When she realises we're there, she glances back at us. Her face is vacant, uncomprehending, although that isn't unusual.

To be fair, I don't know what to do either. Part of me thinks we should try to lead a sortie out and kill all of the eraserheads, but that, of course, is what they want. Silhouetted against the blazing light of the barricade, we'd be little more than funfair ducks lining up to get shot.

A couple of streets away, something fizzes up into the sky. At first we don't realise what it is. I expect a mortar to land in our midst, spraying us with shrapnel and dropping half our number into the dust. When a firework bursts into blue sparks over our heads, I can't say I'm not relieved. Then another goes up, and another, creating aerial vistas of luminous green and pale crimson. Marcello's men are really treating us, trying to soften us up and make us drop our guard.

As the light from the fireworks dies away, leaving just the afterglow of explosions on our retinas, I hear my name again, chanted this time by several mouths. August. August! Then there's Marcello's singular voice calling out: August, bella, come and join us. Come on. We're out here. You know where the power is. Come and join us, or even better - let us in. Let's talk. Let's join forces and save ourselves, and this world.

The honeyed phrases continue for the next half hour, becoming some hideous, flattering backdrop to my thoughts. I don't want to respond, but the calls, with the constant refrain of my name, show no signs of letting up, grinding on my nerves like some combination of water torture and siren song. Eventually I can take it no more. I clamber up Filippa's barricade and crouch at the top, scanning the black street before me, my head barely breaking the uppermost strut. I'm certainly not going to give them a free shot.

What do you want, I yell. Marcello's voice dies in the darkness, as if it were never there, an internal monologue suddenly silenced. The last time we talked, I go on, I thought I was clear enough. Thanks for the fireworks, but you all need to leave. There's a pause as my words sink in. Then his voice again, cloying, needling. Bella, he says, you can't mean that. We have so much in common. So much. We just got off on the wrong foot, that's all. And most of that is probably down to me. If I scared you, I apologise. It certainly wasn't my intention. Let's talk - as friends, as colleagues, as fellow travellers in this grey new world.

I raise my eyebrows and glance down at Joe. He doesn't react at all, which seems pretty much in line with his stoical nature. No, I say, shaking my head. You've got it wrong. We bear you no malice, but we're quite happy here on our own.

This is our town, and you've got to leave.

Silence. I peer into the darkness, trying to see if I can locate the source of his voice, but when the words return, they're just funnelled down the street from some distant, unseen point, as if they're echoing down the throat of hell itself. August. August! That boy you shot... Raphael. He wants to come and see you. I pause, unsure of how to respond. Tell him to stay where he is. I'm glad that he's okay, but if he approaches the barricades, he'll be shot. You've been warned.

A vision of this lad, caked in blood and shuffling towards the barricade, fixes itself in my mind. He's dead-eyed and strapped with explosives. I try to dismiss this dismal image, but he lingers, fuelled by my guilt. As if on cue, the voice emerges from the darkness. But he so wants to see you again, chimes Marcello, just to show you there are no hard feelings. Tell him to stay where he is, I yell, for his own good. My words die away, and as there's no response, it feels as if I'm talking to nobody. After five minutes of silence I come down from the barricade. Of course Filippa's still there, crouching at the doorway, clutching her rifle. If anyone approaches, I hiss, shoot them. She nods once, the weight of responsibility heavy upon her.

We give it another minute or two, but as nothing happens, Joe and I wander back towards the bonfire in the centre of the square. There are now more than enough people gathered at Filippa's barricade to see off any intruders. It's funny, I say. I could have sworn that shot killed the boy. Why would he tell me that he's all right? It's good to know, I guess. Joe gives me a single shake of the head, as if to emphasise my naiveté. He's just trying to get under your skin, he says. Don't let him.

As we're standing by the fire, both given over to gloomy introspection, a scream rends the air. It came from one of the other barricades - the one I returned to this morning. Without a second thought, Joe and I hurry over. There are only a couple of people there, but the sentry's come down off the barricade, another of Mr Moretti's rifles shaking uselessly in her hands. What is it, I yell, breaking into a run, are they attacking? There's no immediate response. The sentry just raises one arm, pointing to the apex of the barricade.

Turning my torch on, I play the flickering light over the top of the barrier until it hits a protuberance. There's someone there! I steady the torch, and then realise what it is. It's the young boy, arms spread over bits of furniture, open eyes staring into the square. It takes me a second to realise he's dead. Another scream goes up, and two of our ghosts flee. Mio Dio, I say under my breath. What bastards.

Thankfully, Mr Moretti arrives a minute

later, coughing and wheezing. Together, we dislodge the body with his pike. It takes several goes, and when we hear the body hit the ground, it's with a mixture of both relief and disgust. Relief that it's no longer hanging there, but disgust with myself for having shot the boy in the first place, and disgust with Marcello for coming up with such a sick ruse. I go over to our sentry and place a hand on her shoulder. She's a youngish woman, maybe ten years my junior, called Angela. She's got the golden hair, pale skin and delicate constitution of an angel, so her name seems apt. Are you okay, I ask. She nods, staring at me with oversized eyes. Don't worry, I say. We'll remove the body in the morning. He'll have to lie there for the time being. At least he won't feel the cold.

Then, several streets beyond the barricade, we see what we've perhaps all been dreading. An eerie, flickering glow that illuminates a pillar of smoke rising into the night sky. I rub a hand over my face. So it's started in earnest. If one block burns, what's to stop the fire spreading to others, and eventually ours? We have no fire-fighting equipment other than hope itself.

We watch the fire burn for the next half hour. There's nothing we can do, other than endure a paroxysm of terror that the flames will spread to nearby buildings, and eventually to our own. Thoughts of how to haul water up from the river plague me, but we don't have enough buckets and a pump will take too long to install. Using our drinking water would be both pointless and dangerous, both in the short and long term. Our little bonfire in the square no longer seems quite so innocent: its evil twin out there in the streets is eating a block of flats alive.

Bella! Bella! As the roof of the burning building finally collapses in a shower of sparks, I'm almost glad to hear Marcello's voice again. He's given us plenty of time to stew and experience the fear of a town-wide conflagration. Still, I reckon that now we've got the advantage. He's done his worst: thrown a dead body at us, and torched a building. From the state of the declining fire, I imagine that it's going to take more fuel than they've got to torch the whole town. The flames from that one building don't seem to have spread to another. Most buildings have probably gone unheated for the last five years at least, and sucked up a fair bit of moisture during that time, turning them into the equivalent of damp kindling at best. As long as there was no one in there... the thought curdles my blood.

What do you want, I yell into the empty street in front of us. There's a pause, and then Marcello's voice again, strong and soaring with the misplaced confidence of youth. Bella - August! So now you see that we are serious. Now you see the new world rising from the ruins of our own. Join us - let us in - that is all we ask! Let us join forces and realise our vision. The times are not our own August. It is not our fault that we were born into this. But we can be reborn again. Seize control, and watch us rise. From the ashes of the old into a brave new world.

I glance sideways at Joe, who simply rolls his eyes. We're too old for ideologies and all the bullshit that comes with them, but how I'm going to explain this to Marcello is beyond me. I should probably just keep my peace, but it's never been my way. What sort of a world is that, I yell back, feeling a sudden surge of anger. The world of the ultras and the Blackshirts?

Very funny, chimes Marcello, sounding as if he's enjoying himself a little too much. In times like these, a strong hand is needed, to be sure, but I think we've moved beyond all such old allegiances, don't you August? I shake my head. This is becoming something of a playground quarrel, but I can't help myself. It looks like quite a society you're building there, I yell back. It's good to see how well you treat your dead, I add, almost on a whim, trying a little psychological warfare of my own. I was surprised to see no bite marks on the body. Well done. Very restrained."

This shuts him up. I have a dreadful feeling that I've gone too far, but I can't see how that would play out. Let him do his worst. They can torch buildings at random, but they'll just be wasting their fuel. And if they come for us across the barricades, we'll shoot them down. My dread turns, by degrees, to something more positive, thanks to the effect of these rational thoughts. What are Marcello and his band - these eraser-heads - other than a small, misguided group of men? They want power where there's none to be had. They want some sense of control in a rudder-less world. For the first time today, I start to feel confident.

It takes Marcello a long time to reply, and I can't help but think that I've won some kind of moral victory. Bella, bella, the voice comes back eventually, with the intonation of a respected teacher who's disappointed with a student. Bella, I had hoped that it wouldn't come to this, but I see now that we have no choice. There are so many buildings to choose from. We have to be se-lective. I think it's time to burn something more beautiful than a block of flats. There's a building on the main square that's caught our eye - it's got a round window and a bell tower. I think you might know it. In our new world, even God needs to be reborn. He must die. Those who support him must die. And, of course, those who are shel-tered by him must die as well.

The feeling of dread returns tenfold, plum-meting through my guts like a dropped rock. I glance at Joe. He wouldn't, I say. Why wouldn't he, Joe replies. He already shoved that kid up on to the barricade. I don't think moral fibre is his strong point. I think he'll do whatever he wants.

I shake my head. As soon as we saw the fire this morning we sent a messenger to the convent, telling the nuns to keep the kids inside, stay locked up and keep quiet. What happened? Did our messenger get spotted? Did the nuns leave a light on? Did one of the children shout out in their sleep? It's impossible to know. And really it doesn't matter. I'm frozen by inaction, and peer at Joe hopefully. Maybe he'll come up with something in the next few seconds. But he's simply staring into the darkness beyond the barricade, looking as bewildered as I feel.

We've got to go and help them, I say. We can't just let him burn that building down, with all of the children inside. Joe just shakes his head. That's just what he wants us to do: head out, break cover. He's probably got his men lined up along the streets leading out of here, ready to pick us off.

I shake my head. We can't take the risk, I say. We've got no choice. To his credit, Joe nods. You're right, he says. Within a couple of minutes we've gathered together the most rag-tag of posses. We've got Angela, our terrified sentry. We've got Filippa, her dark eyes wide and bovine, like those of a cow approaching the slaughterhouse. There's Mr Moretti, who can barely move faster than an animated shuffle. There's' Nick from our block, who looks like he's about to slope off for a fag. The feather in our cap is Hilda, stern and purposeful in the firelight. Then there's me and Joe. The not-so-magnificent seven.

We can't take the most direct route to the square - that much is certain. And we don't have much time to formulate a plan. Instead, we clamber over the barricade furthest from main the square. My hands, cold with fear, struggle to grip and pull me up over the makeshift structure, and judging by the combination of stumbling and swearing, it seems that others are having the same problem. Still, we help each other out, and within a couple of minutes, we're over. Still, it's a couple of minutes too long. As we break into a jog, I realise that we're actually doing quite well: if a sniper had been posted out here, he'd have picked a couple of us off on the barricade itself. The thought of ash-smeared, machete-waving maniacs emerging from doorways is a daunting prospect, but the reality is that we don't have time to take precautions. To be fair, it's hard enough simply navigating our way through the streets, let alone being alert. Luckily the moon lends us a modicum of light, peering hazily from behind fast-paced clouds that scud across the sky.

Despite everything, we move well. If I go wrong, Mr Moretti chips in, offering directions. Angela chimes in too, showing more pluck than

I'd given her credit for. Hilda hisses the odd command as well, but Nick and Filippa, of course, remains wordless, which is fine. Joe brings up the rear, utterly at sea in the town. Still, there's something dashing about how we're moving through the deserted streets like members of the French Resistance on a sortie. Maybe things aren't so hopeless after all.

When we get to the main square, though, my confidence nosedives. The square itself is an odd, elongated shape, but I didn't realise quite how much ground we'd have to cover. Because of our circuitous route, we've come out in the corner farthest from the convent. There are a couple of dead plane trees and the odd bench to our right, but still, after that there's a clear run-in of fifty metres or more. I'm no marine, but even I can see that's a lot.

Plus, two fires have been lit on either side of the convent's door. Marcello's men have created massive piles of furniture and other junk, both of which are now burning. Seething yellow flames burn against the walls and throw sparks high into the air. It's only a matter of time before some part of the building catches alight, and then the endgame will begin. The sheer amount of light the fires produce is also a problem: there's no chance of getting in close before being spotted.

We stand there, aghast. Next to me, Mr Moretti shakes his head. La bocca dell'inferno, he mutters, breathing hard and wheezing. La bocca dell'inferno. A couple of figures flit before the bonfires, patrolling and celebrating. They peer out, then whoop and jig about: military men one moment, ravers the next.

Okay, I say, there's no point in creeping about. We're just going to have to go for it - they're probably too drunk to shoot straight anyway. Are we ready? I take a deep breath, and look at my group expectantly. Hold on, says Joe, pushing his way towards me. It's too far to just rush them. Some people should stop over there, behind those benches, he says, pointing to just beyond the plane trees, and provide covering fire. That way we might stand a chance.

He's right, of course, but I can feel myself bristling at having my leadership challenged. But now is no time to throw a hissy fit. Okay, I say. Filippa, Mr Moretti and Hilda - you stay behind the benches as Joe says. Shoot at anything that moves, but preferably not us. I give Hilda my revolver somewhat reluctantly, take my carving knife from my bag and tuck it under the belt at the back of my coat. Even so, I feel somewhat defenceless. Still, Joe's got his rifle and Angela's got one of Mr Moretti's museum pieces, so we might well be okay. Poor Nick's just got a claw hammer, but it does look like a good one.

Okay, I say, taking a deep breath, andiamo. So we break from the relative cover of darkness at the far side of the square and scuttle forward, looking less glamorous with each step. Before we're even halfway to the benches, though, a cry goes up. One of the guards has spotted us and is yelling incoherently. Then he drops to one knee, suddenly all military and purposeful. A loud crack rends the air, and a bullet zings over our heads. We all clatter in behind the benches, clumsy and catching our breath. We've gone from resistance fighters to Stooge-like in a matter of minutes, but there's no time to think, we just have to act. The flames against the convent are burning harder than ever, clutching at the walls with the intensity of a lover.

Ready, I ask. Hold on a minute, says Joe, clutching my arm. Why didn't they build the fire against the door? That would make more sense. He shakes his head. This is a trap, August, I'm telling you. I stare at him, aghast at his suggestion that we sit back and do nothing. Maybe it is, I say. But we don't have any choice. There are dozens of kids in there, and pretty soon they'll be burning. Joe squints at the beleaguered convent, his taut, stubbled jaw thrown into relief by the firelight. Just be careful, he says, beneath his breath. Then it hits me. I might, just might, actually be in love with this man.

Thankfully, there's nothing like mis-timed emotion to get you moving. I take a deep breath. Okay, I say. Now. We break cover as one, Joe and I in front, Angela and Nick behind. We run towards the fires, charging headlong into the mouth of hell. The man who shot at us has reloaded by this time. Just as he's about to fire again, a bullet scuffs up a handful of dust in front of him. It's enough to put him off. His rifle cracks, but the bullet sails wide into the night. Then he's scuttling backwards, trying to stay low but barely able to keep his feet. As I'm running, I hear Angela's and Joe's guns go off, and our man, who I now recognise as the lumbering tradesman, falls backwards, no doubt gone to join his apprentice in the underworld.

Then there's a flash and crack from the dark reaches beyond the fires. Beside me, I hear Joe grunt and go down. I keep moving, running purely on adrenaline, but manage to glance backwards. Thankfully, I see him come up on one knee, aim and fire. I have no idea if he's hit his target or not, and soon enough I've got bigger problems to worry about. The squat eraser-head looms up in silhouette before me, as wide as he is tall, blocking my way. He's got a knife in one hand, and is in the act of raising it when a bullet hits him front on. He staggers backwards and falls. I risk another glance back. From his kneeling position, Joe's waving me on. Go on, he shouts. I've got you.

To my right the scrawny, parka-clad old man is unloading his gun into the night, emitting a screeching sound as he does so. When a couple of our bullets find their mark, though, he squawks, pirouettes, and plunges head-first into the fire, whether by accident or design I can't tell.

I'm almost at the front of the convent, practically blinded by the two fires, when the small door opens and a man leaps out, as if pushed. At first I think it's Marcello, as he's carrying that hooked machete, but it isn't. He's taller, ganglier, more unsure of himself. I come to a sudden halt, wondering how I'm going to get past this new lunatic, when Nick plunges past me, hammer raised, a throttled war cry emerging from his open mouth. The man raises his machete in self-defence but Nick is on him, hammer swinging, that guttural cry still emanating from somewhere deep within him.

I take my chance. I duck and sidestep, grab the door handle, twist and push. To my surprise the door opens first time. What I'd have done if it hadn't, I have no idea. I step gingerly over the threshold and creep along the dark entranceway towards the next door. I'm just thinking about calling out when a hand closes over my mouth and I'm dragged backwards, legs kicking, arms flailing.

Shhh, bella, the voice hisses in my ear. It's Marcello, the devil made flesh, one hand wrapped around my face, the other around my waist. It looks as if we've been given these few precious moments together, he says, before all your children die. I think we should enjoy them, don't you? Then I'm wrenched round, and he shoves me into the wall. My forehead hits the hard stone, and white dots dance across my vision. Then I feel a hand on my hip, then my backside, and realise that this could get worse. Much worse. Very nice, he hisses into my ear, but I can't miss looking into your eyes. Then I'm wrenched around again and slammed backwards into the wall. This time the back of my head hits hard, and more white dots take up dancing. I shriek, stunned by the impact, but then Marcello's forearm is crushing my throat, and my voice is cut off.

The door to the entrance swings open, letting in some of the ghastly yellow light. I'm saved, I think, and close my eyes, waiting for the bullet that will rip Marcello away from me. But it doesn't happen. When I open my eyes again, I see that the door's swung open, but that there's no one there. Oh, I'm so sorry, he whispers, were you expecting someone? I stare into his dark eyes, at the bald grey head alive with a rippling patina of flame. I'd love to say something defiant and witty, or at least spit in his face. But I can't. I can't breathe. I'm right on the edge of passing out.

Perhaps sensing this, Marcello pulls his arm back a little, allowing me to take a deep, shuddering breath. Then he slams his arm back into my throat, and I'm gasping ineffectually, panic gnawing at the edges of my consciousness. No, no, no, he says. We want you awake for this. There's no point fucking a corpse. With that, he reaches up under my coat, grabs the top of my cargo pants, and pulls.

The ripping sound of fabric horrifies me. Fairly soon, it could be my own flesh that's being torn. Then his hand's pushing hard against my crotch, pinning my entire body to the wall. Make it quick, I manage to mutter. I'm sure that won't be difficult.

His mouth splits. All I can see are his teeth and dancing eyes. His breath, hot with alcohol, swabs my face. Turning aside, I feel my body begin to go limp. Is this some kind of defence mechanism? Then his hand's at my knickers, wrenching them down. The cold night air attacks my sunken belly and enervated thighs.

Then he's opening his flies. I realise that he's already got an erection, and means to use it. I wonder how many women he's raped, how many buildings he's burned, how many people he's killed. And although I have no way of knowing, even one's too many.

As the pressure on my neck increases, his other hand begins prising my legs apart, allowing me some room for movement. As he jams one of his knees between mine, I manage to pull my right hand up to my lower back. I've been looking forward to this moment since this morning, he hisses at me. I'm sure you have too.

My hand fumbles for the knife. Then I've got it, my fingers twisting around the handle. He shoves his hips forward, and just as he's about to rape me the point of the knife makes contact with his midriff. I don't give him a chance to react. Jamming the knife upwards, I feel it enter him and stall, as if it's hit something hard - bone or cartilage. Shifting my grip slightly, I shove the blade home. As he realises the extent of what's just happened, I push him away from me, hard. He staggers backwards and hits the other side of the entranceway. His knees go, and he leers up at me from the grey death mask of his face. You bitch, he whispers. I'll see you in hell, August. I know you won't keep me waiting long.

With that he slumps to the floor. His head lolls forward, dead eyes open. Hitching my trousers up, I run further down the entranceway, yelling. When I reach the doorway just before the quadrangle, I batter on it with my fists, wailing. There's the sound of bolts being retracted, and then Anna's there, her pale face and hands accentuated by the dark habit and the unlighted corridor behind her. Come on, I say, we've got to get the children out. They can come over to our square, but we've got to go now. They'll need coats, blankets, something to put over their heads.

To her credit, Anna doesn't flap. Within

minutes, the kids are ready to go, huddled in the entranceway. They stare, wide-eyed and silent, at Marcello's crumpled body. Okay children, I say, trying to get their attention, you've got to be brave. Put your coat up like this, I say, pulling mine over my head, and run. Feeling crazed, I jump over Marcello's legs and then plunge through the main door. As soon as I jump over the threshold, the heat from the two fires hits me like the front of a forest fire. Luckily, it doesn't last long, and then I'm out into the square, peering around, looking back and beckoning for the kids to follow. I don't know if there are any eraserheads left in the square, but we can't wait to find out. A cursory glance shows Nick standing not far from the doorway, silhouetted by the fire, hammer still in one hand and a body at his feet. It looks as if his whole mechanism has come to a standstill, but I don't have time to offer him sympathy or praise. Some way behind me, Joe kneels, rifle still clutched in both hands. He grins and gives me a thumbs up, oblivious to what I've just been through.

Come on, I yell at the door, unable to see anyone inside. I stretch my arms out, trying to look encouraging. Come on, I yell again, starting to sound a little frantic. Pretend it's an obstacle course! And then a small figure emerges, rendered headless by the coat clutched over him. I rush forward and clasp the small boy to me. He can't be more than eight years old, but has done so well going first, showing the others the way. I ruffle his blond hair. Well done I say. Well done. He looks up at me with expectant eyes and a grin. Come on, I say. Let's see if we can get the others out too. So we stand there, this small child and I, hand in hand, jumping up and down and cheering when each new child emerges. A sense of pure exultation, of gratitude washes through me. Five minutes later we're escorting a long line of children across the square, flanked by a bevy of nuns. The rest of our group emerges from behind the benches and escorts us out like a guard of honour. I should say something, I guess, as they've all done so well, but I'm so happy that words fail me. Instead, I glance back at them, and smile, and nod. Leading the line out of the square, I find that I'm still clutching the blond boy's hand, but as he seems in no rush to let go, I'm fine with that. Joe hobbles alongside me, obviously in some pain, but grinning nonetheless.

We all pause on the edge of the square and look back. The convent - never the prettiest of buildings, a belfried Cyclops - is burning in earnest now, the flames licking and consuming its face, catching its eye-like shutters, the vast dark mouth of the door and the very eaves themselves. And it strikes me that this place that the kids have called home for the past seven or so years is going up in flames, that this place of sanctuary will soon be no more. It's a bitter pill, to be sure, but at least we got the children out. I catch Anna's eye and ask, is that all of us? She nods. Every single one, she says, every single one. Bene, I say, bene, and lead the line off towards our square. Their home may be gone, but we'll just have to see if we can't create another one for them. Seeing what we've just achieved, I'm sure we can.

VII

As soon as we're safely back in the square, I realise my mistake. We've achieved our objective, but at what cost? When we left here not so long ago, there were seven of us. Now? Six. It doesn't take me long to work out that Angela's missing. Too excited from getting the kids out, I forgot to check the members of my own team. It's a cardinal sin. The sort of thing they warn you about on the first day of leadership training. Look after your people, and they'll look after you. It seems like I've failed to do this in spectacular style.

I take back Mr Moretti's revolver and head towards the nearest barricade. When he sees me going, Joe yells out my name. He's standing by a large clump of children, conspicuous by the fact that he's a couple of feet taller than any of them. It's Angela, I say, having made my way back to him, she's not with us. Joe's face collapses, horrified that he too can have missed this fact. Hold on, he says, I'll come with you. He moves towards me, but for the first time I realise he can barely walk. His left thigh is bloodstained. He's taken a bullet to the leg as we charged towards the convent. You're not going anywhere, I say, holding up a hand. I'll be back before you know it. They're all dead anyway. The eraserheads.

So I leave them in the square, disbursing the children into spare flats, each group accompanied by a nun. I push my way through the door on Filippa's barricade and set off at a trot. I've never felt less afraid in the streets. I suppose that's what almost getting raped does to you. The drifts of ash, the looming facades and empty doorways hold no terrors for me now. Even the cold makes no inroads. I wonder if I've been covered in some invisible exoskeleton, wrapped up in something hard and numbing. I wonder if I'll ever feel anything ever again. Good or bad. Euphoric or tragic.

I break into the square from an unfamiliar angle. The fires are dying down, but the convent's roof has caught, smoke and flames snaking through its fabric. The smouldering building is the focal point of this communist-era stage set. A few huddled bodies punctuate the flat expanse of the floor. I move forward, revolver hanging by my side, peering at these approximations of human form. They could be made of cardboard and draped with cloth, so lifeless do they seem.

Angela was to my right as we ran towards the convent. I approach as near as I can to the farthest fire and walk out from there. It doesn't take me long to spot her. She's lying in a foetal position, her brown raincoat giving her the panache of a fallen resistance fighter. Her bobble hat's come off, leaving her blonde hair gleaming in the firelight. I circle round to face her. I can just make out her pale hands clutched to her midriff, dark tendrils of blood leaking between her fingers. I kneel down next to her, slide an arm under her shoulders and place her head on my lap.

The movement makes something spasm inside her, and she coughs. Her eyes flicker open, uncomprehending. Slowly she looks up at me, her irises forming slim rings of opal. August, she breathes, and smiles slightly. Did you get them out? I nod energetically, my words lost. Well done, she says, well done. She closes her eyes. I stroke her hair and make shushing noises. When it finally occurs to me to check her pulse, I can barely find it, but when I do, it's slow and erratic. She's obviously lost a lot of blood, her system losing pressure through the hole in her stomach. Like a central heating system with a leak. But far more delicate, far more precious.

I keep stroking her hair, and find myself talking to this ineffectual sentry, this reluctant combatant. I tell her how well we did, how amazing it was that we got all of the children - and all of the nuns - out without so much as a scratch. I tell her how promising the future is looking, how soon dawn will be with us, playing her rosy fingers into the eastern sky, how soon the ash in the atmosphere will finally fall, delivering us into a bright new world where we can re-imagine what we once had. Where we can create an honest, caring and loving society. A society in which people are no longer afraid. A society in which people come together to sort out their problems, much as we've done tonight.

It's a bright vision, and one I had no idea I actually harboured, but there it is. Spelt out clearly to this dying woman. This woman I knew only by sight. It occurs to me that we could perhaps have been friends, and I wonder why we weren't. Was it my own lack of fellow feeling, or her shyness? We'll never know. It's too late. Way too late. Over the next few minutes she coughs several more times, but doesn't grace me with another glimpse of her opal eyes. With one hand smoothing her hair and the other pressed into her neck I feel her slipping away. There's a final, almost unnoticed breath - a slow susurration - and then she's gone.

And that's when the smell of the ash bears down upon me. The wet, drifted ash beneath my knees, the dark soot billowing above, the smell of so much that's been lost. So much that has slipped in silence by.

And that's when the tears come, leaking down my cheeks. I didn't even know Angela, but that makes her loss so much more unforgivable. I should have done better. I should have befriended her long ago, looked after her, not lost her out here in this wide and dusty square. My own inadequacies pour down upon me, adding guilt to this sorrow. This sorrow for someone I didn't know.

When my tears have subsided I pull Angela on to me. Slowly I worm my shoulder into her belly, feeling the slick blood brush my face. I loop my arms around the back of her legs and lurch up to my feet. She's a mere slip of a woman, but is now a dead weight. It takes all I've got to stand with her in a fireman's hold. The white dots of earlier begin to dance across my vision as I start to shuffle forward. The enormous effort is actually a welcome distraction from my thoughts.

As I stagger from the square, I realise that this woman is my cross, my albatross. Does that make where I'm heading my home port or my Golgotha? Or both? My thoughts bump along like this, speculative and inconsequential. And now thankfully free of emotion. As I approach the barricade I call out. Several ghosts clamber over and help me drag Angela's body back over. As we lay her on the far side, a small group gathers around me. We all stand and stare down in silence at this woman who was so recently alive. I feel the torrent of grief gathering itself again, ready to fall, and I wonder if I can take it, if it won't send me shrieking and spinning across the square, all sanity shed. Then there's a hand in mine, a fragile body pressed up against me. And I turn and cry into Rosa's shoulder.

I wake sometime the next day to grey light and a white, pillowed duvet. Joe's lying next to me, but I feign sleep and watch him sit up on the edge of the bed. His movement and breathing are both laboured, but he still looks lean and strong, his long body still that swarthy, nutty brown, as if he were out in the sun just yesterday. Which is in marked contrast to most of us. If I were younger, less haggard, more elfin, I might get away with describing my own skin as porcelain. Sadly, pasty is a more appropriate adjective.

Joe stands and makes his way around the edge of the bed, limping with each step. He's just wearing his undershorts, and from this angle I can't see his leg, but the way he's moving suggests that this injury isn't something he's going to be able to shake off. I remember reading something about bits of fabric getting punched into gunshot wounds from clothing. If they aren't located and removed, these tiny bits of fabric rot, causing major infection and possibly even death. The thought makes me feel queasy. I've never been much good with gore or gunk, or too much internal stuff. Smear tests have always been one of my worst nightmares. Well, at least we don't have to get those done any more. The collapse of civilisation does have some advantages. Death before discomfort.

When he's made his way into the kitchen, I pull the duvet down a little. I'm wearing my warmest nightdress: a full-length gown of white terrycloth, something my grandmother might have owned. The thing is, I don't remember having put it on the night before, and the idea of Rosa or Joe helping me on with it, actually dressing me, is mortifying. Having to feed my scrawny limbs and torso into this most unflattering of garments is the sort of thing you have to do for people in nursing homes. It would have been better if I'd died out there on the square. And then I remember that some people actually did. Angela. I push her memory aside, terrified that I'll start weeping once again. Chastened, and with a much better grip on reality, I sit up. My head swims, and my whole body throbs. I feel as if I've played a rugby match, or been hit by a car. I take several deep breaths, and squint into the grey light. Here goes.

I lever myself up and lurch round into the kitchen, still squinting and running a hand through my hair as if I've just woken up. Joe's sitting there, sprawled out on a chair, wearing a thick plaid shirt. Thankfully he's already put the coffee on. Good man.

How are you feeling, he asks. It's a kind question, I know, but it feels like we're adopting domestic roles already. The critical husband, the slatternly wife. Not bad, I say, scratching my hip, just like I've been run over. And you? I sit at the table, propping my head up in my hands and widening my eyes at him. Make sure you look like you're taking an interest - taking an interest in itself isn't enough. Not too bad, he says, hauling his injured leg towards him with both hands, as if it's a piece of wood. Although I may have to get this looked at.

Peering at his leg, I realise that it's not as bad as it could have been. I was dreading seeing something like an exploded vulva, but the injury is just a single red hole - fairly neat to be fair. The tissue around it has a reddish hue, however, and his thigh does seem swollen. I reckon you're right, I say. It looks like you really took one for the team there. Joe attempts to smile, but it's more of a grimace. Then I remember Angela. I'm going to keep my mouth shut for a while.

So I pour the coffee, get dressed and head out, determined to put in some aftercare for the rest of my team, perhaps to make up for the unforgivable neglect I showed last night. First up is Nick. He lives in a small apartment at the top of our block, right over in one corner. I have to knock several times before he responds. When he eventually opens the door, he's dressed just as I imagined: T-shirt, boxer shorts and sandals. He runs one hand though his dark, greasy hair. I realise that if he could actually string a couple of words together, he'd be an attractive man. This revelation is curtailed by the sight of his left arm, swathed in a dirty bandage. How are you, I ask. He nods by way of reply. Thanks for last night, I say. There's no way I would have got through that door without you. What happened?

He shrugs, that's what happens when you try to use your arm as a shield, he says, smiling weakly and looking straight at me for once. And that's when I realise that there might be more to Nick than meets the eye. It's obvious that there's a dry sense of humour there somewhere, but he's so closed off that you never see it. It's as if he's got some secret hurt that he wraps himself around like someone sheltering a small child. Sounds like you need stitches, I say. He nods. I head downstairs.

Predictably enough, Filippa's in her cubbyhole, staring at an old magazine about trains. When she sees me she drops it quickly, as if it were something to be ashamed of. How are you, I ask. She looks suddenly bewildered, perplexed by my inquiry into her well-being. Fine, she says. Thank you. But, August, what if... what if I killed a man last night? I step into her cubbyhole and lay a hand on her shoulder. Her face looks puffed and oily in the weak yellow light, like a pastry that's been left out too long. It's okay if you did, I say. Those men... well, you saw what they were trying to do. They were trying to kill a whole load of innocent children, and we couldn't have that, could we? Don't you worry, I say, smiling complicitly. Last night, we were the good guys. This seems to mollify her somewhat, so I pat her shoulder and step out into the square.

I'm glad - if somewhat surprised - to find the bonfire still burning from the night before. Mr Moretti stands by it, wearing a gilet and flat cap, tossing odd bits of wood in, his attention consumed by the flames. I make my way over to him, rubbing my hands. It's much colder than the night before, and the heat from the fire is welcome. I'd say that Mr Moretti looks hale and hearty, but he answers my questions in monosyllables, no doubt scared to start constructing sentences for fear that they'll be cut off by his cough. And sure enough, a racking, hacking cough shakes him every minute or so.

Hilda approaches the fire and gives me a cursory nod. She's supplemented her summer jumpers with a dark blue coat, has her mousy hair tied back close to her head, and still carries a rifle over one arm. How are you, I ask? Fine she says. All of the children and nuns have been allocated rooms in the end block, she adds, nodding over the top of the fire to the block she's talking about. They're all fine, but we need more bedding, warm clothes, mattresses. All that kind of thing. Of course, another generator would be good too, to keep that block heated. Thank you, I say, that's amazing. How about medical supplies, I say - do we have anything for wound care, any antibiotics? We've got plasters and bandages, she says, and that's about it. As for drugs, no chance. And then she's off, striding across the square, her sense of purpose plain for all to see. Thank God she's with us.

Then, on the far side of the fire, near one of the barricades, what I'd assumed was a bundle of old clothes transforms itself into Angela's body. Thankfully, someone's put a hat on her head, and she's facing away from me. What are we going to do with her, I ask, aghast. Bury her, says Mr Moretti, and coughs. No shit Sherlock, I think. But where, I ask. He shrugs. Right here in the square, I reckon. Why not? Then she can be at home, where she belongs. His voice breaks as he's saying this: Angela's death has affected other people, not just me. And I always thought of Mr Moretti as so stoical. We can take up some of the cobblestones in one of the corners, he says, and dig down. I'll go and get my spade in a minute. A few of us can take it in turns to dig. It won't be easy, but, well, she deserves a proper resting place.

Bene, I say. I grasp his shoulder and head over, past Angela's body, to the barricade. I daren't look down at her. I simply can't face another emotional episode right now. Thankfully Mr Moretti's on the ball: burying her is one less thing I have to think about. And that's just as well, as it might be more than I can take. I dismiss Angela from my mind, clamber over the barrier and head out into the streets.

Although I may be ineffective, and although I may have a casual disregard for my fellow human beings, there are some things that I've made it my business to know. Like where Cornelius lives, for example. I've never been to his place, but I know where it is. And let me tell you, following a man as shrewd as Cornelius isn't easy.

Of course, there is the possibility that he has multiple addresses, and that could be a problem. Someone in his position stands to make enemies, so prudence on his part is essential. As, no doubt, are boltholes. But for now I head to the address I know about. It's not the sort of place you'd think - not the smart, swanky suburb you'd expect. For a start, his block is on the outskirts of town, plus it's low-rise and utilitarian. Defunct telephone wires and other cables explode from its weathered front like ascetic teachings being spouted from a prophet's face.

The block's door is ajar, and I know this can't be a good sign. Pushing the door open reveals an entranceway that's empty - thank God - but also shrouded in an almost nocturnal gloom. I ease my way inside and head up two flights of stairs, looking ahead of me, alert to any signs of life. The atmosphere in the stairwell is damp and unpleasant; the steps creak and swathes of paint and plaster crackle dully beneath my feet, leaving white, leprous patches from where they've fallen. Soon I'm where I need to be, standing outside his door. Thankfully - if unsurprisingly - there's no one else around. I knock, and wait.

Come in, says a weak voice from within, it's open. For a moment I wonder if I've got the wrong room - it certainly doesn't sound like Cornelius - but I push the door open anyway. A single figure sits in a chair, staring out of the window, wrapped in some kind of dun-coloured throw. Again, I think I've got the wrong room, but then again Cornelius's large, seamed head is unmistakable.

Cornelius, I say, it's me - August. I know, I know, he replies. Come in and close the door. Let's keep the warm air in, shall we? I do as he says and edge my way into his flat: it's a single room, sparsely furnished, a simple kitchenette to my left and a bedraggled bed tucked in alongside the wall on the right. This isn't the sort of place I'd expected the elegant and energetic servitore I've dealt with so many times to inhabit.

Come in, he says again, take a seat. I move forward slowly, and perch on the edge of a simple wooden chair alongside him. Before us, diaphanous curtains hang like fishing nets set out to dry. Monochrome light pours through them, gilding Cornelius's features with lines of silver. His face still has the quality of an old rugby ball, the ones that used to be made from pigs' bladders, but it's a little more crumpled now, as if some of the air's been let out. The purple fingers of a bruise create an exotic halo around his right eye. He stares past me into the light.

Are you okay, I ask. Absolutely fine, he replies, nodding and pulling the throw more tightly about him. I just had a slight altercation with one of my clients. It's nothing, as you can see. But it has - I must confess - knocked me out of my stride.

I feel myself frowning. Is there anything I can do for you, I ask. Cornelius shakes his head. No, nothing at all my dear. Nothing at all. I'm absolutely fine. Just going through one of my periodic bouts of introspection.

Since I don't really know what to say to this, I dive in. Last night there was something of a fracas, I find myself saying, perhaps unconsciously adopting Cornelius's circuitous way of approaching things. There were these thugs from Monte Fiori. They came to the town and started fires.

Oh yes, says Cornelius, nodding again. I saw the smoke and the flames. Well, I continue, they tried to set the convent alight, with all the kids inside. Luckily we managed to stop them and got all of the kids out unscathed. But we've suffered a few injuries, and we're having to put the kids up in our square. So - in an ideal world - we could really use some medical supplies - including anti-biotics - and as many blankets, pillows and other clothes as you can get your hands on. I know it's a lot to ask.

Cornelius turns the leather expanse of his face towards me. How did you get on with the rat poison, he asks. I give him a quizzical look. Yes, fine, I say. All quiet on the rodent front. He kicks his head back a little and utters an ambiguous, hah! Then he's back to staring out of the window again. It's a wonder they eat that poison at all, he adds, seeing what a livid colour it is. I suppose it stops people eating it by mistake.

Yes, I reply, drawing the word out for as long as I can. Hopefully this will make him realise I've got more pressing matters to deal with than giving him feedback. There are thirty-six kids, I say. Most are between about five and twelve years old. I guess people stopped having babies when they saw what a sorry state the world was in.

Or, says Cornelius, turning a bright eye on me, the would-be parents were already dead. I shrug. Could be. I've never really thought about it like that.

It's an even mix between boys and girls, I add, if that helps. I know it's a lot to ask. And I know it's short notice. And, as they say, winter's coming. So, anything you could get would be... you know...

My words die off as Cornelius turns his unflinching gaze on me. It must be how mariners felt centuries ago when caught in the beam from the Lighthouse of Alexandria: awed and forced to look away at the same time. And how, my dear August, were you hoping to pay me for such a large amount of goods? With another bag of vegetables?

I sit back, caught off guard, and take a deep breath. Please, Cornelius, I say, trying to sound as pathetic as possible without completely letting go of my self-esteem. Two of us are injured, and they could well die if they don't get those injuries seen too. And the kids - well, at this rate, a lot of them won't make it through. They've only got the clothes on their backs. Winter will take them.

Have you considered, he asks, how you're going to feed so many, before you took them in? I shake my head like a student who's been picked on by the teacher for not paying attention. No, I say, I've got no idea. But we couldn't just let them burn to death, could we? I feel my sense of anger and injustice returning. What would you have done in a similar situation?

Me? I'd have let them burn, says Cornelius, his eyes boring into mine. I'm forced to look away. What's out there for them anyway, he asks. I don't say that to be unkind, August. But if there's no sense of hope... nothing to look forward to... what are we doing? Going through the motions, that's what. Treading water, desperately trying to keep ourselves from going under. Is that any way to live? He shrugs and returns his gaze to the curtains.

I shake my head. That may be so, I say, but right now I've got bigger problems to worry about. So I'll go along with the Hippocratic oath for a bit, if that's all right with you. I know it's a lot to ask, and I know a bag of vegetables isn't going to cut it. Still, I add, taking a deep breath, I'm sure we can come to some kind of arrangement. Reaching out, I place a hand on his knee and smile weakly.

Cornelius looks at my hand as if it's a tarantula. Then he looks at me and smiles. Hah, he says, amusement spreading over his crumpled features. My dear girl, I know you've been waiting to throw yourself at me for years. And while I'm flattered - of course - I couldn't possibly accept. Besides the fact that I decided when all this started never to take payment in kind - one must have some morals, after all - I'm afraid that it's really out of the question.

I withdraw my hand slowly, feeling both chastened and foolish, like a lovesick teenager who's made an inappropriate pass at a much older man and been - quite rightly - rebuffed.

There's simply no way, continues Cornelius, staring back out of the window and holding forth, that I could fulfil even a fraction of your request. And to take such a payment in advance would be taking advantage in a most... how would you say? A most scurvy fashion. Besides, he says, turning his watery eyes back on me, can't you see? Even if I'd wanted to, there would be no way I could take up your kind offer. I'm all used up.

For the first time, I realise how frail Cornelius looks. It's as if he's aged ten years overnight. It wasn't the punch that did it, if that's what you're thinking, he says, smearing one hand across his eye and looking to the heavens. That's par for the course. It's just that I feel my energies fading. It's finally got to me - all of this - he adds, waving a hand at the curtains before him. The ash, the grey skies, the death. Too much, I'm afraid. Did you ever read *The Lord of the Rings*?

I shake my head. Well, he says with a shrug, the elves, when they found themselves getting a bit long in the tooth, a bit disenfranchised with life, headed off into the West. The Western Isles or whatever. And I think that I'm going to do the same. But for us it's south, isn't it? I'm going to head south and see what happens. The promise of warmer climes. Who'd have thought it, eh, even a few years before? With global warming, everyone thought we'd be heading away from the equator, not towards it. But still, if nothing else, I suppose that shows us how unpredictable life is.

I sigh and feel myself sagging, the air and

energy leaving me in tandem. So is that what I've done for these children, I ask, and perhaps Joe and Nick too - simply provided them with a slow, lingering death? Don't worry, says Cornelius, reaching a hand out and patting my knee. And in that gesture, I see how platonic his attitude towards me is, and how foolish I was to think that it could ever have been otherwise. Don't worry, I won't let you go empty-handed. Here, he says, reaching into one of the pockets in his tweed jacket and pulling out a small address book. This is my little black book. You won't find the names of any gigolos or puttanas, more's the pity. What you will find are the names of some of my contacts. I've even added - just in case my memory should fail me one day - what they can supply. It should be fairly up to date. If they died, I crossed them out, as far as I'm aware. And as for a doctor, look up old Zambucci: somewhat eccentric now, but used to be a doctor - as far as I'm aware., Zambucci's your best bet - and better than nothing.

I take the book, put it in my bag and find myself welling up. Thank you, I say, placing a hand on his shoulder, and good luck. I show myself out. The last I see of Cornelius is him sitting by the window, staring into the diffuse white light of the curtains. Maybe that's how heaven looks, when you get up close.

On my way back, I pass through the main square.

Unfortunately, the convent's still smouldering, giving off plumes of charcoal-coloured smoke. It's too risky to look inside right now, and besides, I don't know what I'd find. The roof's totally collapsed, the shutters have fallen in and the walls are blackened. There's not much chance of anything inside surviving in any passable state, but at least no other buildings have been set alight. Small mercies and all that.

As I'm about to leave, I notice a dog nosing around a couple of the bodies. It's medium-sized, with perky ears and a curly tale. I try to coax it over, but it just stares at me with its lively eyes, nose testing the air. I wonder if this was once someone's pet, but it probably wasn't. A whole new generation of dogs have grown up since the impact, and this one looks like one of those: mixed breed, not so big that it'll need a lot of feeding, not so small that it'll get easily picked on. I don't know if I've seen this dog before, but it does look familiar. I always wondered about trying to befriend a dog, to get it to come home with me. Those empty, lonely years would have been so much easier to bear. But now it seems as if it's too late. I've managed to surround myself with more people than I'd ever thought possible, and I can't help but wonder at my motives.

Reluctantly, I leave the dog. I'd love to take it home, but it just regards me with disinterested suspicion. It seems far more interested in the bodies, and if one of the eraserheads provides it with a meal, fair enough. At least in death they'll have done something useful. As I make my way out of the main square, I feel Cornelius's pessimism start to work its way under my skin. I feel like I'm leaving things behind: first him, now this dog. I know that's probably just fatigue talking, but suddenly I feel overwhelmed. I can see now why he's ready to leave. Not only have I got to try to keep all of these children alive, I've got to give them something to live for. No doubt the nuns have plied them with countless draughts of Christianity, but surely that vintage has been corked and gone sour by now. For the kids at least, I need to come up with something. Us adults may be past it, but surely new bottles deserve new wine.

Strangely enough, the next day does bring hope. Maybe it's true what they say, that the night's always darkest before the dawn. Yesterday I located Dr Zambucci. He'll be coming over shortly to tend to our injured. Waiting, I stand on my minuscule balcony, coat on and a cup of coffee clutched between gloved hands. Below me, the children rush back and forth across the square. They're playing, as children should. Against the ash-grey ground they look like stick figures in a Lowry painting. If they're having this much fun just playing on the sand pile, lobbing the odd rock and chasing each other, just imagine how much fun they're going to have when it snows!

The fact that the kids are now all housed in different apartments means that the nuns have lost some of their grip on them, which perhaps isn't a bad thing. The result is this: they're running free and no doubt enjoying some much-needed time outside. Watching their movements, though, it occurs to me that they haven't been set loose completely. One of the side effects of the barricades is that we've inadvertently created the world's biggest playpen. Despite the threat from the eraserheads having gone, there's usually an armed sentry about. It's as if, without being told, the sentries have simply carried on with their roles, out of a sense of duty or routine we'll probably never know. I do know that Filippa takes every opportunity she can to sling her rifle over her shoulder and head outside. There's no set rota, as far as I'm aware, but there's always someone to shoo the kids off the barricades if they get too bold.

Also, Angela's been buried. Mr Moretti's seen to that. She's been laid to rest not far from the sand pile. I can't quite see her headstone from my balcony, as this side of the square oddly slopes back a bit, but she's there, with a paving slab as a gravestone. The slab leans back against the wall of the building, like the tomb of some local worthy buried inside a medieval church.

It's blank at the moment, but as soon as we find someone with the necessary skills, we'll get it engraved. I'm sure that time will come. Her name will live on: Angela, the first fallen of the new republic.

Sadly, it's not all plain sailing. Joe's condition has deteriorated a lot. He's lying in bed now, morose and staring at the ceiling, no doubt pondering what's to come. A knock at the door breaks my reverie, drags me back inside. It's Rosa, looking bulky beneath multiple coats. I get a brief ciao as she bustles inside, eyes shining with purpose. Then she's shedding layers, piling them up on one of my chairs and heading into the bedroom, drawing a chair up next to Joe's prostrate figure, taking his hand in hers and telling him that it's going to be okay. She leers down at him with the face of a saint, and I realise that her canonisation is continuing apace without my help. Weirdly, some of these things I've set in motion seem to be continuing automatically. Sadly I don't get long to admire my handiwork: as soon as she spots me lounging in the doorway, her face becomes hatchet-like. Go and put some water on to boil, August, and fetch as many clean towels as you have. Hold on to your hats, everybody, Florence Nightingale has just entered the building.

I do as she says and return to the balcony, leaving Joe in Rosa's saintly clutches. The poor man probably doesn't know what's causing him more pain: the bullet in his leg or her ministrations. I watch the running children somewhat abstractedly. The time of our appointment with Dr Zambucci comes and goes. I start to have misgivings, and my mind wanders back to yesterday afternoon. Were my instructions clear enough? I think so, but it's hard to know when you're making an appointment by writing post-it notes that are hauled up to a flat in a bucket lowered on a piece of string. I didn't get to see Dr Zambucci, although his scrawled responses seemed friendly enough. All I can really recall was peering upwards at this tower-like projection on the top of the building from which the bucket descended. I couldn't help wondering whether the doctor had always lived there, or whether he'd moved in more recently, choosing the spot as it resembles the eyrie of some mad scientist.

Then the door goes again. It's Nick. He shuffles in wordlessly. I make a couple of half-arsed but cheerful remarks, and get him to sit in a chair in the lounge, as if it's some temporary waiting room. I can't help but notice that the bloodstains on his bandaged arm seem to have grown overnight. When I return to the balcony, my anxiety level ratchets up a notch. Where the hell's the doctor? He's obviously eccentric, as Cornelius said, but I thought doctors were meant to keep appointments? Isn't that part of the Hippocratic oath too? Thou shalt not be late. Fat chance.

Then I see some commotion on one of the barricades, the one that Angela manned so recently. A sentry - I can't see who it is from here - is helping someone up and over its slatted apex. The figure seems to be having some trouble, but probably because it's wearing what appears to be a long black dress or gown. It's also wearing a large top hat, and its face seems oddly elongated. When the figure reaches the floor, it proceeds directly towards us, black skirts swishing. Initially, the children scatter at the sight of this apparition with the face of a crow, but soon enough curiosity gets the better of them. By the time the figure gets to our block, a whole crowd of whooping children follow in its wake.

I open the door and step out into the unlit hallway. The figure that emerges from the darkness before me is like something out of a horror movie. Skirts swish and ripple from its corsetted torso; round glass eye-panes glint with reflected light; and the hooked nose of the plague doctor's mask hangs with savage intent.

Doctor Zambucci, I ask. The figure nods. What have I done, I wonder, as I motion this tall, medieval figure into my flat. It feels wrong, all kinds of wrong, as if I'm ushering the angel of death into our company. As soon as the doctor's inside, he pulls off the giant top hat, lays it purposefully on the table and then removes the mask. The face that's revealed is rounder and more delicate than I'd expected, the eyes more sparkling and intelligent, the cascades of grey hair longer and more grizzled. I'm sorry, I say, taken aback. I was expecting a... I shake my head. It doesn't matter, I add, feeling strangely reassured. I hate to admit to myself that I was expecting a man, but there it is. It's good to know that patriarchy's alive and well, even in our heads.

Apologies for the mask, says the doctor. I started wearing it during the Covid era for house calls, just for fun. And you know how it is: old habits die hard. So this is one of your patients, she asks, indicating Nick. And the other is... I point in through the open door of my bedroom. Rosa's still clutching Joe's hand, but is transfixed by our visitor.

Okay, says the doctor. We'll start easy and work our way up, I think. She smiles at Nick, who seems oddly reassured by her presence. She lays her leather satchel on my table and flips it open to reveal a fearsome array of stainless steel instruments: glinting scalpels, scissors and forceps. Let's get going, shall we? If you can remove this young man's bandage, we'll have him sown up in no time. As I start unravelling the bloodied bandage from Nick's wrist, my stomach dry heaves. I'm no good with blood and other human fluids. That's why I asked Rosa to come over. Still, with her attached to Joe, there's nothing I can do but comply. I'm just glad I haven't eaten breakfast.

The doctor's as good as her word. Within fifteen minutes the two horrific cuts on Nick's arms have been thoroughly cleaned and stitched up. His arm looks like something Frankenstein slapped on his monster, but it'll certainly give him a talking point in years to come. If he ever needs to impress a girl, that'll be a good starter for ten. Doctor Zambucci packs him off with a set of out-of-date antibiotics and a smile, and then we turn our attention to the main event: Long John Joe and his skewered leg.

The doctor's appearance really does belie her bedside manner. You couldn't want someone more sympathetic or caring. Before she even looks at the wound, she sits on the edge of the bed and engages Joe in conversation, asking him about what gun he thinks fired the shot.

Only when she's let Joe have his say does she actually look at his leg. She scours her hands with a disinfectant wipe and dons a pair of latex gloves. And then she's peering into the red bore-hole in Joe's leg, pulling the surface skin taught to get a better view, and eventually taking out a small torch and peering into the wound. Joe's grimacing already.

It occurs to me that this is what I've done for him. He was quite content in his cave, but no:

I drag him back into society where he receives what could be a life-threatening injury. Medical care isn't like it used to be. Now people die of things like appendicitis all the time. I find myself swallowing hard, overcome by a sudden stab of trepidation. What if he doesn't make it?

I'm sure I'm being melodramatic: this mounting sense of hysteria has no doubt been brought on by the presence of suffering, and my mind isn't helping by imagining some of the brutal outcomes. I see, in one particularly unhelpful mental image, Joe's gravestone next to Angela's out in the square. What's happened to me? I used to be quite content on my own, but it's as if Rosa's opened a Pandora's box of emotions that had lain quietly inside me for so long. Ever since she appeared as my mother, things have grown steadily more difficult. And now I seem to be dragging other people into my orbit, and making them suffer too. Exhibit one: this tall, bearded man lying on my bed, jaw clenched with the promise of the agony to come.

Okay, says Dr Zambucci, we're going to have a look in there and see if we can't fish that bullet out. Hold on. She returns with her bag of instruments and a smile. This may, she says, sitting back on the bed and coughing into her shoulder, hurt a little. But I'm sure you knew that already. I'll be as quick as I can, but I've got to get that bullet out and anything else that might be in there.

Luckily it's not too near to bone, and it's missed your major blood vessels and nerves, which is a bonus. Here we go.

Oh, she adds, I almost forgot. Do you fancy a slug before we continue? She pulls a small bottle of Metaxa out of her hip pocket, the yellow and blue label brightening the room. He nods and she hands him the bottle; he takes a swig and subsides into the pillows. Keep it, she says, giving Joe a wink, I've got plenty more at home. Then she takes a slim metal probe from her case. I watch in horrid fascination as it descends into his wound.

Suddenly I find myself talking. Shouldn't you have given him something stronger, I ask, my voice sounding high and reedy. Couldn't you chloroform him or something? The doctor looks up at me and smiles, but her hand doesn't waver a millimetre. No, she says, that only works in the movies. Besides, it's dangerous. Without general anaesthetic, brandy's the best option we have. Here we go.

Less than a second later her hand stops and Joe sucks hard at his own lips, his face piqued with pain. Well, there it is, says the doctor, as if to herself. It should be simple enough. She pulls the probe out, takes a pair of forceps out of her bag and re-enters the wound. Immediately, Joe tenses, muscles twitching. Grab his leg, would you, asks the doctor. I sit by Joe's foot and mutely clamp my hands around his ankle.

Okay, she breathes, here we go again. She delves downwards, inadvertently touching the sides of the wound as she searches once again for the bullet. Joe's head thrashes from side to side. Rosa tightens her hands round his, muttering soothing phrases under her breath. When the doctor pulls the forceps from the wound, they're clutching a bloodied, crumpled piece of metal.

Look at that, says the doctor, holding the bullet up to the dismal light. You must be made of stern stuff. It's actually collapsed as it's gone into your leg.

This information doesn't seem to do Joe much good. Now for the fun part, she says. We've just got to see if there's anything else in there. Hold on young man. With that, the forceps disappear back into the wound. As she searches deep inside Joe's leg, he jerks and thrashes. It's all we can do to stop him kicking the doctor. Pulling the bullet out was the easy part. Seconds pass and turn into minutes, punctuated by Joe's gasps. The minutes begin to mount up, and Joe's agony doesn't seem to be subsiding. Just as I think that he won't be able to take much more, the doctor pulls what looks like a piece of his own flesh from the depths of the wound. There we go, she says, smiling with obvious relief, a small piece of your trousers. By now Joe's slicked with sweat, tendons protruding through his thin brown skin.

From another of her pockets the doctor pulls a small bottle of yellow liquid. Iodine, she says, grinning at me. The old ways are often the best. Now this may hurt some more, she says to Joe, patting his leg, but it's all for the best. We're almost there. Do you mind, he asks, his voice little more than a whisper, if I have another shot before we carry on? Be my guest, says the doctor. Be my guest. Joe pulls his hand free from Rosa's grip and takes several mouthfuls brandy. I watch as his tendoned neck and gullet drag the liquid downwards. He wipes his mouth with the back of his hand and passes the bottle to Rosa. Much better, he mutters, a gleam returning to his eye. Go on doctor, do your worst.

And she does. She pours a thin stream of iodine into the wound, and it may as well be liquid fire from the way Joe bucks and writhes. Soon the liquid fills the hole and pools at the top. Then she's pressing the two sides of the wound together, causing the iodine to spill down the side of Joe's leg in fingers of the deepest, darkest yellow.

August, she says, and at first I don't respond, so mesmerised am I by this whole awful procedure. She hands me a pair of latex gloves. Hold the two sides of the wound together, would you, so I can stitch them? I pull the gloves on with some difficulty, struggling to get my fingers in place, stretching the palms and snapping the cuffs against my wrists. Eventually I'm there, pushing at the swollen flesh of Joe's ruptured leg, my breath held and my heart beating in my ears. I'd have made a horrible nurse. Watching the needle pierce Joe's skin and then emerge on the other side - a slim silver worm dragging its own black guts behind it - makes me feel suddenly sick. I look away and concentrate on maintaining an even pressure through my fingertips.

To her credit, it doesn't take Dr Zambucci long. Thank you, August, I hear her say. Her voice sounds as if it's coming from the next room. Then she taps Joe's leg lightly, as if sending a taxi on its way. When I dare to look at him, it seems that Joe's whole body has taken on the colour of the iodine. He stares at the ceiling, eyes glazed, a jaundiced casualty.

He's not the only one to be affected. Rosa's clutching his hands as if he's about to get dragged overboard, and I'm shaking, awash with adrenaline. Dr Zambucci snaps her gloves off, stands and runs a hand through her spray of grey hair. There you go, she says. It couldn't have gone much better. Thanks for your help. I follow her out of the room, muttering my thanks. She hands me a pack of her out-of-date antibiotics, does up her bag and starts fastening her mask back into place. Just so you're aware, she says, he may never walk quite the same again. The wound was deep. He may need a cane or a helping hand at times, but it should heal up well enough. Staring into the giant crow's eyes, I wonder if any of us will ever be the same again.

We spend the afternoon baking. I send Rosa back to her block and she returns with eggs, flour and butter, a small fortune's worth of ingredients. As I can't focus, we make madeleines, with her taking charge. Despite Rosa's instructions and the discrete, methodical steps - the weighing of ingredients, the grating of lemons, the stirring of the mixture - I feel anxiety seething through me. I try not to, but every few minutes I peer in at Joe. He wrestles with a fitful sleep, his corded neck and limbs contrasting with the smooth, voluminous surfaces of the pillows and duvet.

  Each time I'm certain he's still breathing, I feel a sense of relief, as if I've been given a shot of serotonin. Sadly, the effect doesn't last long. Several minutes later I'm fretting even more badly than before, until I have to look in on him again. To her credit, Rosa notices my mounting distress, and takes my hands in hers. Looking into her calm, grey eyes is comforting. He'll be okay, she says. He's strong. He just has to rest. She seems to implicitly understand my suddenly desperate affection for Joe even better than I do myself. In this world of things that fall so easily away, it seems more important than ever to hold on to what we've got.

While the madeleines are baking, we make coffee and stand out on the balcony. A number of kids are still rushing round the square mimicking Brownian motion. Maybe they're just trying to stay warm. It's obvious, even from up here, that their clothes aren't going to cut it when winter really sets in. I can hear them shrieking on the sand pile, but can't see them as it's just beyond Angela's grave. I shake my head. They certainly love that pile of sand, I say. And then it hits me like an epiphany. Mama! I say, turning and grasping a surprised Rosa by the shoulders. This time she really thinks I've flipped - you can see the sudden fear in her eyes. Mama! Your block bought the sand, right? And there's loads left. Hilda ordered it, didn't she? And she wouldn't have got the amounts wrong, would she? There'd be enough bags for sand, and vice versa, right?

It's a Eureka moment, as cheesy as the apple hitting Newton on the head. But no less impressive - for me at least. Rosa nods slowly. She's either being polite or simply agreeing with me so as not to provoke me any further. Don't you see, I ask. Where there's sand, there must be sandbags! Let's go and speak to Hilda. Quickly, before the madeleines burn! Bene, she says, nodding as we don our coats and hurry out of the door. She still doesn't get it, but that's okay.

Less than an hour later we're both sitting in front of my block. A queue of children stretches from the desk in front of us halfway across the square. On the desk is a notebook, a plate of chopped up madeleines and a pile of unused hessian sacks.

Okay, children, I say. Step forward - one at a time. Sacks first, then a slice of cake. These sacks, I add, holding one up for all to see, are all the rage in Milano right now. They're wearing them as coats, but you can use them as an extra blanket when you go to sleep as well. I give them all a big smile that I hope isn't too unhinged, and get the first kid to step forward. It's Massimo, our little chap with the cloth cap. I hold the sack up to his small body, grab our pair of evil-looking dressmaking scissors from the desk and get to work. A hole for his head in the base of the bag, and two smaller ones either side for his arms. As it's my first attempt, my cutting could be neater, but it'll do. I help him on with it, and he disappears entirely. When we finally get his head to pop out, he's still wearing his hat, and he's grinning. I get him to stick his arms out, then turn him round to display him to the rest of the kids. Most of them clap politely; a few of them cheer; and one of them even wolf whistles. Then I give him a piece of madeleine and send him running off, rectangular and cackling like SpongeBob SquarePants.

I soon get my hand in and the process speeds up. Rosa takes the kids' names and writes them in the notebook, just so we know who's been issued a sack. Then I cut the holes, trying to judge each as best as I can against the size of the child, and then we give them a piece of madeleine and pack them off. It takes us less than half-an-hour to get through them all, which is pretty impressive. A lot of the kids I actually recognise from our outings, and what's even more gratifying is that a lot of them recognise us and smile. Cara, the older girl, brings up the rear. She's wearing a long dark coat and - I notice - a small silver crucifix at her throat. She's a young woman now and no mistake. After hugging Rosa and swapping a few words with her, she takes a sack, but folds it neatly and puts it in her pocket. For my bed, she says, and then strolls away, casting a watchful eye over the younger children.

She's a good girl, that one, says Rosa. Just what we need around here. Someone from the next generation who's sensible. I slump back in my chair and thrum my fingers on the greatly diminished stack of sacks. Absolutely, I say. But I do feel for her. There are no other kids of her age around here. When they get older, says Rosa, it will all even out. And who knows what we'll be able to do when the ash clears?

The sky above us is a dull, oppressive grey, heavy with snow. I can feel my mood souring by the second. True, I say, who knows. We've just got to keep the kids alive until it actually does. And then I remember Joe. I feel almost guilty for having forgotten about him for so long. Come on, I add, let's get all of this cleared away and go and check on Prince Charming.

He hasn't missed us. To my relief, he's sleeping soundly, but a sheen of sweat covers his face and forearms. I actually shut the door to the bedroom and step out on to the balcony with Rosa. The kids are still running around. Incredible, I say - look at them! The energy of youth, Rosa says, taking my arm. The energy. We must look after them well, August. We must. It's our duty.

I smile. Thank God for Saint Rosa. Looking out over the square, it seems as if their new attire has made the kids more uninhibited. They rush around in their sacks, lobbing handfuls of wet ash at each other with wild abandon. Where the ash balls hit, they clog the loose weave of the hessian, leaving grey smears. Typical kids, I say, looking to the heavens. Sackcloth and ashes, says Rosa. Sackcloth and ashes.

When he finally wakes, Prince Charming isn't quite so charming any more. This is compounded by the fact that it's the middle of the night, and I've barely got any sleep myself. First he asks for a glass of water, then asks if I've got any alcohol, which I haven't. He necks the rest of the brandy that Dr Zambucci left him, and then falls back into a fitful sleep. Despite the fact that one of his legs is out of action, he still manages to thrash around a fair deal with his three other limbs. I'm surprised by how quickly my overbearing concern for him the day before morphs into annoyance. Still, it's perhaps not surprising. I'm used to getting my beauty sleep, not to being woken every fifteen minutes by a gangly, thrashing man. Again, nursing wouldn't have been my career of choice.

In the morning, Joe's not much better. He peers at me with bleary eyes and licks his dry lips. August, he says, you've got to help me. It's as if someone's stuck a hot poker into my leg. It burns, he says, peering down his body at he leg that pains him. It burns.

Isn't that what you say, I ask, when they flick holy water on you? He narrows his eyes at me. Very funny, he says. But you've got to help me with this. I thought I was pretty tough, but... his voice trails off. I smile and lay a hand on his shoulder. I'd have thought this would be right up your street, I say. A bit of pain and discomfort and all that. Joe retrains his puffy, slit-like eyes on me. It's as if he's got two tiny pillar boxes buried in his face. I'm used to sleeping under canvas and in caves, he says, not getting shot.

Fair enough, I say, patting his chest. But I can feel the insincerity in my voice. I guess I'm annoyed that we didn't have that connection again when he woke up. There's been no acknowledgement of what we've got - what we've been through - just a dull acknowledgement of his pain. Which is unsurprising, I suppose. It's just as if we've skipped several years' worth of niceties in the last forty-eight hours, and now find ourselves well into what should be a new relationship.

Of course, this isn't surprising. These days, children grown up fast, and so do relationships. It's a sign of the times, perhaps, but I'm still annoyed by it. Then I realise that I have - to some extent - belittled the amount of pain that Joe's actually in. This annoys me even further. Oh well, more black marks against my nursing career. Hopefully I'll get fired soon.

What do you want me to do, I ask, knock you out with a baseball bat? End your suffering with a pillow? You heard what the doctor said. There's precious little left in the way of pain management, unless you've got any ideas. Booze, he says, smiling weakly. That's the only idea I've got.

I raise my eyebrows. People have been hunting for booze from the first day this all kicked off, I say. Joe shrugs. Okay, okay, I say. I'll see what I can do. I grab my coat and rucksack and sweep out of the room, banging the door behind me. I leave without saying goodbye, and a few minutes later I'm stalking through the empty streets in dawn's early light, seething with anger. A smile, a hello August, a how are you, August, would have been nice. Anything. Not a, could you go and get me some booze August? I've half a mind to see him off, go for a desultory walk and come back empty-handed just to watch him suffer. But of course I don't. I'm not that callous. Instead I head to Dr Zambucci's. I figure the doctor's an early riser, and I'm right. A couple of post-it notes are exchanged and soon I'm the proud owner of another 20cl bottle of Metaxa. It's very kind of her, but it'll barely last Joe beyond noon.

Foreseeing this eventuality, I was wise enough to pick up my crowbar before leaving the house. I've always found it comforting knowing that it's there by the front door, tucked away behind the broken umbrella. There's something about its worn spike and dual, curved prongs that lends you a sense of security. I'd love someone to lurch out of the shadows and try it on. Images of the blackened steel sinking into the pasty white flesh of some man's skull flit through my mind. When I become more conscious of my train of thought I'm not appalled, but I am surprised. Thinking like some thug isn't my normal modus operandi. Still, I suppose that's what almost getting raped does to you. I know there's going to be emotional fallout from that whole episode, but I can't face thinking about it right now. Instead, I push Marcello's grey, grinning head from my mind and focus on the dead buildings about me.

I'm not sure where I'm heading until I find

myself back on the road above the ravine. Why here? Bigger houses, more likelihood of a drinks cabinet perhaps? Thankfully there are no fires fluting the sky, and the whole episode with the eraserheads feels as if it happened years ago. I suddenly feel tired and old, as if I've experienced a great deal. Continued existence will be a battle, a struggle upstream against the current. Sometimes I feel like kicking my heals up and going with the flow, letting apathy and depression take me where they will. But of course I can't. The realisation that some people need me has come to me somewhat later in life, but it's inescapable.

The villa that the eraserheads torched looks like it's been hit by artillery or a flame-thrower. It's still standing, but it's been gutted by the flames. Above its broken windows soot is smeared like excess mascara. It's a sad sight, and one I'm not keen on investigating further. The first house along from it has already been rifled. I stalk through its shattered depths like Jonah wading through the bowels of the whale, finding nothing but filth. The next few houses are just the same: damp walls, broken furniture and crumpled paper. There's enough to start a fire with, but not much else. I feel like a beachcomber at the end of the universe, stalking through the detritus of a long-dead alien civilisation. And all I'm trying to find is some booze, for God's sake.

In the sixth house, just as my morale has

taken an almost terminal nosedive, I strike it lucky. I think it's because the cabinet looks like an unused panel in the kitchen that it's been overlooked. But the slightest of pushes brings it rolling out, its two wire shelves filled with bottles of brandy, Kahlua, vodka, gin and whisky, many of them nearly full. Whoever lived in this house must have left in a hurry. The fools! I pack my rucksack with as many bottles as I can. Outside I take a quick glance at the front of the villa so as to remember it. As Arnie once said, I'll be back.

I leave Joe with the small bottle of Metaxa, stash the rest in the kitchen and head back out into the square. I'd love to have a sharpener with him, but it's a bit early. A sense of restlessness sloshes through me - I need to be doing something. Kids pass me, running around in their ash-smeared surpluses. At least they've still got them on - well, most have, anyway. I head for the end block where most of the kids are housed. To my surprise the large front door's ajar. I wander into the damp hallway and head up the stairs.

I knock at the first door and step inside. The whole of this flat has been turned into a dormitory. Couches, blow-up mattresses, camp beds and rickety single beds have all been pressed into the service of our troop of urchins. The problem doesn't seem to be the lack of beds - the place is crammed with them. But they're all at odd angles, with little floor space between, and clothes are strewn at random over chairs and furniture. I can't think that the inside of the convent looked like this.

A nun moves through the middle of this chaos, a boat navigating treacherous waters. It's Anna but I don't realise it at first, the habit rendering her nondescript. For her part, she doesn't notice me either. She proceeds between the beds, sweeping imaginary crumbs from the ill-made sheets. Occasionally she'll pick up a small piece of clothing, shake it out, fold it and leave it on the end of a bed. She's got that far-away, vacant look that we usually associate with people suffering from shock.

When I say her name, it takes her a second to react. Eventually she looks up at me and smiles weakly. I thread my way into the room, take her hands and sit with her on the side of a camp bed that looks like it's from World War I. How are you, I ask, looking into the soft confines of her face. She can hardly meet my eyes. Fine, she says, fine. The children are doing well. As you can see, they've got a lot of energy. And I think it will do them good to be elsewhere. Somewhere different. Here.

Her barely concealed suffering is plain to see, and heart-rending. I'm sure, I say. But how are you? Okay, she says, nodding but looking down into her lap. It's then I realise that she's clutching a string of rosary beads, her thumb clicking each bead along with the unconscious accuracy of a doorman counting people into a club. I'm fine, she says. It's just a big change, you understand. When she looks up at me, tears are brimming on her lower lids. Most of us lived in the convent for the majority of our lives, she says. I lived there for almost thirty years. Change can be hard, you know? I clutch her hands and nod. And now, she says, waving a hand to indicate the inside of the flat, it's as if, well, the children don't need us any more. They're free - as they should be. And our purpose has gone. She gives me another weak smile, and this time two tears leak down her cheeks in tandem. But please excuse me August, she says patting my hand. Self-pity is simply a sign of weakness. And I have work to do.

I push down with my forearms, putting some torque through Anna's wrists, keeping her seated. Her eyes flash defiance, but she doesn't complain. Listen, I say. You and your sisters have done an amazing job, and we're all thankful for that. But you're amongst friends here. We all have to work, but we can work together. These children are getting older, and a lot of good people live in this square. I'm sure some of them would help to house the kids, to adopt them, if you will. Think about it. It would take some of the pressure from you and your sisters. And besides, the worst of winter's yet to come. We need to work together to get through it.

Anna nods, even though she's obviously holding her tongue. We'll talk, she says, no doubt meaning her and the other nuns. But still, August, there's one thing that I don't understand. I know we live in difficult times, and I know that the church has enemies, but even so, who would want to hurt innocent children? Her hands clutch at mine and she looks into my face imploringly. It's obvious that she's come up against something outside her ken. The giant rock smacking into the face of the planet she could no doubt label an act of God, but that was impersonal in the misery that it spread. The arson of the eraserheads was specific, personal and inexplicably malevolent. Looking at this nun now, her body bent forward, her palms clammy, you can see that her faith's being tested. And - if I'm not mistaken - her jury's still out. And it occurs to me that faith must take a lot of maintenance, like a bikini line.

I don't know, I say, at a loss for words. These have been testing times. Some people's judgement becomes warped. Things lose their value. It's nihilism, I suppose, or something more than that. And I know it sounds preposterous, but those men were using the fire to get to me - to us, to everyone who lives here. They knew we'd come, and they were right. Still, we won. Of course, no victory is ever free. And that's one of the reasons I came to see you, I say, ploughing on before my own tears start to fall. I'd like to have a service for Angela, the woman who died, in the square, tonight at five. I wondered if you would lead us in prayer. It would mean a lot to everyone.

Anna reaches forward and puts a hand on my shoulder. It would be my pleasure, she says, brightening. If it weren't for you, we'd no longer be amongst the living. I smile back at her. Spread the word, and I'll see you at five. I leave her there, sitting on a camp bed, somewhat broken. Where would they all be now, I wonder, if we hadn't interceded? With God? That doesn't sound like such a bad result, but of course I know it isn't true. They would be ash and bones inside the burnt-out shell of a building. The dead only exist as memories, or as lights to guide the path of the living. And that's exactly what Angela and Rosa will do, God willing.

That evening, we all gather round Angela's grave. It's a magical scene. I've topped her gravestone with tea lights, and have given each of the mourners a small taper. This seems extravagant, as you never know when you're going to need candles in the coming months, but we can't skimp. The result is that this whole corner of the square glows with a soft yellow light. The added benefit is that each person has to keep their taper alight. There's little wind, so this is possible, but it still takes concentration. It's quite a sight, all of these dark, hunched figures, cradling tiny flames that glow within their hands. It's a visual metaphor for the coming months, when each of us will have to nurture our life force to survive the cold and the hunger of those melancholy days.

My friends, I say, opening my arms wide, we are gathered here today to remember the life of Angela Lorenz, who died in the defence of our community. She gave her life - the ultimate sacrifice - but we can all be assured that she now resides with angels. She is gone from us, but not forgotten. As we gird ourselves to survive in the teeth of the oncoming winter, she looks down upon us and smiles at our efforts. For she died so that we could live, and to go on living is our solemn duty. I would now like to hand you over to Anna, who will lead us in prayers for the dead.

I step back, allowing our nun to take the space before Angela's grave. It seemed a bit cheeky, almost an imposition to use Anna's first name, but if the nuns are to live amongst us, we need to be on first-name terms. If she's put out, she certainly doesn't show it. We bow our heads and the serious, solemn words of prayer wash over us. The Italian language renders them more beautiful than one could believe - their power heightened by the nuanced and unctuous vowels. The references to Christ, the faithful and the removal of sin have both a calming and uplifting effect. As I feel myself relaxing, I scan the crowd.

The kids are here too, interspersed among the adults, smaller trees in the forest. And it strikes me that this is the first meeting of our new community. A new beginning. Even Nick and Joe have made it down. They stand on the edge of the group, towering pines.

The thing is, I've always scorned organised religion. But now I see its power and potency. It's something more than just a combination of the aesthetic and the wistful: it's an acknowledgement that the lives that we lead - with their triumphs and tragedies - actually have meaning and resonate through eternity. I've always loved churches - their windows, architecture and words - but I've never loved the church itself. Now I can see why people are so seduced by the calm reassurance of faith, whichever one we choose or are born into.

As Anna's words tail off, I'm brought back to the present. She steps aside, leaving me to speak once more. The truth is, I've done my homework. I've gleaned as much knowledge about Angela from Rosa and a couple of others as I can. I've scratched her name on to her headstone in white chalk, and even added the dates of her birth and death. It may sound ghoulish, but we also raided her flat, found old photos of her with family and friends, and have tacked these up on the wall behind her grave. The candlelight reveals the smiling faces of those nameless, departed faces,

faces that now brighten our square. Still, I never knew Angela, and so am going to have to entrust the next section of our remembrance to those gathered before me.

Of course, I'm no fool, and have set up our first anecdote. When I ask the crowd for memories of Angela, Mr Moretti dutifully raises his hand. He tells a rambling tale of how, when they were fixing some roofing tiles last summer, he began to slip. On the slick tiles, he couldn't arrest himself. And then Angela reached out, he said, grasped his hand, and held on to the apex of the roof like a mountaineer. At this, Mr Moretti makes a bracing motion, like someone hunkering over an ice axe. To be fair, I can't see the waif-like Angela in this very muscular, gritty position, but there we are. When I joked, he continues, about the hand of God, she said no, just the hand of Angela. And there you have it, he says, opening his arms wide. She saved my life, pure and simple, as if it were nothing. As he says this, his candle goes out, and I'm not sure if I find this amusing or disturbing.

More anecdotes follow, though - to be fair - of decreasing length and quality. When we get to some old dear chiming in about how Angela once helped her carry her shopping up the stairs, I know it's time to move on.

Thank you one and all, I say. Thank you. I never knew Angela, I add, my voice breaking slightly, although I knew her by sight. I never spoke more than a handful of words to her. I never knew what it was to be her friend, though I wish I had. But now, of course it's too late. So I tell you all, don't neglect each other. Speak to each other, cherish each other, because the road before us is long and winding. And I would just like to add this to our memories of Angela. When we stormed the convent, facing those ghastly men with their dead eyes and dead souls, Angela was with me, on my right. As soon as we started running, I lost sight of her. But I felt her presence, and I felt that no harm could come to me from that direction. And sure enough, it was true. Angela died to protect me, to ensure that I could get to the convent to save the lives of the nuns and children here among us. So in my heart, I thank her for saving me. For saving us.

I pause to let my words sink in. I'd love to have hammed it up even more, but people who were there that night are in the crowd, and I can't bend the truth too much.

Thank you all for coming here tonight, I add. In her death, Angela has shown herself to be a saint. So when you pray tonight, make sure you ask her to intercede for you. She interceded for us in life, and I have no doubt that she will do the same for us in death. Thank you.

I watch the crowd disperse with a beatific smile upon my face. I collect in smoking tapers, pat shoulders and swap words of encouragement and commiseration with the departing. My work here is done. Angela has just been canonised. She has become the first of our saints. The first of my martyrs.

VIII

After the small consolations of Christmas we are turned out naked into the new year. Winter has come down from the mountains. The wind shrieks and hisses, rattling the shutters. Dry snow is driven through our square like sand, never settling. We persist.

For the most part we stay inside, hunkered down. I tend the vegetables in our basement and run food parcels round the square. The children still play outside, but less frequently now. The nuns continue to lose their grip, both on the children and reality. With the destruction of their convent, so much of their confidence and assurance has disappeared. Anyone's would. We try to help out as best we can, but there's only so much we can do. Rosa bakes, I have small groups over to the flat to play games, often with the masks that we got from the Calle d'Oro. I even try to fashion a few of the children into a Commedia dell'arte troupe, but with mixed results. My grasp of the topic is a little shaky, and it turns out that improvising is harder than it sounds. Plus the little ones just end up fighting. Hey ho.

I leave if for as long as I can, but two weeks into January I tackle Joe on the subject of adoption. Literally. He's just in the act of hauling himself up out of bed when I grab him by the shoulders and pull him backwards. Despite his inarticulate protests, I take his knees and haul him bodily back on to the bed. He's lost weight being bed-bound for weeks, and I'm enjoying my physical superiority. I'm more mobile, more dynamic. Just to underline the point, I straddle him and sit there, staring down at him with my arms folded and a smug look on my face.

He sighs. Not now, August, he says, couldn't you at least wait until I've had a couple of drinks? I widen my eyes in mock consternation. How dare you, I say, aiming a half-hearted slap at his head. He intercepts my hand easily and gives my wrist a squeeze for good measure, just to let me know that that he's still stronger than me. Poor man. I've been riding him pretty hard - literally - since he's been here. I tried to resist, telling myself to leave him alone, that he's injured, but I just couldn't help myself. After so many years of enforced celibacy, it's like a dam of lust inside me broke. And although he can't take charge - in the bedroom or in any other way - I know he enjoys it really.

You need to cut down anyway, I say, else our supply's not going to last until the end of the month. You keep banging on about potato vodka - well I've upheld my end of the bargain. We've got potatoes galore in the basement. You just need to pull you finger out and set up a still or whatever.

In truth, my careful management of the potato supply is all that's keeping us all from starvation. Our meagre supplies of flour and rice are dwindling by the day. In the summer, I have visions of us venturing out into the fields, of planting wheat, barley and corn. I see us idling the days away beneath trees, watching our crops grow, enjoying the halcyon days of a season that we thought we'd never see again. Of course, it's all up to the sun. Well, it isn't. The sun's not at fault. It's the one constant here. We just need the ash in the upper atmosphere to thin out a little, to let the sunlight hit the land with enough intensity to grow crops. Up until now, no one's bothered with large-scale farming around here. All attempts in the past have failed. But this year - I don't know. There's something in the air. I think things are about to change.

And to be fair, I'm feeling a little better within myself too. I think having sex on tap helps: how can it not? Let's be honest, coming is cathartic. And at the moment, it's a release that we're lucky to have. Exercise sure as hell isn't happening: we're all too enervated, and the weather's too awful.

I still have odd moments, of course. Times

in the middle of the night when panic rises up within me like a dark wave, when I have to go into the kitchen to calm my breathing before returning to bed. But it's good to have Joe here, that human presence. Like I said, I'm still waiting for the fallout from being almost raped. But so far, nothing particularly untoward has cropped up - just the usual anxieties, fears and paranoias. As if they weren't enough to deal with already. Maybe I'll dodge the fallout entirely, like stepping back on to a pavement just as an articulated lorry thunders by. God, it's crazy to think that such things - cars, lorries, mopeds, motor vehicles in general - existed at all. It seems such madness now, that you could step out of your front door and get knocked down. How times change.

Listen, I say, leaning forward and catching Joe by the wrists. He lets me push his arms down. He's good like that - a real sport. Listen carefully. I know you haven't been over there for a couple of days, but the nuns are struggling. Really struggling. Can you imagine being stuck in a room with fifteen kids twenty-three hours of every day, seven days a week? Joe shakes his head dutifully. He knows how to play this game. We've got to help them out. Not just you and me, but all of us, I say, indicating the rest of the square with a flick of the head. The nuns are going to lose it if we don't get involved.

Okay, my lady, says Joe, exhaling dramatically, what did you have in mind? I know he doesn't necessarily like where this is going. Maybe it's because he hasn't got involved with the kids much - ostensibly because of his leg. It's funny, because he's the kindest man. If they've ever needed anything, he's over there straight away, gammy leg and all, helping out. In fact he and Mr Moretti - who's still clinging on, despite his cough - have become the firmest of friends, bound by their mutual love of DIY. What we need to do, I say, weighing my words, is to parcel the kids out.

What, he says, smiling, like send them all off somewhere? He's being deliberately obtuse, of course, trying to get a rise out of me. He knows that I've become attached to the kids - more so than I'd ever admit - and that the thought of sending them away, or losing them somehow - is horrifying to me. He calls me the pied piper, and keeps threatening to make me a coat of motley, but I know that he hasn't got the sewing skills or the patience to carry it off. An empty threat if ever there was one.

No, I say, not to be put off. You know very well what I mean. The kids - or some of them, if not most of them - need to be parcelled out to people around the square. He frowns. You mean adopted? Are you sure the nuns are going to go for that?

I sit back on my haunches. No, I say, I'm not.

We've talked about it before, and they've been resistant. But now they're on their knees. I think fatigue will get the better of them. I'm going to call a meeting today. We've got to help them before it's too late, before something bad happens.

Like what, he says, still frowning. I throw my hands up in the air. He can be exasperating at times. I don't know, I say, before one of them gets injured, or before one of them wanders off at night and dies in a doorway. I don't want that on my head. There's enough blood on my hands already. Joe raises his eyebrows, but doesn't say anything. He's hard to read at the best of times, and sometimes taciturnity descends on him like a cloud.

So, he continues, not letting this go, what did you have in mind for us? I can feel myself bridling. What do you think I have in mind, I ask. I have no idea, he replies, that's why I asked. Now it's his turn to wear a smug smile. The bastard. So, you want the truth, I ask. He nods. I lunge forward again, pinning his arms back, and lowering my head to within inches of his. You want the truth, I ask again. You can't handle the truth. Try me, he says. Okay, I say, widening my eyes at him in a mocking manner. I thought we could adopt a couple of girls. There are two who I reckon would be perfect.

Okay... he says, but that process usually involves a lot of checks, introductions and visits. It can take a really long time.

Do you see a bureaucracy around here ready to impose those things, I say, flaring up, sitting back and putting my hands on my hips. And we don't have time, Joe. The nuns don't. The kids don't. We don't. And for your information, winter's going to get a whole lot worse before it gets better.

Okay, he says, nodding. Good idea. You're right. Now get me a drink, would you?

As soon as we call a crisis meeting with the nuns, I can feel their relief. We meet in what I've come to call Anna's dorm. Half the people in the square are there, sitting around on beds. We've kicked all of the kids out to play in the sub-zero temperatures. They're becoming more feral by the day.

The nuns sit in a protective crescent, and do their best to look put out. They're even dutiful in how they employ their sense of guilt. To be fair, the conversation is thoughtful and sober - how you'd imagine a real democracy would work. A socialist democracy. All the big guns are here: Rosa, Hilda, Mr Moretti, me and Joe, plus another dozen or so. Even Filippa's made an appearance, although Nick's conspicuous by his absence, but that's fair enough. He probably isn't the paternal sort.

At the end of the day, it's got to be up to the kids, I say. It'll be their choice on whether to be fostered or adopted - and it'll be their choice if they want to return. Of course, we can't have them coming back and forth on a daily basis, but you get the idea. Common sense has got to prevail here. We can't have hard-and-fast rules like an adoption agency or the government. But the joy of this arrangement, ladies, I add, nodding at the nuns, is that you can check on the kids every day if you want to. In fact that might be a good idea. In that way everyone's accountable: no kids will get a raw deal, and new parents will have support on tap. What do you say?

Of course, that sounds great - in principle, says Anna, leading from the front. But the adults would have to choose which children they want to adopt: we can't leave that to the children, otherwise they might all choose the same person. At this, Anna glances at me. I know what she means, and I can't say I'm not flattered.

It's really important that we only take as many kids - and the type of kid - that we can handle, I add. If we, as carers, get overwhelmed or aren't happy, that's no good either. At this a low murmur of assent fills the room. Everyone seems to be on the same page, which is a massive relief, as I'd envisioned a fair bit of to-ing and fro-ing, if not downright argument. And perhaps the most gratifying thing is that there's no one in here who I wouldn't trust with a kid or two. The old, infirm or antisocial have stayed away, which makes things much easier. Of course, a couple of the older folk will need support, but that's what our nuns were born to do.

Another of the nuns raises her hands, as if she were in class. She's slight, dark haired and would have been pretty in another life. Go on, Alessandra, says Anna, patting her leg by way of encouragement. What we could do, says the younger nun, is have times when the children can all see each other. They've been together for so long, they're like a big family. It would be cruel to keep them apart.

That's a good point, I say. What did you have in mind? She shrugs. Well, we could set it up like a school day. They could have a break and a lunch-time when they can meet, and maybe before din-ner - at, say, four o'clock. When it's summer they could play out later, of course. And on Sundays we should all go to church, as we have been.

Again, there's a low murmur of assent. I nod. That sounds good to me, I say. It's essential that we remain a cohesive group, what with winter closing its talons around us.

But Alessandra's mention of summer has sent my head spinning off to imagined days in sun-bleached fields, with blue skies and moun-tains visible in the distance. Is this just a pipe dream, or might it actually be possible this year? Is it too much to ask? I'm not dreaming of a for-eign holiday, just the resumption of vaguely normal weather patterns. Romantic, I know.

By the end of the meeting, we've all dropped the names of the kids we'd like to adopt into a damp woollen hat. This is important - we've got to know who we might be taking on. The process may be a little unfair - cruel even - as some kids may certainly get left out, but we've got to do something. And at the end of the day, the nuns will be the arbiters. They'll have the final decision, which is as it should be. If we can't trust the servants of God, who can we trust?

The nuns reckon the whole process will take a couple of days at least, which means the best part of a week. As we struggle back across the square, my arm linked through Joe's, his free hand heavy on his stick, I can't help wondering if some of us haven't bitten off more than we can chew. Despite the snow falling steadily from the grey skies above, despite the ash drifts and biting wind, the kids run around the square as if each has a small nuclear reactor inside them. Getting away from the convent has released something primal within them - a supply of inexhaustible energy and enthusiasm. They now seem unbowed by life, despite its past sorrows, present hardships and future uncertainties. How are some of the older folk going to contend with such unbridled enthusiasm? In truth, it'll probably do them good. And, to be fair, most of these kids could do with another dose of socialisation.

We decide to call on Nick, as we haven't seen him for a couple of days. Sadly, as soon as we get to our floor, Joe dips out, claiming exhaustion. He's certainly made hard work of the stairs so far, grunting and stabbing at the steps with his stick. Part of me reckons he just wants to get back inside so he can have another drink, but that would be unkind.

So I hike on up to the top floor on my own. Nick's the only person left up here now. We've taken a few hits over the last couple of months, but I don't like to dwell on these things. It's easy to become maudlin. When I get to his door I knock and stand there dutifully, soaking up the damp and darkness. No response. Of course, he might be in the loo or otherwise indisposed. I cringe at the thought. How single men spend their time is not something I want to dwell on. I give it a minute, knock again and call out his name. Still nothing.

I try the handle. To my surprise it turns, and the door opens. It only takes me a couple of seconds to work out that something is wrong. It's the smell. It's not particularly unpleasant, but is sweet and sickly, like spilt syrup that hasn't been cleared up. Nick? I move slowly down the short hallway. Meagre January light leaks in through the half-closed curtains at the end of the one-room flat. As soon as I enter the main room, my hand reaches up to cover my mouth. I can't help it. I didn't know what I'd expected to see, but somehow you always hope for the best.

Nick's lying in his bed, a grey sheet wrapped around his legs like a boa constrictor. He's wearing shorts and a t-shirt, and his dark hair's an elegant bird's nest. His eyes stare up at the ceiling, and his hacked and bandaged left arm is stretched out above his head. Bloodstains have leaked through the pale crepe, and here and there a smear of yellow-green pus is visible.

Nick? I reach out and touch his chest, but there's no response. And no warmth either: the fires of life have long-since left his body. He's thinner than I remember too, his once pale face having assumed the drawn tallow of death. It looks like infection did for him. My sometime-saviour brought down by bacteria. It's an ignominious end, and I wonder if he suffered. I guess we'll never know. If he had, he wouldn't have told anyone. He died as he lived - in quiet, dignified silence.

I sit on the edge of the bed and stare at his sprawled form. In truth, I don't know how to feel. I never really knew him - he was a pleasant acquaintance at best. And after Angela's death, it feels as if I'm all wrung out, emotionally spent. This, of course, might not be such a bad thing: I don't think I could face another bout of intense soul searching. But still, perched here alongside the latest of our dead, the bleakness of our situation presses itself upon me, as if the pressure in the room has increased tenfold. But I suppose there is some consolation: Angela's got company.

We bury Nick next to Angela that same day. The earth is harder now, and several pickaxes have to be employed. We're so underfed that the work is harder than it should be, so a group of us ghosts take it in turn to dig. We each throw the metal blade a couple of times into the caked ground before passing the pick to the next person. The digging takes us the rest of the day, but it has to be done. When we wrap Nick's body in his bed sheets and bring him down, it seems as if there's nothing left of him. I'd never realised how much he'd declined in the past few weeks. When one of his skeletal arms flops from the stained sheets, it should be a reminder of his suffering. But it isn't. It turns out to be one of those macabre yet ridiculous moments that seem to crop up in times of extreme stress. Several people laugh, and I don't blame them. It's as if he's waving us goodbye.

Having said that, this time the burial's a far more sombre affair. We conduct it as soon as Nick's safely in the ground, which is just as dusk is falling. This way we escape the plummeting temperatures that night brings. Despite the fact that it's not quite dark, we do light a few candles, which adds a certain solemnity. We follow roughly the same format as before. Anna does the prayers; I give them some spiel about how Nick died so that we - all of us - could live. We owe him, I say. He is the second of our saints.

As these last words echo across the square, no one bats an eyelid, even the nuns. They're probably all just freezing their knackers off, waiting for me to shut up. Still, canonising someone is usually a lengthy process. It seems I've managed it in a couple of sentences. Well, I'm not going to complain. The old order changeth, yielding place to new. And in this new order, people can die and be named saints on the same day. Amen to that.

With the service over, we scatter as quickly as we can. Looking back, I catch a glimpse of the red roofing tile topped with tea lights that forms Nick's temporary headstone. We haven't dug it in - it's just propped up against the side of the building. I've scrawled his name on the tile with white chalk. Overall, the effect is underwhelming. It looks like a pet's grave that some child might have made. Rest in peace Nick, my unlikely knight-at-arms.

Back inside, I find that I'm shaking, and not just from the cold. Come on, says Joe. Come and sit down and I'll pour you a drink. It looks like you could do with one. I join Joe in the kitchen. He flips open a couple of cupboards and then bangs a bottle of single malt whisky down on to the table, along with two tumblers and a small pottery jug of water. We slump down either side of the table, throwing our long legs out. He picks up the bottle and reads the label with the expression of someone who's just found something they thought they'd lost, a favourite book or a treasured toy from childhood. This should be good, he breathes. I've been saving it for a while, but if not now, when?

He pours the copper-coloured liquid into the glasses and tops it off delicately with water from the jug. I'm no expert, but even I can see that the whisky would have cost a fair bit back in the day. Now, it's probably priceless. Here's to Nick, he says. We clink glasses and sip. I can just about see what whisky drinkers bang on about. There's a sour, pervasive note must contain a level of complexity for those who care to engage with it. For me, it tastes like peaty water from some highland bog, fortified with ethanol. I don't say this to Joe. I murmur appreciatively and wait a few seconds before setting my glass back down. If this is the best the Scots or the Irish have to offer, they can keep it.

Joe holds his glass up to the light and inspects the single malt as if it's the piss of the last Pope. So, he says, not meeting my eye, what are you up to August? The question catches me off guard, and I'm totally flummoxed. What do you mean, I reply, squinting at him. I'm sitting here with you, drinking whisky. No, he says, I mean earlier - just now. Running the burial is one thing - someone's got to do it. But unilaterally declaring Nick a saint? There's something off about that. And it isn't the first time it's happened, if I'm not mistaken. Are you shooting for a place in the priesthood, or something a little more esoteric? To be crowned our lady of light, perhaps?

This irks me. Am I so transparent? Are my motives this easy to see for anyone with two eyes and a brain? What do you mean, I ask. Joe smiles at me. Okay, so it's not kind enough to be a smile - it's a smirk. Come on, he says, your taking charge I can understand, but adopting a pseudo-religious role - with a bunch of nuns kicking around - what's all that about? Do what you're good at, August. If I were you I'd stick to bossing people about and sorting out the logistics. I'd leave all the spiritual stuff to the God squad. You can't compete.

Now I'm really put out. I'm glad you think so much of me, I say. I shunt the glass of whisky towards him. Here, you can have that. It tastes like piss. I'm going to bed. I stand and step forward, but Joe extends his injured leg, blocking my way. The merest of kicks would send him sprawling to the floor in agony. But I'm glad to see he's recovered enough to be able to hold it out. Truly I am.

Be careful, he says, tipping his glass at me like some lecherous old lecturer, you don't know what you're dealing with. Whether he means the powers of organised religion or himself, it's hard to say. And quite frankly, right now I don't care. And then it strikes me that he's drunk. He's been drinking all day, and now it's finally caught up with him, and given him Dutch courage to boot.

Don't think, I say, placing my hands on my hips like a truculent teenager, that you can start telling me what to do. I'm the only reason you're here. If it weren't for me, you'd still be out there in that cave, freezing your arse off. Joe raises his eyebrows. I see, he says. Is that a threat, August?

I wonder if I've overstepped the mark: people shouldn't purposefully make me angry - I lose all sense of perspective. Of course not, I say, adopting a conciliatory tone. All I'm trying to do is give people a bit of hope, that's all. Is there any-thing so wrong with that? But why should I have to explain myself to you? You're not my dad.

Joe shrugs, takes another sip of his drink and places the glass back on the table. Then, slowly, he retracts his leg. I bet he couldn't hold it out any more, that the pain got too much, or the muscles were too weak, or both. Either way, it looks like I've won. As I step past, he sits forward quick as a snake, and one of his bear-like hands clamps around my wrist. I try to pull away, but I can't. Let go, I say, you're hurting me. Let go or what, he says, his voice slurring slightly, you'll put me out in the snow, like a dog? I'm sure you can take it,

August. I inhale slowly through my nose. Let go, I say, my voice steady and ominous.

Looking up at me, I can't tell if his eyes are hurt or simply bleary with alcohol. A little hope can be a dangerous thing, August, he says. Just remember that. A little hope can be a dangerous thing. Don't give people hope where there is none.

What are you talking about, I ask. I'm just trying to get everyone through this wretched winter. Is that a crime? We can do it, but we've got to believe we can - otherwise... I wave my free hand above my head... otherwise everything just fizzles out. If we don't believe we can make it, we may just as well curl up and die. Now, can you please let go of my hand?

Joe releases my wrist with a theatrical gesture, as if his fingers have just been blown open by a grenade. The problem is, he says, that you never want to talk about anything serious. You just gloss over it and chat about stuff that doesn't matter. Joe may have let go of me physically, but he seems intent on keeping this conversation going - God knows why. What are you talking about, I ask, genuinely confused this time. We're talking now, aren't we?

Yes, he says, grinning up at me, his teeth luminous in the gloom of the kitchen. We're talking now, but only because I made you. Your first reaction was to storm off, right? I throw my hands up in the air. I'm so sorry, I say. I can see that this lack of communication is all my fault. But as you may have noticed, I'm here now. What do you want to talk about?

It's true, he says, staring at the whisky glass on the table, that objectively I've got nothing to complain about. You brought me up here, and you've looked after me. I've only got you to thank you for that. But sometimes I find myself wondering why. Why did you bring me here, August? Is there some ulterior motive? Did you think it might be handy to have a man around to reach things from the top shelf, do a bit of DIY and occasionally kill things? Did you think it might enhance your chances of survival?

I'm gobsmacked. I couldn't be more surprised if Joe had got up and slapped me across the face. As his words sink in, I realise that some previous version of myself might have got upset at this point. But right now I'm too angry to get upset. Whoa, I say, holding up one hand in a talk-to-the-hand kind of way, which I immediately regret. Let me get this straight: I feed you, fetch you booze and fuck you, and you've got a problem with that?

No, he says, looking up at me again. And it may be the half-light, or my imagination, but he does look like an animal that's been maimed by a trap, that's asking to be put out of its misery. No, he says again, of course I don't. Though I think if the genders were reversed we'd be in interesting territory.

No I don't have a problem with what you've done for me. Sometimes I just wonder why, that's all. Do you even like me August?

Again, I'm flabbergasted. And I'll admit it - this time he's found a weak spot. Expressing myself has never been something I've found easy. I'm sure that in the past I've been guilty of being undemonstrative. Hence perhaps the love of masks, the Italian language, the theatrical gestures of the people. Maybe these things gave me a system of semiotics to help me express emotions that were contradictory, fleeting or too strong. But doesn't everyone feel like this to an extent? Just because I'm not the gushing sort - is that a crime?

I find myself shaking my head. Jesus, I say. I'm really sorry that I haven't brought you flowers lately, but as you may have noticed, all of the petrol stations are shut. What do you want from me - a declaration of undying love? Me to fall into your arms? Maybe I could find some stupid fucking song to put on. If you can't read between the lines, that's really not my problem.

I realise how this must sound. And I realise that I'm simply strengthening Joe's argument, giving body and substance to what he's trying to say. Looking down at his sprawled form, I realise that he's probably just seeking a bit of reassurance. And it's flattering that he's looking to me:

it certainly highlights our positions of relative power. The need for comfort, affection and recognition is simply human after all. At the end of the day, he probably just wants a hug.

I step past him, go into the bedroom and close the door.

A week later, our girls arrive. They look as if they've been packed off to a posh picnic. Cara, our teenager, wears a red beret, a black coat and a smile. She's got a grey satchel slung over one shoulder that no doubt contains all her worldly possessions. She's holding hands with the little girl with the wavy hair and dark eyes, Abril. Getting both of them was a stroke of genius on my part. I love Cara and get on with her really well. She's almost a grown woman, and can certainly take care of our little one if I'm otherwise engaged.

Hello, I say, lapsing into English despite myself. I lunge forward, giving Cara a hug. She responds, and it's good to know we share a level of understanding and affection already. Then I drop to one knee and place my hands on Abril's shoulders. She's wearing her brown corduroy dress, thick tights and leather shoes, but also a grey felt coat and a shapeless black bobble hat. Abril, I say, smiling, it's good to have you here. You and Cara. I hope you'll both be really happy. She doesn't respond, just stares at me with those dark, shining eyes. Who's this, I ask, pointing to the small teddy she's clutching in one hand. She holds the teddy up for me to inspect. He's got glossy black fur and purple eyes. Inscrutable. He's lovely, I say, does he have a name? Abril shakes her head by way of reply.

I'm sure we can think of one, I say, still smiling. Come on in, both of you, and make yourselves at home. I usher the two girls in, closing the door quietly behind them. Joe lurks in the background - a smiling and benevolent presence, if a little standoffish. Still, we want to give these two some space on their first day. You'll both be sleeping in here, I say, indicating the lounge. They wander in, between the sofas and side tables, like animals exploring a new cage. This one's a sofa bed, I say, slapping the back of the largest sofa. You can both sleep in it, or one of you can take that other couch - they're both the most comfortable things ever. Glancing back at me, Cara smiles and sits on the couch. Abril goes to the windows that open over the balcony and peers out, still clutching her teddy.

Oh, I say, moving towards the windows, not wanting to crowd our new arrivals, but unable to help myself, look what we've got here! To the side of where Abril's standing is a small flat screen TV on a stand with an old and somewhat battered DVD player underneath. Next to this relic is a stack of films, documentaries and kids' programmes that I've managed to filch from other flats. I don't reckon our little one has probably ever seen anything on TV. Maybe we can all sit down a bit later and watch something, I say. She turns and stares at me with her wide dark eyes. It's a date, then, I say, ruffling her hair. I do like a challenge. Baby steps and all that.

So we all settle into a somewhat uneasy alliance. But like they say, you've got to be careful what you wish for. As the days turn into weeks, I find I'm marginalising myself more and more. I visit Rosa on a daily basis and find myself spending more and more time with her, listening to her clawing her way back in to the past. Why I'm doing this, I have no idea. Suffice it to say that I find myself superfluous. Joe makes a surprisingly good dad - attentive, kind and affectionate without being overbearing. Everything I'm not. Cara - through no fault of her own - adopts my role seamlessly. It's not that she means to - she's just one of those genuinely helpful people who gets on with things. And since there isn't a lot for me to do around the square, I find myself at a loose end.

I should spend more time being motherly: baking cakes and reading to the kids. I know that. It's just that I don't have it in me, and when I force myself to do these things, I become tense and edgy. The kids soon pick up on my vibe, and we all breathe a sigh of relief when the activity's over. I'm more of an entertainer - someone who should be hired for birthday parties and then left to wend her sorry way home.

Perhaps I should just admit to myself that it'll soon be time to move out and adopt the role that was always going to be mine, that of the distant mother. It's a role I've given a lot of thought to: the distant mother is despised, and yet offers hope at the same time. She's despised by her children for being physically and emotionally unavailable. She's the antithesis of what mothers are supposed to be: present and caring, a fixed point in the lives of her offspring. By adopting the role that's usually reserved for men – the absent father - the distant mother becomes something monstrous.

Yet at the same time she offers hope. She does this through her very independence, her rejection of society's expectations. The distant mother shows that you don't have to adopt the role allotted to you, that you can go against it, despite the damage. In these days where autonomy is a simple necessity, the distant mother is empowering, a beacon of hope. She is an emblem of conduct, a figurehead for feminism. And the most delicious, most indulgent aspect of this role is that you don't have to declare who you are: you don't have to care for others, don't have to share your innermost feelings and emotional states on a daily basis. You can smirk behind the mask.

Joe, of course, isn't stupid. Maybe he can't describe exactly what's going on with me in so many words, but he knows something's up. When I head over to Rosa's these days, I get a raised eyebrow. When I return, he routinely says, you've been gone a long time. He's so suspicious of me – so aware of my comings and goings – that you'd think I were seeing another man. And the irony of our situation is that now he's back to more-or-less full fitness, the sex has dried up. Maybe it's that I've enjoyed being sexually dominant, and don't want those roles reversed now he's able-bodied again. Or maybe it's having the kids in the next room that's put a dampener on our lust. Who knows? We're like a couple that's ten years into their relationship, not ten weeks.

This time, though, when I say I'm going to Rosa's, he doesn't just raise an eyebrow. I know what, he says, putting his book down and pushing himself upright, we'll come with you. But Abril is playing at his feet with a family of salvaged dolls, and Cara is busying herself in the kitchen, no doubt cooking up a three course lunch: it's a scene of domestic bliss that I'm loathe to destroy. It's okay, I say, waving him back into his chair, stay here, I won't be long.

This, of course, is a lie. Joe knows that I'll disappear for the best part of the day. What do

you reckon, bambinos, says Joe, shall we go and
see Aunty Rosa? Where he gets the term aunty
from, I've no idea. Abril stops what she's doing,
looks up at his towering figure, and nods solemnly. She absolutely adores Joe, which I find
galling, especially as she seems indifferent to me.
They each possess a certain calm, a certain still-
ness in their natures, and both seem to have
found a kindred spirit in the other. Leaning back
into the kitchen doorway, Cara says, Mama, wait
ten minutes. Then we can take this cake too.
The word Mama, which I use so freely with Rosa,
grates every time Cara uses it to address me. Still,
I'd better get used to it. I find myself nodding, giving her a rictus grin and acquiescing all too easily. Okay, I say, okay. I slump down on to a sofa,
clutching my bag like a disgruntled pensioner
who's been kept waiting in the doctor's surgery.

Soon enough, we're wending or way across
the windswept square. Cara and I are in front,
Joe and Abril walk behind us. Abril's carrying a
naked blonde doll with one hand, and holding
Joe's hand with the other. So, what do you think,
asks Cara, nodding down at the cake under its
square of hessian. I smile my false smile. It looks
absolutely stunning, I say. I didn't know that such
things could still be made these days - let's hope
it tastes as good as it looks!

My comment about the cake - though effusive - is honest enough. And although it galls

me that Cara now possesses all of the positive womanly qualities that I lack - youth, warmth, even curves - it's plain to see that she looks up to me. She's a sweet girl, and there isn't a bad bone in her body. In contrast to the stereotype of the grumpy teenager, she's quietly upbeat, industrious and yet likeable. I don't know what she sees in me - some kind of strength or independence, I suppose. Or maybe she just enjoys my sarcastic asides. Whatever it is, we get on well. Which makes it even harder to contemplate leaving her. But still, I'll only be across the square. The distant mother is often a tantalising presence.

Despite the fact that Joe's formed this little entourage, effectively forcing himself and the kids on me, we do feel strangely carefree as we step into Rosa's block. It's pleasant to duck out of the icy winds, to leave the grey sky behind, and even Hilda seems glad to see us. As we troop up the dark stairs, we could be heading out into the sunny hills on a picnic, not going to see an old lady in a flat.

But as soon as Rosa opens the door, I feel the mood shift. She's made an effort as usual, wearing her black skirt and top with its neckline of white lace. And over her shoulders she's wearing not a shawl, but a slate grey army blanket. That's fair enough - it is pretty cold, even inside. But it's her hair that does it, sticking out from either side of her head like wire wool. And the fact that her dark lipstick looks as if it's been applied by a two-year old. And that she's clutching a blood-soaked handkerchief to her nose.

Cara, though, bless her, doesn't miss a beat. She steps in, encircling Rosa's shoulders with one arm, the cake still held firmly with the other. Ciao Nonna, she says, kissing the old lady's cheek. Rosa leans in to Cara's arm, and smiles slightly, but doesn't kiss her back - she's in too much of a funk. Then Abril pushes past me and gives Rosa a wordless hug, throwing her arms around her waist. Everyone loves Rosa, even children who don't speak.

Come in, come in, says Rosa, dabbing at her nose. The bloom of fresh blood in her handkerchief is shocking - it's the brightest, most vivid thing in the room, a red peony resurrected in the middle of winter. Joe shuts the door behind us, and as we move in, I realise how similar the layouts of our flats are. Rosa's has higher ceilings, a more genteel sweep to it, but the basic positioning of the rooms is the same. Even so, I doubt this is some kind of sign. How many different ways can you arrange a handful of rooms?

As the kids escort Rosa to a seat, Joe gives me a look as if to say, is she all right? I shrug. Why do you think I've been coming to see her almost every day, I say in English. I don't know, he says, sneering slightly, I just assumed you were bored with our company. I snort, take the cake from Cara and head into the kitchen. But there's no escaping Joe. He leans his long body against the doorway, peering in as I cut the cake. The chocolate mirror glaze that Cara has managed to achieve is a miracle of rare device. I can almost see my reflection in it, but not quite, which is perhaps no bad thing.

You can talk to me, you know, says Joe. I sigh, clatter the carving knife on to the worktop and look to the heavens. I'm just not very good at being part of a couple, I say, rounding on him, okay? I'm sorry. He shrugs. Hey, that's okay. We're all a little out of practice. He smiles at me, his teeth and thin lips made more pronounced by his short beard. His wide-brimmed hat throws his eyes into darkness, lending him a sense of mystery. He is the quintessential tall dark stranger.

I want to go and kiss him, to encircle his slim waist with my arms, but I don't. Instead I turn my attentions to the cake. The knife cracks the mirror glaze and plunges slowly into the still-warm flesh of the chocolate sponge. It's going to be rich, but I cut fair-sized slices even so. We could all do with the extra calories. And then it strikes me that I never used to bake - or to even eat cake - before the impact. I suppose we bake now to keep our morale up, to show that we can still produce something beautiful with the simplest of ingredients in a world gone to seed. That and the fact that there are no shops left.

I've been worried about her for some time, I say, levering the slices out and placing them on small plates. I didn't tell you because I didn't want to burden you with something else. We've all got enough to worry about, without adding to each other's woes. Plus you've been recovering. I offer him the barest of smiles as a glide past, clutching portions of cake. He doesn't move.

It's hard to fill an awkward silence with a mouthful of cake. It's like one of those Christmases when all the relatives come over - even the ones you don't like - and the forced conversation suddenly dies. The white elephant in the room is Rosa's health, though none of us enquire after it. She pecks at the cake like a small bird, and when she's nowhere close to being finished she puts the plate down and pats Cara's arm. Bene, she says, bene.

Then she rests her head back against the cushion and stares out of the window. Cara gives me a wide-eyed look of alarm. I counter with a thin-lipped shrug as if to say, what can I do? Abril - ever the most independent of our little troop - has taken her place on the floor, and is walking her plastic doll goose-step-style around the legs of the coffee table.

Chewing and swallowing quickly, I set my plate aside. Somebody's got to say something before this visit nosedives. This looks like a job for me. If there's one thing I've discovered about myself in the last few years, it's that I can talk. Usually to myself, of course, but it really makes no odds. I can blather away for hours by giving voice to my internal - some might say interminable - monologue.

She's a sweetie, isn't she, Mama, I say, nodding at Abril. She doesn't speak, but you can put her anywhere – and as long as she's got a toy or two, she's happy. Rosa doesn't respond, just keeps staring out of the window. I don't let her lack of attention put me off though. I'm too much of a pro for that. Abril's mother was Spanish. An expat like us. What a little group we make! Thank God we've got Cara to help us with our Italian when we get things wrong! At this, Cara smiles weakly, but it's obvious that she's still concerned by Rosa's apathetic state. The only problem, I say, pressing on regardless, is because Abril's name's so similar to the English month, I end up just calling her April by mistake. I shrug again. Still she doesn't seem to mind, do you April? To this inquiry, I get no reaction from the younger of my adopted children, which is no more than I'd expected. But whether she's simply ignoring me or doesn't recognise her new Anglicised name is open to debate. However, I don't think Rosa is able to make the distinction in her current state. It doesn't really matter - either way I'm a terrible mother.

I keep going, but as the minutes pass, things

don't improve. Rosa simply sits there, staring out of the window, her upper lip stained with blood and the handkerchief clutched in one claw-like hand. I realise that my default setting when communicating with Rosa recently has been to talk at her while she remains silent, responding less and less as the days pass. With just the two of us, it hasn't seemed so bad. But now, with an audience, it's painful. Plus, I'm not getting a lot of help. April's playing in her own little world. Joe and Cara just sit there in shocked silence. I'm not surprised. They all came over expecting to see a warm, effusive lady, not this empty shell of a woman.

When a trickle of fresh blood descends from one of Rosa's nostrils and she doesn't even notice, I realise it's time to go. We say our goodbyes with enthusiasm in an effort to conceal Rosa's vacant confusion. Still, we leave her another slice of cake in the kitchen. As I'm hustling the others out of the door, I notice that Rosa's irises are glowing with a luminous, otherworldly quality in the grey light. If we don't have this inner light, I think as we trudge back across the square, we're just dead stuff. When the skin is sloughed away, the inner light will shine through, unimpeded. It won't be long now, Saint Rosa.

We don't talk about what we've just witnessed as we walk, but as soon as we're back, I round on Joe in the kitchen. That's why I go on my own, I hiss. I didn't want you and the kids to see that. That's what I do when I'm over there, Joe - I talk to her. I talk to her for hours at a time, without so much as a word in response. So if I'm a little ratty or distant of late, I'm sorry. It's hard watching someone die in front of you, day by day. I've seen it too many times - we all have - and I'm sick of it.

I can only hope that this outburst reveals a well of hurt that I'm trying my damndest to hide. I think it probably does. Joe scratches his beard and gives me that ponderous silence only men can manage before saying something conciliatory. I don't give him the chance, pushing past him, grabbing my coat and slamming the door of the flat behind me. I venture out into the streets, wandering between the empty eyes of the buildings. Soon it starts to snow. Great clumps of the stuff fall from the greasy heavens above, and it strikes me that we're still a long way from summer. Usually walking calms me, but this time it doesn't. The clumps of snow fall about me, the souls of the dead returning to the Earth.

The next morning, Joe visits Rosa. This isn't something I'd foreseen, but it's a free world. And maybe his being there will take some of the responsibility from me. After a vain attempt to play with April, I leave her with Cara and descend to the basement to tend the vegetables.

The plants - without a single exception - look amazing. The chillies and peppers are in bloom - their small white flowers lolling like snowdrops amidst their luxuriant winter foliage. The courgettes are flowering too, their fleshy mouths opening like invitations to hell. I wonder how long this can continue, this preternatural luxuriance, this riot of vegetation. It's so healthy it looks unhealthy, like a society that's peaked, become decadent, and is about to decline. I really should do something to counter this - maybe lay in some fertiliser for the next few months. What about bone meal? I seriously contemplate going and digging in the town's cemetery before I realise how ghoulish this would look.

Still, I've got to do something: I can't lose all of this just because of a lack of Nitrogen and a few other trace elements. What about blood meal? Even worse. All the slaughterhouses shut down a long time ago. Who'd have thought a giant rock hitting the Earth would have been good for animal welfare? From out of nowhere I realise that saving coffee grounds will be a less lethal way to procure fertiliser. I also decide that I must show Cara all of this. The next generation need to know the tips and tricks we've used to survive. Maybe - God willing - they'll be able to improve on them. I harbour vague hopes of being able to plant crops in the fields this year, but of course that may well not happen. Still, I have a feeling that it's going to be a good summer. With images of sun-drenched fields held firmly in my mind, I head upstairs.

To my surprise, I find that Joe's already back. He's got coffee on, and is lounging in the kitchen, his legs taking up most of the space. I smile at him and nod at the ancient coffee maker. We've got to start keeping the grounds, I say, for fertiliser. If we don't the plants are likely to... my voice trails off. On the table stands the packet of rat poison that Cornelius sourced for me so long ago. The one with the sitting rat, his eyes crosses.

I didn't realise, says Joe, looking up from beneath the rim of his hat, that Rosa had a rat problem in her flat. I shrug. I'm pretty certain that Joe has never seen this packet before now. Still, better to be on the safe side. A flat denial could easily backfire. I shrug. She does periodically. I sometimes put some of that out for her. There are a couple of holes. I'd have preferred one of those all-in-one traps, but that's all I could get. And anyway, why did you bring it back over? I'm pretty sure that we don't need it here. There's nothing to bloody eat anyway. And I'm sure the rats aren't too keen on courgettes.

Joe fingers the packet, lifting it several centimetres from the top of the table before letting it drop. I was just thinking, he says, almost drawling, that - well, you know what a state Rosa's in these days - well, I was thinking that it might not be safe to leave this over there. What if she starts spooning this into her coffee by mistake? Really, I ask, raising both eyebrows. I know she's a little far gone, but I think even she's not mistaking that for Tate and Lyle's finest.

Well, he says, exhaling through his nose, you say that, but the physical symptoms she's displaying at the moment are in line with consuming rat poison - or something like it. He peers up at me from the shadow beneath his hat. His eyes are as hard as chips of wet rock. I feel myself stiffen. What do you mean, I ask, as carefully as I can. He shrugs and glances at the coffee. It's about to start bubbling up - we can both tell. Well, he says, looking back at me, most rat poisons work - as far as I'm aware - by thinning the blood. Eventually this causes the rat - or whatever - to haemorrhage internally. If it's a big enough bleed, they die. I think it builds up cumulatively in their system, but I could be wrong about that.

You seem to know a lot about it, I say, holding his gaze. Joe raises one shoulder and lets it fall. Lots of rats in mountain refuges, he says, plus - after all - I am a scientist. So, I ask, what makes you think that Rosa has been swilling this stuff?

Nosebleeds, he says. She had another one this morning. Not great for someone of her age, in our situation, to be losing blood on a regular basis - even a little bit. Now, of course I can't say that she's been spooning this stuff into her coffee, but it pays to be on the safe side, don't you think?

He looks up at me with his hard eyes, and I find myself nodding. Absolutely, I say. Why take the risk? But if she has been treating that like a bag of sherbet, we've got more than just a few nosebleeds to worry about. That's something you'd do in the last stages of Alzheimer's.

Joe shrugs. If she's that far gone, he says, there's nothing we can do. They couldn't do much for dementia before the world fell apart. But we can stop her poisoning herself. Agreed, I say. With that, Joe unfolds himself and places the offending packet in one of the high cupboards. Just so April doesn't get her hands on it, he adds with an avuncular smile. He pours the coffee and we go into the lounge, sit next to each other on the couch and watch Cara playing with April. It's another idyllic scene in the life of the modern reconstituted family. Joe tries to take my hand, but I find myself pulling away. Neither of us makes an issue of it. We just continue watching the children. A nice normal family.

They used to say that Hell hath no fury like a woman scorned. Well, I'd like to change that a bit. How about, Hell hath no fury like a woman thwarted. It's not as catchy, but it makes sense to me.

There's little sense in rushing things, but you've got to strike while the iron is hot, so the next morning I pack Cara and Joe off to inspect the vegetables and forage for coffee grounds. Joe knows what he's doing, and can probably explain how everything in the basement is set up better than I can. Even for starters, his explanations will keep them both occupied for some time. Sadly, it's not Cara I'm trying to kill.

I'm also determined to improve my relationship with April. To that end, we're going to bake a cake together, whether she wants to or not. We're going to bake a cake, mother-and-daughter style and then take it over to Rosa. Three generations under one roof.

Red Velvet cakes aren't the easiest to make, but I do like a challenge. We've got a little butter that we've got to use up - it's like gold dust around here - probably produced by some poor cow - excuse the phrase - that's been locked in a basement for her own good for the last seven years. Which brings me on to wondering how long cows live for - I guess we'll never know. So I set April up on the kitchen table and get her creaming the butter into the sugar while I start measuring and sifting the dry goods. Luckily, we've got some red food colouring. It's about fifteen years old, but I'm sure it'll do the job.

It's an exhausting process. Baking usually is - I'm not a natural like Rosa who can just throw stuff together and come up with the goods. Throughout the whole process April just stares up at me with her wide, dark eyes. Occasionally she'll push a strand of hair away from her face. It's such an adult gesture that I find it unnerving. When she looks at you, it's as if she's peering into the very depths of your soul. I wonder what horrors she's seen, what traumas she's suffered. Stories about kids trapped in flats with their dead parents abound. And it strikes me that when you adopt kids, they usually give you a whole load of background about them. I realise - to my dismay - that I know nothing about April. I really should go and ask the nuns about her. Still, they probably don't know much more about her than I do.

Eventually we get the batter done. As I spoon it into the tins I shoo April away to go and play with her dolls in the lounge. We've only got two cake tins, but this makes the whole process much easier. All of the mixture goes in, and the tin on the left gets a dose of rat poison. Of course, as the mixture itself is the colour of fresh blood, you can't see anything untoward. I wonder what it'll taste like, or what the texture will be like when you eat it. Do you remember chocolate that used to contain popping candy? I'm guessing something like that.

So the cake with the special ingredient goes into the left hand side of the oven. Left, sinister. It all makes sense. Then I set about making the icing. In the absence of cream cheese, I'm going to have to improvise a little. It's not traditional, but I go for a white frosting - I've got a tin of cream of tartar left over from the Stone Age. Maybe I'm doing myself a disservice - it seems I can improvise.

While the cakes are cooking I try but fail to engage April in play, even grabbing another doll and trying to get the two of them to talk, but she's not having it. She just looks at me with her wide, dark eyes and then shifts her focus and slides away to play on her own. I feel like a rejected lover. And I have to admit, it's starting to hurt.

Before long we're slapping frosting on to the cakes and then hauling the finished product - which looks like it's fallen from a two-storey window - across the square. Still, we've done the best we can, and it certainly looks like a collaborative effort.

After a quick hello to Hilda, we're up the stairs and knocking on Rosa's door like a couple of kids running a bake sale. To my surprise, it doesn't take Rosa long to get to the door, and when she opens it she greets us with a warm smile and ushers us in. The grey blanket's still draped over her shoulders, but the nosebleed's disappeared. Thanks to whatever ministrations Joe performed the day before, Rosa seems in much better form.

August, she says, smoothing my arm, you shouldn't have. I should be the one baking cakes, bringing them to you, not the other way round.

Five minutes later, we're sitting in the lounge, each with a slice of cake in front of us. April perches deliberately on a chair next to us, and peers at me with such intensity that I feel myself forced to defend myself.

You wouldn't have liked the bottom layer, I say to her, it was too dense, too moist. It had a soggy bottom. So you've just got the top bit - more icing, I add, smiling. April doesn't appear to have understood a single word I've just said. She simply stares down, bereft, at her single layer of cake with its gouts of white icing. You can't be too careful. You don't want to go killing your own daughter.

I glance back at Rosa. In the brief time my attention's been directed towards April, my mother's slumped into the sofa and is staring blankly out of the window. And it occurs to me that nature may end up doing my work for me. Come on, Mama, I say. Eat up. I'm sure you and me can deal with a soggy bottom, eh? She brightens slightly, smiles and chops at her cake with her fork. She spoons a bit into her mouth and chews half-heartedly, before lapsing back into what some might call a settled apathy. I think she got a bit of the base layer. Sweet Lord, I think to myself, this could take a long time. This stuff isn't Novichok.

Come on Mama, I say, reaching over and cutting her cake for her. You've got to get your strength back. What could be better for you than cake? It's what all the old strongmen ate. Then she turns to me, a picture of sorrow. Her eyes have a downcast look, as if the skin around them's slipping. She reaches out a hand and pats mine. It's okay, August, she says. I don't think any amount of cake will make a difference. I don't think I'm long for this world, she says. August, you and the children must go on without me. You've always been a wonderful daughter, and I've always been so proud of you.

I well up. I can't help it. I clutch her hand fiercely. Come on now, Mama, you'll get through this. You're just going through a low patch - that's all. It's the time of year. Everyone knows that January sucks. All of our Vitamin D levels and our patience are exhausted. Just hold on a little longer - until spring. Then things will look better. It's incredible what a few degrees and some sun can do.

I don't have the heart to sit there, egging her on. So I get April to shove a few mouthfuls in and then drag her out of there, leaving Rosa staring out of the window. I leave the rest of the cake in her kitchen: she might get peckish a little later, you never know.

But when Joe turns up several hours later, clutching a bucket of mouldy coffee grounds, he's appalled. Why did you leave the cake over there, he asks, virtually shouting. She's not going to eat more than a slice or two before it goes off, and meanwhile the rest of us are over here, starving. Cara looks awkward and goes off to play with April. It's the first time I've seen Joe's calmness crack. He's sometimes morose, sometimes distant and sometimes withdrawn, but never angry. Get yourself back over there and bring it back, he says.

This fires me right up. Excuse me, I say, who the hell do you think you're talking to? April and I made that cake for Rosa, in the hope that she'll get better. It's her cake. Not ours. And it'll stay over there with her.

Fine, says Joe, dropping the bucket of grounds to the floor, I'll go and get it myself.

And I realise, for the first time, that hunger might well be getting to him. He's a tall man, and there isn't much of him, so his body's probably eating into his meagre reserves. Just leave it there, I say, eyes flashing, and for a moment I consider attacking him, beating him back into the corner by the door. Of course, this isn't how things would play out, so I let him go. I'm too angry to shout down the corridor, so I simply slam the door. The impact creates a hollow, booming sound, that of a fist rapping on a coffin lid.

It doesn't take long for him to return. He seems more at peace, more subdued now, as if he's got something off his chest. That's the effect that soon-to-be-Saint Rosa usually has on people.

She's a calming influence, thank the Lord. Still, I'm appalled to see that he's carried the cake across the square with no cover: a couple of flakes of ash sit atop the white frosting. Joe probably hasn't even noticed.

Okay, he says, exhaling through his nose as if he's just accomplished some major task. I'll go and cut us each a slice. He heads into the kitchen. Hold on a minute, I say, slipping past him and facing him, you can't do that.

Why not, he asks, raising an eyebrow, I'm famished. And just look at it - what a lovely colour! You didn't tell me you were making a red velvet cake.

Why should I have, I say, sounding petulant. I don't tell you everything. I was managing very well before you turned up. Joe doesn't take the bait. He just shrugs and says, where's that knife gone anyway? As he pulls a kitchen drawer open, I grab the plate that the cake's on, and dump the whole thing in the bin.

Joe turns on me slowly. Why did you do that, August? He's smiling slightly, but only with his mouth. His eyes have a look of knowing sadness about them. I did that, I say, trying to control my breathing, because that was Rosa's cake. Not ours. You can't just go and take things from people just because you're hungry. We're living in a society here Joe. We're not out there, living in a cave, killing stuff when we feel like it. He shakes his head and fixes me with his stony gaze. And that's why you threw the cake in the bin, is it, he asks.

He leaves the room before I can reply. I remain there for some time, my body shielding the bin, my whole being pulsing with barely contained rage.

I consider going out and walking around all night. Sadly, it's not safe for a woman to be out on her own, even a woman as pissed off as me. Still, I'd pity the fool that ran into me right now.

The problem is, I can't get away. As I said, it's as if our relationship has been put on fast forward, and now I desperately need some time out. Joe and I need to do our own thing for a while, but that's not going to happen. This stupid nuclear winter has seen to that.

Instead, I do the next best thing. After the kids are asleep, I stay in the lounge, reading by the pitiful flame of a single candle. This is probably how you end up going blind, or short sighted, or getting cataracts or something, but I don't care. I just don't want to have to talk to Joe. It works. I wake up early in the morning, with the candle guttered out at my elbow, the book in my lap and streaks of grey in the sky. I curl down into the chair, pulling the thin blanket up around me, and promptly fall back to sleep.

When I wake again, just before eleven, Joe's

done a real number on me. The kids are nowhere to be seen. He's put the sofa bed up, folded the duvets and is sitting staring out of the window. When he realises I'm finally awake, he gives me a sad smile.

It was a bit of a risk, he says, leaving the kids in here with you at night. But what choice did I have? I figured you wouldn't hurt them. I guess I was right, but I still didn't get much sleep.

Where are they, I ask, sounding flat and disinterested. I can't be bothered to debate the likelihood of my having hurt them. It's ridiculous.

Oh, I sent them over to Rosa's, then to go and see Anna and the other kids, and then told them to play until lunch. They won't be back for hours, which gives us plenty of time to talk. He glances at me. Great, I add, I can't wait. I sigh. Who knows where this is going? And suddenly I feel tired. Not just the tiredness you get from a broken night's sleep, but a fatigue of the soul: ennui as deep, empty and delicious as the universe itself. It occurs to me that I don't want to be here any more. Not in this room. Not in this town. I don't want to be anywhere. Maybe I've felt like this for a long time. I could try to goad Joe into killing me. After all, he is ridiculously strong. The only trouble is that he's one of those mild-mannered men who's got a fuse as long as a football pitch. Still, it might be worth giving it a try. Stranger things have happened.

So, he says, raising and dropping his hands to his knees. We might as well get into it. Why in God's name are you trying to kill Rosa?

What are you talking about, I say, widening my eyes theatrically. Come on, August. Don't bullshit me, he says. Just answer the question. Why are you trying to kill Rosa?

I roll my eyes and wave a hand at him, as if to dismiss the topic. I wouldn't expect you to understand, I say, my voice a scornful drawl. She's outlived herself. If the clinics still existed, she'd have checked herself in a long time ago. She doesn't want to be here. She's said as much many, many times. But you know how it is. I can't just go in there and knife her. Social norms and all that. I'm just trying to put her out of her misery, Joe. That's all. And the fact is, in her death she'll be much more powerful than she is now. Her memory will live on, a beacon for us all, a beacon for future generations. Don't you see that?

To my surprise, my voice is raised in the lilting, mellifluous tone used by preachers the world over. I know that sounds crazy, I add, but it's the truth. It was meant to be a humanitarian gesture, but often the best-laid plans go astray. I shrug and look at him with mournful eyes. He doesn't meet my gaze, just keeps peering out of the window.

So, let me get this straight, says Joe, you're trying to kill two birds with one stone. You're trying to spare Rosa years of suffering and, at the same time, turn her into a saint. I let a sad smile surface on my features. Inside, my inner child is doing cartwheels. And for the first time I realise that I might - just might - actually get away with this.

IX

I'm ecstatic. I figured Joe would never understand this, being a scientist and all. He's generally one of those infuriatingly logical types who doesn't do well with grey areas or human motives. But it seems I've done him a disservice. He's understood my intentions exactly. Or he's able to parrot them back to me, at least.

There's only one problem with that August, he says, staring at me. I feel my stomach sink a little, and study his face. At least he's not wearing his hat inside, as he often does. Then it's impossible to see what he's thinking. Even so, I'm struggling to read him. Maybe I am actually on the spectrum and have been struggling to understand humans my whole life. It would explain a lot of things. Sadly I don't think this is true. I can't think of any autistic people who've wanted to kill their adoptive mother. Just me. And that's what makes me so special. So very special indeed.

What's that, I ask, having no idea what he's about to say. He sighs, as if he really doesn't want to go on. The problem is, he says, that as an idea, it's totally insane. Saints don't exist, August, he says, still staring at me. Celebrities or whoever-else-has-replaced them don't exist. Everything's been pared back, stripped away. If Rosa dies, that's just another person dying, nothing more. It's just sad.

Oh, he says, as if catching himself. And there's one other problem as well. I shrug. What's that, I ask, folding my arms. He's already rubbished my life's purpose. What more can he do? The problem, he says, is that this isn't just some isolated incident, some one-off aberration. Months ago, before I even met you, I saw you kill that woman down by the river.

I experience a sudden dizziness, a staggering sideways shift, as if I've been hit by a car.

What, I ask, Ursula? Joe holds my gaze like a counsellor talking to a patient. I don't know what her name was, he says, measuring each word. I'd just got back to my camp when I heard the noise. By the time I got to the edge of the woods, it was all over. I didn't have any idea what had just happened, other than there'd been a fight. I saw you standing there on that spit of sand. It was obvious that you'd been struggling with someone. Even from that distance, I could see that you were breathing hard, and that you were soaking wet. Then the other woman came up out of the water a little, and I watched as you fetched your stick, waded out and killed her. I'll be honest with you August, I've hunted my whole life - even before all of this. I'm not some squeamish tree hugger. But even so, I've never seen a more cold-blooded killing.

Thankfully, by now tears are coursing down my cheeks. I shake my head sadly, at a loss for words. You don't understand, I say. Ever since the impact, that woman - Ursula - made my life hell. I don't know why. Maybe she was just jealous of me. Maybe she thought I was an easy target. She thought she could live off me for a while, and she did. She'd bully me, threaten me. Make me give her stuff. Food, clothes, you know. She seemed to love... causing me pain. She lived over in Rosa's block. Once, in the corridor, she grabbed me around the neck, and punched me so hard that I started coughing up blood. Then she just left me slumped there, thinking I was going to die. Eventually I managed to stagger back over here. And I vowed, if I lived, that this was going to stop. Everyone else around here got on well, despite everything. I don't know why she picked on me. Maybe because I was a foreigner. The irony was that she was a foreigner herself. And I knew that I couldn't do anything to her up here, where people could see, and judge.

So that's why I followed her down to the river. It was a risk - she was much stronger than me, and I've never been much of a fighter. I had no idea what would happen. When I first confronted her, I just gave her a warning.

I shrug and wipe my nose with the back of my hand, and hope I'm looking pathetic. I tried, Joe, I really tried. But you know what bullies are like. I told her to leave me alone, and she laughed in my face. I stare at him, unashamedly tear-stained.

So I knew I had to follow it up, I say with a shrug. Or the beatings would get worse, and I'd end up with nothing. So I swung for her. Luckily I had that stick. If I hadn't... who knows what would have happened? But I never intended to kill her. I just wanted her to feel what it was like, being on the receiving end. But things never go according to plan, do they? We ended up in this great big fight, and I knew one of us was going to die.

I stand up and move towards Joe slowly, like some penitent child. I sit next to him on the sofa. He doesn't flinch, doesn't move. To be fair, I say, after that, I don't think I've ever been quite right, you know? I've had my suspicions, but you just brush them aside, don't you? You've got to survive. And there was no one I could go and see. No one I could talk to. I couldn't even turn myself in. I couldn't even put myself in jail and deal with my guilt that way. I knew I'd done a bad thing - an awful, hideous thing - but what could I do? I just had to get on with life, or end it. That was it. I did contemplate suicide for quite some time. Instead

I decided to carry on, thinking that maybe I could help other people, perhaps make up for what I'd done in some small way. But the damage had already been done.

I stare into Joe's face, but he doesn't meet my gaze. He just keeps staring out of the window. There's nothing more I can do. Nothing more I can say. Instead, I just lean my head against his shoulder. The tears continue to course down my cheeks, but slowly now. We sit there for some time, both simply staring out at the grey light of this broken world, and I have absolutely no idea how this is going to pan out. Seconds pass, turning into minutes, and still we sit there, unmoving.

Eventually he takes a deep breath, and shakes himself. I sit upright. He turns to me. Okay, here's what's going to happen, he says, fixing me with his hard, dark eyes. We carry on. We look after these two girls, he continues, and we give them the best home we can. We act like the perfect little family.

I hate to say it, but I feel a sudden wave of attraction to this tall, serious man. Maybe it's because he's finally taking charge, finally being assertive. Finally getting involved. For too long now he's felt like an outsider, like someone looking in, an observer. And it seems that to me, having someone around who'll get stuck is something of a turn-on.

You leave Rosa alone, he continues, and I, in turn, will brush all this madness under the carpet. I don't know if you're telling the truth, August, but what else can I do? I could just leave, but then... then you'd be alone with the girls, and I've got to wonder how safe they'd be.

I shake my head frantically, wide-eyed and desperate. Joe, you've got to believe me, I'd never hurt them - why would I? They're the future. They're our children. His eyes scan my face, his mouth set. He's trying to work out if he can trust me. I wonder if a part of him now resents me for trapping him - as he might well see it.

I stand and make my way to the window. As I peer down into the swathes of ash in the barricaded square, I can't help but wonder if Cornelius was right. Get out. Run while you can. Head south into the ephemeral, Elysian dawn. Perhaps he was the smartest person around here all along: keep yourself to yourself, make yourself indispensable, but depend on no one. It's hard to tell how much the last six months have taken out of me, but I can't help but feel that I've lost something. I watch a child running across the square: a dark, rushing comet, and I'm glad to see that she's wearing her sackcloth coat. Not everything I've done around here is bad. It's too easy to be negative, to berate yourself when the odds are stacked against you.

Okay, I say, turning back to Joe, another sad

little smile on my face. If you're up for it, we'll give it a go.

You're looking well, says Rosa, reaching a hand up to my face. The roses have returned to your cheeks. I smile and usher her back inside. You too, Mama, I say. You're looking ten years younger - twenty! Hush, she says, waving a hand at me. That would still make me an old woman!

I follow her back into her flat. It's true. The blanket's gone and the spring has returned to her step. Look Mama, I say, we baked you a cake. Bene, bene, she says, barely glancing at it. She makes a flicking gesture with her hand, indicating that I should take it into the kitchen and serve it. Looking down, I can see why she's not impressed. The sides of the coffee cake are a dull brown, and despite my attempts to hide it with white icing, the middle has sunk a little. Mediocre at best. And besides, she wants to be ready for the main event - and the main event is April. She rushes in with a doll and throws herself at Rosa, who's now seated, braced for the impact.

Bene, bene, says the old woman, clasping the young child tightly. Cara follows her into the room. She's grown her fringe out and it really suits her. She's well on her way to becoming a raven-haired beauty, a touch of darkness amidst the oceans of calm within her. Joe brings up the rear: tall, smiling and wordless. He leaves the chattering to the girls, choosing to look on with pride rather than joining in. I've never seen him happier.

So I slope into the kitchen with the sunken cake and place it on the worktop. Days have passed into weeks, and now we find ourselves at the end of March, on the threshold of spring. The days have got lighter, the temperatures have risen, and we're all waiting expectantly for what the summer may bring. We've even planted seedlings down in the basement with the expectation that we'll be able to plant them out at some point. Fingers crossed.

But I still can't shake that feeling that something's been lost. And as I stare at it, I can't help but feel that this cake is a metaphor - somehow - for my life. The vivacious white frosting, applied with such theatrical gusto, hides something. Well, that's not quite right. The frosting hides an absence, a void where something satisfying should be.

As we sit there chatting like any happy family would, I feel myself phase out. It's then that I realise the banality of it all. Like a fly on the wall I watch these humans jerk and quiver, empty sounds being emitted from their mouths. Gestures lost upon me. Where has the light gone, that glimpse of metaphysics that meant so much, that illuminated us from within? Now we all just play parodies of ourselves, flat characters with no attachment to eternity. We are empty slabs of stuff that will one day line the inside of graves and be forgotten. There must be more than this, I think. There must be.

I give them gracious smiles, but they don't mean much. When we've finished our little visit to Nonna, we troop back across the square. It's become part of our humdrum routine to visit her every other day. We just chat and laugh about nothing much. When did Rosa - when did we all - become so banal? She could have been so much more. And I have to ask myself whether the price of happiness, or perhaps contentment, is banality. Are we now damned, as the ash seems to be clearing and the days brightening, to remain forever grey?

That evening, sensing the emptiness of my mood, Joe starts drinking. And I know what that means: it means he'll want to have sex. It's become a tacit part of our agreement that if he wants to have sex, we have sex. I go along, but I never really want to any more. When we do, I just imagine that I'm some animatronic doll moaning and grinding against him for his pleasure. To massage his ego and make him think that he's doing a bang-up job, that I can't get enough of him. Of course I don't tell him how I really feel - where would be the sense in that? Plus, I'm not sure how I really do feel, so to articulate my innermost thoughts or feelings would be nigh on impossible. I get glimpses of my mind through the dark, shifting tides of my moods. There are rocks there, items discarded long ago, and pale, unspeakable things that sometimes look like bodies, sometimes like mannequins.

The girls are going over to help Anna tomorrow, so we get April to bed early and leave Cara in the lounge with her, reading. I give her a smile and look in on Joe. He's in the kitchen, drinking Tequila. We've been out foraging a few more times, but our alcohol supply's on its arse. He keeps banging on about how he's going to make potato vodka, but he hasn't got round to it. I've fulfilled my end of the bargain: we've got buckets full of potatoes in the basement, all ready to be mashed and fermented and distilled down to their essence. Or whatever.

Care to join me, he asks. Joining a sprawled, half-drunk man in a small, half-dark kitchen doesn't seem like much of an offer, so I politely decline. I'll go and take a bath, I say. I give him one of my sad little smiles, and notice that he's put two shot glasses out on the table. One that he's drinking from, and another that's empty. He's trying so hard to normalise me, poor dear Joe.

The immersion heater is still working, thank God. I lock the bathroom door behind me and marvel at the tepid water that pours from the tap. In the chill, white-tiled confines of the bathroom a slight mist rises from the pooling water. That's more due to temperature difference than anything else. Still, I imagine the generator downstairs running overtime, eating half the year's worth of diesel just to give me this one luxury.

I strip off and wallow for as long as I can. The water's not unpleasant, but it's certainly not hot, so it's something of a tempered treat. As I lie there, I realise that the water has the tint of weak tea: it's like water from a bog or moor, stained by peat. I ply my hair with shampoo that I've been saving for years, and immerse my whole head to wash it out. I feel the weightless, floating sensation that astronauts must enjoy. I also feel myself immersed in light, my old dowdy skin being sloughed away by this tarnished water.

When I push myself back up to standing, the rusty water pours from me in rivulets: I am a tall, scrawny goddess, encased in a new white skin that is tough but translucent. Unless you looked very carefully, you wouldn't notice the change, but I do. I can feel the light flowing from me, and I can't help but smile.

I towel myself off as best I can and put on my cream-coloured babydoll nightie. It's the sexiest thing I own, despite a coffee stain down the front that I can't get rid of. To be honest, I don't think Joe will notice. He's not one of those picky, particular guys, and for that I'm thankful.

So as I sashay past the kitchen, I give him

a flick of my hips, but don't make eye contact. Then I settle in and pick up a book that I've been reading in a desultory, half-hearted fashion. It's Anna Karenina. It's very good, but I don't think I'm doing it justice with my patchy efforts. I wonder if I'll ever get to the end.

I give Joe forty-five minutes at the outside. Sure enough, after half an hour I hear him pushing his chair back. I imagine he's been necking tequila to get a quick buzz before I fall asleep. He wants his cake and to eat it too. But isn't that like most men? Most of them don't realise that life is an endless succession of compromises. Buoyed up by testosterone, they don't see the landscape of their lives for what it truly is. That's where we come in.

He dunks himself in the now-cold bath. I listen as he splashes himself in a cursory, haphazard fashion. He doesn't want to appear a complete Neanderthal, and a quick, occasional dip is his concession to keeping up appearances. It's a thoughtful gesture, but I don't mind the smell of him, within limits of course.

When he comes into the bedroom, he's got a towel around his waist and is still drying his dark hair. The feeble light highlights the hard ridges of his still-wet body. It's as if someone constructed a man out of leather and bone. There's not an ounce of fat on him - it's all been stripped away by years of near starvation. But the deep tan of his skin is what's most impressive: after almost a decade without sun, he still looks as if he's spent the last fortnight sunbathing. He's quite a specimen, really, and a lot of women would be pleased to have him.

It's at this point that I realise he's already got the best part of an erection going on. It's impressive how easily he's aroused. Just the thought of having sex and, well... I lay the book down and push myself back on my elbows, playing it slightly coy. There's no escape, though. He climbs up over me, half mantis, half man, and kisses me on the mouth, his bristled face pricking mine. One of his hands clamps down on what's left of my left breast, and then he's inside me. I gasp and push back again, still playing it coy, but there's no escaping him, and soon he's building up a rhythm. I let my body go, head lolling to one side, eyes glazing with an approximation of mounting ecstasy.

Two machines, grinding against each other. Friction the deciding factor. I reckon we must look like a couple of wooden puppets, automata going through simple motions. My head gone, his hips thrusting. A simple biological mechanism, stuck on repeat. Come on, I mutter under my breath, come on. It's a cryptic little phrase: am I willing him on to greater efforts, or am I urging him to get it over and done with quicker, so I can get some sleep? This is just an example of the things I think about when we're having sex. The tricksy, ultimately ambiguous nature of words. Context is everything of course, but even that doesn't help sometimes.

And of course there's my resentment to nurture. When he's fucking me, it seems as good a time as any to sharpen the blade of my bitterness. I think of Marco's abandoning me, my parents' silence, the mountain-sized slab of rock that did for most of us. I think about what I could have been: the vivacious teacher, the sexy older woman dangling a string of toy-boys in her wake. Strong, in control, seizing life by the horns. And even lately, I could have been a redeemer, an arrow pointing the way to a bright new future. A maker of saints, a bringer of hope. And all of that has been taken from me. Life is full of compromises, to be sure, but sometimes you can make one too many, and lose yourself.

To be fair, although I'm pretty sure Joe can't see the change in me, I'm pretty sure he can feel it. He's more than usually ardent tonight, pawing at me, pulling me to him, thrusting hard and deep inside me, as if he wants to become one with me. Poor man. I can't say I blame him. I flex my hips, my buttocks, my vagina, pulling him in to me again and again. Clutching him ever tighter. The light that he can't see pours from me, illuminating the room with a white glow. This is the inner light, the radiance that resides within saints, angels, and ultimately within God himself. And now it burns deep within me. A beatific smile rises up to my lips. It should be warning enough.

Nothing will stand in my way. I'm done with compromise. I'm about to become who I was always meant to be. And for a moment, I actually enjoy Joe's ardour. His mounting sense of urgency. We live our lives one moment at a time. An infinitesimally slow and fleeting mix of thoughts, impressions and emotions. And just before orgasm is perhaps when we realise this most. When time becomes strung out, each second essential. Don't lose it, we think to ourselves. Don't lose it. And it saddens me that I can't share this moment with Joe. But I can't lose control. Not now. I feel my right hand creep to the edge of the mattress, as if it has a life of its own.

As my hand grips the handle of the knife, I realise that he's close. Really close. Come on, I whisper, come on. Joe redoubles his efforts, frantically pushing towards his orgasm, perhaps wondering if he'll take me with him. But no, Joe. Not tonight. I can't lose control. And then he's straining against me even more so, slowing down to savour the moment. As I feel his cum flooding into me I pull the knife back and slam the blade into the base of his spine. I feel it catch and twist slightly, and then I'm pulling it home with both hands, jamming my hips up against him, adding to the leverage.

He grunts and falls forwards slightly, but I can't tell if this is a result of his orgasm or the six inches of steel that's embedded in his back. He takes a hollow, shuddering breath and cries out, a sort of smothered scream. It's the sound I imagine soldiers make when they get shot, groaning while trying not to give themselves away, wanting more than anything else their mothers.

Joe starts thrashing in the half-dark, arms coming within inches of my face. But I turn away, push down on his hips and feel that odd sense of suction as his penis is pulled out of me. With both hands I wrench the knife out and shove him away with my whole body, twisting out from underneath him. Joe rolls, unable to control himself, and collapses by the side of the bed in a tangle of long, wooden limbs. I get slowly to my feet and pull the nightie down over my thighs. Despite this, the white light from my skin still illuminates the room. I am ablaze.

I can still feel myself smiling as I make my way around the bed. This was how it was always meant to be. I have that deep, serene sense of things aligning, of edges locking into place. Joe's wild, staring eyes show me, however, that he's not quite on board with this. It's the look of an animal caught in a trap. The frantic anxiety of an animal that can't escape, that foresees his own death but is powerless to avoid it.

Joe shakes his head, once, twice, in mute

denial. I can see the drops of sweat in his hair, flung away and leaking down his face. He really did excel himself tonight. What a sterling effort. Still, it wasn't enough to save him. Why, he asks, wide-eyed, why?

I laugh. Because you were in the way, trying to turn me into something I'm not, I say. Trying to stop me becoming who I was meant to be. I notice that his legs aren't moving. They lie there, one over the other, like broken branches. You can't hold out a little hope, I say, and then not see it through. We're not just dead stuff, Joe. There's more to us than meets the eye. Much more. You've got to let the light out. You can't cheat people of that.

I close the distance quickly, not wanting to lose momentum, not wanting to muck things up at this stage. He tries to stop me. His hard, sinewy arms flail in the light of my radiance. One of them catches me across the back of the head as I lean in, knocking me forwards. I feel my vision swim for a second, but I catch myself with a forearm against his chest. He pulls me down, and I lose my balance. My knee hits the floor, sending a bolt of pain up my leg. I cry out, more in exasperation than anything. It seems I've underestimated him: he's a strong man, and still has the use of his arms. But instead of pulling away from the pain, I press my weight down into it, grinding my knee-cap against the floor, anchoring myself. And then my right hand comes up, burying the knife in his solar plexus. I push hard, feeling the knife shearing through what must be his diaphragm.

I lean in and kiss him, then pull back and stare into his amazed eyes. I'm sorry it had to be this way, I say, my voice little more than a whisper. I'll take good care of the girls - don't you worry. And I'll miss you. I really will. Slowly I pull the knife out, feeling the warm slickness of his blood on my hand and arm. Crouching next to him, I press his unresponsive head to my chest. It's true. I will miss him. And for a second the memory of everything I've lost wells up within me, a giant wave of loss. How has it come to this? How? I pull him harder to me, making shushing sounds. It's okay, Joe, it's okay. But, in truth I don't know whether I'm saying this to reassure him, or whether I'm saying it to reassure myself. In the glare of my newfound radiance I stare down into his eyes, and watch the life slowly leaving them. Goodbye dear Joe. Goodbye.

This should be one of those moments where time pauses, emotions are expressed in a torrent of tears, heartfelt clutchings and whispered words. It should be one of those moments. But of course life isn't like that. No sooner have I said goodbye to Joe than the door of our bedroom creaks open. Standing there against the lemon-yellow light of the lounge is the silhouette of a small girl. A small girl with wavy hair. The yellow light strikes Joe full in the face, revealing his ghastly, staring eyes, his hanging, jaundiced face.

I smile, but it's more of a rictus. And I realise that this little girl must see me as a ghoulish, grinning figure, knife clutched in one hand, crouching next to the body of her lover. The best laid plans and all that. If only Joe had locked the door. Stupid man. I guess the sight of me lying there in my nightie was just too much for him. Everything else left his head. Who knew you could be too seductive for your own good?

I rise smoothly to my full height, as if my legs are pistons. There doesn't seem much point in dropping the knife now. She's seen everything. Even so, April stands there in the doorway, a mute, passive observer.

My words don't come, so I reach out my free hand instead. And again, I realise how this must look. Come here child, it seems to say, come to your bloodstained Mama and meet your maker. Of course, this isn't what I'd intended at all. It's meant to be a calming, conciliatory gesture. Instead I must look like Salome, gloating over the dead. It's not an edifying image.

And then I realise that I could still get away with it. April's a small child after all. And small children aren't known for their powers of inference. I'm about to step forward, about to start giving voice to a story of how Joe attacked me, of how I tried to fend him off, of how I had to kill him...

I'm about to do all of that, but before a single syllable can escape my mouth, a taller figure joins April in the doorway. Cara puts a protective hand on one of April's shoulders and stares in on what - for her - must be a scene of horror. A butchered man, a bloodied, knife-wielding woman. Damn. When things go wrong, they go spectacularly wrong.

Before I can react, Cara reaches forward, grabs the handle and slams the door shut. This throws me and - I'll admit it - I'm slow to respond. I grope my way around the bed in the sudden darkness, shuffling like an old lady. Where has my radiance gone, I wonder, just when I needed it most? Still, only saints shine with a continual light, and I'm not quite there yet. But it won't be long. It won't be long.

Girls, I call out, girls! It takes me too long to get round the bed. And when I pull the bedroom door open, I'm in for a shock. The front door's ajar, revealing the blank darkness of the hallway. Where could they have gone? An abandoned room? The basement? That doesn't seem like Cara's style. She's not a little kid anymore. If she thought I'd killed Joe, that I'd lost the plot, she'd go and get help, alert others. So where would she go first? She'd go and see Anna, or perhaps Rosa. She's known the nuns longer, but she's formed a bond with Rosa over the last few months, and they know she's my mother.

Still pondering this, batting it back and forth, I pull on my dark coat and a pair of boots. Then I half-stagger, half-run down the hallway. I tell myself that there's no time to lose, but the fact of the matter is that they're gone, that no amount of calling will get them back, no amount of chasing will overtake them. I clatter down the stairs and realise that Filippa's not in her cubby-hole. The weak, fly-specked bulb is on, but there's no one home. No one I can get information from, but also no one I'll have to deal with. Shoving the front door of the block open, I step out into the square. Thick clumps of snow are falling, flaring briefly in the light from the doorway. I remember once, as a kid, standing in our garden, trying to catch snowflakes on my tongue. The sudden joy of catching one was reinforced by the icy, quick melt of the snowflake itself.

As I stand there at a loss, I realise that the weather has done my guesswork for me: two sets of scuffed tracks in the snow lead directly across the square to Rosa's block. I'm not quite up to skipping, but I walk purposefully through the snow, hands thrust deep into my pockets. The summer doesn't seem so far away. With Joe - who was always a source of objections - out of the way, I think I'll go ahead and flood the square. It'll be a real feat of engineering for us, but what a spectacle! The thought of floating across a rect-angular expanse of water in a gondola, punted by some young man, is delicious. What an achieve-ment that'll be! I can't wait. I can't.

The front door of Rosa's block is open. Since we dealt with the eraserheads, security has gone to pot. I shake my head. That victory and the barricades have given us all a false sense of secur-ity. I stalk past the concierge station, expecting - almost incidentally - to have to kill Hilda. Luck-ily for both of us, she isn't there. Tomorrow we're going to have a meeting. We need Hilda and Fil-ippa where they should be, and also a sentry on each barricade and one on the roof. I don't want to go crazy, but you've got to be careful. And I don't want anyone accusing me of not running a tight ship.

I smile as I rise slowly up the stairwell, my inner light burnishing the wood around me with a cold white sheen. It's true. Things have fallen off quite a bit while I've been away, lost to myself, but there's no lasting damage done. We'll soon pick up again where we left off. And then it'll be summer. Those halcyon days are not far off.

As I stalk down the corridor, I take Rosa's key out of my pocket. I was always worried that I'd have to use this in an emergency, and here we are. I slip the key into the lock, turn it and push the door gently ajar. I push my face through, hop-ing that they're not blinded by my light, and ask, is anybody home? Rosa? Girls? It's me. It's August. I've come to see if you're okay. It scared me how you ran off like that. I realise that things might have looked bad back there. We need to talk. I'm coming in, okay? I need to set things straight.

I walk in unopposed, like a ghost. There's only one light on, apart from the one that burns deep within me. I glide through the lounge and am confronted with a beautiful little triptych in the kitchen: Rosa, flanked by the two girls. And then I realise that Cara is taller than Rosa. Rosa's wearing a grey sweater, and her lips look sunken without their customary lipstick. She eyes me, her grey hair exploding from her head. What have you done, August, she asks, her chin trembling, what have you done?

I look down at my front, see the bloodstains on my nightie, take in the hand that clutches the knife, sticky with Joe's blood. I look up. The time for lies is past. It's time, finally, to tell the truth. I smile at them. Cara's wearing a pink T-shirt and pyjama trousers, April a full set of pinstriped terrycloth pyjamas that we looted from someone's house. They both look wonderful. But it's only then that I realise that neither of them are wearing shoes, that meltwater is pooling at their feet.

I take a deep breath. Joe, I say, got in the way. He tried to stop me from achieving my goals. He tried to take the real me prisoner, and for that

I couldn't forgive him. But I'm back - can't you tell? I look down at my left hand and marvel at the light shining forth. This is what we are, I say, holding my hand up for them to see. Creatures of light, not this dull stuff that surrounds us. And you, I say, pointing at Rosa, are going to be a saint - a fixed star in the sky that others can guide themselves by. She stares at me, vacant and uncomprehending. A look of stricken senility is etched deep into her features. Mother, I say, I'm going to kill you. I'm going to make you immortal.

Needless to say, this doesn't go down too well. Her jaw starts trembling, and she shrinks back against the counter. It didn't have to be like this, I think. She could have died with so much more dignity, so much more grace. Why do we cling to this paltry little thing that we call life? Why do we cower and cherish it when the hand of fate is laid upon us? She should give herself willingly to me, for the service I'm about to do her.

I don't understand, she says. What have I ever done to you, August? All I ever tried to do was love you, look after you. And you, you did the same for me. She shakes her head, uncomprehending. What you did, I say, was give me hope. You gave me hope that everything could be okay. And it can be, but not like this. A little bit of hope is a dangerous thing, Mama. You've got to see it through.

I lunge forward. Someone screams. I plunge

the knife downwards at Rosa, but she puts her arms up to block me. Somehow, she succeeds. Maybe I should have stabbed her from below, swinging the knife up from my hip.

With death hard upon her, Rosa finds the strength to grab my knife arm in both hands and leans away, gasping. Another scream registers on my hearing, but I pay it no heed. I wrench my arm free and retract the knife, ready to strike again. The smile returns to my face. My purpose will soon be achieved, all of the pieces aligning.

And it's then that I feel an icy, searing pain in my midriff. Looking down, I see another knife buried in the white fabric of my nightie, and red blood starting to bloom there. I stare down dazed. Then I look up into Cara's eyes. They're wide with shock. Shock at what she's done. And I realise that her eyes are an unearthly, glowing green at odds with her dark hair. And I see a light there, even as I feel my own strength ebbing away. The light burns deep within her.

And that's when I feel my legs go. I fall forwards, and end up in a kneeling position, a sacrificial victim enduring her final few seconds of life. Rosa peers down at me, aghast, and Cara's up against her now, shielding her, staring down at me with her luminous green eyes. Yes, I think, there's radiance there. Three generations of women. Life being handed down, not exactly in the way I'd envisaged, but still. And then April comes into my vision. As I'm kneeling, she's the same height as me. She's going to be a tall girl, and strong. Her eyes are dark, her hair unruly. A slight smile plays upon her lips. She reaches out a hand and strokes my hair. Mama, she says, Mama. I feel myself smiling back at her, tears pooling in my eyes. And I realise that this is the first time she's spoken to me. I couldn't be happier. These may be the last days of August, but they're also the first days of April.

Printed in Great Britain
by Amazon